11/11/15

LEGIONARY – A CALL TO ARMS

LEGIONARY – A CALL TO ARMS

John Waite

Forget not, Roman, that it is your special genius to rule the people;
To impose the ways of peace, to spare the defeated, and
to crush those proud men who will not submit.

Virgil, The Aeneid

SERENDIPITY

First Published in 2005 by
Serendipity
Suite 530
37 Store Street
Bloomsbury
London

British Library Cataloguing-in-Publication data
A catalogue record for this book is available from the British Library
ISBN 1-84394-134-1

Printed and bound by Antony Rowe Ltd, Eastbourne

To my wife Helen. For always being there and believing in me.

Semper Amemvs

ACKNOWLEDGEMENTS

First and foremost my eternal gratitude to Steve 'Fronto' Rogers for his unconditional support in making this book happen. And to Guy 'Secundus' Story for providing me the push to 'Go for it'. And to Aden O'Dea. Thanks also to my good friend Paul Harston and to Tony Cornish for his advice and the benefit of his experience. And finally to the many members of the Roman Military Research Society who have provided me with so much inspiration for this book.

My most sincere thanks to you all.

FOREWORD

If I was ever going to write a book such as this I'd decided, right from the off, that it would have to meet certain criteria if I was ever going to be happy with the end result. Maybe I was going down a line of limiting the marketability of the book but my resolve was firm. The central character was to be a nobody in terms of status or extraordinary ability. His story would have to adhere to the version of events that history provides for us, relative to his time, and there would be no fanciful or improbable plot lines injected to spice up his story.

No. Vepitta's story was going to be an eye on the world of an unremarkable young man striving to fulfil his life's ambition as he takes up arms and plays his role in one of the most significant events in British history.

The Roman invasion of 43 AD.

As well as providing an accurate story I also wanted the book to offer the reader an opportunity to learn about the Roman army and the kind of world they operated in. Something that would entertain and surprise but, at the same time, impart knowledge in a less intense form than reading a text book.

I drew my inspirations from two sources. The excellent *Roman Woman* By Lindsay Allason-Jones and the meticulously produced TV series *Band of Brothers* produced by Steven Spielberg and Tom Hanks and based on the book by Stephen E Ambrose.

Lindsay's book, *Roman Woman*, was a perfect example of how a fictional character could be used to teach historical fact in an informal and easy to read style while still providing the reader with an entertaining story to follow as they absorbed the information cleverly injected into the text.

Band of Brothers provided me with the path that I wanted Vepitta's story to take and also gave me an idea of the accuracy and impact that it needed to make the story work. As close as you can get it, the series provided the viewer with a 'warts and all' account of historically accurate events as they impacted on the American airborne soldiers of late WW II. Now armed with the bones of what I wanted, all that was left for me to do was take those ideas back 2000 years and apply them to our current understanding of those times!

It should go without saying that when one decides to undertake such a task it is inevitable that certain difficulties will surface that just cannot be easily resolved. This then is really the purpose of this foreword. To answer some of the questions that I think will arise for both the casual reader and those more specialized and knowledgeable in the period.

Whilst my research into the many aspects of life in the period has been extensive and ongoing, there are certain areas that remain grey or unknown to historians at this time. Areas that can only be coloured in by informed speculation and sometimes even that old favourite, best guess. Of these areas, the facts of the actual landings and initial pushes inland still remain beyond absolute certainty. Nobody can yet say for sure just where the invasion force landed and what happened to the various units once they actually began the push inland. Perhaps the most universally favoured landing site is Richborough in Kent, the one that I personally favour. This does not however sit well with such theorists who favour sites such as the area around Chichester in Sussex. Much has been forwarded by way of evidence and opinion over the years but, until such time as matters are proven beyond doubt, then this book must stand, not only as a piece of historical fiction, but also as my best guess as to the events of that time. Subsequently, as the reader works their way through the book they should be aware that those suggestions that I have made have been based on current available information and what I personally think is the most logical version.

Very little is known about the movements of the invasion force and its constituent units. Classical sources such as Tacitus and Cassius Dio shed very little light on the activity of the invasion forces and it is left to informed speculation and archaeology to try to fill in the blanks. Anyone who researches the period would not hesitate to point the more curious reader in the direction of the work of the late Dr Graham Webster, a brilliant mind who published many books and papers on Roman Britain, providing us with a rich and detailed source of information which will be used for many years to come. Since Webster's time, however, much more has been discovered and further theories put forward for the movements of the army.

First published in 1987, *Conquest – The Roman invasion of Britain* by John Peddie is a work I have drawn on much whilst describing the movement of the legions. Peddie draws on his own military background and compares more modern logistical considerations to offer a clear and concise explanation of the problems facing the invasion force. The amount of relevant, detailed and credible information put forward in the book made it impossible for me to ignore and it is mostly his version of events that I have used to guide me through the landings and subsequent engagements between the Roman forces and the defending Britons.

The more observant reader will notice that I never refer to the native tribes as Celts or Celtic. Certainly the indigenous population of Britain were Celtic peoples but the term 'Celt' is generic and covered a very widely distributed population extending right from the shores of Britain to as far afield as modern Turkey. The population of Britain at the time was made up of various separate tribes who, by and large, tended not to mix too well with each other. Ideally, it would therefore be best to describe the people by their own tribal group or, if a more collective name needed to be used, then 'Briton' would be more appropriate.

When dealing with the Britons I have also made use of the descriptions given by Julius Caesar in *The Gallic Wars*. Caesar is an excellent contemporary source of descriptive material for many aspects of the lifestyles and attitudes of the Celts of Northern Europe around one hundred years before the Claudian invasion. His descriptions of the native Britons and their use of chariot warfare, long after the practice died out in mainland Europe, is particularly useful as it would have been little different to the deployments experienced by Vepitta and his colleagues.

As a last word on these people the reader may like to look at *The Celtic World* edited by Miranda J Green. The book is a series of papers covering all aspects of the Celts as we currently understand them. A source which is becoming increasingly more useful as I plan further books in this series which will see Vepitta's contact with these people become more intimate.

As it is with the operational facts, so it is with the main players. We often know little about the key Roman characters and even less about the leaders of the defending Britons. Once more I have referred to classical writers to shed a little light and combined that with current scholarly thinking to bring them into the story. I have, for instance, given an eyewitness account of the death of Togodumnus. Several versions exist as to when Togodumnus met his end so I adapted one of those versions to further illustrate the devastating effect of attracting the attention of the lethal Roman artillery crews.

A warrior's death for a noble prince! Why not?

As to the rest?

Well, I have used the same formula in an attempt to give what I hope is a credible illustration of the many aspects of the Roman world as a whole such as social activity, religion and military procedure; to name but a few. If I wanted to achieve an end result it would hopefully be an entertaining and informative book which would stand as tribute to men like Vepitta and his colleagues who, by their valour, skill and fortitude, carried the influence of Rome to the edges of the known world and laid the foundations for the society we live in today.

This book is my opportunity to pay tribute to the extraordinary and unique soldier that was the Roman legionary.

John Waite
21 October 2004

PROLOGUE

No. I'm not afraid.

It's my turn to go now. Death is waiting to lead me beyond the realm of man and into the shadow world where my ancestors await me. Strange that it should be like this. Lying in my bed, strength long gone and the man I once was nothing more than a distant memory.

Once. Long ago it seems. I wanted the warrior's death. To die, gloriously, in the service of the Emperor. Now that death has finally found me, I welcome a passing like this. I have seen so many good men die in battle. Comrades and enemies leaving this world in gory, ferocious combat. There is no honour in the frenzied butchery one witnesses when men fight for their lives and homes. Much better that my life finishes in my bed, in the home I have built with the woman I love here by my side.

It can't be much longer. This thing that eats at me has grown strong in recent times. Whatever it is that slowly started to grow in my very core now seems to drain every last drop of vitality from me. It has grown large in recent weeks. My stomach felt hard and then grew, very quickly. Before I knew it I could not rise from my bed or even hold food down. So quickly did this curse fall upon me. The agony that is its close companion now seems to have faded. As if it knew that its work was done. I have been grateful to the physician for the drafts he gave to ease my pain but now I seem to have no need of them. I feel the warmth of the brazier in the room. I can feel Salviena's hand holding mine and stroking the arm that once was so strong. She speaks to me quietly, telling me to sleep and that she loves me. She is going to stay with me until it is over. I am aware of all things around me. And yet. It is as though an invisible hand pulls curtains of shadows slowly around me. Until, at last, all the light will be gone.

How wonderful it would be to still have the power of speech. Than I could tell Salviena that, contrary to appearances, my mind still functions and I still love her as much now as I ever did. How marvellous to be able to tell her that I am happy that she is with me and that I know she will be safe and secure when I have gone. If only I could do that. All I can do is whisper words that she cannot hear. My weakness will not allow me to give them substance and form.

It must be soon. I am minded to recall tales told to me by men who have faced certain death and survived. They told me that the gods laid out their whole lives in front of them so that they were able to have a measure of the sort of man they were before the final reckoning. I feel myself drifting back now. Back to a time when I had nothing but a mere handful of memories to look back on. Born to the Legion and growing up next to the biggest fortress for miles around. A scruffy little urchin running around, stealing fruit and bread from street traders. Running errands for the Legionaries in the taverns for a bronze coin. I knew that my destiny lay with the service of the Emperor. I knew that, as I rolled in the dirt, fighting with the other boys, my destiny would bring more than bruised knuckles and skinned knees.

As I drift images start to come back to me with greater clarity. Scoldings as a child, the innocence of a childhood romance, the flush of adolescent passion and lust as I grow towards manhood. Everything I learned as a child. Moving toward the fulfilment of my ultimate destiny.

Those invisible hands seem to draw the drapes closer together. But. As it darkens so my senses attune to the sensations of the past. Gods. It's true! I can even smell the incense on the altar. The priest making the offering on the altar of the Legion as we young boys were taken into the mightiest war machine in the world. The army of Rome.

I want to see it, just once more. Then I will pay *Charon* to ferry me to the other side . . .

Chapter 1

Beginnings

I had taken Quintus's advice and waited just a little longer before joining the army.

'Stay the urge boy. I know you want to be gone, but think! Take a trade into the Legion with you and your life will soon become easier than those who do not have skills.'

Quintus lived close to us in the *Vicus* with his wife Curatia. He had served as a Legionary and then set up a business in retirement manufacturing and repairing armour. He learnt the trade whilst serving and it was now providing him with a comfortable living. A kind and generous man. Quintus had given me a home when my parents had fallen ill and died within a year of each other. Although retired, my father was still part of the brotherhood of the Legion and the Legion always looked after its own. No payment was expected but I vowed to father, on his deathbed, that I would follow his footsteps into the Legion and lead my life by the code that he had observed all of his adult life. I was glad that he heard my words, and, knowing them to be true, passed to a more peaceful realm.

Quintus had willingly housed, fed and mentored me. His advice was always sound and, even with the impetuosity of youth, I always felt it wisest to follow his counsel on important matters. Even when my mind was set to join the army early I found it changed by the train of the man's reasoning.

The day I decided to announce my big decision I found him at his bench, in the workshop attached to the house. He was sat in front of one of the windows, preoccupied with the task at hand, amidst broad shafts of sunlight that illuminated the dust motes drifting in the air. The top half of the door was open allowing more of the precious sunlight into the working area. Quintus' attention was fixed on the stubborn hinge pin that he was fighting to remove from the damaged cheek piece of a bronze helmet. He hissed through his teeth, muttering something fearful as he wrestled to extract the pin, totally oblivious of my presence.

'Quintus!' I blurted out in the most assertive manner a fourteen year old could muster.

Instantly there was a metallic snap and a screech of metal. The old armourer sprang up off his stool waving his hand around frantically then clapping his other hand over the back of it.

'Great flaming *Jupiter* boy!' he bellowed. 'How is it you wish me to die? Am I to bleed to death from this cut you've just caused? Or do you prefer that my heart explodes with the shock of how you prefer to announce your presence?'

'I ... er ... I wanted ... erm' .... It was no good. The moment was ruined and the resolve I had set myself with was fast ebbing away as I watched the old man dance around the workshop, gripping his hand and uttering hair-raising oaths as the wound began to sting.

'For the love of *Augustus* boy. You've started now. Get on with it.' Quintus grabbed a piece of oily cloth lying on the bench and clapped it onto the wound. His face contorting once more as the cloth increased the stinging sensation.

'This had better be good!' he snapped, breathing through his nose as the pain grew.

'I ... I'm ready to join the army now. I want to be with my brothers in the Fourteenth!'

He looked at me then. Stopping the tormented dance he had just been performing and setting me with a long probing look. As though he could count the thoughts running around inside my head. After a few moments he gave a half smile and slowly nodded his head.

'So! The young wolf would like to try out his new teeth eh?'

'Of course,' I replied, feeling as though the old man was mocking me with his tone. 'I am man enough for the life now. There are some younger than me in the Legions and I'm just as good as them.'

My confidence was returning now and I felt myself pushing my chest out to show the old man just what fine young warrior material I was. Then, slowly at first, a grin began to break on Quintus' face which threatened to separate the top of his head from the bottom. Once more the confidence trickled from me as of water from a spilt cup.

'What's so funny Quintus? Do you mock my ambition?'

Pride was badly tattered now and my bottom lip began to tremble. Quintus knew I lived for the day that I could enter the fort and fulfil my pledge to my father. So why was he doing this to me? The old man walked over to me and grabbed me by the shoulder, squeezing it lightly.

'It's not mockery Vepitta.' He shook his head and spoke softly. 'I know how much you want this. I have waited to hear you say that you are ready and I knew that you would say it before you really were ready.'

'But ... ' I protested.

'Hang on,' he interrupted, 'listen for just a moment.'

Quintus led me over to a stool and sat me down before squatting down in front of me. He still smiled but there was affection in there now and no trace of the imagined mockery I thought I saw earlier.

'You know that your father and I were comrades for many years and that you live under my roof because of the closeness we all shared. When we knew he was dying I and all of his old comrades sat down to discuss what would become of you. Decisions were made and I visited your father to tell him of what we proposed. He was happy with the arrangement and felt that he could depart this world knowing that you, his only son, would grow up being guided to fulfil the destiny you both wanted. That guidance is not yet over and there is more for you to do before you are truly ready.'

'But what now?' I huffed like an impatient child. 'I read and write. I can do numbers and I am fit and strong. I can box any of the boys in this part of the *vicus*. I am learning the bow and I can throw a javelin better than ...'

Raising his hand for a pause, Quintus sighed and smiled again.

'I know all of that and I don't doubt your abilities as a man but, to help us survive, we have to have a little something to help us along the way. I promised your father that I would not let you go until you were capable of standing alone, and I mean to keep that promise, young man. Stay a little bit longer and I will pass on as many of my skills to you as I can. That way you will have a trade to your name and the ability to earn more than a labourer's wage if you need.

'What point is there in being just another dogs body?' he asked. 'Life will be hard enough without making it harder. Listen to my counsel and give yourself an advantage over the others'

I felt myself unwilling to consider the points raised, knowing that the wisdom of his words would outweigh my yearning to go. As usual the old man was right. Were I to enter service with no real trade then I would be consigning myself to a life as a labourer. Those who had been wise enough to bring a trade would eventually be granted the title of *Immunis*: a valued soldier who was exempt from such drudgery as guard duties, latrine details and all the other soul-destroying jobs that were the lot of the ordinary *Miles* in camp. Did I want to break my back building military roads and aqueducts? It was not the fear of hard work that changed my mind but the plain fact that I would work hard enough without adding to my burdens. Quintus was right. With much reluctance I agreed. It wasn't time just yet.

* * *

I followed his advice and learnt everything I could from him. Over the course of around three years Quintus taught me enough to give me an excellent grounding in the skills needed to make and repair armour. Skills invaluable to any unit of the army. I could make and repair every type of body armour the soldiers wore. I repaired weapons of all varieties and learnt to smelt metal from ore. I could beat and fashion metal plate and acquired enough skill to be able to perform maintenance and repair on the various types of *catapultae*. As I laboured and learnt my muscles grew in strength. During those years spent hammering red hot iron, twisting metal, bending and shaping things, and pumping the great leather bellows of the workshop, I had changed from the skinny boy of fourteen into a fit and strong young man of seventeen summers.

When the day arrived that I was finally ready to depart Quintus supplied me with the necessary papers attesting to my new qualifications. He also presented me with the most important document that I needed to become a Legionary. A diploma attesting to the fact that I was born a citizen of Rome. Along with this he gave me a letter of introduction that my father had written before his death. Without these I would never be accepted for service with the Legion. Quintus had kept it all safe until I was ready to leave. I wrapped them in cloth and carefully placed them in my pack. Time to go.

Curatia had gone off to market. She didn't want to be here when I left, preferring to say her goodbyes earlier in the day and then take herself off. She would return home when she felt ready.

We didn't speak, Quintus and I, just closed the door to the shop and walked out onto the busy street. People were bustling by, trailing in and out of shops and houses and conducting themselves as normal. Everything sounded the same, looked and smelt the same as any other day. But this was not any other day. It felt so strange to be surrounded by normality when, for my part, it was anything but normal. My mouth had gone dry and I couldn't decide whether I was wildly excited or utterly terrified at what lay ahead. This was all I had ever wanted but, now it was here, my head boiled with a mass of mixed emotions. Walking next to me was a man who had given me a foothold on life and now, in front of me, rose the walls of the massive fortress. *Mogontiacum.* Where I would have to part with the man who had guided me here. Still we said not a word and the gates came closer. Many times I had seen the fort. I grew up within its protective shadow. But there never was a day when it seemed as huge and imposing as it appeared to me this day.

He walked with me up to the imposing stone fortress that had once been home to him, my father and all of their comrades. Now it was my turn to enter within and acquit myself well enough to be accepted for training in the twin Legion. I stared at the doors of *Mogontiacum*, convinced that I would be accepted and my new home lay within its walls. As my mind tried to imagine what life would be like a familiar voice entered my consciousness.

'Remember young Vepitta,' Quintus said, ready to deliver that last piece of good advice, 'keep your head down, your mouth shut, and work hard. Never dishonour the Legion or the memory of your father. And always remain loyal to your Emperor. Heed my words and you will retire with honour and respect.'

Then the weathered old face cracked into a gap toothed grin and he gave me a great hug followed by a thunderous whack on the back.

'Now go damn you. And don't bother coming back until you've conquered the rest of the world for us!'

Instinctively I reached out and hugged him as hard as I could. Looking into his eyes I thanked him one last time.

'Thank you. May the gods always watch over you.'

He smiled gently and I turned and began to walk. I could feel his eyes in my back. I didn't want to look back. I knew Quintus would wait to see me through the doors and a show of emotion at this time would be disastrous. How could I convince the Legion that I was ready if all they saw was a snivelling boy? As I struggled along with those pieces of my father's old kit that remained I preferred to look to the future. I had no family left alive anymore and no real reason to stay. Quintus and Curatia had given me a home and much more but we all knew that this day would come. Our life was more of a business arrangement than a family. I had learned and flourished with them but they were not my blood. Still, I felt as though a mighty wrench was required to pull myself free of this life. My roots lay in the fort, not the *Vicus*, so what was it that made me reluctant to go? I knew not but this was something I had waited all my life for and nothing was going to deny me that. I walked quickly down the street until I reached the door of the fortress, my mouth opening to state my business to the sentry ... ...

'I know you boy! You're Gaius's son.' His battered but friendly grin was reassuring and the fact that I was accompanied by the memory of my father lifted me considerably. 'In you go and see the *Tessararius* in the gatehouse. He'll show you where you need to go.'

It was as simple as that. I passed from one world into another without even uttering a word. The wicket gate shut behind me and I knew that the ties that bound me to my old life had been so well cut by that heavy, iron shod door. The Fourteenth Legion was going to become my life and my family and, as far as I was concerned, the outside world had ceased to be. For now at least.

This day was the day that the Legion set aside, about once every three months, for the reception of potential recruits. Around fifty of us stood in the courtyard of the *Principia* and waited in silence to be told what was required of us next. Clear blue sky hung above the courtyard and the midsummer sun chased the shadows under the porticos surrounding the fountain. On any other day I would have found the gurgling of the waters relaxing and pleasant but today was not ordinary. Nobody knew what to expect, or indeed what was expected of us. You could feel the anticipation, and apprehension, as we all stood there gawping at each other in the silent courtyard. Two soldiers stood, one either side of the door to the *Sacellum*. Were it not for the fact that their faces were reddened and glistening with sweat from the heat of midday then I would have taken them for statues. Unmoving and yet poised. The sun glinting on polished metal and leather. The bright colours of plumes and shields enhanced by the light. Through those doors lay the standards of the Legion and the unit coffers. Any man foolish enough to attempt entry without prior authority would be cut down instantly. As I slowly took in my surroundings I became aware of more soldiers. The *Principia* was the heart of the fort and, on any given day, had its own unit to defend it. A fort within a fort.

Nobody spoke to us at all as we stood there, save for an *Optio* who was moving amongst us and recording names with the assistance of one of the unit clerks. It seemed to take for ever until I heard one of our number behind me whispering to his neighbour. I could not hear what was being said but it did not matter. The *Optio* heard it, his head snapping up from a document he was reading. Instantly his gaze settled behind me and he waded into the group, swatting candidates aside as he went. He planted his hand against the side of my head and shoved me away like he was parting rushes. As I recovered my balance the *Optio* stalked past me again. This time moving to the front of the group, dragging the unfortunate whisperer as he went.

'Discipline is the key to your future survival, if you are chosen to remain here,' snarled the *Optio*.

By now he had adjusted his grip and was leading his squirming victim along our lines by the neck. One strong hand applying tremendous pressure to the lad's neck to such a degree that he was obviously trying hard to stifle the sobs of pain as he lurched alongside the *Optio*. The boy could have been no more than fifteen and his face was a mask of pain as the *Optio's* iron fingers bored into the soft skin of his neck.

'Indiscipline will bring you the ultimate downfall. If you are slack and lazy and inclined not to listen then, at the moment of truth you will fail and die!'

Slowly the *Optio* walked along our lines, staring at us, each in turn, as he went. The man's eyes seemed to burn with anger and contempt. His jaw was set hard and his neck was akin to twisted rope. His unfortunate captive arched his back in torment, his head swelling and turning purple from the fierce pressure exerted by the tough veteran of many years hard soldiering. The ferocious grip exerted on his poor captive made his arm muscles stand out in bold relief, as though cast in bronze. This was not a man to be crossed.

'You will speak when you are spoken to by your superiors and at no other time unless otherwise instructed.' He stopped, standing straight as a spear in front of us, his prey squirming feebly now in his powerful grip.

'Whispering is the province of weak men and gossiping women. When you speak you will make yourselves heard like men, not mutter like shy virgins. Do you understand? he growled.

Still we were shocked and the reply came as a few muffled responses which only served to annoy the man further.

'Do you understand?' He railed.

'Yes *Optio*,' came the crashing response, delivered as one.

'Good,' came the growled reply as he shoved his unfortunate victim back into our ranks, satisfied now that the first lesson had been learned. A muffled gasp came from the lad who lurched towards us, eyes popping from his head. The look of rising panic now turning to blessed relief.

'Now get back in line you stupid bastard. And learn from what I have taught you.'

The lad stood, fighting to remain upright, and struggling to regain some composure.

'Yes *Optio*,' he managed to blurt out.

For a moment it looked as though he would faint as he rocked backwards and forwards, fighting for balance. I'm sure everyone felt the same as I. I wanted to help him, give him a hand to steady himself, but I dare not. It would have been the decent thing to do but, if the *Optio* thought otherwise, it would be me getting the throttling. 'No friend. You stand on your own two feet!' I concluded.

Eventually all of the names were taken and, one by one, we were led inside the building. The *Optio* led us in with a quiet and efficient manner, totally different to his earlier demeanour with the unfortunate whisperer. As soon as he had dealt with the boy he just went back to the task in hand, calm and unhurried. How is it done? How does a man switch from calm, to ferocious and calm again at the blink of an eye? It didn't seem personal. As soon as it was over it was over. The *Optio* never even looked at the boy again until it was his turn to go in. And even then he had just ushered him in with very little being said.

Finally, it was my turn to go in. The *Optio* called my name and I was led under the portico and into a stairwell which led to an office above the gateway. The *Optio* pushed open the door and held it open without actually entering the room, motioning with a nod for me to enter. The room was a spacious square with whitewashed walls painted with a scarlet border around the bottom. Thin green lines formed open square patterns on the walls and a marble bust of the Emperor surveyed the room impassively from its place adjacent to the table. Racks stood against one wall containing scrolls of various sizes. Two large iron lamp stands stood either side of a heavy wooden table which was covered with parchments and writing materials. The planking of the floor was unpolished but scrubbed clean. This last detail being something I felt compelled to pay particular attention to as I came under the scrutiny of the three figures seated behind the table.

'Do you have your papers?' A warm, intelligent almost friendly voice enquired.

I looked up and saw a young man in his early twenties, holding out his hand for the requested items. Without reply I stepped forward and gave him the documents that I had been instructed to have ready. The young man took them and began to read them, his chin resting on one finger of an elegant, manicured hand whilst his other hand engaged idly in twirling round a stylus backwards and forwards through his fingers. He wore an immaculate white tunic of linen with red trim and his short dark brown hair was oiled and neat. His wealth was apparent from the exquisite jewellery he wore on his neck, wrists and hands. The finery was eye-catching but, at the same time, it was not overmuch. It gave the young man the required show of status but did not exaggerate the point. If memory served me well then I was sure that I had seen this young man at the head of a very large column of troops only recently. Was I actually in the presence of one of the Legion *Tribunes*? Oh Gods! Now I felt nervous. This was no provincial Roman but a real live resident of the city of the seven hills. A high born from a place I could only imagine in countless dreams.

As if he were absorbing all of the available information from the papers, the young man mused over the papers for some time until .... .

'You are Marcus Sulpicius Vepitta?'

The clear green eyes looked out from the flawless complexion and one eyebrow raised slightly.

'Yes. Yes sir. I am.' I tried so hard to moderate my delivery but it must have just sounded to him like I was some sort of bumpkin. My lack of poise embarrassed me and I felt my face redden.

The young man slowly reclined in his chair and began to stroke his jaw line lightly with his finger. Oddly enough, as I watched him, I began to feel more at ease.

'I am *Tribune* Scribonius. I preside over your *Probatio* today. I am fortunate to have at my disposal the assistance of these two fine gentlemen to guide me in assessing which of you will become soldiers in this Legion.' With that he indicated to the two figures seated either side of him.

'Sextilli is a well respected physician who has served the Fourteenth well for many years. He will assess your physical suitability for the life ahead of you. *Centurion* Scaurus here will assist me to determine whether or not you are a worthy candidate for entry. Should you be successful he will also be overseeing your training.'

Sextilli sat at the table leaning forward with his hands clasped together. A sharp featured man, well into his sixties, he exhibited a slight smile and acknowledged me with a small nod. He was of thin build but, even though seated, it was apparent that he was taller than the average man. His grey, receding hair swept back across his head and he was clad in a light woollen tunic in a dark red hue.

Scaurus sat at the table unmoving. A flat expression on a weather beaten face of around forty years betrayed nothing of what was going through his mind. He wore an off white woollen tunic with scarlet *clavi* running vertically down the garment. A blue cummerbund was worn under the beautifully ornate *cingulum militare* and strapped to that was a heavy *pugio* with elaborate enamel work on the scabbard. Seemingly of medium height and build the general impression he gave was very formidable. Cold blue eyes appraised me as he wrote notes on a parchment in front of him. Once more the flutter of nervousness returned.

'I am pleased that you have seen fit to bring a trade along with you.' Scribonius continued.

'There are many who come to us in the hope of finding a regular wage, a decent meal and companionship. Not all realize that we prefer something more than a two legged pack horse. My compliments. You seem to have done well under this Quintus chap and you have skills that will be most useful.' He paused. 'If you are accepted that is.'

This was good. Thank you Quintus. For giving me this and thank you me for having the good sense to listen. I had only just entered the room and already I was receiving praise from a senior officer. The smug feeling didn't last long.

'You needn't think, however, that your future is bright and life will be spent tapping on bits of metal.'

His tone changed discernibly and he leant forward onto his elbows.

'I am sure that you have heard all about the role of the *Immunis* in the Legion, and the fact that, as one of their number, you will be exempt from the majority of the more mundane and labour intensive tasks of a soldier. Am I right boy?'

'Yes *Tribune*.' Thank the gods. This time it didn't sound like I was about to trip over my own tongue.

'No doubt you have got the facts essentially correct.'He continued. 'What you probably are not so clear on is how you get to that special status.' He paused momentarily to look me up and down once more.

'Along with Scaurus, it is my task to see that whichever of you are selected for service become first rate combat soldiers. In order to do this you will be trained to the pinnacle of excellence and maintained in that state for the majority of your service. If you are required to fight you will do it, and do it well. You will be part of a war machine that is ever ready to deploy anywhere in the world and fall, without mercy, on the enemies of Rome. Forget your civilian trade. You are not here to be a metal basher in a soldier's uniform. You are here to fight.' Scribonius continued with enthusiasm.

'Only after the rigours of training and a period of assessment with your new *Century* will the decision be made as to whether you are worthy of the title of *Immunis*. If you get that far then you will have rightly earned your title as you will have proven yourself to be at least as good as the better soldiers in your unit. Make no bones about this Vepitta. If we decide that you are to join us then you set yourself on a very hard path. The only things that will end your journey are completing twenty five years service, disability beyond usefulness or death.' Scribonius looked me squarely in the eyes and I was aware of Scaurus scrutinizing me also.

'Do you wish to continue this, boy?' asked Scribonius.

'By all the gods, yes sir. I do!' I felt stirred by my answer. I was on the point of fulfilment and I was sure Scribonius knew it was my heart answering as well as my head.

'Then the *Probatio* will continue. Sextilli will examine you medically to determine your fitness. If that is satisfactory then we will speak with you further.'

'Thank you *Tribune.*'

This is it then. Now we will see, I thought. Now we will see if I am good enough.

Sextilli rose from the chair and approached me. Still wearing the half smile he sported earlier.

'Disrobe boy,' he said in a quiet, but firm voice.

'Sir?' I felt stupid almost as soon as I had said it.

'If you are going to be a part of this army then bashfulness will not help you to share a dormitory with seven of your new companions. Now. Get em off!' The order was almost like the lash of a whip and totally unexpected from the placid looking medic.

'Yes sir,' I replied as I hopped around the room trying to remove my boots.

I felt extremely vulnerable as I stood there, naked as the day of my birth. All three of them assessing every inch of my frame.

'Scaurus. Will you be so kind as to record my observations regarding this fellow?'

Sextilli was a civilian in the employ of the military and, as such, was not required to observe the formality of rank with superior officers. Common respect, however, was due at all times. Being an old soldier Sextilli knew this and was aware of what was required.

'Naturally doctor. Carry on,' came the response.

'The candidate Vepitta is of strong enough frame with good proportion,' he began.

'There is good muscle tone and I see no external evidence of disease of any kind.' The medic took hold of my hands and turned them, palms up. 'There is extensive evidence of callusing to both hands, indicative of a past spent at honest toil. I estimate him to be $5'.10''$ in height and his build, as previous, is proportionate to this. Bend, your head boy.' I leant forward.

'The hair is strong and shows no sign of lice infestation. Do you keep clean boy?' He asked.

'I use the baths regularly sir and use a fine tooth comb daily. My guardian also treated me with sulphur powder and fine ash when required.'

'Good. Open your mouth.' I did as I was bidden and the medic shoved a short wooden stick down my throat. I gagged instantly. The stick was withdrawn and Sextilli held my lower jaw down, peering inside my mouth.

'His gag reflex is sound and, apart from one back tooth on the lower jaw, the teeth are strong and fine. The offending tooth will have to be extracted to avoid any infection.'

What's wrong with my tooth? I thought. It doesn't hurt. I get a bit of food stuck in it now and again but I can pick that out. It's fine I don't want it yanked out.

'Your breath is somewhat pungent young man. Are you a great eater of meats?'

'Yes sir. My job was quite taxing so my guardian recommended that I eat more meat to give me strength.'

'Hmm.' Came the reply. 'You are too young for that sort of diet. If you are taken into service you will eat a more varied diet with more vegetables. You need the goodness from all foods. Understood?'

'Yes sir!'

'Good. Now take deep breaths in and out until I tell you to stop.'

I started to breath as requested while Sextilli placed one hand on my chest and one hand on my back. He stood to the side of me, seemingly measuring the rise and fall of my chest. When he was done he placed a hand lower down my chest and put his ear to my heart. After a short interval he declared:

'Chest expansion is satisfactory but will develop with more exercise. The boy has spent overlong in sooty workshops and needs clean air in him. I'm sure you can help there Scaurus.'

Scaurus responded with a short. 'Huh!' Shrugging his shoulders.

'The heart is strong and beats well with good rhythm.' He began to probe my stomach with his fingers. 'No anomalies with the abdomen.'

I flinched as he took hold of my manhood with one hand and cupped my scrotum with the other. As if by reflex I stared up towards the roof beams as my face reddened once more.

'Cough boy.' Came the instruction.

I managed something that would just about manage to clear my throat.

'Oh for pity's sake!' Sextilli gasped. 'I'm not going to pull them off and run away with them. Now. Put your chin down and give me a cough. Not a ladies' excuse me!'

'Sorry sir!' I replied as I tucked my chin down and gave him my best cough.

'Fine. Thank you for that,' he retorted. 'The candidate's Venus organs are sound. The appendage carries no evidence of infection and the seeds behave normally when tested.'

He looked down to my feet and inspected both of them in turn.

'The feet show no signs of disease and the toe nails are of normal shape and colour. Both arches are slightly lower than perfect but boot packing for the arch should eliminate any problems on the march.

My examination is complete and I declare that I have found nothing to bar entry. Dress yourself young man.'

I scraped my clothes together and dressed as quickly as I could. Such a hurdle to pass and now it was done. Physically I was what they wanted and now it remained to find out whether they would accept me as a man. Once dressed I stood once more in front of the table, straight as a rod, trying to look like a soldier. Arms clamped to my sides and looking straight ahead.

'Loosen off and look at us Vepitta.' It was Scaurus who spoke first. His deep voice filling the room.

'I have read your papers and, essentially, I find no fault with them. Your father was wise to write the letter of introduction that he did. It was very efficient of him to leave you such a valuable legacy. His death was mourned by many of us who remembered him.'

Scaurus knew my father! I had to fight to stop myself asking him for his memories. This man was a *Centurion*. He would beat me half to death if I were so disrespectful to ask that now. Perhaps there would be opportunities to find out later but for now I needed to concentrate on the task in hand. Scaurus continued.

'You have been very fortunate in that your guardian Quintus, not only gave you a home but taught you a trade to boot. How is it that you have been so fortunate boy?'

'The Legion sir!' I replied.

'Explain.'

'Sir. I would have probably been a beggar or a corpse on the street if it had not been for the Fourteenth.' I drew breath and paused. Now I needed to make them understand, clearly, what drove me. Please *Iovi,* father of gods, guide my speech now.

'Quintus served with my father. Along with his other retired comrades, they secured my future when they realized that I was about to become an orphan. Men such as Gemmelus, Capito and Priscus, to name but three, assured my father that I would live to serve the Legion. After my father passed they funded my upkeep whilst Quintus gave me a home and a skill.'

The three men listened impassively as I continued.

'None of this would have come to pass had it not been for the special connection between my father and his friends. They were more than just friends. They considered themselves brothers. That made me family. Those men guided me here today and now I stand before you to request entry.'

'But why Vepitta. Why do want to join us?' Scribonius asked.

'Because I owe those men a debt that I will be unable to repay. But there is a way that I can make it good. I can take my place in the Legion and aspire to become as honourable as those men. I will serve with loyalty and dignity in an attempt to honour their memories and carry their names forward with me. When the time comes I will retire. Perhaps then I will have my own opportunity to make a difference to somebody like me and carry on the tradition of the brotherhood of the Legions.'

'Do you not wish for glory Vepitta?' Again Scribonius asked the question as Scaurus took notes.

'I have no doubt that glory will come my way as my service passes. Such a great Legion will always follow the path to glory and honour. Until that happens I wish only to serve my Emperor, the Senate and people of Rome. That is enough.'

'Anything further?' Scribonius looked at the men seated either side of him.

'Nothing sir.' Answered Scaurus.

'No. Nothing from me sir.' Said Sextilli.

'Wait outside the door Vepitta,' said Scribonius. 'I will summon you when a decision has been made.'

I turned on my heel and left the room, pulling the thick wooden door shut behind me. I was so tempted to leave it ajar but who knows what would befall me if Scaurus spotted it. It didn't bear thinking about. The latch snapped shut and I stood to the side of the door. For what seemed life a small lifetime I stood there. What if they didn't think I was good enough? What if they thought that my reasons were just a load of invented claptrap. Oh *Fortuna* don't fail me now. I beg of you. My mind raced with all the things they could be identifying that meant failure. Even my bladder was beginning to fill. Just to pile on the agony. Why are they taking so long, it must .... .

'Vepitta. Return to the room!'

'Oh gods!' I whispered. 'Yes sir!' I shouted and opened the door.

I entered the room and Scribonius was sitting quietly discussing something with Sextilli. Scaurus was stood up behind the desk and staring straight at me as I came to a halt in front of the table. Scaurus picked up a scroll from the table and handed it to me.

'Take this to *Optio* Fuscus downstairs and then get yourself directed to the quartermaster. You're in. Now move!'

Chapter 2

A Soldier to be

I had scarcely had time to blink, let alone savour the fact that my *Probatio* had been successful. We had charged around the fortress for most of the day going from one office or department to another. We had been numbered, sorted, measured, documented and filed. We had been issued with very basic kit and our heads had been shaved as a precaution against head lice. Once they had done that they had sent us over to the hospital wing where we had stripped once more and been dusted with a foul smelling powder which we were not allowed to wash off until the next day. We were now divided into five groups of eight and allocated billets in a barrack block. These groups would now be the *Contubernia* we were to stay in for the duration of our training. Any personal items we had brought with us deemed useful to our future service, such as weapons and armour, were placed in storage until needed.

'Until you evolve from a load of arse licking nobodies into decent soldiers you will have no need of a soldier's accoutrements,' taunted Fuscus as he locked them into a storeroom.

We stood, once more, under the portico in the Principia courtyard. Each of us now wore a clean wool tunic, off white in colour and belted at the waist with a simple leather belt. We had been given old *caligae* of a near enough size until we took possession of our new ones which we had been measured for earlier. We must have looked like a detail of corpses as we stood in our light tunics, bereft of hair with our powdered white limbs.

It was clear now how it was going to be with Fuscus. As we had charged all over the fortress trying hard to accomplish the tasks we had been set, Fuscus would appear at random and torment anyone that merited it. One lad's nose still bled copiously after he had been set upon by the *Optio*. Fuscus had found him after the lad had lost his way to the Quartermaster's. He had assisted the lad by seizing his nose in a vicious grip and leading him to the store personally, bellowing at him as they went. Another of our number was limping from a kick the *Optio* had administered. The lad had bent down to retrieve a wooden bowl that had fallen from the pile of kit he was carrying. Fuscus had delivered a vicious kick to his backside. The studs on his *caligae* had cut the lad's flesh and blood trickled down the back of his leg as he stood in the queue wincing at the withering tirade Fuscus was bringing down on him.

'You stupid pig! How am I supposed to teach you how to march across the empire in full kit if you can't even keep hold of a poxy bowl?'

Fuscus glared at the lad spitefully then stalked off to the head of the queue.

There was nothing to be said, we just looked at each other. Resigned to the fate we had brought down upon ourselves.

The double door of the *Sacellum* was now open and Scaurus was within, along with the two sentries and a clerk. I could just see a large wooden table illuminated by flickering lamplight. It was now dusk and shadows danced from the room and cavorted on the cobbles of the courtyard. Although I couldn't see clearly, I perceived the odd glint from inside the room.

We had been instructed to place our old clothing in piles in the centre of the courtyard and Fuscus now directed us as to its fate.

'You now have no need of civilian clothing so, when we are done here, it can all be carted down to the furnaces of the baths and burned.' He waited for any protest, grinning nastily, but none came.

'These rags are lice ridden and not even fit to be torn up for arse wipe so burning is the best thing for them. It matters little anyway because, like it or not, you are going nowhere for the next month. I'm not having you wandering abroad amongst decent folk, telling them you're soldiers, when you're not yet fit to scrub out the latrines. Is that clear?'

'Yes *Optio!*' came the bellowed response. We knew by now that what he wanted was blind obedience. If it was not forthcoming then we suffered.

'You are shortly to receive your *viaticum*. That is to say you are going to be paid seventy five *denarii* just for turning up and offering your miserable carcasses for service in my Legion.'

He began to walk slowly along the line, eyeing each and every one of us as he went.

'You will enter one at a time in the order that you are now. Once inside you will speak only to confirm your name and to acknowledge receipt of your payment. Once this is done you will then form a line under the other portico on the far side,' he said, indicating casually with a sweep of his hand.

'Once there you will count out twenty five *denarii* from your new found wealth and wait for me to come over to you. Don't go thinking that you will be flouncing down to the *vicus* after one month and throwing your money around. If you have any ideas about frittering your money on painted whores and cheap, pissy wine then forget it! You may be allowed out but you will be under curfew and you will be disciplined if you come back here either drunk or with a dose of Venus' curse. That is the first and last warning you will receive on the matter. Clear?'

'Yes *Optio!*' Once more the response thundered round the courtyard.

'Right. First man. Get in there!'

One by one we entered the room of the *Sacellum*. Slowly the queue went down and a new line grew under the opposite portico. Then it was my turn. I walked along the top of the courtyard and turned into the room. I may as well have walked into a wall as I came to a shocked halt about two paces short of the table. My mouth fell open as I gazed on the standards lining the walls of the room. Wall paintings in rich colours. Depictions of the gods and legendary heroes provided a backdrop to these glittering icons of the power of the Legion. Crimson silks glowed in the lamplight along with gold braiding. Everywhere the glint of gold and silver shimmered around the room, reflecting on the polished wooden shafts of the standards.

I gazed agog at the bright unit *vexilla* and brought my eye around to the *signa* of the Cohorts present at the fortress at this time. They stood either side of the *Aquila*. The magnificent golden eagle stood atop a polished wooden shaft. Wings spread and beak open. Seeming to scream defiance. Its golden talons gripping flashing gold lightening bolts. It seemed the very embodiment of the power and spirit of the Legion. Resting next to it, the most sacred image of all. The *Imago*. The face of the Emperor gazed out from its ornate bronze and silver surround, its face a shining mask of bright gold. The standard rested against a laurel bound with gold ribbon and draped with gold edged purple silk. The unexpected awe of the scene left me breathless.

'Close your mouth and step to the table you idiot!'

Scaurus' bark jerked me back to reality and I quickly took in the rest of my surroundings. Scaurus sat behind a broad oak table with an iron bound chest in front of him. A padlock and ring key lay next to it and the sentries stood to either side. The clerk was sat next to Scaurus and was scribbling away seemingly oblivious to my presence. Behind them lay an open hatchway in the floor. I could see a set of stone steps leading down into the *sacellum* and wondered if I would ever get to see what lay down there.

'Name?'

'Marcus Sulpicius Vepitta Sir!'

'Vepitta will do!' came the grumbled response.

'Seventy five *denarii*. Witness my count and proclaim it correct.'

With that Scaurus began to count the coins out as I watched. I had never had this much money in my life. Even if Fuscus was about to relieve me of some of it. The count finished, Scaurus looked up at me.

'Pay correct?'

'Correct sir!'

'Then sign next to your name!' Scaurus pointed to the ledger in front of the clerk who handed me an ink pen. I signed and took the money.

'Next!' Scaurus bellowed.

I left the room and joined the new line. The satisfying weight of the coins felt good in my hand.

When we had all collected our payment Fuscus appeared at the top of the line, a smug grin spreading across his face as he held out a cloth bag in front of the first man. Scaurus was with him. But his face exhibited its usual, impassive mask as he cast the odd glance up and down the line.

'Right then!' shouted Fuscus. 'The *Centurion* and I will now collect twenty five *denarii* off each of you. Such payment represents your board and lodging and sundry other expenses whilst you are undergoing your first month's training!' He indicated to the first man to drop his coins in the bag and began to work his way down the line as Scaurus watched from the end.

'If you are thinking that you are going to short change us then I would advise you to think again. There will be a count at the end of the collection. If the count falls short then you are all up to your necks in it. I loath dishonesty, and if any of your number is a cheat, then by *Iovi* I will teach you to hate it too!'

Each of us looked at their neighbour as though pleading for him to put the right money in the bag. If there was just one coin short then all hell would break loose.

Only the gods and Fuscus knew what would happen to us but every last one of us knew it would cost us in pain and humiliation.

Once the collection was finished Fuscus and Scaurus retired to the *sacellum* table and began to count the money. It seemed to last for ever and every one of us began to cringe when they began the count a second time. Finally they finished and the coins were put back into the cloth bag. Fuscus shoved the stool back he was sitting on and stalked briskly into the courtyard. Scaurus was behind him carrying his *vitis* which, we knew, he would beat every single one of us with if he felt the need.

Fuscus stood in front of us slowly looking up and down the row. His eyes glinting in the light of lamps and torches as dusk blackened to night. You could have cut the atmosphere with a knife. It was so charged with nervous anticipation. Silence was king as Fuscus initiated an agonizing pause.

'You are a shower of useless, good for nothing bastards. Nothing more than the lowest form that *Iovi* saw fit to create!' He fairly spat the words out.

'Oh *Juno* strengthen my bones,' I thought. 'This man is about to smash us all into a million bits.'

Fuscus continued.

'The one thing you do appear to have, however, is honesty!' His voice lowered then. You could almost hear the collective sigh of relief rise from our lungs as we realized he was happy with the collection and nobody had cheated them.

'I now have something to work with. You have now given me something and I, for my part, will do my best to elevate you all to the status of Legionaries!'

Still Scaurus remained silent. He continued to survey the line. As though he were able to identify the strengths and weaknesses of each individual merely by laying eyes on them. As he surveyed us he idly tapped the thick end of his *Vitis* into the palm of his hand. Fuscus spoke again.

'You will now leave, in *Contubernium* order, for your allocated barracks. The first two men in the column will carry torches to light your way. There will be no talking and you will keep file or I will spring from the shadows and visit untold misery on you. Do you understand?'

Once more we bellowed. 'Yes Optio!'

'You have one half hour to reach barracks and turn in for lights out. Anyone outside their beds after that will answer to the *Centurion*. Tomorrow you are sworn in and, after that, you learn to become soldiers. Now go! And sleep soundly, you will need it!'

With surprising efficiency we fell in in the required order and moved off towards barracks, moving silently through the fortress, not even daring to acknowledge the sentries and fire pickets along the way. Even as we entered the barracks and made for our respective billets, there was silence. I don't think anyone wanted to run the risk of Fuscus springing out on us like some sadistic *Lemur* from the spirit realm. We had not even had the opportunity of introducing ourselves to our new comrades and, for now, that was how it was going to stay. I had managed to secure a low bunk in the dormitory and I swung my legs in, pulling the blanket up to my chin and sinking into the straw stuffed mattress. The day had not been physically taxing but our minds had raced for most of it. Everyone was exhausted and sleep descended in an instant.

It was over, almost as soon as my head had sunk into the mattress. My eyes stinging to open as the racket travelled up the corridor from the commotion of Fuscus entering the first dormitory. His now familiar tirades booming around the walls to the accompaniment of groans and complaints.

'Don't snivel about it you lazy bastards. You wanted to be here. Live with it!'

The commotion drew closer, accompanied by the thud of bare feet running around on the cold stone of the floor. The outside door of our billet crashed open and then the door of the dormitory flew open and Fuscus roared in like a wild animal about to rip us all to shreds.

'You filthy lizards. It stinks in here! Has some scabby old mule been bedding down in here? Well?

'No *Optio*.' We groaned with as much energy as we could summon.

'Hah! So! Instead of spending the night sleeping, you've obviously all been up all night farting and playing with yourselves! Well that's just typical. Get up and get out to that well. Go and wash that shit off they dusted us with yesterday!'

Oh that! Everyone had forgotten that we still had a coating of that foul smelling powder they doused us in at the hospital. I swung my legs out, scratching my scalp and fighting to suppress a jaw cracking yawn. My bunk mate swung down and lifted his tunic over his head, about to put it on.

'What are you doing you stupid animal?'

Fuscus snatched the tunic from the lad's grip and landed a stinging slap to the back of his head, causing him to lurch forward, eyes almost bursting from his head in shock.

'How in the name of *Dis* do you expect to be able to wash that stink off your body when it is covered in clothing? You idiot! Now shift. All of you!'

Fuscus was off next door, leaving like a whirlwind to wreak devastation on some other poor devils. We scurried through the door, jamming ourselves in the frames in our panic to get out then running up the corridor that travelled the length of the barrack block. The billets we passed that Fuscus had visited were already empty with the sight of just a few white backsides in front of us disappearing through the top door. As we spilled outside the chill hit us and I blinked in surprise. No sun! It was still dark!

More naked bodies blundered out into the cold air, the shock registering on their faces. We stood, still half asleep, steam billowing from mouths and nostrils, each one of us with our arms crossed tightly around us in a vain attempt to warm up.

'Well well! Cold are we?' Fuscus emerged from the door sporting that now familiar sadistic grin.

'Why are you not in your *Contubernia*? Why are you all standing round like a load of Greek pretty boys snivelling in the cold? Right! If you're cold then you need warmth. Five times around the block. Get moving!'

Still dazed, we started off on a trot, not sure what he wanted.

'You idle pigs! Shift! Woe betide the last man back.'

Fuscus had just introduced the element of fear and that did it. We were off. Every last one of us wide awake and tearing round the outside of the barrack block like wild horses. We jostled, pulled and tripped as we went. Skittering and slipping on the dewy paving as we rounded the corners. None of us wishing to be the recipient of the loser's prize. On the second lap I was elbowed in the face and lost my balance, sliding painfully across the paving scouring my knees and elbows, and instantly throwing myself back upright. I recall jumping over the prostrate carcass of one of my comrades and then running like a madman to catch up. I made the middle of the pack and fought to stay there. As we rounded for the fifth lap my heart was pounding away in my chest so much that I thought it would burst from my mouth. Phlegm rose from my lungs and gathered in my mouth, forcing me to spit as we ran. We finished by Fuscus. A now sweaty mass of bodies heaving from the exertion, coughing retching, spitting and puking. Sobs and groans being cast into the night air. The shock of our rude awakening now dawning on us.

As we stood, so the last one of our number cleared the far end of the block and came lurching towards us. A thinly built lad of my age, he was grazed on his chest and face and his knees were cut. As we watched he staggered to the group and collapsed to his knees. Fuscus setting him with a malevolent stare.

'So! All your comrades finish standing up and you think you are entitled to a rest do you?'

The lad was trying to speak and shaking his head violently. Trying to get air into his tortured lungs. Fuscus stepped over and delivered a swift kick to the ribcage causing the small amount of air in the lad's lungs to be expelled with a whoosh. He grabbed the lad by the throat and lifted him upright. The lad's breathing was spasmodic now and foamy mucus drooled from his nose and mouth.

'Right. Let's have another lap out of you for being such a waste of space and thinking you can rest while your comrades can't.'

Fuscus shoved him in the back and commenced running him round the block again. Harrying him as he went. It was obvious the lad was on the point of collapse.

'He'll kill the poor bastard!'

A tall well built lad of perhaps twenty took a step forward, as if to follow Fuscus and his unfortunate victim. I and another instantly barred his way.

'Let him have his sport,' I said. 'Interfere now and you will suffer greater brutality, along with the rest of us. The lad failed. There's nothing to be done.'

We all stood and waited for them to return. Eventually they rounded the top corner of the barrack. Fuscus was still bawling and the lad was virtually crawling on his knees. Instinctively we all started to shout encouragement to the lad. Fuscus stared at us and the lad seemed to take heart from the cheering. He lifted himself to his feet again and stumbled towards us, eventually lurching to a halt in front of us. When he had done he stood there swaying like a poplar whipped by the wind. His chest falling and rising heavily and his breath rasping through cracked lips. He was near to collapse but still he stood.

Fuscus nodded grudgingly. Turning to address us.

'This boy has learnt to finish the job. He suffered. But he finished. You have all started to learn the value of the team. Your encouragement caused him to finish with pride. Remember this lesson.'

He looked over at the lad, still swaying and panting.

'Whose *Contubernium* does he belong to?'

A hand shot up in one of the other groups.

'Two of you. Clean yourselves up, and him. Then take him to the infirmary to have those cuts dressed. We have an important day today and he needs to be with us!'

Two of his *Contubernium* fell out and helped him over to the well. We all watched quietly as his two comrades washed the dust off him and cleaned his wounds with the icy water from the well. I was beginning to realize that, perhaps, Fuscus could guide us along a path of learning, and not just meaningless brutality. Yes, what he had inflicted on his unfortunate victim was harsh. But we all saw how much our cheering gave him that extra desire to finish. We also saw how we, as a group, wanted a common goal and collectively urged the lad to achieve it. Fuscus had not set about us for opening our mouths without permission because he identified the start of our desire to work as a team. For his own part, the exhausted runner had won his first personal victory and showed us all the spirit of success. No one had lost from this.

Once they had finished cleaning the lad, the two volunteers took him off in the direction of the infirmary and Fuscus spoke again.

'Get used to this! You will rise every morning, one hour before the sun and your working day will not finish until one hour after sunset!' Again he paced along our lines, eyeing us as he went.

'You have one half hour to clean your carcasses, dress and break your fast. After this time I will return to collect you and I expect you to be formed up here in your *Contubernia*. Clear!'

'Yes *Optio*!'

'Good! Shift!'

With that he turned and walked off.

We broke ranks and rushed to the well, individuals snatching buckets up and scooping water from the trough at the side, already beginning to wash themselves. A clamour to get hold of a bucket soon developing into pushing, shoving and cursing.

'Together, together. Help each other not yourselves!'

Someone from inside the press shouted over the clamour. It made good sense. We would be done quicker if we exercised order. The crowd broke into the now familiar groups and organized themselves collecting water and washing each other down. We were soon finished and ran quickly back into the barracks to dress. Still in our groups we presented ourselves at the bread ovens and collected bread, honey, oil and cheese for breakfast and then swiftly back to our billets to feed.

Finally, back in the ante room of the dormitory we sat and spoke to each other for the first time.

'This is going to be tougher than I thought, perhaps.'

The lad was around my age and of slim build with nut brown hair. His eyes carried a roguish glint and his accent was local to mine. He gnawed enthusiastically on a thick hunk of cheese and slurped water down as he ate.

'Pudens. That's me!' He said. 'Lucius Calpurnius Pudens.' Now shovelling a large wad of bread in to his mouth.

Now we were breaking the ice. It felt good to have the freedom to speak without Fuscus waiting to deliver some hideous punishment.

'I'm Vepitta. I come from *Mogontiacum*. I was born here!'

'Lucky you! It took me an age to walk here. After all that, I've done nothing but race round like a headless chicken since I got here!'

This was Secundus, the oldest amongst us at twenty two. He had come from the North of Germania and was a farmer by profession. He would become notorious for complaining and wished only to be sent back north so he could go and slaughter the raiders who burnt his farm and stole his cattle.

'Let's make the most of it. Life is going to get hard but at least we have food, a decent living and, I would hope, a lot of new friends.'

Surus was sixteen years old and, already on the way to developing a sound physique. He had spent much of his time working in his father's employ as an assistant stone mason. He had received qualifications but felt that his skills were better employed serving the Legion. Provincial life was dull and if you could do a bit of scrapping, and building, then so much the better.

'Huh! Let's wait and see, eh?' Came Secundus' response.

'Every time I feel as though I was lucky to have made it, my brain shouts, Fuscus! And my heart is in my boots again!'

This was Firmus. He was a year older than me and grew up in another part of the *Vicus*. I had seen him around but had no dealings with him, until now. I knew he had spent most of his life growing up in, and around, one of the town brothels. He gave the impression of being somewhat of a rogue but, I reasoned, he had been required to prove his credentials as much as the next man. Even at this early stage I noticed that he was constantly looking about him and seemingly listening for ... I didn't know!

'Hey. You're the whisperer who got his arse tanned aren't you?'

Firmus pointed accusingly at the young boy sitting quietly in the corner, picking at his food.

'What's your name friend?' asked Surus.

'Lupus,' came the quiet response.

'Hah! The little wolf!' Firmus quipped.

'The *Probatio* must have been touch and go for you after what happened, eh friend?'

Secundus posed the question.

'Yes, I struggled but eventually they allowed me entry. I'm only fourteen and haven't done much with my life yet. The board said that I should be given the chance as they felt I had some soldierly potential and am already trained in accounting and record keeping.'

'Ho ho! Great steaming *Dis*! A boy genius!'

'Leave him alone Firmus!' I said. 'We're all in the same boat here!'

'Fine!' He huffed.

'It strikes me we need to learn how to work with each other, and learn quickly.'

Pacatianus stood in a corner pulling a piece of bread from a round loaf and dipping it in some oil. He was the same age as me and hailed from one of the town's outlying villages. Another to become bored with the rural drudge he had made his way to the fort for a better life.

'Somebody had better have a look at that water clock in the corridor. We'll all be dog food if we're late outside!' Pacatianus reminded us.

'I'll go!'

Lupus jumped up and ran out into the corridor. He had hardly touched his food.

'If he's done with that, I'll take care of it. I'm starving!'

'Starving? You've managed to get hold of, and eat, about twice as much as anyone else!' Observed Pudens. 'By what name does this human rubbish pit wish to be known as?'

'Aebutius. Primus Aebutius! It takes a generous amount of fuel to keep a body such as mine in perfect functioning order.'

The room erupted into gales of laughter as Aebutius sat on his bunk, smiling stupidly, and chewing on his bread. How could such a body need so much fuel. He was fairly tall but looked as though he had been built of twigs. Undoubtedly, Aebutius was the thinnest man in the entire intake and, as we were to find later, had it not been for the incredible amount of qualifications he held regarding armour and weapon production, probably would have been refused entry. He was twenty years old and had trained for twice as long as I had. His credentials were enviable and all obtained under the tutelage of master craftsmen. The Legion had its rules regarding physical standards but even they could be bent to obtain such a useful man.

Lupus came scurrying back into the room, snatching a hunk of bread from his plate and plunging it into the communal bowl of oil.

'We need to go. Now!' He said as he stuffed the bread into his mouth, wiping it with the back of his hand. Everyone of us took a last mouthful of food and then rushed out into the corridor. The other billets were emptying again and together we moved outside, forming up in the half light of the new day.

Silently we waited for the return of Fuscus. The spreading light of the morning sun touched me with a feeling of well being, even after such a harsh awakening.

Fuscus appeared again, and this time Scaurus was with him. Both were fully kitted in armour, but without helmets. Fuscus wore a set of iron *lorica segmentata* which gleamed in the dawn light. His *cingulum* glittered and jingled as he approached and he bore a beautiful bone handled *gladius* carried in a red leather scabbard decorated in chased bronze plates. A light brown *paenula* was draped over his shoulders with the body of the cloak draped over his left arm.

Scaurus was resplendent in a shirt of *lorica hamata* which was sleeveless and terminated at hip height. Over the shirt was worn a harness of leather straps on which seven *phalerae* were hung. The silvered discs of the *Centurion's* decorations captured the colours of the morning sky and gleamed as though gifts from the gods themselves. He carried his *gladius* on the left side and it hung on the end of a plated waist belt, unlike the baldric arrangement worn by Fuscus. A second belt of bronze enamelled plates supported a highly ornate *pugio*. On his legs he wore silvered greaves which flashed reflected light as he strode along. The whole assembly was completed by the *sagum*. A rich dark blue with a black border. It was brooched to his left shoulder and draped over his right forearm. The ever present *vitis* was carried in his left hand.

Scaurus took up position in front of us while Fuscus remained to one side of the formation. Everyone was conscious that he was casting a critical eye over everyone present, a mental roll call being carried out as Scaurus addressed us.

'Today you pledge yourselves to the service of the Emperor, the Senate and people of Rome!' He began, unhurried and thoughtful as he delivered his address.

'In a few moments we will march off to the temple of *Iuppiter* and there you will declare your oath of allegiance, in the presence of the standards and the priests, and in the hearing of the Gods. Your oath binds you to the Legion and requires you to adhere to the regulations laid down which govern your service. This day marks your first as soldiers in the service of Rome. Do you accept the honour you are about to receive?'

'Yes *Centurion*!' Forty voices roared the proud response.

'March them off, *Optio*.'

'Turn to the left!' ordered Fuscus. 'Move off in your *Contubernia* and stay silent! Follow me!'

Fuscus led from the front and Scaurus walked alongside the formation, now and again casting a glance back to the rear to see if the line had developed stragglers. I couldn't imagine that there would be any such thing on a day such as this if all of my comrades felt as I did. My heart was beating with intense pride and excitement and I could hardly wait to take the oath and affirm my loyalty to my new family. What a great day this was!

By the time we had reached the temple the sun had climbed high enough to shine down from behind us and light the steps of the huge edifice. White marble gleamed in the morning sun and gilded capitals and plinths blazed with fiery reflections. Shadows fell into the area under the pediment and I could almost imagine Gods hiding in the darkness, waiting to bear witness to what was about to happen. At the base of the steps stood a stone altar, draped in garlands, the lettering carved on its face picked out in red and attesting to the fact that it was dedicated by the Legion in honour of *Iuppiter,* Greatest and Best. On the top of the altar, embers glowed in the focus, waiting to be fed with libations and offerings of incense and *libum,* the sacred cake baked for the consumption of *Iovi* himself.

On either side of the altar stood *Cornicens* and *Tubicens.* Resplendent in full armour and wearing wolf skins attached to their helmets. Vicious white teeth still snarling the defiance of the beast that originally wore the skin. Their polished instruments were held poised, ready to blast out a fanfare to welcome the Father of heaven into our presence.

The *Haruspex* stood ready, along with his assistant, close to the altar. Clad in their white priestly robes and with their heads covered in deference to the God they were about to invite down. Close to the temple steps a large ox stood accompanied by the *Auspex* and his assistant who carried a large poleaxe. The ox stood placidly, blessedly unaware of what was about to befall it.

We were halted in front of this assembly and silently we watched as Fuscus and Scaurus advanced to our front and stood directly in line with the altar. I clenched my fists with the anticipation of the moment, impatient to swear loyalty and begin my new life. Suddenly the musicians raised their instruments and the melodic blasts echoed around the open area in front of the temple. The ox shifted, startled by the noise and snorted noisily, the *Auspex's* assistant calming the beast as the clack of hobnails on the slabs came from our left side. As we watched the two standard bearers halted in front of the altar and turned to face us.

The defiant golden eagle seemed to stare down at each and every one of us, as though it expected, no demanded, just and proper reverence. By its side the golden visage of the Emperor, *Claudius,* surveyed us from inside its own portable shrine on the polished wooden pole of cornell wood.

Scaurus and Fuscus snapped to attention, the *Centurion* raising his right hand in an open palm salute, first to the standards and then to the priests at the altar.

'Greetings! Those men assembled here today have been accepted for service in the Fourteenth Gemina Legion and wish to proclaim allegiance!' Scaurus addressed the priests solemnly.

'I ask that you take their oath and confer on them the blessings of *Iuppiter,* Greatest and Best!'

'You may proceed with the oath *Centurion!*' Said the chief priest.

Scaurus turned, and again raised his hand in salute towards us. Fuscus stood between the standards grasping each of their handles and facing us. Both men now absorbed in the dignity of the proceedings. Scaurus paused momentarily and the scene was akin to a painted frieze from a rich man's town house.

The *Centurion* and *Optio* were frozen in time with the two standard bearers for that brief moment, the only clue to real time being the gentle breeze which tussled at the soft fur of the great bearskin worn by the *Imaginifer.*

'Raise your right hands and repeat the oath!' Scaurus instructed us. We did as we were bidden and then it began.

'Now that I am accepted for service in the Fourteenth Gemina Legion,
I do swear allegiance to the divine Emperor *Caesar Augustus Claudius,*
I promise to obey all that are placed in command,
And will follow them against whatsoever enemies they lead me before,
I pledge not to desert the standards,
Nor in any way break the laws of the Roman people.
If I break my vow of loyalty thus given to the Emperor,
Or violate the oath that I have thus accepted,
Then let my life be forfeit to *Iuppiter*, Greatest and Best.'
After a short pause Scaurus boomed.

'So say you ?'

'So say us!' crashed around the square.

Shivers still ran the length of my spine as the priest stepped forward and, raising a finger to us he announced;

'You will remain silent, your God is at hand!'

We waited silently, expectantly. The priest raised his hands to the heavens, as though to implore the great God to descend.

'Banish thoughts of impurity or evil from your minds. Make *Iuppiter* welcome with your piety! Evil spirits, leave this place now!'

Again the horns of the musicians blasted out the notes needed to drive out the entities unfit to remain in this sacred gathering. An acolyte approached the altar and poured water over the hands of the priest and his assistant to purify them, then each were handed a small cloth with which to dry themselves.

The acolyte bobbed in a low bow and moved to one side.

'*Iuppiter*! Great father descend for us now and grace this precinct with your presence. I beseech you!'

The acolyte returned with a small open box from which the priest took incense, placing the resin on the glowing embers, as did his assistant. The aromatic smoke rose into the morning air to welcome the god as he descended.

'Now the air is pure, I offer food and drink to sustain you great father!'

Again the priest raised his hands skywards and then took the silver jug offered him by the acolyte, pouring the libation onto the altar once more and causing a cloud of steam as the liquid doused the red hot charcoal. Again the assistant repeated the act and the process continued, libum then being placed on the embers in an identical procedure ensuring the God had food with his wine.

'Banish those evil spirits remaining here still. Great father *Iovi* is amongst us!'

Again the horns blasted out the notes to purge the assembly of bad spirits.

'Great father! These men have declared their loyalty to you and to Rome. Give us a sign that you accept their pledge and will take them into your protection for the rest of their service!'

With that the priest indicated to the *Auspex* whose assistant stepped swiftly in front of the ox. Before the animal could react in any way the assistant had raised the poleaxe and brought it crashing down between the animal's eyes, mercifully stunning the beast and laying it flat on the flag stones. The *Auspex* stepped forward, and drawing a large knife, he stooped next to the beast and pulled it across the ox's neck and throat. Blood sprayed into the air and a thick, crimson pool spread around the prostrate animal glinting and steaming in the morning air. The animals legs twitched momentarily, its cloven hooves clicking and skittering on the flags, then it was done.

'Accept the carcass of this humble beast great *Iovi* and show these men your will!'

The *Auspex* sliced open the stomach of the ox with the razor sharp knife and steaming entrails slumped out onto the flag stones. At once the *Auspex* began to sift through, eventually cutting the gleaming liver free and scrutinizing it in detail. At last he stood and faced the *Haruspex*.

'Are the *Auspices* good?' asked the *Haruspex*.

'I can find no fault,' came the reply.

'Soldiers of the Fourteenth Gemina, you have the protection of *Iuppiter*, Greatest and Best. Go now. And fulfil your pledge!' proclaimed the priest, throwing his arms wide and nodding to us approvingly.

Now it was done. The oath was taken and my heart swelled with pride. Now I was truly where I belonged.

Chapter 3

Strong Foundations

Most of the remainder of the day was spent, once again, addressing outstanding administrative and logistical details for our future service. One of these tasks was the tattooing of the Military Mark on our left arm, just below the shoulder. Black ink and a bronze needle marked in our initials and year of enlistment followed by the letters SPQR. Naturally all of this was conducted at breakneck speed under the direction of Fuscus. Despite the fact we had taken our sacred oath and received our mark it seemed to make little difference to him. Still, we were given no more consideration than the lowest form of slave. It was the most important day of my life so far but, to Fuscus and Scaurus, it was just the first rung of a very tall ladder that we needed to be taught to climb.

As the day was drawing to a close I was sent, along with several others, to report to Sextilli at the infirmary. I wasn't definite about why I had been summoned but I had a good idea and already I was filling with trepidation at the thought of what was likely to happen.

I poked my head slowly round the door when told to enter and saw Sextilli standing at a low table. The top of the table was laid with four squares of linen upon which rested some of the most fiendish looking instruments I had seen so far.

The medic cast me a sideways look as he leant over the table.

'Ah! You're .... .' He wagged his finger quizzically. 'Who are you again?' He beckoned for me to come further into the room.

'Vepitta sir!' I stood in front of him, shifting restlessly.

He tapped his chin with a *stylus* and looked down a list inscribed on a wax tablet in front of him.

'Vepitta .... . Vepitta .... . Ah yes! Rotting tooth. Good, good!' He announced cheerily. Clapping his palms together.

He turned from me and began to carefully measure something from a glass bottle into a small pottery cup with dimpled sides, tipping small amounts at a time into the cup until he was satisfied with the quantity.

'Sir. I .... . the tooth gives me no trouble, it .... .'

'Good.' He interrupted. 'When we have finished it will be of even less consequence to you!'

He smiled benevolently, handing me the cup, my fumbled attempt to wriggle out of the situation a dismal failure. I took hold of the cup, holding it down low as if something were about to leap out and latch onto my face. I slowly held it level with my face and sniffed gingerly. Instantly I thrust it back to arms length,

25

screwing my face up, disgusted at the foul smelling brew lurking in the bottom of the cup.

'Down in one then. It may smell like it's just come out of the latrine drain but it's excellent at its job!'

Sextilli smiled again and gestured for me to drink up.

'Its job!' I thought. 'And what in the name of all the gods might that be?'

Swiftly I tilted my head back and threw the contents down my throat, swallowing hard in an attempt to speed the progress of the evil smelling draught along quicker. An orderly entered the room as I did this and, seeing the obvious change in my expression, picked up a wooden pale and advanced towards me, the bucket outstretched towards my face. My stomach felt as though it would erupt and went into gripping spasms while I coughed and retched. I arched my back over and began to heave violently, although thankfully nothing was produced. When the worst of it was over I stood upright. My eyes were watering heavily and I had drooled all down my chin and onto my tunic.

'Good show boy!' Shouted Sextilli. 'Not many people can keep hold of that stuff. Tastes like shit doesn't it?' He grinned at me once more.

'Now! Come over here and sit down. I expected you to throw some of that back and allowed accordingly. As you have kept hold of it, it should work much faster!'

He gestured to a wooden chair with a padded back and the orderly took hold of my arm to lead me over. I moved towards the chair.

'Sir. Really, the tooth is ... ...'

The power of speech left me in an instant as the draught took effect. It felt as though *Iovi* had struck me with a lightening bolt as myriad coloured lights flashed in front of my eyes and my blood began to roar in my ears. My legs gave way and my mouth dropped open as I gasped like a stranded fish. The orderly hauled me across the room and I became aware of the support of the chair as I slumped into it. Almost at once, my head flopped backwards and I felt my mouth fall open again, I must have looked like some sort of senseless simpleton as my head rolled around and I groaned feebly.

I tried to tell them that I felt stranger than I had ever felt but all I could muster were the inarticulate mumblings of a gibbering idiot. The orderly was securing me to the chair with large leather straps. He tightened them up and then applied a strap across my forehead to stop my head from rolling around. Eventually announcing to Sextilli that I was now ready for treatment. Although Sextilli's potion had rendered me totally paralysed I was still aware of everything around me. As I sat there, the orderly picked up a small oil lamp and a mirror, holding both up to my face. The light flashed momentarily into my eyes and then Sextilli leaned over me, his face now a mask of concentration as he probed my mouth, probably with one of those infernal instruments from the table.

'Good. Keep the light there!' I heard him speak but it seemed to come from miles away.

I felt, rather than saw a large metal object enter my mouth. I could hear a squeaking noise as my mouth expanded slowly to the point that I thought my jaw would crack. Then it stopped. Again Sextilli's face floated around in front of me and another tool entered my mouth scraping around and knocking my back teeth.

I was aware of pressure being applied but could feel no pain. Another instrument. This time centred in one place as Sextilli stood above me, his eyes narrowing in concentration.

'Right, hold it just there. Steady!'

Now the orderly appeared above me as well, peering intently into my mouth. I felt a heavy impact in my jaw bone, still with no pain and heard a crack, as though inside my own head. Gods! What were they doing to me? Sextilli moved out of view then quickly reappeared. Another unidentified instrument entered my mouth. This time I could feel a few small shakes and pulls. My mouth had dried out now with my breaths but still I drooled from the corner of my mouth. Next came the taste of warm salty blood as Sextilli announced:

That's it. Done! Let's get that expander out before he chokes then!'

Again the squeaking noise and I felt my jaw relaxing, able to close once more, then the blood and drool slipped down the back of my throat and I began to choke. Quickly Sextilli and the orderly loosened the straps and pushed me forwards, head between my knees. When the retching and coughing stopped I was sat upright once more and another cup was presented to me.

'Try to drink boy!' It was the orderly. He poured a small amount of extremely salty liquid into my mouth and I swallowed. This time there was no holding onto the contents of my stomach and a stream of vomit erupted into the well placed bucket, the orderly slapping me on the back repeatedly as I gagged and retched.

Slowly I regained my senses, the ability to move my limbs gradually returning, carefully testing them for function as I remained sprawled in the chair. I remained there as the others who had accompanied me were brought in, one at a time, and treated for whatever it was that ailed them. Some seemed quite quick, others took longer and were accompanied by yelps of pain on occasion. Everyone I saw looked at me, apparently in stark fear. I must have looked hideous, flopped in the chair like a corpse with dried blood all over my chin and tunic. Perhaps they thought that was their fate as well. Eventually I recovered enough for Sextilli to send me back to barracks, although my head still spun and I was very unsteady on my feet.

'Take this poultice with you and place it in your mouth over the hole where the tooth was,' Sextilli advised. 'Place it in boiling water for a minute then coat it liberally in honey and keep it there for as long as possible. If you can manage to sleep with it there, then so much the better!'

He handed me a small cloth package which felt as though it contained leaves, perhaps herbs. It seemed big enough to keep in my mouth without falling down my throat and choking me whilst I slept.

'It contains certain ingredients to take away pain from the area and to start hardening the edges of the hole. Be sure to use plenty of honey until it is healed as this will help to prevent it festering!' He went on. 'Don't let any odd bits of food get in the hole and rinse your mouth regularly with as strong *acetum* as you can stand. Now. Any questions?'

He smiled and spread his hands. Awaiting the response.

'Lo Shurr.' I replied. Oh gods! I can't speak anymore. A look of dismay must have crossed my face then for he quickly responded.

'Don't worry. That is the lingering effects of the draft I gave you. You needed it because the tooth was a large and deep one. If it was a lesser tooth from the front then I would have just yanked it out!' He demonstrated a swift twisting gesture with his hand, grinning broadly as he did it. I held the side of my face and winced at the tenderness.

'I have held back a couple of your comrades to assist you back to barracks.' He turned to the table and began to start cleaning his instruments.

'If the hole turns sour then come back and see me. Now, go and get some sleep!'

He dismissed me with a wave over his shoulder and continued his cleaning. The orderly opened the door and led me out to two of the other patients who had been kept back to assist me. Gratefully I placed an arm over each of their shoulders and together we shuffled back to barracks where, having followed the medic's instructions, I fell into a deep, dreamless sleep.

* * *

I cannot speak for many of the recruits in the other *Contubernia* but, as to my own, most of us, with the possible exception of Lupus, were very confident of our own physical abilities. We believed ourselves to be strong and fit young men capable of demonstrating durability and stamina. How hard could it be to raise ourselves to the fitness of a Legionary? Over the next few weeks we found out the painful truth of just how far we had yet to go. Our main advantage was that we were young and fit. The hard fact of the matter was that, at the beginning we didn't even come close to what we needed to be able to give.

Through arduous training, in a variety of conditions, we began to forge the stuff of the Legionary. Slowly we began to build bodies capable of marching across continents and develop the mindset that would allow us to go into battle with unwavering confidence in the abilities of ourselves, our comrades and our commanders. Hardship was borne with quiet resilience and the spirit of the team was all that mattered. If one man suffered then he would be helped to complete his goal. Everyone learnt that if this rule was followed then, the day that you struggled, your comrades would be there for you.

We would not be allowed to go anywhere near weapons and equipment for a long time. Those would be mastered later. For now we were to work on forging ourselves into one efficient body. Each man knowing his place and how to move swiftly and correctly in relation to his comrades. *Mogontiacum* would serve as our base while we strived to master the basics. Scaurus and Fuscus would ensure that those skills were properly learnt before we progressed to the next level of training.

Initially we began with basic marching skills. We learnt the regulation marching pace along with static foot drills. Both Scaurus and Fuscus tutored us in equal measure. Sometimes we worked as a large group, other times we would be split into smaller groups for ease of tutoring. We were separated on occasion from our own *Contubernia* in order to learn how to adapt to co-operating with other, less familiar groups of men. We learnt the value of demonstration as one or two *Contubernia* illustrated to the rest what they had learnt. Sometimes it was easier to learn from demonstration than participation as one could not always see what was being taught whilst stood in the centre of a group.

Four *Veterani* assisted the *Centurion* and *Optio*. All were equally as harsh as the senior ranks and were merciless when it came to failure and stupidity. Beatings and humiliation were a common feature of their techniques. For the duration of their time with us they were anonymous. It wasn't our place to learn their names, such information was of no use to us. They were all addressed by the collective title of *Veteranus*. If we had aspirations to achieve such a status then we were told to forget about it. We were the lowest form of scum and didn't show any real potential to evolve further!

As Fuscus promised, our working day started one hour before sunrise and finished one hour after sunset. Every morning we bathed outside in the trough by the well and then we ate a very swift, light breakfast before starting our work. Physical excellence was a priority and we initially started with running outside the confines of the fort to build stamina. We progressed to gymnastics and boxing in leather gloves to build toughness and fighting spirit. We were deliberately pitted against our closest comrades and urged to beat them into submission to encourage aggression. Such exercises caused us great concern for a time with regard to Lupus. He was the youngest of us and weaker than all of us. Initially he suffered badly and sustained terrible beatings. Both from the boxing and from those who trained us. If we could not grasp the necessary on our own the only solution was to beat it into us. Lupus was so close to despair at one point that we thought he would take his own life. Then, suddenly, it all changed.

Shortly before a boxing session we had tried to fire his morale and enthusiasm, but without success. The boy was becoming increasingly downhearted as he struggled to achieve the required standard. It was hard to have to try to build him up and then be expected to box him to the floor but we all knew that our trainers would spot it if we went easy on him. If that happened we would suffer dire consequences.

So it was that day that Lupus went into box with Aebutius. The bout began, as expected, with Lupus taking a few good hits to the ears and ribs. We watched his suffering and could see the frustration of his failing defence building up in him. Longer in the arm, Aebutius evaded the boy's blocks and swipes with ease, delivering precise, painful punches and jabs. Urged on to finish, Aebutius planted a stinging blow on Lupus' nose. There was the familiar wet smack of the punch landing and blood began to flow from the boy's nose. Lupus backed away shaking his head and rubbing his eyes, which watered heavily from the punch.

Aebutius stepped back momentarily, allowing Lupus to recover. The *Veteranus* accompanying Scaurus was just about to bawl at Aebutius when he caught sight of Lupus from the corner of his eye. Lupus had backed off and dropped his guard, watching Aebutius carefully. Then, surprisingly, Lupus beckoned him forward. Everyone started shouting for Lupus to re-engage and for Aebutius to get in and finish the boy. The older fighter approached, intent on putting an end to Lupus' continuing humiliation. Still Lupus stood, gloves down, seemingly waiting for the final assault. Aebutius shuffled forward quickly, toe to heel, intent on delivering a hard right to the jaw. The blow licked out and .... The target was gone! With tremendous speed, Lupus ducked the blow and hammered two fists into Aebutius' kidneys as he passed. Aebutius swung round, grimacing with the unexpected pain, and flushing with rising anger and embarrassment, swinging his fist with him as he tried to back hammer his attacker. This time Lupus had dropped to the floor, evading the swipe, and hammered his fist into his opponent's stomach. Now aware that he was the defender, Aebutius doubled up, punching downward in an effort to stun his unexpected tormentor but Lupus had rolled out to one side and sprang up, landing a volley of punches to his hapless opponent's exposed side. A loud grunt of pain emanated from Aebutius as he leaned to the side that had been hit, in doing so he opened his arms wide to the sides. That was all that was needed. Fired by his new found confidence, and presented with an open target, Lupus darted to Aebutius' front and delivered a single, punishing blow to the older lad's sternum. Aebutius creased over in agony and dropped to the floor, retching and gasping for air.

For a moment there was silence. Even Scaurus, presiding over the session, stood with his mouth open. Trying hard to suppress a shocked grin. As skinny as Aebutius was he was a good boxer and had a fair turn of speed. He knelt on the floor cradling his midriff whilst Lupus stood over him, wearing a look of disbelief. He had done it. He had won.

Suddenly the assembly erupted into cheers and laughter. So! The little wolf had finally bared his teeth. He had used speed and his wits to deliver his opening attack and his confidence to achieve a win had grown with every landed punch. At last. Victory was his. Everyone cheered for the little cockerel as his victory registered with the spreading smile on his bloodied face. Our pride in him was obvious as he was patted, pummelled and his hair was ruffled by his comrades.

To our relief Lupus developed at an astonishing rate after that. Once he realized that he did have the ability to achieve his goals his spirits soared. With the worry of wondering what would become of Lupus now a distant memory, the rest of us were able to apply ourselves fully to the tasks ahead, and just as well, as much hardship still lay ahead of us.

* * *

As our stamina increased with our ability to run over greater distances we incorporated swimming into our training regime. *Mogontiacum* lay on the River *Rhenus*. It was a huge river and offered little in the way of narrow crossings or gentle currents. The river could only be swum on calm days in reasonable weather. Poor conditions resulted in increased currents and swelling from rains meant that even the strongest swimmers risked being swept to their deaths. Our swimming lessons took place just upstream from a large wooden bridge, the pilings of which were great timber trunks driven into the river bed. Spaced at regular intervals, the gaps could be hung with large rope nets to catch any swimmers that succumbed to the strength of the current. The nets would prevent you from being swept down stream but there still existed the danger of being dragged down by treacherous under currents that swirled unseen in the black waters. No swimming was therefore allowed in bad weather, or heavy rain.

On our first crossing, as with subsequent ones, we entered the river around two hundred paces upstream from the bridge. The drag of the current was incredibly fierce, even on the mild sunny day that we first swam the river. You could feel the surge of the current against your legs then your feet left the riverbed and you were swimming furiously to reach the other side which lay some hundred and fifty paces away.

The *Veterani* swam amongst us as we struggled, kicked and flailed in the swirling, muddy water. They shouted encouragement and kept an eye out for those who struggled to stay afloat. Fuscus observed from the bridge, calling out to individuals as he walked across and looking for any of us who may have hit the nets. Several of our number were swept down to the nets and had to struggle up ropes to reach the deck of the bridge. They were met by Scaurus and Fuscus who made them wish that they had been drowned before they were ordered to the far side to assist those about to reach land. I made my crossing with much splashing, coughing and spluttering. Determination almost giving way to blind panic as the river threatened to pull me to a watery grave. I felt its power as it shoved me downstream while I fought for the opposite bank, unseen river nymphs grasping at my ankles, trying to pull me down to their world. The experience was, for me, truly terrifying.

I crawled from the water, exhausted. Instantly I was kicked in the ribs by a *Veteranus* who yelled obscenities at me and yanked me to my feet, ordering me to assist those coming out of the water. I waded up and down, waist deep in the surging current, grabbing at wrists and armpits and dragging exhausted comrades into the slippery mud of the bank. Once we had retrieved everyone we clawed our way up the steep sides of the grassy bank and stood, dripping and exhausted, on the grass above the bank, coated in stinking black river mud.

Scaurus had kept the recruits who had climbed from the nets to one side. A roll call was then taken and, miraculously none of us had been taken by the river. Once we were all accounted for Fuscus sprinted those separated by Scaurus back across the bridge to collect our tunics. Then sprinted them back with the armfuls of clothing to distribute it amongst us, berating and insulting them as they went.

It had started to dawn on some of us by this time that Scaurus and his staff were participating in all of the running and swimming that they subjected us to. They, however, were eating up the punishment, with enough strength and energy left to look fresh enough to do it all over again. We, meanwhile, flopped around in states of near collapse during the initial stages.

For the remainder of the month we continued to be subjected to this blistering regime of punishment and pain. We all knew how much it hurt to endure this training but none of us had quite realized how fit and powerful we were becoming. Nor did we completely realize how close we were knitting together as a group or how strong were the ties that now bound us. We were brothers. A family forged in the harshest of environments.

When we thought it could not become harder we were shown that it could hurt much more. Our runs doubled in distance. Packs were introduced and weights increased as we grew used to the load. The *Rhenus* held less fear for us as we advanced further into our training. The struggle to cross had now been replaced with the need to cross in faster times, first in clothing and then with packs. The river claimed three of our number during that time. They were never found again. Their deaths served only to illustrate that, if we didn't master the crossings, as instructed, then we would share their fate. Our brothers had demonstrated the ultimate price of failure to us and we would not forget them for it.

Towards the end of this period of basic training it became noticeable that Scaurus and his team were having to spend less time running backwards and forwards, shouting and railing and pulling stragglers along. Our aim to succeed had become our motivation now. Little else was now needed to urge us to engage in gruelling marches, exhausting river crossings or flattening friends pitted against us in increasingly more vicious fist fights. Injury was ignored, borne until we returned to *Mogontiacum*. We knew that Sextilli and his assistants would be there to fix it. All we had to do was get ourselves back. And come back we did. Time and again, through the great gates, each time a little less exhausted than before. Spirits higher than the last time as we finally realized the extent of our achievements. Finally, we knew we were the raw material required to forge the world's finest soldier.

The Roman Legionary.

Chapter 4

The Welcome Break

With reluctance, I decided that I would not visit Quintus and Curatia. Once I had known that Fuscus was going to honour his word and let us have an evening's leave I had wrestled with the question of whether to visit them or not. There was no question that they held a special place in my heart but I could not go back. Not yet. Our time out would be limited and I needed to finish my training. Then I could go back with my head held high. Then I could tell them that I was a fully trained soldier and had earned my place in the Legion. I knew they would understand. Once the next phase of training was complete I would return to *Mogontiacum* and I would be able to see them whenever I chose. The Legion had been garrisoned there for years and we lived in a time of relative peace in this area of the Empire. There was every chance that I could spend the majority of my service engaged in peacekeeping duties around this part of the world. There would be plenty of time for visits.

By now we were entitled to wear undress kit, along with a *cingulum militare* and *pugio*. These were the trappings of the soldier and people would know that we belonged to the fort. Our superiors also knew that it would be unwise to let us wander abroad without any protection. Even Legionaries got their skulls cracked by thieves and cutpurses. The chance of any prospective thief ending up on the needle sharp point of an iron dagger would minimize the risk so we were allowed to order them through stores, their cost being met from pay stoppages. My excitement rose as it drew closer to our release. A whole evening with no Scaurus or Fuscus breathing down our necks or tormenting us with that pack of bears known as the *Veterani*. It seemed almost a dream come true. I had a pouch full of money and a desire to see a little of the good life. We could find whatever we needed just outside those gates.

'Oh, for pity's sake. Will you get a move on! Do we have to wait all night for you!'

Secundus was complaining loudly, as usual, whilst Pudens rooted around in the wooden chest at the base of his bunk.

'How can I possibly go into town without my lucky dice?' Pudens looked incredulously at Secundus. 'How in the name of *Fortuna* am I to win so much as a *quadrans* if I don't use my lucky dice? Tell me that if you can, you miserable farm boy!'

Secundus stabbed a finger at Pudens, his mouth opening to deliver a retort when Pacatianus cut in.

'The only reason why you're so keen to take those dice with you is because they're fixed!' He said, crossing his arms and nodding with a grin. As if challenging Pudens to refute what we all knew was the truth of it. He did not disappoint.

'That's outrageous you bastard! Why my old toothless granny carved those dice herself from the knuckle bones of her favourite cow!' Said Pudens, feigning indignation. 'She gave them to me as a leaving present when I left for this temple of suffering. It wounds me to think that you think I could be so devious as to carry loaded dice!'

Most of us were smiling or chuckling quietly as we locked our things away before we left. Pudens was starting to gather his audience. He loved nothing more than to provoke Secundus. Why on earth Secundus fell for it every time was beyond me. Still. It was entertaining to watch and I was certain that both participants enjoyed it. Even if Secundus did bluster and rant most indignantly at his taunts.

'Oh, you're so full of it Pudens!' spat Secundus. 'How can anyone as irritating as you have been tolerated by a family for so long. Your Granny probably took poison in despair years ago!'

Secundus was biting well. Pudens seized the opportunity to introduce even more fantastic claims and lace them with taunts directed at Secundus who, as usual, took the bait. As he blustered, he gestured wildly with his arms and held his hands high in the manner of a righteous man, as if beseeching the gods to silence the lies of his tormentor. Pudens was grinning stupidly, lapping up the attention as Secundus became more infuriated. The rest of us leaned against the bunks, grinning at the free show, knowing that, soon, the now seething Secundus would be able to take no more.

'Did you keep pigs on your farm Secundus?' Pudens gave another cheeky grin, totally unperturbed by the earlier insult he had received.

'I only ask because every time you are close to me I can smell pig shit. I was told that once you'd worked with them you never got rid of the smell!'

That provoked hoots of laughter as Secundus struggled to find a comeback to fire at Pudens, who now sat on his bunk smiling serenely at his flustered opponent.

'One day I'm going to push your teeth straight down your damn throat!' Secundus roared pointing his finger at Pudens like a weapon.

Pudens again smiled sweetly, placed his hands behind his head and leaned back against the wall, goading Secundus to react. This was too much. Secundus sprang unexpectedly onto the bunk and grabbed Pudens by the throat. Feigning shock Pudens began to squeal like a girl.

'Ooh gods. He's going to kill me. Help, help!' Still he ridiculed Secundus, now beside himself with rage, his face purple with fury.

Aebutius and Firmus jumped in and dragged Secundus off Pudens who was now laughing like a loon. Secundus shrugged the pair off and stepped back, pointing venomously at Pudens once more. His mouth opened but the gift of a smart retort not forthcoming. The pointed finger curled back into a fist, which he shook at Pudens, a low growl under his breath before turning and stalking out into the anteroom.

'You can't help it can you?' said Firmus, gesturing accusingly at Pudens. 'He'll brain you one day. I know it. You mark my words!'

'Course he won't. He loves the banter. Just like me!' Pudens said with a wide grin.

'Look Pudens, just don't go mentioning farms will you?' said Surus. 'He's never really said what happened to his and you just don't know what he might be thinking. You know he's all fired up for killing any raiders he finds. They must have done something pretty bad to him!'

'Hmm, perhaps you're right!' Pudens said in a dismissive manner. 'Anyway! Haven't we got an appointment in town?

The object of his entertainment now gone, he quickly turned to other, more important matters. Jumping up from the bunk, a sudden look of excitement replacing the mischievous mask of earlier.

'That we have!' I said, clapping my hands together. 'Let's waste no more time!'

As we left the barracks we walked past the other dormitories, shouting in to those still present that we would meet them in town. Lewd promises made about securing girls and handing them over to latecomers only when they were worn out. Laughter rang around the barrack block and the air was filled with excited chatter and boasts about drinking ability and sexual prowess as we left. We found Secundus down by the latrine block and Pudens slung his arm around his shoulder, smiling and making his apologies. Secundus initially maintaining a face like thunder then shoving Pudens away with a grin as the rogue squeezed his neck with his arm, drew his face close and planted a large sloppy kiss on his cheek.

None of us could have been happier.

'Shut up, shut it now! Scaurus is down at the gate with the sentry!' hissed Firmus. 'Too much of this carry on and he'll never let us out of the gates!'

We all quietened down dipping our heads as we approached the gate. The sentry opened the wicket but barred the way as Scaurus stepped in front of us, his *vitis* held low across his hips in both hands. He too was wearing undress kit. He surveyed us all, once more seemingly able to read what was going on in our heads. A silent pause now falling on the assembled group. All of us now wondering whether we would now be getting out or not.

'This is your first period of leave,' Scaurus announced, 'and, as such, I expect that you will enjoy this opportunity to relax a little. I don't intend to repeat the warning that Fuscus gave you a month ago, I merely expect you to remember it ...'

He looked at the stone flags momentarily and adjusted his cloak .... 'If I have to take disciplinary action against any of you tomorrow then I will make no allowances for the fact that you are all very young in service!' He looked up, seemingly being able to achieve eye contact with every one of us.

'Tomorrow we march to the north, to begin the next phase of training. If any one of you renders themselves unfit for the march by virtue of tonight's activities then you will pay the price.'

Scaurus switched the *vitis* from his front to his back, a double-handed grip holding it horizontally in the small of his back. His head tilting slightly back. Releasing us from the unnerving eye contact he held us in, he walked slowly along the side of the group.

'Over the last month you have begun the long transition from civilian to soldier.' He continued in a measured, thoughtful tone.

'You have all acquitted yourselves well under difficult conditions and worked hard to reach this point. You are, however, not out of the woods yet! As far as I am concerned you are being forged into a weapon. A weapon held in the grip of Rome and directed by the will of the Emperor. So far we have smelted the ore and beaten it into shape. Now we must hone the blade, and sharpen it to a deadly edge. Only then can you be truly effective. Whilst you learn the skills required you will maintain strictest discipline. As of tomorrow, I will employ every regulation to ensure the maintenance of that discipline. That can range from everything to restricting rations and imposing fatigue duties to beatings, floggings and ultimately, execution.

'You will rise tomorrow, at sunrise this time, and be ready to depart for our new base two hours after that. I expect personal kit to be packed by then and baggage trains to be loaded with the items on the lists that you have been given. Everyone will be fit for the march!'

The emphasis on this last part was clear and we all understood perfectly well what was required.

'Enjoy your evening! Stand aside Gellius, let them out!'

The sentry stood to one side, allowing us exit. Scaurus stood, the *vitis* now in front of him as he leant forwards on it, silently watching us file through the wicket of the great, iron-bound gates. Every one of us now the picture of solemnity.

He would kill us! If that were what was called for, then we would die! There was not a shadow of doubt in any of our minds. If anything were going to guarantee our good behaviour tonight then the friendly little word that Scaurus had just placed in our ears would ensure it.

We walked out of the gates, initially subdued by Scaurus' words, but becoming more vocal as we put distance between the fort and ourselves. We had soon climbed to the cheerful pitch that we were at just prior to leaving the great fortress. Chattering and laughing noisily as we strolled along, although careful not to offend the civilian population present. The fortress had maintained a good working relationship with the surrounding populace over the years. We were put on trust not to sully that arrangement.

Whenever a community grew up next to a military base a closely interlinked relationship developed between the two communities. The *vicus* would start as a small collection of tents and ramshackle buildings, mostly dwelt in by traders of one description or another. Permanent fortresses saw small towns developing next to them as the *vicus* evolved and became more permanent in its own right. This was the case with *Mogontiacum*.

From its earliest beginnings, the *vicus* was protected by its military neighbour until, eventually, the town would be ringed with its own defences and become an integral part of the life of the garrison. On occasion, the military would move on, leaving just the settlement to grow into thriving new towns and cities.

When such settlements grew next to garrisons the military, albeit unofficially, adopted the growing community as a welcome link to civilization. Border garrisons worked very much on untamed frontiers in difficult and dangerous conditions. The presence of such little settlements offered the chance to escape temporarily from the rigours of service in a potential war zone. Soldiers needed the ability to drink and be entertained. The presence of taverns and prostitutes catered for the needs of the soul whilst traders plied their wares, providing creature comforts, essential items and the odd luxury.

As the civilian settlement prospered so the relationship grew even closer between the two groups. Peace prevailed as the areas to the north and east of our particular fortress were pacified. Soldiers were able to turn their attentions more towards life and less towards war. The Divine *Augustus* had forbidden marriage for Legionaries but, inevitably, unofficial unions were formed and resulted in children, the male children becoming an obvious and useful source of recruitment for the Legion in years to come. This was the way that my mother and father met and, in time, how my own life was to begin.

It felt unbelievably good to be able to walk down the familiar streets of my hometown in the clothing of a soldier and in the company of my new found friends. Truly this was what I had always yearned for and now I had it. As I walked, I passed people I knew. Some nodded acknowledgement and some hailed me with a shouted greeting and much backslapping. Firmus also received his share of this as we encountered his friends and acquaintances. Now and again we would pass by a girl that one of us had known. Invariably, they would walk past with their heads held low, a quiet half smile on their faces and a sideways glance as a protective mother ushered them along. Even so, I couldn't help but puff my chest out, proud of the fact that I could show these girls the trappings of the man that I had now become. I felt truly alive, vivacious, surging with the energies of a young god. Strong and fit, commanding respect. And money. I had money to spend for perhaps the first time in my life. Never had I had so much as I had now.

'Is there anyone in this town that you two don't actually know? If we have to stand much more of this hugging and blowing kisses I think I'll puke!' Secundus claimed bitterly. 'All I want is a drink and a laugh! Is that too much to ask?'

'Give it a rest can't you Secundus?' Aebutius checked him. 'I didn't even realize that you were capable of laughter! That must be a new innovation!'

Secundus grumbled something under his breath as Firmus took hold of Pacatianus' arm, dragging him towards a tavern and beckoning the rest of us to follow him.

'In here. This little place has wines from all over the place and the owner brews a decent beer on the premises!' Firmus didn't have to work hard to get us to follow him.

The building was one of the older generation of permanent structures that had sprung up with the growth of the settlement, its main structure being a two storey construction with a frame of wooden beams filled in with panels of wicker, plastered over with a mixture of mud and straw then painted with white lime. We stepped up from the muddy street onto a porch area covered by an overhanging pitched roof supported by sturdy timber uprights. This was tiled with wooden shingles, as was the main roof of the building. A heavy oak door sat in a wide frame with two windows either side housing cross pattern wooden frames. Both windows were fitted with shutters for keeping out the cold, damp night air when needed. A sharp squeak emanated from the broad iron hinges as we pushed the doors open and excitedly spilled into the tavern.

The interior of the building was reasonably airy with more windows allowing in the pleasant breeze of the early evening and shafts of sunlight beamed through one side of the building and lit up patches of the wooden floor which, although swept clean, was stained from years of spilt drink and the gods knew what else. A painted border of a reddish brown colour covered the bottom of the walls for about the first three feet in height. Above that was a pale yellow colour with thin white and green lines following the edge of the rectangular panels between the timbers, which remained in their natural finish. Fixed to the upright timbers were iron brackets upon which sat various sizes of oil lamp. Some containing only one wick, others accommodating up to three wicks. A further series of fine iron chains suspended larger lamps, with multiple wicks, from the ceiling timbers.

A staircase crossed the back wall diagonally to the second storey and, underneath the stairs, a sizeable amount of large wine *amphorae* lay stacked on their sides. The missing bungs indicating that the contents had already been consumed. At the base of the stairs a small doorway led, presumably, to the storage sheds and brewery at the rear of the main building. A wooden counter stretched along a sidewall, behind which were various vessels, jars and jugs including pot and wooden beakers for the use of the customers. The smell of stale drink was intoxicating enough without actually having to start quaffing any more.

The innkeeper was sweeping around under the rough timber benches and tables with a rush broom as we entered. A squat, heavily built man, he wore brown checked leggings with ankle length leather boots. A heavily stained, long sleeved cream coloured tunic was worn over his rotund body. A woollen cord tied around the man's midriff threatened to burst under the strain of supporting the globe-like belly underneath the tunic. He had a couple of days' growth that sprouted grey on a ruddy face of at least forty-five years.

A large, bored looking woman stood behind the counter leaning both elbows on it and resting her chin in her palms. This last action having the unfortunate result of pushing the fat in her face upwards, creating a mask of supreme ugliness. This frightening visage was crowned by her long dirty blond hair dangling in front of her face from a badly tied, disintegrating bun sitting on the top of her head.

The place had a scattering of customers who had evenly distributed themselves around the tables. The room was more spacious than from the impression first given by the exterior. They sat, either engaged in conversation or gambling their money playing various forms of dice. A noisy hum of voices and laughter filled the room as we headed towards one of the corners to secure our seats.

'Ho Atilius! Any chance of a drink for some thirsty lads then?' As Firmus shouted, the innkeeper instantly looked up from his sweeping. His gaze fell on Firmus who stood with his arms open wide and a wide grin on his face.

A puzzled look melted to one of pleasant surprise as Atilius recognized the face behind the voice.

'Can it be?' Atilius rubbed his eyes in a mock gesture of dreaming. A wide grin revealing a collection of uneven yellow teeth. 'Look at young Firmus. Proper little soldier he is!'

The man lumbered over and clamped Firmus in a bear hug, slapping him on the back as Firmus slowly went scarlet under the immense grip.

'Nice to see you too, Atilius!' He managed to gasp.

By now the remainder of us had taken a seat and were watching the fond reunion of Firmus and the innkeeper with mild amusement. Atilius had now released his grip and planted a winding slap on Firmus' back as he shouted over to the woman behind the bar.

'Livilla! Look what the dog fetched up!'

The woman took one hand away from her face, creating an unfortunate lop sided look. She squinted over to where Atilius and Firmus stood, pausing to register recognition for a brief moment.

'Firmus? Great gods, it is you Firmus!'

Her face lit up in a toothless grin and she moved swiftly towards the gap in the counter. Clearing the gap she bustled towards Firmus at an astonishing turn of speed.

'My little soldier. Come and give me a big kiss!' She shouted and flung her arms wide as astonished customers looked up to see what all the fuss was about.

'May Hercules grant the boy great strength!' muttered Pudens. 'He'll need it when she gets hold of him!'

'She'll kill him!' observed Surus casually.

Livilla reached Firmus and almost knocked him off his feet as she grappled with him. Again he was placed in a bear hug, this one even more stifling than the last as she planted huge wet kisses all over his face. Despite it all, Firmus bore the onslaught of affection with a grin and, when it was over, he gestured over to where we sat.

The couple joined us and greeted us warmly. Both of them remained talking to us for the duration of our time in the tavern. They would take it in turns to attend their customers whilst the other pressed us with questions about what our new lives were like and how much we had learned so far. We shared jugs of wine and beer with them and learnt, very early on, that they both had a tremendous capacity for consuming strong drink, seemingly with no ill effects. When it was time to move on they bade us farewell, as though we were departing family, and made us swear to return.

'Make sure you all come back and let us know how you are getting on!' Atilius shouted from the door, letting go of a thunderous belch as Livilla waved us off down the street. 'And look after that young rogue Firmus for us!'

We all shouted and waved back, promising to return as soon as we were able and scrubbing Firmus' head, shoving him around between us to the obvious delight of Livilla who hooted with laughter and pointed, elbowing Atilius in the side as he drained another beaker of wine. As we continued down the street, I looked back with a smile as Livilla snatched the beaker from Atilius' grip gesturing for him to get back inside, shooing him with one hand and shoving him in with the other as he turned towards the door, his protests falling on deaf ears as she imposed her will on him.

Inevitably, we ended up at a nearby brothel. A young male slave allowed us entry and we stood, gawping around us in the reception room. Built from stone, the building was not very old and was a reasonably sized structure with a courtyard and a modest garden at its centre. It was now around sunset and the reception room was well lit with lamps, small cressets and braziers. There were no furnishings in this room and the walls were painted only with geometric designs in a variety of bright colours, interspersed with garland and candelabra patterns. On the floor was a simple mosaic consisting of a white background with black detailing. Geometric meanders traced the outside, comprising of interlinked swastikas. This framed a portrait of *Cupid*, riding a great, leaping dolphin, his wings spread wide and carrying a bow and quiver of arrows.

'Soldiers are always welcome, just as long as they remember that this is no brawlers' tavern. We are a respectable establishment and require that you behave accordingly!' She stood framed in the doorway of an adjoining room and leant against the frame surveying us all curiously and wearing a half smile. Aurelia was a slightly built woman in her late thirties and, I surmised, native to this part of the world.

'My ladies are both freed women and slaves!' she continued. 'All, however, are valued members of this household and I demand that you treat them all with equal respect. Follow these simple rules and you are welcome to return as many times as you wish!'

She continued to scrutinize us. Her blue eyes twinkled, seeming to laugh at each one of us, making us feel slightly uneasy. It was obvious to her that most of us were novices when it came to this kind of establishment. She drew closer to us, grinning wickedly now. As she came closer I could smell her perfume, almost overpowering in its strength. She stopped before Pudens who stood there, gawping. Looking out of the corner of her eye she gently bit her bottom lip and grasped his groin area. He flinched, gasping with the shock and surprise.

'You can stay, sweetness!' She breathed quietly in his ear. He flushed red with embarrassment and she laughed loudly.

She moved around the group asking names. Everyone of us jumpy now as she ran her fingers through the hair of one then pinched the backside of another. Now the proud, tough young soldiers had all been reduced to nervous young boys as she had her sport with us. Throwing her head back and laughing as we stammered nervously, flushed with the colour of bashfulness.

'So! Maybe one of you has visited me before, after all!' She proclaimed, stepping back with a smile and pointing at Firmus.

'Greetings, Aurelia!' Firmus said softly, returning the smile and cheekily raising an eyebrow.

'Greetings indeed, you slippery young boy! How is it that you finally succeeded in being accepted for the service of the Legion? I thought them to be more discerning!' She scoffed, still smiling at the grinning Firmus.

'My credentials were adequate and I have proven my worth, so far!'

'Oh, I don't doubt that a resourceful young man such as you could have done that easily!' Aurelia said laughing as she clapped her hands to her thighs, leaning forward and shaking her head at Firmus who maintained his ground, smirking back at her.

'So!' She said, clapping her hands together. 'Now that we are all friends, shall we repair to another room for drinks and the company of the fairest girls in Germania?' She walked towards the doorway she had emerged from, beckoning for us to follow, and still setting us all with those laughing eyes. Like a flock of sheep we obediently followed her.

We proceeded down a dimly lit corridor until we reached an open doorway, a little more light spilling from this room into the darker passageway. As we entered I found myself surprised, and impressed, by the opulence of the room. Humble soldiers we were but it appeared we were going to be treated to top class hospitality.

The room was a large rectangular shape with a three coloured mosaic of various shapes and patterns bordering the floor. An alternating pattern of black and white squares made up the rest of the floor. It would have been pointless to have adorned it with a more elaborate mosaic due to the amount of furnishings that filled the room obscuring the pattern. Besides, the wall paintings more than compensated for that. The perfectly smooth, plastered walls were divided into panels. Bordered by whites and greys, the main panels were a deep red in colour and divided by broad vertical black stripes. Inside the panels were depicted all of the gods and goddesses associated with love and the erotic. Men and women in the act of love and passion adorned the walls while mischievous *Satyrs* and *Cupids* cavorted around them, hiding in trees and behind clouds. Almost lifelike as the flickering lamplight seemed to bring them to life.

Couches were placed around the room and, here and there, a chair or stool placed next to the walls was occupied by one of Aurelia's ladies. Three other men were present in the room, all sat on couches engaged in conversation with one of the resident hostesses. The men were middle aged and dressed in everyday clothing of woollen tunics, their cloaks for the journey home lying on the couches next to them. The women flirted and giggled as they plied the men with drink and fed them morsels from nearby tables set with a variety of snack foods and sweetmeats. Slowly the men were edging closer to their new companions, slurping from their wine beakers and leering at their young prizes. Without a word, one of the girls stood and pulled gently at her client's hand, beckoning him to follow. The man stood, grinning broadly, and followed her through to another room, snatching up his beaker as he went and chuckling lecherously.

As we entered the room the remaining girls stood and walked over to our party. They moved gracefully amongst us, smiling, stroking faces and casting alluring glances towards us as we stood grinning foolishly. Their practised seduction techniques fully employed now as they silently split us up and led us towards couches. Although divided, we remained close enough with each other to carry on conversation, which is what we did, jabbering nervously to each other and forcing nervous laughs. Our attempts to convince these *nymphs* that we were experienced men of the world failing dismally. Brows were being stroked and ears playfully nipped as the girls giggled and cooed softly for us to relax and enjoy.

My new companion introduced herself as Julia. She was around twenty years old and reasonably attractive. What really set her apart were her eyes. Piercing green eyes that seemed to hold the very fire of life and passion. When she spoke and laughed they flashed with that fire and sent a tingle of excitement down my spine. Her glossy dark brown hair was put up in braids contained within a fine golden hair net. Black eye make-up enhanced the edges of her eyes and lashes, creating the perfect frame for the flashing green eyes whilst a dark pink colouring was dusted onto the eyelids. Sharp contrasts created prominent cheeks as the rouge stood out from the lead whitened skin. Finally a seductive smile came from a pair of full lips carefully enhanced with the application of a deep red colouring.

As my eyes traced a path down Julia's body, I admired the slender elegance of her neck, spreading into soft shoulders then travelling down to a modest cleavage, tantalizingly revealed by the low neckline of a soft linen dress in a rich scarlet colour. The dress hung in soft folds down to a braided woollen belt of a bright red and cream diamond pattern, tied just under her breasts. The material then fell onto her thighs outlining their shape in the plush scarlet colour. At the top the dress was fastened together at the shoulders by a pair of delicate circular brooches of silver. A simple chain of round silver links hung around her neck and tiny silver earrings finished the adornments off, set with small red garnets glinting like fire in the lamplight of the room.

She held, not surprisingly, no inhibitions and instantly I began to feel at ease with her. Surely this must be the same reception that had been given to many a man before me but it still felt special and unique to me. Clearly she had developed a talent for her profession and I was benefiting from the experience of all those other men before me. Still, it did not seem to matter about that as far as I was concerned. She excited me, made me feel wanted.

'Does the soldier have a name?' Again the eyes flashed alluringly and I swallowed hard.

'Vepitta. My name is Vepitta!' I deliberately said it slowly, and carefully, so as not to stammer and make myself look foolish to her.

'You are young and sweet. I fancy that you have not soldiered for very long. Am I right, Vepitta?'

The emphasis she placed on my name sent a shiver down my spine. My desire for her now growing by the second as I stared, almost mesmerized, into those amazing eyes.

'I have spent one month with the Legion. We leave tomorrow to continue with our training up country!'

She leant forward, placing one hand gently round the back of my neck. The other hand came to rest on my thigh as she came closer, placing her mouth next to my ear.

'Then why do we waste time talking?' She seemed to breathe the words into my ear, the warmth of her breath arousing me. 'Time is short! We need to make sure that you remember this night for all time!'

She kissed me lightly on the lips, taking hold of my hands and standing slowly, smiling enigmatically and fixing me once more with those eyes. I felt my blood surge and thought that I would burst, there and then, if she did not take me soon. I stood and followed her through the door as my remaining comrades carried on, engrossed in their own girls, not even noticing my departure.

Swiftly, Julia led me along another partially lit corridor to a staircase. Occasionally she would glance back at me, smiling seductively, biting her lower lip and fixing me with those eyes from a lowered brow. We had carried on down another passage to her chamber where she silently pushed the door open and stepped inside. I followed and stood, watching her as she stood momentarily with her back to me, bathed in the warm glow of the light of four small oil lamps. Then she spun round to face me, giving a girlish giggle as she reached up to her hair net, carefully removing it and placing it on a stand near to the bed. A swift pull and a carved bone hair pin was removed, causing the twisted braids to fall. She tussled them then and gave a final flick of her neck, loosening the hair and allowing it to fall, bouncing down onto her delicate shoulders.

I felt as though I could take no more. My ability to control my soaring lust was almost non existent as she turned sideways to me and began to release one of the silver brooches from her shoulder. As she freed it so the two halves of the shoulder fell away revealing a tantalizing glimpse of a small, ivory breast. She turned her attention to the other brooch and soon it was free, then, using her arm to hold the dress in place, she bent to place the brooches on the stand.

She stood then, the smile now gone and her mouth slightly open, staring provocatively now as she released the dress. It slid silently down her body revealing the perfect globes of her firm breasts. Her flat stomach and trim waist appeared before me as I was engulfed by yet another wave of intense desire for her. In the half light the shadows danced on her naked body, creating a soft dark area between her legs and shading the small, perfect circles of her nipples. The dress lay around her feet like a dark scarlet pool as she stepped from it and crossed to the bed. I watched, smitten, as she lay down, reclining on her side and raised her head with her elbow. One leg drawn up to her waist to reveal the exquisite curve of her buttocks. Slowly she extended her hand towards me and flicked her head, throwing the long hair over her shoulder. Once more the light picked out the details of her form in shadows and the garnets and silver twinkled in the half light.

'Come here soldier,' she said softly.

There had been times, as with most young boys, when I had shared the company of a girl who appeared as anxious as me to experience the flush of passion. Always, for me, it had been a snatched moment in some stable or store house. Fumbling around in a hurried attempt to satisfy that gnawing lust. Inevitably failing to achieve the goal of the ultimate prize. The fear of discovery quelled the passions of the once willing girls I had persuaded to join me. Never had I even got close to the heights of pleasure that Julia took me to that night.

The pleasure of the physical act was made much more intense when combined with the way she captured me, spellbound with her sensuality and natural beauty. As we joined, we seemed to melt into one being. Completely wrapped in the pleasure of the moment. Aware of nothing but each other. So intense were the feelings that I physically shook as they seemed to wash over me like waves. All too soon did it seem to be over.

Julia dressed me as I stood in front of her. Once more I looked into her eyes, no fire now but perhaps a sense of warmth and contentment in them. Or was I imagining it? When she had dressed me she gathered her dress up and I took the opportunity to survey her slim beauty for one last lingering moment. Her pale flesh glistened in the half light. A light sheen of perspiration laying on her skin. Evidence of our passion lit by the gentle, flickering light of the lamps. The dress now moving up her legs and veiling her body as she pinned it in place with the two brooches. Beauty now unseen as I immediately strove to recall every curve.

Julia quickly scraped her long dark hair, slightly damp with sweat now, into a tail which she wound into a tight bun on the back of her head. She reached into a small wooden box on the stand and took out a pair of bone hair pins which she used to secure the bun. Smiling, she crossed the room and opened the door, standing in the doorway and holding her hand out to usher me from the room.

As we walked down the shadowy corridor she held my hand then lightly pushed me back against the wall. Pressing her warm lips to my mouth, giving me another taste of her sensuous touch. She laughed softly as she nipped at my ear. Then I felt the leather purse being slipped from behind my belt. She turned her back to me then and pushed her body back onto mine rubbing herself up and down me as I sighed in pleasure. I heard the faint chink of coin as she giggled and turned round once more to face me. Julia placed her hand against my face and stroked my lip lightly with her thumb as she replaced the purse.

What did I care how much she had taken? For what she had given me tonight I doubted that I would ever have enough money to pay her adequately. I felt so invincible now, as though I surged with a mighty power. How could I ever be more alive? I had youth and strength and I served the Legion with pride. To crown my sense of completion *Venus* had bestowed the gift of Julia upon me. Truly I was a fortunate man.

'Oh! Finally he decides to show up!' Pudens exclaimed as Julia and I entered the reception room. 'What happened? Did you get your balls stuck in there?'

The others hooted with laughter as a wide grin spread across Pudens' face.

Julia stood in front of me, a gentle smile on her face, ignoring the crude jibe. She raised a finger to her lips and kissed it softly, then placed the finger lightly on my lips. Before I could say a word she had gone, moving swiftly through the door we had just came from. My mouth wide open as the door slid shut behind her.

'Well, well! one of us seems to have done well for himself. I didn't get that treatment!' Sniggered Pacatianus. 'Was she a good ride then, or what?' They turned to look at me then. Poised for the blow by blow account of what had gone on with Julia.

'Where's Firmus?' I enquired. Grateful that I had spotted his absence and used it as an excuse to steer the conversation elsewhere.

'He left some time ago!' Aurelia had entered the room to see us out and stood by the door, examining her finger nails. 'He seemed rather pale and claimed that he felt unwell. As far as I know he was going back to barracks. At least, that's what he said!'

'Oh! That's just the limit that is!' moaned Secundus 'We all had the decency to wait for one another. He flounces off whenever he pleases. Never mind his so called friends!'

'It is of no surprise to me that he did this to you!' Aurelia said, as she pushed the slipped shoulder of her dress back up her arm. 'I have known him since he was no taller than wheat in a field. Firmus cares only about Firmus. You would do well to minimize the trust you put in him!'

'Why?' Surus asked. 'What do you know of him to say such things?'

'Only that he is a devious old man in a young man's head!' she answered quickly. 'He has always had a talent for underhandedness and is prepared to stoop very low to get what satisfies him. Where do you think he got his introduction to the Legion? Do you really think those credentials are genuine?'

Aurelia smiled bitterly, the jovial, easy manner of earlier now nowhere to be seen on her painted face.

'It is a matter for yourselves, but you should be wary!' The smile reappeared as she beckoned to the door and clapped a hand on Lupus' shoulder and led him towards the door, now being opened by a large male slave.

'You are most welcome to return to the house of Aurelia, good soldiers. As long as you remember to bring with you the good manners and plentiful money that you had tonight!' Again she laughed and planted a kiss on Lupus' cheek as he walked out into the cool night air. The lad was grinning broadly and seemed to be floating on a cushion of air. So! We were all made men tonight then!

'Now! I must bid you goodnight. I have not seen Claudia since she disappeared with Firmus and need to make sure that he has not spirited her off anywhere. She is a valuable girl, and talented!'

With a final laugh and toss of her head she closed the door behind us and we stood, staring at each other in the street. Grinning faces lit by sputtering torches, slowly we started to laugh. Then the laughter grew to great gales as we slapped each other on the back and scrubbed each other's stubbly scalps. Congratulating ourselves as if we had been awarded some great trophy.

'I did it! I did it!' Squeaked Lupus in the unmistakeable voice of a teenage boy. A huge grin splitting his youthful face. Again we hooted with laughter and playfully slapped him and pushed him between us as he laughed uproariously.

'Now that is what I call living!' Pacatianus said as we began to stroll up the street.

'Did anyone notice the time on that water clock in there?' I asked 'If we break curfew then we're for it, and no mistake!'

'I reckon we are close to it, we'd better get moving!' Secundus added and began to break into a jog.

We followed his lead and began a steady run back to the fortress. Plenty of people were still wandering abroad, even though it was dark. We dodged our way through the streets, street prostitutes calling after us with lewd offers and hawkers trying to sell us one thing or another, despite the fact that we were running swiftly now through the streets. The hawkers would run alongside for a short distance holding up whatever it was they wished to sell. Frantically they would jabber their sales pitch to us. Then, when they realized there was to be no sale, they would stop and shout after us. Scolding us for not giving a few coins for the goods and helping to feed their starving family, or helping to keep a roof above their heads.

Finally, we arrived back at the gates of the fortress. The sentry stepped out of the wicket gate to greet us, a torch held up to identify and count us in. His polished armour reflecting the flickering orange light of the torch as he peered over our heads, accounting for us all.

'Ooh, you lucky bastards!' He smiled and shook his head, wagging a finger towards us accusingly. 'You ain't half pushed your luck tonight!' We looked quizzically as he followed a list on a wax tablet and began to mark it with a *stylus*.

'If I've got it right then you lot are *Tiro's* from second training *Contubernium*! Yes?'

'You're quite right my man, but why all the fuss?'

We all cringed at the way Pudens decided to address the sentry. The soldier lowered the tablet and looked incredulously at Pudens who stood there with a foolish smile on his face. Now realizing that he had perhaps overstepped the mark.

'Oi, snot nose!' blustered the man indignantly. 'Just who do you think you're talking to? I'm on this poxy gate all night and I don't like the idea of *tiros* going out and enjoying their little selves while I'm stuck here!'

The sentry clapped the tablet shut and thrust his finger at Pudens who was forced to jerk his head back to avoid his nose being speared on the man's finger.

'Listen, you little shit! If I say you came back in after curfew time then that's how it will be! Do you follow?' The smile had fallen from Pudens' face by now and it was crystal clear what the sentry was implying.

'I'm sorry friend!' Pudens was crestfallen at having to grovel to the triumphant looking sentry. 'A small consideration? To restore good relations perhaps?'

'You're damn right there son!' He thrust his hand forward, palm open. 'Two denarii ... Each!'

Muttered curses were spat accusingly in Pudens' direction as we retrieved the money from our purses and handed it over to the now smug looking guard. To make matters worse, his companion had joined him and stood there sniggering mockingly at us.

'The next time you come to my gate you'll show some respect. You are the last ones back and you had a quarter hour to go. Cutting it fine is one thing but sending your mate back on his own and drunk was not very pally. You've just paid for his mistake and he should be in bed by now. That's if he made it through the lines without getting caught by Scaurus or Fuscus. Now! Get lost you idiots, before I turn the lot of you in!'

Like scalded cats we ran through the gate, the clatter of our boot studs echoing around the buildings. Finally we reached the barracks. Slowing down to a walk just before we reached the entrance, hoping that Scaurus or Fuscus would not hear us. We took our boots off outside and crept into the long corridor, hardly daring to even breath as we past Scaurus' door, then Fuscus'.

'If you had been just five minutes later I would have flogged the flesh from your backs!' The voice behind us was quiet and measured. We all knew whose voice it was. Scaurus.

'At least you all appear sober!' He said quietly. A thin smile parting his lips. He stood there for a moment, his arms folded across a light linen under tunic, viewing us as though reading us once more. As was always his way.

'Get to bed. Tomorrow is a long day!' He turned and slipped silently back into his room. The door latch shutting with a light 'snick'!

Simultaneously, we looked at each other, like a bunch of frightened rabbits. The breath we held in our lungs now being released with long slow hissing noises. Heads were shaken and hands wiped imaginary sweat off brows. Not a word was said to express the intense relief we felt. We had made it back just in time. Quietly we made our way down the corridor and entered the billet, undressing quickly for bed, not even bothering to kick or slap Firmus as he lay snoring in his bed. In an instant we were all bedded down, lamps were extinguished and I lay there, smiling in the darkness until sleep descended upon me.

Chapter 5

A Lesson Learnt

The area outside our barrack block was a hive of activity that morning. Mules and ox carts had been brought round and we streamed backwards and forwards like a column of ants, ferrying kit and possessions out to the waiting transports.

During our first month's training we had been fitted for armour and equipment and our weapons had been ordered for us. Some of us already possessed inherited items of equipment and these had been duly inspected for suitability in service. The examining armourers had passed the items once carried by my father, declaring them adequate for use. I had worked hard on their restoration as the day approached for me to join the Legion. I saw their being approved as a vindication of the standard of my craft. Quintus had taught me well.

The most important part was the mail shirt. Made of narrow diameter iron links, even the armourers conceded that it was a finely made shirt. Far too good for a *tiro*. It extended to just above the groin area and, as was common with Roman shirts, it was fitted with doubling flaps over the shoulders, increasing protection from downward blows to the shoulder area. Its fabric was made up of a row of stamped iron links, connected with a row of riveted links, a method of construction that delivered maximum strength to the garment. The doubling flaps were secured by a pair of bronze hooks which were riveted to the centre of the chest. These extended outwards and held the doublings in place by looping on to bronze studs, themselves riveted to each doubling flap. The edges of the doubling and neck part were dressed with leather which I had recently renewed when I fitted the garment to my own size. In truth, I was extremely proud of that shirt.

Before the end of his service, my father had acquired one of the newer shaped short swords, his old *gladius* had become badly notched and the blade was becoming weaker with time and the battering of constant post drills. Again I had given this my best attention and the weapon was pristine with new a bone hilt, brand new wooden fittings and a refurbished blade. The weapon held a needle sharp point, needed to fulfil its primary role as a stabbing weapon, and the straight edges of the blade were honed to a wickedly sharp edge.

These pieces, along with a few sundry cooking items and tools, were all that I had brought with me. The rest of the required equipment had been issued to me, as with my belt and dagger, on the understanding that it would be paid for by deductions from my pay. Non essential items would have to be accumulated as we progressed through our service.

Of the new kit I acquired, I prized the *scutum* overall. I had managed to purchase a brand new one. It stood to just above waist height, having a curving surface and straight edges trimmed with bronze strips. Its horizontal handgrip was protected by a large iron boss riveted to the body of the shield. What really filled me with pride for the piece was the fact that it carried the devices of the Fourteenth on its face. The white wings of *Victoria* spread to the four corners of the shield whilst jagged yellow bolts of lightning zig-zagged up and down the centre of the shield. These fiery bolts would tell our enemies that *Iuppiter* walked with us. The symbols of our might stood proud on a deep red background which also bore the inscription 'LEG' and 'XIIII' to either side. There was to be no mistake about who we were.

The iron helmet that I carried was of excellent workmanship. A comfortable fit, the helmet had been totally refurbished with a new lining of soft leather padded with horse hair. This would complement the light woollen cap I wore underneath it to increase padding and comfort. The body of the helmet bore decorative raised chasings around the dome and neck guard. This increased the strength of the helmet as well as improving it aesthetically. Above the brow it mounted a thick iron cross piece. There to protect against frontal blows, it also deployed well when butting someone in the face. The broad cheek guards almost completely enclosed the face with just ears, eyes, nose and mouth left visible. A soldier needed, after all, the benefit of all of his senses.

In addition to our weapons and armour we were all to carry *impedimenta*. As well as a few small personal items, this consisted broadly of cooking and eating equipment and kit for the construction of defences. Combined with a pair of *pila* and *pila murali*, the load was to be a formidable burden for our first outing in full marching order.

The morning had been very busy and we scarcely had time to chatter as we moved swiftly to complete the allotted tasks. A brief conversation was centred around Firmus at breakfast, who received not a little criticism for leaving without us the night before. Despite the fact that he knew we were all displeased with him, he offered no real explanation for his conduct and remained quiet for the rest of breakfast.

We completed our work well within the time allowed and formed up, outside the barrack, fully armoured and marching kit propped against shields waiting for the order to move out. This was the first time I had worn everything I would be expected to from now on. It felt like I was carrying a horse on my back! 'So, now the real training begins!' I mused.

My comrades stood either side of me and I could hear their kit creaking and clanking and the groans of discomfort as they too learned of the uncomfortable nature of their burden for the first time. This was to be a painful start. From this point on we would learn about how to carry our loads and how to adjust it for greater comfort. It took time to learn though and, until then, there would be more than a few blisters, sprains and chafes.

The moaning and complaining stopped abruptly and we snapped to position as Scaurus appeared and called us to attention. We stood as though statues as Scaurus walked along our column appraising every detail of our new look. Fuscus accompanied him as he went and, now and again, one of them would adjust a strap on a man or reposition a piece of kit. Briefly explaining the improvement to the individual concerned. Both of them were fully armoured and equipped. Scaurus carried the ever present *vitis* and Fuscus now carried his knobbed staff of office. Both of them looked infinitely more comfortable than we with our, as yet, unfamiliar loads.

Scaurus paused at the head of the small column as Fuscus went back into the block briefly, returning momentarily with a *vexillum*. The red banner was trimmed with gold braid and carried the image of *Victoria* on it above a Capricorn and the letters XIIII.

'Aemelius! Fall out with your kit and stow it on that ox cart. Then come before me!'

I heard the noise of someone falling out behind me and then saw Aemelius march to the cart and place his gear on it, lashing it down with rope. Then, as ordered, he marched smartly to Scaurus and came to a clean halt before him.

'Aemelius!' Scaurus' tone was very formal. 'Your superiors consider you to be the most improved of this *vexillation* of *tiros!*'

Aemelius said nothing, glancing briefly down at his boots then swiftly back up again. The most serious look set upon his face to mask his pride.

'I wish you to bear this *vexillum* with pride and reverence as we journey to our new quarters!' Scaurus took the banner from Fuscus and placed it in front of Aemelius. 'Do you accept the honour we have bestowed on you?'

'Gladly *Centurion!*' said Aemelius. His chest swelling visibly with pride as he took the *Vexillum*.

'Fall in at the head of the column. Well done!' Said Scaurus as he raised his hand palm upright towards us. We took our prompt, banging our fists on our shields and shouting our congratulations to Aemelius. He had done well to earn that place. He deserved our praise.

Scaurus and Fuscus went to the top of the column and Fuscus turned the unit to face them.

'Now listen!' boomed Fuscus. 'We are just about to ... !' He trailed off as a messenger appeared and began to relate something quietly to Scaurus, who seemed to listen intently. Fuscus turned and began to listen in also. Both men developing deep frowns as the messenger continued.

'Stand at ease!' barked Scaurus as he pointed towards us then went off with the messenger. A slight muttering rose above the column which Fuscus instantly checked.

'Shut it, now !' He pointed the staff towards us. 'Keep it shut! You'll all no doubt soon find out what's up. Until then keep order!'

I don't think any of us had the slightest idea of what was happening until Scaurus returned some half hour later. Instantly Fuscus called us all to attention as he recognized the company that Scaurus kept. *Tribune* Scribonius was with him along with Ademetus.

'Gods. This must be serious!' I thought. The *Praefectus Castrorum*, third only to the *Legate,* was attending the departure from barracks of a band of *Tiros.* 'Something has to be seriously amiss here!'

Yet another brief and secretive conversation took place between the party as we stood, straining to hear details. Then they began to part with nods of the head. They appeared to have reached agreement on some point. Scribonius and Ademetus approached the column halting before us. Scribonius with a strangely sad look on his face, Ademetus looking as though he would explode with fury.

'Turn and face me. Now!' he hissed. Instantly we swung to face him as he stalked along the column pointing a shaking finger as he went.

'Who did it? Which of you bastards has sullied the name of this fine Legion!' The prefect was absolutely beside himself with fury. All of us could see it and we cowered at the prospect of what such a powerful man could do to us if he had a mind. There was no response to his question.

'So! There is one among you who would shit in his own nest then try to evade responsibility for his actions!' Seethed Ademetus as he stalked the lines. 'Where are you, you bastard? Own up now! If I have to find you I'll make ... !'

'Sir ... It's me you want!'

'Who? Who said that?' roared Ademetus homing in on the voice.

Firmus stepped quietly from the front rank. He swallowed heavily and braced himself. The Prefect strutted furiously up to him and fixed him momentarily with a withering stare. We, Firmus' companions, just stood, dumbfounded at the unexpected drama now unfolding before us.

'Stand over there!' Ademetus boomed, pointing to an area in front of the column where all could see Firmus who quickly darted to his place. The prefect turned to address us while the assembly of officers looked on, preferring to leave this business to the Prefect now.

'Last night you were all allowed a brief period of leave!' Ademetus began. 'I am pleased to report that, with the exception of one, your behaviour did you credit! I am less than pleased to receive an allegation that, of a party of men visiting a brothel, one of them decided that he did not need to pay for services rendered. Add to that the fact that the same man saw fit to throttle the unfortunate girl half to death and beat her for insisting on payment and, I think you will agree, that I have a serious allegation on my hands!'

Ademetus pointed to Firmus.

'Get back to your position. I wish to be sure that you are not covering for someone!'

Firmus ran back to his space while the Prefect returned to the group and gave an instruction to Fuscus who quickly disappeared around the corner of the barrack, returning momentarily with two women. Both had their heads covered and I struggled to pick out features until ... . Aurelia! She was supporting the other girl and helping her towards the group of officers. I caught a brief glimpse of the girl's face, she looked badly bruised.

'Please feel free to approach the column and try to identify the guilty man!' Ademetus told Aurelia. 'Once the slave girl Claudia has indicated the man responsible then inform me and we will deal with the matter appropriately!'

Aurelia and Claudia approached, the older woman's arm wrapped tightly around the girl as if to protect her from further harm. What in the name of the gods had possessed Firmus to do such a thing? As they got closer I got a better view of Claudia. I vaguely remembered her from the previous night, a petite blonde girl of around fifteen years, she had a pretty smile and an obvious charm about her. That was, until this morning. Her hair was unkempt and her face red and tear stained. A fierce bruise grew under her eye and the corner of it was reddened by burst blood vessels. An ugly cut extended up her swollen upper lip where it had been split on the tooth below. I could just perceive the purple finger marks around her throat that showed above her tightly drawn up garment. It was not just the physical pain on her face that struck me but the hurt and shame of having to face a column of soldiers this way. She was used to making the best of herself and presenting an attractive package to her prospective clients. Now she stood before us, beaten and broken of spirit. Firmus may have finished beating her last night but, in reality, the assault still continued as she suffered the humiliation of standing before her attacker in this way.

Silently they walked along the column as they hunted for Claudia's attacker until, almost immediately they halted, about three men down from me. That was about where Firmus had fallen in.

I strained to see from the corner of my eye. I could just see both women as Claudia gave a sob and raised a trembling finger to the line. Aurelia hugged her and kissed her gently on the forehead, leading her back to the watching officers. Again they engaged in discussion. Firmus' fate was being sealed as we watched, and he would know it!

Scaurus stepped forward a few minutes later and coolly began to issue orders.

'Firmus take three paces forward!' He waited for him to complete the order then ... 'The two men either side of Firmus. Fall out, disarm him and remove his armour and belt.'

Swiftly the two who had stood next to Firmus, Aebutius and Lupus, fell out, placing their marching kit and shields to one side. They stood either side of the shamed soldier then, his face set in a mask of stone as he stared to the front. Lupus and Aebutius quickly carried out their orders. Firstly removing his weapons then his armour. Finally the woollen belt that gathered his tunic above knee height was taken and Firmus stood, stripped of his soldier's identity. Not even being given the grace of wearing his tunic above his knees, it hung like a sack to the middle of his shins. When it was done they stood, either side of the deeply humiliated Firmus.

'Leave the equipment where it lies for now and fall back in!' barked Scaurus. Instantly both lads turned and hurried back to their places. Their roles played out, it was obvious they wished to have no more to do with the affair.

Tribune Scribonius was writing on a tablet now and accompanied Ademetus as he approached Firmus who stood, rigid and unmoving. Ademetus stood in front of Firmus and appeared to indicate to Scribonius that he wished this part to be recorded. Scribonius stood poised with the *stylus*.

'Tiro Firmus!' Ademetus began slowly. 'By your own admission, and by the complainant's identification, you stand accused of wrongdoings against both a citizen's property and the Legion which you serve!'

We could clearly hear the address and waited anxiously to find out exactly what had passed to bring about this shameful and extraordinary event.

'You are charged that, last night, having engaged the services of the slave prostitute Claudia, the property of Aurelia Severa, you committed the following offences!' The Prefect paused and looked over to Scribonius, making sure that the record was being kept up.

'One! You failed to discharge a lawful payment or debt when required! Two! You maliciously inflicted damage on the property of Aurelia Severa, namely the slave prostitute Claudia and three! You have brought dishonour on the good name and proud tradition with which this Legion has served and protected the neighbouring community!' Ademetus paused as the charges were committed to record. 'What is your plea?'

'Sir, I ... .!'

'Your plea!' Ademetus hissed!

'I am guilty of all, sir!' said Firmus, his head lowered to the ground now.

Ademetus seemed to stiffen and gave a small shrug of his neck, as if to ease his growing tension and annoyance.

'As senior officer present in the garrison at this time I will pass judgement on the offender now!' Again he made a brief check to ensure Scribonius was keeping up. Satisfied that was the case, he continued. 'For the two offences relating to the business of Aurelia Severa you will receive thirty strokes with rods. For that of bringing dishonour to your Legion you will receive a further fifty strokes!'

Firmus visibly paled as the sentence was pronounced but, more was still to follow.

'In addition, your money and personal property is to be confiscated and the resultant proceeds will go to discharge your debt and provide payment for medical treatment. This to restore the slavegirl Claudia's fitness for duties! Finally you are to be kept in service, on quarter pay and basic rations for one year while performing fatigue duties. Your case will then be reviewed as to whether you resume your training or face dishonourable discharge!'

Crashing silence reigned over the scene as Ademetus turned on his heel and approached the two women. He strode over to Aurelia, not even acknowledging the existence of Claudia, as he halted directly in front of her mistress.

'Madam! I trust that, from your perspective, the matter is concluded satisfactorily?' His manner was brusque. It was obvious that he was absolutely furious at having to preside over such a sordid matter. A valuable recruit was to be broken and possibly killed because a slave prostitute could not handle her client properly. Some whore mistress had come complaining about one of his men and, in the interests of justice being seen to be done, he had been forced to hold this farce of a tribunal in front of them.

'The sentence is just, Prefect!' Aurelia said as she bowed slightly to the simmering Ademetus.

'My thanks for bringing this matter to my attention Madam. The sentence will be properly published and posted outside the fort for the benefit of all. Now! If you will excuse me!' Aurelia bowed once more as the Prefect spun on his heel, beckoning for Scribonius to follow.

'Scaurus. Get these men out of here!' he bellowed. 'They should be miles away by now!'

Scaurus snapped to attention. 'Yes sir!'

'And get that man locked away pending punishment!'

'Yes sir!'

Scribonius and Ademetus disappeared around the corner of the barrack block, billowing cloaks trailing them as they went. Ademetus' curses could be heard disappearing with the distance as they returned to the Principia from which they had been so urgently summoned.

Still shocked by what had passed, once more we formed up, ready to leave for our new home. Short now of another man.

Chapter 6

Forging the Blade

As if to increase the down at heel mood, it began to rain. Lightly at first, as we left the fortress, then becoming steadily heavier as we passed through the *vicus* and onto the open road. Here and there children stood silently watching as we marched out. The dirt on their faces beginning to form streaks in the rain as they stood with their mouths open, staring blankly. Our escort of about thirty Legionary cavalry brought up the rear of the column. They sat their mounts wrapped in long cloaks, looking as miserable as we as they plodded slowly along. No talking could be heard. Just the fall of hooves on the stone road and the jingle of harness. The ox cart rumbling along noisily to the rhythmic crunch of boot studs on the road.

Soon we had reached the bridge over the *Rhenus* where we had spent so much time practising fording the great and powerful river. As we passed over the surging waters, already swollen by the rains, the reality of the situation hit home once more. We had been here only one month and already we were four men down on our original number. Three of us were dead, swallowed by the *Rhenus*. The fourth was just about to be flogged, back at *Mogontiacum*. His reward for surviving such a punishment? To spend a year being treated not much better than a menial slave. I did not condone Firmus' actions but, frankly, I would rather have been executed than to undergo the humiliations that had started back there.

We marched for many a mile. On the way we passed small settlements and farmsteads, set close to the roadside as if to draw reassurance from the presence of passing travellers and military traffic. The countryside was remote and vast areas of woodland stretched out before us as we passed. Seldom, however, did we pass close to dense areas of trees.

The massacre of three Legions under *Publius Quinctilius Varus* had taught Rome a valuable, if not costly lesson. Roads were heavily used by the military and, as such, gave opportunity for ambush. Even in this controlled area attacks were not unheard of. A strictly employed policy of deforestation near to roadways meant that any attackers would no longer have the advantage of cover and surprise.

The journey grew harder with each mile. Sodden kit started to weigh us down and water leaking into clothing and armour softened skin, causing agonizing soreness as shifting equipment rubbed us raw. All the time the rain fell hard. The iron grey sky warning us that there would be no let up for hours to come, perhaps days. We could do nothing but live with it, knowing that eventually there would be respite and dry buildings somewhere along the road.

Scaurus set a brisk pace for the march with only three rest stops along the way, pointing out that we should finish the march quickly and not risk encountering even worse conditions. As we forged through the steadily falling rain it became a war of the spirit just to complete the task. Tender areas grew worse as the journey progressed and the weight of armour and equipment now tested muscles to the extreme. My lower back grew tight and stiff with the weight of my unfamiliar burden. The mail shirt was pressing down on my shoulders causing the tops to ache, forcing me to shift and shrug them to adjust the load. I could feel the soles of my feet swelling under the extra pressure and my calf muscles felt as though they were tearing apart under the strain of maintaining the pace. I did everything to occupy my mind, recalling old fireside songs in my head and taking myself through my unforgettable time with Julia. Anything to divert my focus from the pain of the march.

At regular intervals during the march, the cavalry would send four riders forward of us to scout the ground. They would gallop about a mile or so out, depending on the terrain and then return perhaps a half hour later, passing their replacements who would ride out upon seeing the first riders returning. That way a constant watch could be kept on any problems up front of the column.

After what seemed like an eternity of trudging along in the worsening conditions a scout party returned and announced to Scaurus that our destination was in sight and appeared to be in order. Scaurus had been reading the mile posts and started us off on a trot when we were two miles out. Now our loads began to take their toll even more as the extra movement loosened pieces of kit and doubled the friction which already tormented us. As we drove ourselves across open heath land I squinted into the now driving rain to snatch a first glimpse of our new home. In front of me, iron helmets bobbed in time to the movement of the column, rain running off the neck guards and onto the sodden cloaks we wore. The cloaks were hooded *paenulae* but they had been blown back by the growing wind so many times that, eventually we had all given up trying to keep them on over our helmets.

Rolling black clouds billowed across the slate grey horizon as I first spotted the fort. We were just starting to touch the base of a gently rising hill as the ramparts appeared on the crest, about half a mile away. Pain was shoved to the back of my mind as we began the gradual, painful ascent, and the reason to push on slowly grew in form. As the quick time thud, thud, thud of the boots rang out off the road I watched the ramparts slowly rising up. The timber palisade atop them clearly visible now as the road in front of us pushed, spear straight, to the gate tower. Men became visible, posted on the defences, watching our approach. The scouts had reached the fort and informed them of our impending arrival. I saw the welcoming smoke of small fires curling up to be taken away by the wind and could almost feel the warmth from the fire and taste the comfort of the hot food that must be within. With each step the defences grew in shape and form until at last we were twenty paces away from the thick double gate. As it swung invitingly open to allow us entry, sentries appeared all over the tower, fully armed, to see us in. We followed the road as it crossed over the double defensive ditch ringing the fort and passed through the wooden portal and along the *via principalis*. Only when we were in front of the *principia* did Scaurus halt us, turning us to face the building.

Scaurus and Fuscus briefly checked up and down the column, presumably assessing our state and then Scaurus stood us at ease as he disappeared inside the *principia*. Fuscus paced slowly up and down the column, casting his ever critical eye as we stood waiting. The white horsehair crest on his helmet, soaked and wilting with the weight of water, swayed back and forth as he moved. As we waited you could hear the entire column sucking in air and the odd cough and snort as men slowly started to recover from the immediate effects of the march. The cavalry immediately made their way down towards the stables to tend to their mounts. Their priority being to dry and feed their horses before anything.

Eventually, Scaurus reappeared and approached Fuscus, quietly relaying his instructions to the *Optio*. I heard him say something about completing formalities with the commander while Fuscus got us accommodated and Fuscus nodding his understanding then ...

'Right, sling kit! Prepare to move!' shouted Fuscus. We heaved our loads onto our shoulders once more and made ready. Again we marched, this time only as far as the lines of barrack blocks and once more we were halted and turned to face the doors of the buildings.

'On my order!' Fuscus yelled from the top of the column. 'Get fell out and take your kit into block Three. Dump your *impedimenta* in your billets then get out here and start to unload these carts and mules! Right. Fall out!'

On Fuscus' order we turned smartly and fell out, making swiftly for the allotted barrack to dump our heavy loads. There was no pause to linger in the shelter of our new home, we knew that the quicker we finished the job, the quicker we would be able to dry off and get some food in our bellies. We returned again to the worsening weather outside and began the task of unloading the small baggage train that had accompanied us. At least we did not have to bother about the beasts. They were accompanied by handlers and would be led away to be tended to when we had finished. Spurred on by the conditions, we soon completed the task and stowed the extra pieces of equipment where Fuscus directed us to. At last we were able to take shelter and look to the task of preparing some hot food and drying ourselves out.

The rooms inside the barrack building soon achieved a lived in feel as we lit braziers and small fires and began to dry clothing and equipment. Weapons and armour were treated as a priority and were dried, checked over and lightly oiled, leaving us with the task of unpacking individual loads and donning dry clothing. Each of us carried a spare tunic and undergarments in our leather packs but, as some of us were soon to discover, if incorrectly packed, the spares would also be sodden. It came as a blessed relief for me to learn that my spare clothing was dry and that the packing arrangement I had used would be suitable for use in the future.

Soon the block came alive with our presence. The temperature slowly began to rise to a cosy warmth and the smell of wood smoke and wet wool and leather pervaded the entire interior of the building. A little later came the smell of hot food as everybody gratefully settled down to vegetable and lamb broth with bread and beer. We ate, our spirits raised up by the reviving food, and complained of the aches, pains and sundry injuries picked up along the march. Notes were compared about how the kit had felt and handled. What to avoid for next time and better ways of securing loads. We were glad to be here now and the events of the morning in *Mogontiacum* were all but forgotten as we settled in.

As with all Roman forts, our new home followed the same layout as most other forts. The perimeter followed a rectangular shape with rounded corners topped by guard towers. A double ditch encircled a fifteen-feet high rampart built of turfs and topped by a defensive wall which broke to accommodate four gateways, also with defensive towers. The interior of the fort was then laid out in a standard pattern with the *principia* at its heart. Essentially, a Roman soldier could go to any fort in the empire and become instantly familiar with its basic layout.

Our new home was constructed entirely of timber and sat directly on the road we had just travelled. As well as a training garrison this fort was also used as a check-point, monitoring the traffic along the road, which had to pass through the middle of the fort along the *via principalis*. Once inside the fortification the traveller would be checked, recorded and have carts or loads of any description searched. Although we were still stationed in a Roman controlled area it was not uncommon for weapons and other contraband to be smuggled backwards and forwards from the frontier.

Because of its dual role the fort had one or two refinements that set it apart. Two store sheds had been constructed close to the *principia* to accommodate any seized items from searches. In addition, the fort had a large training compound situated just outside the defences. The area was fenced off with a palisade and contained a large timber drill hall with a sand floor, providing a dry training area when poor weather set in. The fort itself had been established about five years previously and already a thriving *vicus* had grown on the plateau to the west of the defences.

We had been taken over to the training compound later that evening and Scaurus had addressed us in the drill hall, outlining the next phases of training. Once more we would be subjected to route marches which would grow in duration and in varied conditions, as and when they saw fit. From now on, everything would be conducted in full battle order, unless otherwise directed, and the unit would move around venues in the training area at quick time. We were informed that the march we had just completed was eighteen miles in duration and, therefore, short of the expected daily distance of twenty miles normal march or twenty five miles forced. Scaurus assured us that we would be trained to cover these distances with ease. Finally, we were reminded of the existence of the *vicus* and conditions were promptly imposed on our visits there. Once more we would be under curfew and visits would be limited. Drunkenness and over fraternization would be punished accordingly and, as though we could forget, we were reminded of the example of Firmus.

The next day saw us catapulted into our new training regime as we charged around the fort and training areas as though our lives depended on it The pace of training was utterly hectic and, the added burden of heavy armour and weapons increased the discomfort dramatically. Down in the training stockade were set a series of upright wooden posts, six feet tall and as thick as a man's waist, enough to accommodate two men to a post and these were to be our new enemy for the duration of our stay at the fort.

Under the super critical eye of veteran weapon masters we drilled at these posts day in and day out. Initially, we were issued with heavy wicker shields in the shape of a *scutum* and weighted wooden swords as long as a *gladius*. Both items were considerably heavier than the normal weapon and it was with these that we began to learn the craft of combat. We would be set against the posts and directed to perform a series of combinations against them. We would attack the post from its front or flanks, feinting, dodging and defending. Low stabs, high stabs, upward stabs, shield lunges. All expected to be delivered with as much venom as you would if the post were a living enemy.

In the beginning we were lacking in the strength and stamina needed to wield the heavy training weapons for prolonged periods. The relentless pace saw us flagging as the stamina drained from moving around in full armour, muscles failed under the pressure of wielding the sword and holding the shield high enough to be of value. Always, the drawn *gladius* should be at waist height, ready to dart out and pierce your foe. The *scutum* should be presented to the front, covering your entire body so that the only visible parts were your lower legs and your head, from your eyes up. This too could be punched out to smash into your opponent's face or the edge of the shield thrust out to cause vicious injury at varying heights. Slowly this basic defensive stance was mastered, the muscles able to hold the position for hours and the deployment being swift and clean at every turn. We progressed from the exhausted, flagging bodies, flopping wearily onto our beds at night, to tireless young warriors, keen to take on any new challenges that tested our new abilities.

Those challenges came in the form of our own comrades. What we had learned from the posts, we were now to test out on each other. The weapon masters had carefully watched us as we trained and identified strengths and weaknesses as we progressed. Scaurus and Fuscus knew our personalities well by now and, together with the weapon masters, they decided on the initial pairs that would fight each other in the *armatura*.

My first pairing was with Surus. We fought each other with vigour and spirit but quickly learnt that there was more to the fight than delivering swingeing blows with wooden weapons. The training proved extremely painful to the enthusiastic beginner as he tried to land strikes on his opponent. Unlike the post, the opponent moved freely and, on top of avoiding you, he would strike back. In the initial stages of *armatura* the training was just a trading place for shattering blows of the wooden weapon and smashing yourself in the face or legs with the edges of your shield as your opponent moved against you. The venom and accuracy of the post training now had to be complemented with tactical thinking. It was the pain of receiving the painful bruises and split skin, the smashed knuckles and bloody noses that instructed you of the dangers of rash engagements.

Once this lesson was learned, the business of developing our technique began. Soon we were able to move even faster than before and sustain the effort for even greater periods as we tested our opponents. Now we moved in heavy armour as lightly as though we were dressed in linen tunics. As we learned our trade the injuries grew less as the new-found speed and tactics were deployed automatically. Eventually we were regularly swapping fresh opponents to test our ability to quickly assess and overcome unknown quantities. By the end of this phase of *armatura*, we were all perfectly capable of engaging in serious sword work. That may have been so, but we were still not ready for battle. Still, there was much to be done.

We moved next to the use of the *pilum*. Once more we returned to the posts. Once more we practised with heavier than normal training weapons. Although primarily a throwing weapon, the *pilum* could be used to thrust and stab opponents at close quarters, and so we started there. Standing and thrusting the blunts into the posts. Initially without *scuta*, then from behind them. When that was done we put distance between ourselves and the posts, now throwing the heavy weapons, simulating distance between ourselves and the enemy. Gradually the distances increased as we grew more proficient in our accuracy. Ultimately we reached the point where we could achieve central hits on the posts at distances as far out as forty to fifty paces on practically every throw.

The time came when we were to demonstrate our proficiency at these weapons in an examination of our new found skills. *Tribune* Scribonius had travelled in from *Mogontiacum* and would preside over the occasion. The weapon masters would dictate the disciplines to be demonstrated and Scaurus and Fuscus would mark and record results. Individually we demonstrated our dexterity with set formation exercises and then we moved onto personal combat exercises against opponents. This time we carried real swords and shields of the proper weight, although the *gladius* was tipped with a thick leather button to prevent serious injury. The difference in the handling of the weapons was truly astonishing and rapid adjustment had to be made to compensate for the increased speed of deployment as the fights turned into ferocious, fast moving skirmishes which displayed a tremendous degree of skill and agility. Scribonius was delighted and addressed us all at the end of the contest. He congratulated us on our progress, stating that he would be honoured to lead us into battle if the time ever came. We were all delighted by this and Scribonius left the fort, with his cavalry escort, to raucous cheering and the rhythmic banging of weapons against shields.

Now that we had become skilled in the use of our practice weaponry we returned, once again, to the posts. This time we were striking at them with real weapons. The techniques learnt with the heavy practice weapons now became honed using the arms that we would carry to war. Again the posts were subjected to all the aggression and skill that we had developed during our time at the *armatura*. Once more we were set against each other but, this time we were moving without conscious thought. Our actions carried out as if in a reflexive manner. The drills and techniques now burnt deeply into our minds.

Every day saw some form of weapons drill, only this time other skills were being incorporated into the training. We received basic instruction in horse riding with a view to identifying any potential talent for service in the Legion cavalry. This training included instruction in mounting a horse by vaulting onto its back in full armour. Having undergone this training it was clear that I would remain as a foot soldier for the foreseeable future.

The range of our offensive capabilities grew with the introduction of basic archery and slinging training. Specialist trainers visited from auxiliary units to teach us these new and amazing skills. Pantera was a veteran archer from a unit of *Hamians* stationed close by. He instructed us on the use of the recurve bow. A composite construction of wood and strips of horn which delivered terrific power to its shots. The weapon itself became absolutely deadly when used by a skilled

Hamian bowman. Ample testimony to the rigours of training with a bow from the age of around three years.

The trainers of these weapons really held our attention with their demonstrations of skill. Both slingers and archers could easily hit man-sized targets at ranges exceeding three hundred paces. As the ranges got shorter, so the accuracy became more and more impressive. We eagerly set up *scopae* at the far end of fields and began to rain arrows and stones down on them. In the beginning it would have been extremely dangerous for anyone standing around twenty paces either side of some of us as projectiles whipped off in all directions, hitting most things other than the intended targets. With time and patient instruction however, most of us were able to acquit ourselves quite well with these weapons. During our time spent acquiring projection skills we also improved our ability to throw fist sized stones. A few of us still possessed these skills from chasing rabbits and fowl when we were boys and developing the skill would prove to become most useful. If accurately delivered, a stone of such a size could easily shatter an unarmoured skull or even break a limb.

Although learning the art of weapons handling was our first priority, we also needed to learn fieldcraft skills if we were to be truly effective. As our marching practice continued more elements were introduced to the training. We would be taken on long distance marches which would negate the possibility of returning to camp the same day. We would need, therefore, to erect a marching camp for protection at night. This was basically a small fortification which had its own ditch and rampart topped by *pila murali*. This ringed our tents and would buy valuable time to muster troops in the event of the position being attacked. Sentries would be posted in addition to this which taught us the importance of this particular role. On one occasion Scaurus had gone prowling round at night and discovered a man from another *Contubernium* asleep at his post. His colleagues were tasked with administering disciplinary action the next day and they viciously beat him unconscious at Scaurus' bidding. It was explained to us that, had we been attacked, the alarm would not have been raised in time and we would have been overrun and slaughtered. Nobody disagreed with the punishment.

So much we had learned to transform ourselves into what we had become. We had mastered weapons and marched to the point of exhaustion. We had foraged for food and constructed fortified camps in the middle of nowhere. We had toiled with pick and shovel in full armour. We had learned the discipline of attacking formations and rehearsed them again and again until they were perfect. Now we had acquired all of the attributes we needed to return to *Mogontiacum* and tell them there ...

'We did it! Now we are Legionaries!'

Chapter 7

The Blooding

'Come On! I'd be quicker doing the damn job myself!' Yelled Fuscus. 'You are like a bunch of old hags this morning, shuffling around moaning about your aches and pains!'

For once Fuscus was wearing a slight grin as he tried to fire our enthusiasm for the job of getting loaded up, ready to return to the fortress at *Mogontiacum*. The problem had arisen from the night before. Officially, the night was regarded as our last as *Tiros*. As such we were expected to give dedication to the gods and to prepare our own celebration feast.

As the dusk had approached we made libations and gave prayers to *Iuppiter* Greatest And Best. Next, we dedicated an altar to *Mars Loucetius* and made a great sacrifice to him. From our savings, we had purchased a bull, a boar and a ram and offered the *Suovetaurelia* to the great god of war. The animals had been paraded around the fort before being taken before the altar for the completion of the *lustrum*. Sacrificing them before the newly dedicated altar in order that we would invoke the blessing of his protection in time of battle. The performance of this sacrifice would also ward off evil forces and bring us luck, as well as purifying us as a unit, in sight of Mars. As though to hedge our bets, our choice of god also influenced healing, should we become injured or sick whilst serving the Legion.

With the formalities over and done with, we abandoned piety for the joys of drink and celebration. Once again we used our savings to purchase supplies for the feast from the *vicus* and local farms. We ate heartily of the finest food available, making sure that food was also supplied to the sentries of the host garrison in appreciation of their assistance whilst we trained. Raucous laughter rang out as unofficial awards were presented to individuals for such things as the most times late on parade or the most ridiculous injury from weapons training. That particular award went to Statilius, of the first *Contubernium*, for being struck in his manhood by a practice *pilum*. The wounded member had to be bathed and salved daily for a week and a half before normality returned. He received the award of a clay statue of *Priapus* with a livid blush as we banged the tables with our fists and hooted uproariously.

A wheel amulet was given to Lupus, the youngest of our band. He had developed so much over the past months and his transformation was complete. He stood and took the amulet as we all cheered, his face beaming with pride. Almost fifteen years old now, he was a fine, strong young soldier and his body radiated the energy of his time spent in hard training. He was indeed a fully trained *Miles* now but we all hoped that the amulet would bless him with the protection of *Fortuna* and keep our 'Little Wolf' safe and well.

Finally we bestowed gifts on our trainers, or tormentors! Call them what you will! Scaurus and Fuscus had been with us since the very first day. They had accompanied us through every aspect of our training and, whilst we suffered on marches and in gruelling exercises, they had remained alongside us. They had covered the same distances and born the same privations as we had. But, all the time they had guided us towards this point. Yes, they had been cruel and unforgiving. The constant tariffs imposed by both had bled us dry of coin but everyone realized that, without them, we would not be celebrating at this feast. And so they sat, on their own table at the head of the room. When they required food or drink, we served it to them, our thanks to them for serving us so well. Finally we gave them our gifts. Fine presents were hard to come by all the way out there but we eventually succeeded in acquiring two large amphorae of fine quality Greek wine. It was not something that was easy to find and it cost an awful lot of money to bring them out to the fort but we managed. A merchant in the *vicus* had been approached early in our training and managed to bring it in for us. It took about a month to arrive and remained in the merchants store until we collected it the night before the celebration. Again, palms had to be greased in order to slip into the fort, just before curfew, with two bulky and heavy amphorae of contraband wine. But, we managed. The effort of obtaining such items was not lost on the two and they thanked us heartily, smiling friendly smiles now and slapping nearby backs as they ate and drank their fill.

It was inevitable that too much indulgence would lead to sorry men and sore heads in the morning, and so it was as we rose just after dawn to assemble the equipment for departure. Once more mules were burdened with heavy packs and the ox carts slowly filled with leather tents and heavy equipment. Men dragged their feet around, circles under their eyes and reeking of stale drink. Nobody was surprised to see men sloping off now and again to the latrines to spew up the sour, curdling mess that sat in the pit of their stomachs.

Seemingly immune to over indulgence, Fuscus stalked around, moving amongst the men and bawling orders at them as if he had been on bread and water the night before.

'Get your arses moving will you? I want you idle pigs on the road by mid morning! At this rate we'll be lucky to get out of here by the end of the week!'

My head spun as I tottered along carrying a rolled *papilio* and heaved it into the back of a cart. Sweat beginning to ooze from my forehead, despite the chill of the late Autumn morning. Surus was up on the cart, stacking the load evenly.

'Can't he ever shut his face?' he mumbled, nodding towards Fuscus.

'I don't know!' grunted Pacatianus as he slung a large wooden crate on board. 'But if he doesn't give it a rest soon, I'm likely to go over there and stick my fist in that noisy hole in the middle of his face!'

'You wouldn't dare!' sneered Pudens as he approached the cart. 'He'd kick your arse all over the fort and then nail your balls to a tree. No mistake!'

'Oh yeah? Well that's what you .... ' continued Pacatianus, stopping in mid flow as a mounted *Speculatore* galloped through the east gate towards us. 'Hello. What's all this then?'

The rider reigned the horse in, next to the cart. His face was cherry red from the cold of the fast morning ride and a large droplet hung off the end of his nose which he quickly wiped off with the back of his hand before addressing us.

'Greetings you fellows!' He said in a very refined accent. 'Be so good as to tell me where I can find Centurion Scaurus would you?'

'That's his *Optio*, Fuscus!' I pointed over to Fuscus and told him. 'He'll be able to tell you where the Centurion is Sir!'

'Many thanks soldier!' Said the rider who kicked his horse off once more and headed towards Fuscus who was now ranting at one of the men for dropping a sack of grain. A brief discussion ensued between Fuscus and the rider who then dismounted and entered the barrack block with the *Optio*. The horse now stood in the care of the soldier who had dropped the grain and he in turn stood there looking first at the burst bag and then back at the lathered horse. The horse now and again giving an irritated snort causing the soldier to flinch and wipe his face.

'What did you call him sir for, arse licker?' Pudens scoffed, beginning to adopt his familiar mocking tone.

'Oh, so could you tell what he was, wrapped in that cloak?' I quickly retorted. 'And when was the last time you heard any of our cavalry speaking in an accent like that?'

'No squabbling now girls! Let's try to find out what's going on!' Pacatianus cut in. 'This could be very interesting!'

We waited for somebody to emerge from the barracks while we dawdled around the carts trying to look busy. Speculation now rife as to why a messenger would roll up in the fort at so early an hour. It had to be urgent or he wouldn't have tried to get here so early, or so quickly. It seemed obvious that he had ridden hard to reach us. Eventually the trio emerged from the building and the *Speculatore* took the reins of his mount and led him away towards the stables.

'Gather round you lot!' Scaurus shouted and beckoned us over to him. We quickly made our way over and, as we did I noticed that Scaurus looked pale and decidedly jaded. No doubt from last night's celebrations. At last! Evidence that at least one of them was human after all!

We assembled around the Centurion as he cast his eye around us, making sure that we were all present before he began to speak. Fuscus stood behind him, his lips moving quietly as he conducted a mental role call. Once we had stopped moving around, Scaurus looked back to Fuscus who nodded and he began.

'Right, let's end the guessing game and put you out of your misery! That was a messenger from the personal staff of the Legate!' I gave Pudens a smug 'told you so' gesture which received a grin in return.

'We are not to return to *Mogontiacum*, as planned, but to travel north, as a unit with our own special agenda!' continued Scaurus. 'Some of you may be aware of the increase in activity of cattle raiders in the areas just north of here. Intelligence suggests that one band of between fifteen to twenty men are responsible and are systematically working their way through the outlying properties. They are raiding livestock, destroying properties and attacking the inhabitants, often with fatal consequences!'

A muted chatter broke out amongst the assembled men and several of us cast glances over to Secundus who stood, staring at Scaurus, a harsh cold look etched onto his face.

'Alright, alright. Shut the chatter and listen!' Scaurus went on. 'The Fourteenth Gemina is due to be committed to a large scale operation of which I have no information at this time. Because of this the main fortress at *Mogontiacum* and forts such as this one are to maintain their garrisons and make winter preparation for movement of the entire Legion the following year. Because of this you now find yourselves in the unique position of being the only unit of troops available to deploy!'

Again a low grumbling emanated from the assembly as Scaurus gestured for quiet once more.

'You may not like the idea of this task but it comes directly from the governor who wishes us to hunt down and bring these brigands to justice. It cannot be seen that armed bands wander the countryside with impunity whilst the occupying Imperial forces sit back and do nothing. We are losing face with the community and therefore we need to make an example of these men. We have a larger task to complete for next year and we do not need to be diverted with civil unrest while we do it. We ... you, are to march out and destroy this band.' Scaurus paused, looking at each and every one of us, then shouted. 'Are you ready boys?'

'Aye!' We roared and punched our fists into the air.

So! This was to be our first real mission. Not a massive battle against thousands of enemy but a small policing job with apparently wide-reaching consequences for both success and failure. It may not be the stuff of glory but it was an honourable task. One that I, and all of my comrades, were happy to undertake.

Within an hour we had formed up ready to march out. The ill effects of a night's heavy drinking now swept aside by the enthusiasm to be off and to complete our task. All of us buzzing with anticipation. All, except one. Secundus had remained silent since Scaurus had delivered his impromptu briefing to us.

He had said nothing despite being pressed by us about getting his own back on some raiders. Not one of us really knew what had happened when his farm was raided. He never elaborated on it and we respected his right to privacy. Now it had become disturbing. While we were all being driven by duty, Secundus was driven by something darker. He said nothing but the flames of a freshly stoked hatred burned brightly behind his eyes. What had they done to him? I knew not, but I did know that if the hate consumed him that much, it could affect his decision making and endanger any one of us. I resolved that I would be keeping a close eye on him from now on.

Briskly we marched out of the fort's north gate, our boots crunching along rhythmically to the accompaniment of the steady hoof falls of a *turma* of Legionary cavalry, sent along to act primarily as scouts whilst we hunted this band down. The cavalry followed behind our column with the small baggage train bringing up the rear. Fuscus kept pace at our side whilst Scaurus led the column, the white horsehair of the *crista transversa* bobbing above his shining, tinned helmet. He strode out in full armour, his *vitis* swinging in his right hand as he seemed to forge along, carrying the column in his wake.

* * *

For five days we had marched in search of the raiding party. We passed by remote settlements and farmsteads, collecting information as to the whereabouts of the criminals we were tasked to bring to justice. Cavalry outriders had called us over to a ramshackle old farmhouse where an old couple stood outside waiting for the column to arrive. Scaurus went over and spoke to them. We listened intently as the toothless old man told his story as he hugged the distraught old woman, thick cataracts clouded tearful eyes as she sobbed onto her husband's chest.

He shook with indignity as he told how the mounted band, around twenty strong, arrived at his property early last evening. There was nothing that they could really plunder so they ran through the house, smashing pots and furniture, laughing as they went. Around a dozen of them had remained outside, pushing the old man and his wife back and forth as their friends hacked the couple's three old ewes to gory pieces. When they had finished their sport they took the couple's small supply of grain and rode away. Never did they say a word, just laughed as they left their victims to starve.

Night was drawing in and Scaurus decided to camp at the old farm for the night. The raiders would be making camp now and wouldn't be that far away. We were close now, very close. As we erected the camp and defences a few of us broke off and did what we could to repair the damage to the property and make good some of the neglect that it had suffered. The farmer was old and things had slipped into disrepair, through no fault of his own. As we busied ourselves, he followed us round heaping thanks on us. Every time we went near his wife she held out her hand and smiled at us.

'Good boys. You are good Boys!' She would whisper.

In the morning we broke camp and left the couple with what meagre rations we could spare. The old man thanked us for our kindness and the old lady patted our cheeks and kissed our hands.

'Such kind boys!' She would repeat to herself.

As we marched off we knew that the raiders had tipped the balance of the fine knife edge that the couple lived on between survival and death. Their quiet little world had been turned upside down by these men, their living equilibrium destroyed, this winter would be their last. By the Gods, these scum had to pay!

Shortly before midday two of our cavalrymen returned at the gallop. Scaurus halted the column as they drew rein in front of him. Panting breathlessly one of the riders quickly related what they had spotted.

'About one mile directly in front of you lies an attacked settlement!' said the rider, pointing in the direction he had come from. 'There are about four buildings surrounded by a low stockade. We can't see any movement and one of the buildings is well alight. They are single storey thatched jobs. Usual for this area!'

'Where are your other two riders?' asked Scaurus.

'They're still up front. I've left them to do a cursory sweep of the ground. See if they can pick anything up. They won't go far!'

'Good!' Scaurus praised him. 'Go back up there and keep an eye on the settlement, but stay short of it. I don't want you getting run down by superior numbers. The rest of the *Turma* will stay with me until we reach the settlement. Any trouble and you ride straight back here! Understood?'

'Yes Centurion!'

'Good! Now go!'

The two horsemen galloped off, back towards a now visible column of light grey smoke that curved up into the dark grey sky. Scaurus advanced us at quick time until we could clearly see the stockade and the buildings within. About two hundred paces short of the settlement he halted us and got us to down our packs and get into fighting order. Once he had instructed us to stack our kit with the small baggage train he ordered the cavalry to protect it and took us forward in a double extended line. My heart was thundering in my chest as we approached the silent settlement. All you could hear was our equipment clanking and jingling and the odd crack or pop of burning wood from the blazing building as we drew closer. Scaurus halted us just before the low stockade. Its sole purpose was to keep livestock in and it held no defensive value at all. There was ample evidence of this as we could see over the fence top, into the central yard. Smashed implements lay on the ground and here and there a body lay. Indistinct for now, but definitely bodies.

Scaurus picked the *Contubernium* nearest to him which just happened to be ours and instructed us to leave our *pila* with the others who would remain outside. He then had us draw swords and slowly we walked into the stockade via its main gate.

'Right! Fan out and stay in pairs!' he said in a low voice. 'Search the buildings slowly and carefully. If you find trouble of any sort, call out. Now move!'

We broke into four pairs with Scaurus moving to the centre of the stockade to monitor developments. As we moved around the edge I began to smell the fires and a raw, sickly smell. Not like old, decaying death but fresh slaughtered carcasses. Lupus moved silently beside me as we approached the first two bodies. A young girl of about eighteen lay on her back in the black sticky mud of the yard, sightless eyes stared skywards and her mouth hung open above a grisly slash wound across her throat which had been cut almost to the bone. Broken fingernails and blood around her mouth pointed to the fact that she had not succumbed easily. A shallow stab wound in her side must have added to her pain while the torn dress pulled up around the waist and the bruised and bloody thighs spoke of the final indignity.

An old woman lay sprawled across her. Hands tied in front of her and the look of stark fear screamed silently upwards, frozen in time by the sword strike that had cleaved open the back of her skull as she had no doubt tried to plead for the honour of the younger girl. I fought to control the rising bile as I moved silently by their pitiful carcasses. The blood had only just started to thicken. This had not been done long.

As we approached the first hut, Lupus moved quickly forwards, *gladius* pointed towards the door, and crouched behind his *scutum*.

'Lupus! Slowly!' I hissed under my breath. 'Just be careful!'

'Don't worry about me!' He looked back over his shoulder at me, smiling as he moved towards the door. 'Just watch your back!'

I raised my hand to caution him as he turned towards the door then heard the scream, full of animal terror, as the thick log of firewood swung from inside the door and smashed into Lupus' face. A pair of filthy arms appeared at the end of the wood as blood splattered across my face and into my eyes. Instinctively I crouched and raised my shield to protect my head as I thrust the *gladius* forward into the body mass that was now emerging from the doorway.

'To me!' I screamed as the tip of the sword cut effortlessly upwards into the soft body and hot blood sprayed onto my hand. A face appeared from behind the door then. Imploring, terrified. Silently asking why I had killed him. The mouth falling open as he slid to the floor. Eyes wide open. A final gasp leaving his lungs as he died in the defence of his home.

Within seconds I was surrounded by Scaurus and the others as they heard my shout and came running over to investigate. By the time they had arrived terrible screams started to emanate from inside the hut where the man had come from. Everything seemed to be moving in slow motion as Scaurus and two others entered the building. I looked down then and saw Lupus lying there, unmoving on the muddy ground. The right side of his face held a quiet, peaceful look as one eye seemed to stare wistfully at my boots. The left side was almost unrecognisable. The impact of the log on his face had creased his cheek guard in and shattered the bones on that side of his face, blood ran in a thin trickle from one nostril and a pink socket contained the remnants of his burst left eye. The Little Wolf was dead.

I was being bombarded with questions from the others about what had happened. I ignored them, choosing to follow Scaurus inside to find out what the commotion was. Inside I saw two young boys of around ten or twelve years old, with them were an old man and three middle aged women. A young girl of around five years old huddled close to the women. All wore looks of abject terror and the women continued to scream hysterically as I approached. The old man fell to his knees in front of Scaurus and began to beg for his life. His hands clasped tightly and offered up to Scaurus in supplication as he sobbed for his life and that of his surviving family.

'Please sir, please. We thought they had come back. We didn't mean for a soldier to die!'

The Centurion paused over the wretched form of the old man for a moment then slowly placed a hand on his shoulder.

'The man who made the mistake is dead. Killed by my soldier. You have nothing to fear from us now!' A look of extreme sadness crossed Scaurus' face as he motioned over to the women and children. 'Calm your people father. No more harm will come to you and yours!'

The man sobbed as he turned and hugged the remains of his family. Tears of relief now flowed freely as the family realized that their ordeal had ended with our arrival. I felt nothing for them as I turned and walked outside, seeing once more the two bodies lying in the gore-soaked mud of the farm yard. One moment we had, all three of us, been alive. In the blink of an eye two were dead. A mistake. That was all it was! A stupid mistake which killed an innocent farmer and an unwary boy.

'I saw, I saw it!' Pudens grabbed me by the shoulders and looked into my eyes. 'you couldn't have stopped it. The Little Wolf got too far ahead of himself. There was nothing you could do!'

'Perhaps you're right friend!' I nodded slowly 'But it's a bad day's work we've seen here today!'

Scaurus emerged from the hut and ordered the rest of the *vexillation* inside the stockade. Fuscus could be heard confirming the order and moving them inside. Quickly he diverted them off to the rest of the compound and the searching continued as he strode over to Scaurus. I tapped Pudens on the shoulder and gestured for him to look over to Secundus. He had knelt in the mud next to the bodies of the girl and the woman. He was saying something that we couldn't hear but it seemed as though he were talking to the corpses.

Pacatianus came up behind us and nodded in Secundus' direction.

'Do you get the feeling he's seen something like this before?' He ventured.

'If he has then we really need to watch him!' Pudens replied, echoing my earlier thoughts. 'There's no telling what he'll do when we catch up with these murdering bastards!'

A little later that day Scaurus dispatched the cavalry to make a sweep of the area and try to follow the tracks left by the horses of the brigands and their stolen cattle. We remained at the farmstead and began to piece together the events of the day. They had apparently struck at just before sunrise and moved very swiftly, identifying any valuable livestock and smashing down the fences of the pens, driving the animals clear of the stockade. While a handful of the group went with the stolen animals the rest remained to search the buildings for valuables and supplies. They didn't find much to steal so they decided to have some sport with the farmer and his extended family.

The dead women were his eldest daughter and his wife. He had been forced to watch while his wife had pleaded for mercy with the raiders as they raped her daughter repeatedly. She was bound at the wrists to stop her slapping them and pushed contemptuously away as the men continued to brutalize the girl. Eventually she became too annoying with her interruptions. One of the raiders had cleaved her skull with his sword, laughing at the daughter's screams as her mother slumped dead across her breast. The same man then knelt down and cut the screaming girl's throat with a single vicious slash of a knife.

Two more bodies were found in the compound. The farmer's ten year old son lay dead in a cattle pen. He was the twin of one of the boys in the hut and had been slain whilst trying to protect his charges. The farmer's brother in law had a twenty year old son who was speaking of leaving to join the Legion. No longer was he alive to fulfil his ambition. His head parted from his shoulders, the body lay there in the filth, still holding the wood axe he had tried to defend himself with. I later learned that the man I had killed was his brother in law. The man had been completely taken over by fear and shock and had attacked the first thing to come near their hiding place. Truly, the farmer had paid a heavy price for simply earning a living from the land.

Firewood was collected later that afternoon and we began to build funeral pyres for the dead. Two were built for the dead of the farmer's family and their bodies were washed and dressed. Their hair combed and small offerings placed with them on the pyre as the distraught family stood, wailing their grief to the gods for such an outrage of fortune.

Carefully we had stripped Lupus of his armour and weapons and cleaned up the damage to his face as best we could. Aebutius placed a square of linen from his pack over the injuries to hide the brutal wound. We built his pyre next to a small copse with a silent green pool at its heart. There were only six of us left in our *Contubernium* now and we felt his loss deeply. We made our way into the copse and I held out the wheel pendant that Lupus had been given at the feast. 'Much luck it brought him' I thought as I snapped the loop suspending it from the strap and cast it into the silent green waters. An offering to the *nymphs* from a man unable to save his friend.

'Look after our friend, you *nymphs* of water and trees. Join with the *Lares* of this farmstead and ensure that Lupus is untouched by evil. Accept this pendant in return for your protection and as a sign of our gratitude. Be at peace little wolf!'

Pacatianus placed a loaf of bread on a tree stump for the woodland *nymphs* whilst Pudens poured a beaker of wine into the little pool, a libation for the spirits dwelling there. Together we returned to the pyre where we were joined by Scaurus and Fuscus, who had brought a lighted brand. Silently we watched as Secundus took the flame from Fuscus and knelt at the pyre, igniting the kindling at its base. Gradually the fire grew and flames licked around Lupus' body, casting dancing sparks into the darkening sky.

We all stood there for a while, watching and reflecting on the life lost. A young boy who fought hard to reach his goal, succeeding against all odds and to our intense pride. We had lost him but he would always be with us in our hearts. His determination was the embodiment of the fighting spirit we all possessed so, in a sense, he lived still. Scaurus nodded gently at the flames and looked to each side, seeing the sadness on our faces as we watched the flames claim our comrade.

'Remember this day lads. There will be many more like it!'

Slowly we turned and drifted silently back to the farmstead. There was work to be done.

Chapter 8

Justice

The cavalry had returned just before nightfall with the news we all wanted to hear. They had found the brigands sheltering in a woodland clearing about four miles from the farmstead. Immediately Scaurus and Fuscus sat down to plan how best we should approach and deal with the band.

Upon seeing a small trail of smoke just in from the tree line, a small party of the cavalry had dismounted and approached on foot. They had seen eighteen men and horses camped close to an outcrop of rock in a clearing. Makeshift pens held the stolen livestock on one side of the clearing whilst a track way led into the wood on the other. A further broad track came directly off the heath and continued for about one hundred paces, opening onto the centre of the clearing. Makeshift shelters had been erected against the outcrop which appeared to be used for both sleeping and dry storage areas. Further observation of the position revealed that the horses were tethered between the two tracks and the track on the side of the encampment surfaced onto the heath about three hundred paces further on.

A plan was soon formed which relied on the raiders having enough time to escape down the side track in order to spring it effectively.

Scaurus reasoned that, if our cavalry approached the main track at the gallop, then the raiders should mount up and attempt flight down the side track. They were blocked by the rock at their rear and escape through the animal pens would be too risky and hampered by the presence of the panicking livestock. They would either have to run into the cavalry or make off down the safety of the side track. Once on the track they would be dealt with by the Legionaries. Two groups of men would sit either side of the track way and a third group would block the road and fell the advancing horse with *pila*. There would be little danger of the riders leaving the track due to the dense pines on either side.

The ambush would be sprung about two hundred paces up from the camp and, once inside the track, the cavalry would seal the rear, cutting them off in a killing ground. The prime function of the engagement would be to secure prisoners. If men had to die, then so be it, but this was not to be a slaughter. That was made absolutely clear to all of us.

As luck would have it, *Luna* had provided us with a bright moon that night and the sky was relatively clear. We moved out three hours before the dawn and were in position to await the coming of first light. As soon as there was a little light, then the cavalry would make their approach. We slipped silently into position and waited expectantly. None of us had slept that night, but there was no tiredness in any of us. Fuscus and two Legionaries, stripped to tunics with their *gladius* drawn to prevent noise, crept down to the encampment. Seeing that all were still present they made their way back and re armoured to wait with the rest of us.

I and eleven others lay in the trees, waiting for the sound of hooves which would signal us to deploy across the track in a shield wall and bring down the lead horses with our *pila*. Scaurus was with us to give the order to throw. Judging distance in the half light would be critical if we were not to be overrun by terrified horses.

Slowly the grey light of the dawn began to filter into the trees. Blurred, unnatural shapes began to take substance and form before my eyes as the first of the birds began their morning song. I could see a helmeted head, here and there, or the edge of a shield as we lay, silently waiting. By the time the raiders had spotted any of this, it would be much too late for them. Faint noises began to filter up the track as the men in the clearing began to wake and move about, perhaps relieving their full bladders or starting to prepare breakfast.

Suddenly, shouting! The sound of panic rang through the trees and above it, the sound of thirty horses could just be heard thundering down the track into the camp, their riders whooping to cause maximum panic. Scaurus stood and gestured for us to rise. He signalled to Fuscus who readied the men at the other side of the track. Quietly we waited but my pulse raced like a wild horse and my heart threatened to leap from my mouth, so fiercely did it pound. A new noise now as the shouts were accompanied by drumming hoof beats on the soft woodland floor, approaching ever nearer with each second. Swiftly Scaurus snapped his fingers to attract our attention then thrust his arm out, directing us across the track with a swift chopping motion of his hand. In an instant the shield wall silently formed and the *pila* lay poised over our right shoulders, ready to fly. Two lines of shields could be seen, just inside the trees, either side of the track, as the flank ambushers took position. Every hair on the back of my neck was standing now. In second they would be on us.

The din of the hooves grew steadily louder as the fleeing band approached. I felt the ground begin to vibrate with their approach and could hear the men shouting and yelling to spur their horses on, away from the pursuing *Turma*. My eyes widened as the charging shapes took form in the eerie grey light. The lead riders looking over their shoulders as they lashed their mounts with tightly gripped reins.

Eighty Paces, sixty paces. 'Come on! Now!' My mind bellowed out as I looked to Scaurus, the flat of his hand poised at shoulder height. I focussed on him now, ignoring the great weight of frantic chaos approaching me, trusting him to judge it right. Scaurus was facing the horses, slightly crouched, mouth open and breath held. Poised to give the signal, then, the hand snapped down.

'Now!'

The twelve *pila* tore across the space between us and our targets like bolts from *Iuppiter*, a low and flat trajectory, impacting with the first of the charging mounts. The first five horses all pitched forward, screaming their terror as the lethal shafts hammered into their chests and necks, felling them instantly. Their riders soared briefly into the air, arms and legs flailing wildly, then crashed down in front of their fallen horses. Mud flew into the air as the horses in the rear collided with their speared companions. More screaming, this time men, as they were trampled by flailing hooves. The trees echoed with the chaotic sounds as horses thrashed around in their torment, trying to rise, oblivious to the injury they inflicted on their riders as they desperately tried to flee the scene.

The second wave of *pila* tore out of the trees simultaneously from both sides on Fuscus' barked order. A low delivery ensured there was no risk to the Legionaries opposite each other. The missiles sank deeply into ribcages, flanks, necks and legs alike as the unfortunate horses fell in all directions, their riders scattered all over the track or trapped under dead and dying beasts.

'*Gladius* ... Present!' Scaurus bawled over the mayhem of screaming.

Instantly we drew our swords and raised them to the pale sky.

'*Iuppiter, Optimo, Maximo!*' We yelled as we slammed the blades out horizontally against the edges of our shields.

'Quick time! Advance!' The order boomed out.

We rapidly moved to surround the killing ground with three straight lines of shields, presented to the devastated pile of meat in front of us as the flanking soldiers burst onto the track from the trees. Four men rose from the carnage and ran at the walls, bellowing now like cornered animals. One ran in our direction and was slammed to the floor by Surus who swatted him with his *scutum*. Aebutius swung the flat of his blade against the man's temple and stunned him instantly. As we watched, we witnessed the other three choose death over captivity. All three were armed with long swords and ran screaming at the shield walls to the sides. In a heartbeat they were smashed to the ground and impaled on the wicked points of the lunging swords.

Five riders had kept their mounts and had turned tail to escape, back towards the camp. They had just turned and set off when the *turma* swept them up like a huge wave. The Roman cavalry would not toy with mounted opposition. Again we watched as the luckless riders were speared with lances or, in the case of two of their number, swiftly decapitated by razor sharp *spathas*.

Terrible carnage had been brought down on the brigands. I had witnessed so many things happening that I thought I had watched for an age, but, the reality was that it was over in seconds. Part of the *turma* was stood, breasting the trackway and surveying the aftermath of the ambush. Scaurus approached one of the riders and asked him:

'Where are the rest of the *Turma*?'

'Back down in the clearing *Centurio*. Some of the stupid bastards panicked so much they missed their exit and had to front us out. Suffice it to say, they don't fight well on horseback!'

The cavalryman looked round at his comrades, grinning as they burst into gales of laughter and began recounting the elements of the brief but bloody encounter.

'I take it there are no prisoners down there then?' Scaurus snapped at them.

'Sorry *Centurio!*' The cavalryman composed himself. 'I think that there were two survivors, although one may not live to see the day out!'

'Fine!' growled Scaurus sarcastically. 'I suppose that will have to do then!'

He stalked back towards us, scowling deeply as he approached. It was obvious he was annoyed and disappointed that all had not gone entirely to plan. He stabbed a finger at the shattered pile of men and horses littering the track.

'Start working your way through that pile of shit!' he snapped. 'If any of those bastards are alive, bind them and tend to any wounds. I'd like to take at least some of these murdering scum back with us! As for the hopeless cases, cut their throats and be done with!'

The Centurion turned and walked briskly down the track, back to the encampment where he would no doubt find more to displease him. Once he had disappeared Fuscus yelled at us to get on with the task in hand and we set about searching the twisted mass of men and horses. Now and then a horse still screamed or snorted its pain and misery as it lay dying. Trapped men groaned in pain as we began to pull out the survivors worth recovering. Eventually we retrieved four men from the blood sodden mess. Three other men were close to death and two were dispatched with cold efficiency. Secundus knelt over the third.

Most of the troops had gone back down the track with the prisoners and only I remained behind with Surus, Aebutius, Pudens and Pacatianus as Secundus leaned closer to the dying raider and whispered softly in his ear. The man lay pinned under a dead horse. The animals shoulder had rammed him into the ground, breaking his back with the force of the impact. His body twisted at an impossible angle as he still sat astride his mount which lay lifeless on its side. A *pilum* had fixed his thigh to the side of the animal and the man lay there, trying to speak but merely mouthing words, a froth of bloody bubbles popping on his lips.

'Secundus, just do him and let's go will you?' Said Pudens, walking over to the kneeling Legionary, as he cooed softly to the doomed criminal. The scene took on a compellingly bizarre quality as we watched Pudens hold his hand out to help Secundus up.

'Back off, or I'll spit you. You smart mouthed bastard!' spat Secundus as he tore his *gladius* from its scabbard and lunged at Pudens. The blade flashed in the quickening light as Pudens darted out of range of the lethal sword.

'Great gods!' Yelled Pudens. 'What are you doing man?'

Secundus held the blade out rigid before him and hushed Pudens with a finger lifted to his lips. We watched stunned as Secundus stroked the man's hair and whispered to him. Aebutius stepped forward, poised to speak and was met by the keen point of the *gladius* as Secundus stared at him uncompromisingly and slowly shook his head. Again he gazed back down at his helpless captive, smiling almost benevolently.

'I know you brother, don't I?' he whispered as he nodded his head at the raider, whose eyes were now filled with terror as he tried to answer, managing only a bloody gurgle as he stared up at Secundus.

'Two years ago, not far from here, yes? You remember? The woman on her own while her husband tilled distant fields. Just her and those two little boys of hers!'

Secundus nodded knowingly as the raider's eyes grew even wider and a strange whistling noise began to sound from his throat.

'Secundus. This isn't right he . . . ' I tried to reason with him but he thrust his open palm towards me and raised a finger for quiet. He continued to torment his prize.

'I know you remember. How could you forget such a lovely woman and those fine boys?' A great blackness spread over his face now as Secundus gripped the mans tangled, bloody hair. A tear slid down Secundus' cheek, falling onto the captive's lips as we listened to the story unfold. For our part, we just stood there, silent witnesses now, beginning to understand where this was all going.

'I remember!' He nodded to the raider. 'I remember coming back to my smouldering house and finding them dead in the dirt!' Secundus' chest heaved deeply now as he sobbed with the pain of the memory, hateful venom about to explode from him in a fury of violence. He grabbed the man's head up by the hair and his jaw, bellowing in his face.

'You must remember how sweet she was as you all raped her precious body you scum! Don't you remember skewering those poor lads on your filthy swords?' He screamed, almost deranged as he thrust the raider's head back to the ground and brought the *gladius* down on the twisted neck.

It cleaved into the neck with a sickening smack as Secundus screeched at the face!

'You took my life you animal bastard!' Again and again the blows landed, splattering Secundus with bright blood as he raged at the ruined corpse until, at last, he stood. His prize dangling from his left hand as he stared it in the now sightless dull eyes and whispered to it.

'You took my life, so now I must have yours!'

I said nothing as the sword slid from his grip, just turned and walked off down the track, the others following silently behind me.

None of us ever said a word to Secundus about the events of that morning. What could we possibly say to a man who lived in the presence of such dreadful phantoms. Neither he, or we, would ever know if these were the very raiders that destroyed his previous existence so cruelly. Condemning heart and soul to a living purgatory, suffering for the gross wrongs of other men. It was perhaps likely that they were the ones but I believed, with all my heart, that Secundus had laid nothing to rest or managed to assuage the pain that he felt so fiercely.

The Roman cavalry had slaughtered almost every man remaining in the clearing when they had fallen upon them. They had hurtled into the camp and began spearing and laying about with their swords, war cries shattering the peace of the woods as they butchered their vastly inferior opponents. Of the two immediate survivors, one had died shortly after we arrived in the encampment and the other, having almost lost his sword hand in the fight, was losing a lot of blood. Bodies lay strewn on the ground close to cleaved limbs and bloody lumps of flesh. Stark evidence of the deadly effectiveness of the razor sharp, slashing *spathas* wielded by the cavalrymen. Of the eighteen, we had managed to capture only five to stand accountable for their crimes. Scaurus was not pleased but it would have to do.

Bodies were stripped where they lay and their weapons retrieved, to be taken back with the prisoners. Nobody moved to afford the dead even a simple funeral. They could all rot! Supplies of grain and other stores were piled in a corner of the encampment for collection later. Scaurus had decided that the last farm raided could claim the foodstuffs and reclaim their livestock as compensation for their suffering. Obviously, it would never make up for the terrible tragedy that had befallen them but it would go some way to restoring their living. Besides. We did not have the means to transport it.

The injured captive's ruined hand was amputated there and then and a brand from the camp fire used to cauterize the wound. The unconscious body was slung over the back of a captured horse. When he regained consciousness he could walk, like the others. Briefly we stopped at the farm to tender the news that their tormentors, if not now dead, would be publicly executed. The prisoners would return to *Mogontiacum* with us to receive their punishment. As capital of *Germania Superior*, it would ensure that many saw the administration of Roman justice and that word would spread swiftly of the fate of those committing such outrageous acts of brigandry and lawlessness. Along with publication of the executions, personal effects and weapons of those slain in the camp raid would be displayed at the execution site.

The weather grew steadily worse as we marched south to return to the fortress. Autumn was now turning rapidly into a bleak, cold winter as we pushed the prisoners to their limits in our hurry to reach base before the weather took a real turn for the worst. On the way we encountered people who lived and farmed the raided areas. Some knew people who had fallen victim to our charges and, worse, the odd few were survivors of their raids. Many a time we had to threaten injury or worse to get them to stay clear as they spat, punched, clawed and kicked out at the now shattered men, shuffling along in chains. Whilst fully understanding the rage of these folk it was more important for all to see the price of their actions than to allow them to be torn to pieces by enraged peasants. We protected them. For now at least.

Their leader was a man called Castex. He would speak little with us and endured the privations of the journey with hard jawed arrogance for the most part. He hated us. That much was plain. A man of around fifty years he was of the *Chatti* tribe, subdued and pacified many years before. Bending the knee to Rome had not been everyone's choice and men like Castex despised Romanization and preyed upon those who embraced it. On his quest he had been joined by wasters and hangers on, out for an easy meal and cruel entertainment. They did not embrace his ideals but they loved his methods and so he became feared. For a brief moment in time he could aspire to be a Chieftain with his warriors. Only now it was over and the time to pay the price was upon him.

Our escorts had ridden ahead of us and notified the fortress of our approach. As we entered the town the roads were lined with locals, eager to see the barbarian terrors who had finally been brought to book. Sleet flitted around on a sharp wind as we marched in. We were grimy from the march and must have looked a mess as we arrived. The filth and rust on the equipment was honestly earned though and we wore it like laurels as we marched proudly up to the fortress gates. As we approached I looked to the crowd, here and there a familiar face until ... Quintus!

He stood close to the front of the crowd smiling, as he spotted me he nodded his head and I swelled with pride as we passed. When last he saw me I had entered the gates as a boy, now he saw me returning with my captives, as a soldier! I would see him as soon as I was allowed leave. I had much to tell him.

Castex and his men were thrown in cells whilst decisions were made regarding their fate. In the interim a *Quaestionarius* and his staff employed their special talents to extract information from the men about how many farms and homes had been raided, where and when. Once they had finished with them a report was sent to the Magistrates who would then decide on the appropriate punishment.

Two mornings after our return, the executions were carried out. We were kept inside the fort until that morning when we marched them out of the gates and onto the far side of the *Rhenus* bridge where a large crowd had assembled. As the soldiers who had captured these foul criminals, we were to have the honour of crucifying them for the public.

Proclamation of the sentence was read out to the people gathered at the execution site and the document was then nailed to a short post next to where the crosses would be erected. Once this was done, we began our task.

Five, rough timber crosses lay on the ground, next to five narrow holes in the frosty soil that would take their bases. The five prisoners were, by now, in very poor health. They had been beaten, whipped and tortured without mercy, two of them now holding on to life by the finest of threads. We divided into five parties and lay them onto the crosses, lashing arms to cross members and tying both ankles together, just above a small foot shelf. When all of them were securely tied we awaited a signal from Scaurus to start driving the nails home. After a moment he nodded left and right and we began.

A small wooden pad was placed over the forearm and the iron nail was then placed over it. As the heavy iron hammer began to drive the nails home the screaming began. Animal wailing and howling as the huge nails tore into the flesh and tendons above the wrist. The men began to writhe like snakes, trying desperately to free themselves of the torment they were enduring, but to no avail. High pitched shrieks stung my ear drums as we stood waiting to drop the crosses into their holes and begin propping.

The screams starting to lower to loud groans and sobs as the men suffered for their cruelty.

Scaurus gestured with arms outspread, pushing his palms upwards.

'Lift!'

I heaved at the arm of Castex's cross and began to shove it into the air with Surus. Secundus and Pudens took the other side, Pacatianus shoved the head up and Aebutius guided the base into the hole. Castex snapped his head to the side, glaring at me as he rose into the air, teeth bared and gritted with the pain. Still the hatred boiled in his eyes. He let out a low, tormented moan. 'That's right you bastard!' I thought. 'Suffer! If not for you we would still have our friend!' The cross thudded into place, its neighbours dropping down one by one.

We drove packing stones into the holes and, at Scaurus' order, we moved away from the crosses and looked up, surveying the morning's work. The brigands' weapons, equipment and clothing was laid out before them for all to see and guards were posted while they died. The crucifixion would take its course with no intervention from the crowd. No merciful knife wound or broken legs for them, theirs was to be a painful death. They were straining now, we could see their arms beginning to spasm and shake. Straining to keep their bodies rigid enough to breathe. As time passed they would weaken through blood loss and muscle fatigue and their bodies would sag, sliding down the cross and slowly, very slowly, suffocating them with their own weight.

We had brought Lupus' ashes home with us and, later that day, as the tortured Castex and his men breathed their last agonized gasps, we buried the Little Wolf by the roadside.

Chapter 9

Winter in Mogontiacum

'Come on then lads, give an old man some war stories!' Quintus beamed as he sat down behind the kitchen table, poised to listen to our exploits of the past weeks. I had taken the rest of the *Contubernium* to visit Quintus and Curatia and we were welcomed like conquering heroes. Curatia moved around the table offering drinks and food as Quintus eagerly pumped us for information concerning our final phase of training and the hunting down of Castex and his band.

It was so good to be back in the old house again. My memories of so many things sprang back to life as I walked back through the door to the warmest of welcomes. I had many new memories to share with them and my friends had also possessed lots of interesting tales to satisfy the couple's curiosity. Quintus was delighted. It was like the old days for him. Sat with a group of soldiers swapping exaggerated tales of personal valour and prowess. In truth, we had little to tell as our experiences were, as yet, somewhat limited. Quintus cared little about that as he listened to the tale of the hunt from all of our sides and then threw in a few amazing tales of his own. We watched the afternoon light fade to dusk and finally night laid its shroud on the town as we chatted, laughed and drank.

They were both pleased with the young man I had grown into since they last saw me. Curatia remarked that I reminded her of a young Quintus as he scoffed, reminding her he was much fitter and better looking than I at that time. She giggled mockingly and he threw his arms wide in mock indignation, staring at us with mouth wide open. We laughed happily at the display.

Quintus wanted to know more about Castex. What was it that had driven him to commit his crimes? Why had he become such a murderous fiend that needed to be hunted down like a crazed dog? I don't think any of us really had the right answers for him. There was little to say about the man as he had said very little to us during his time in captivity. Perhaps he had given more to the *Quaestionarii* but we had not become privy to much of that information. I closed the matter with the possible explanation that the world had changed catastrophically around Castex and he had not been able to move along with it. For a while he fought it and in the end it had killed him.

'Maybe you're right Vepitta!' Quintus acknowledged. 'But, even on that chunk of wood you nailed him to, you could see the hatred in his eyes!'

Briefly, my mind's eye opened and I remembered the look of pure hatred that he had fixed me with on the day that we had nailed him to his cross and planted it in the ground. Not a moment that I would easily forget!

'He knew the risks!' snapped Secundus, drawing a large gulp from his beaker. 'He knew and yet he continued. He got what he earned!'

For a brief moment there was an uneasy silence. The topic was painful for him, especially as we had learnt from the interrogation that Castex and his band were indeed the raiders that had destroyed Secundus' farm and murdered his family. This news had not helped to lay any of Secundus' ghosts. If anything he had become more detached from us and spent a lot of his free time on his own.

'So!' sighed Curatia, tactfully trying to change the subject. 'More wine or beer for anyone?'

'Not for me!' Secundus replied, waving his palm over his beaker as he pushed his chair back and stood. 'I am away back to barracks. I have equipment that needs attention! My thanks for a fine evening's hospitality. Vepitta is fortunate to have been taken in by such kind and generous people!'

He drew his cloak over his shoulders and made for the door as Quintus rose to see him out. As the old man opened the door and the cold air drifted in from outside he squeezed Secundus' forearm in the greeting of the Legionary.

'Please feel free to visit again friend. You will always be welcome. As are you all!'

There was something about the look in Secundus' eye as he placed his hand on the old man's shoulder and smiled at him.

'You are a fine host sir. I hope that I will share your company again, one day!'

Secundus waved briefly over to us and then walked out into the chilly night air. Quintus waved him off and closed the door, turning to us with a puzzled look on his face.

'Another time perhaps Quintus!' I said. 'It is a long and sad story and not for a night such as this!'

We shared a drink or two more with the couple and then made our way out into the street. The air temperature had fallen dramatically now and already timbers began to sparkle with a fine dusting of frost. Our breath billowed in front of us as we pulled our cloaks tight around us and began a brisk walk to the house of Aurelia.

Perhaps it would be odd to say that we felt at home there, especially as we had only ever been there once, but the expensive surroundings of the brothel felt safe and welcoming as we entered its rooms once more. Again we were welcomed by Aurelia who teased us playfully and led us through to the meeting room. She remembered us but said nothing of the events of our last visit. For the deeds of one bad visitor it would have made little business sense to turn away his former companions. Drinks were given to us as the girls sauntered over and began to work their tender charm. I sipped my wine and helped myself to some oysters lying on a wide *Samian* plate as a I looked around for Julia. She was nowhere to be seen as I searched around, politely declining the advances of her companions. I decided that she must already have a client and resolved to wait for her to return from upstairs. Eventually I grew impatient and made my enquiries with Aurelia.

'You wish for Julia's company, my sweet?' She said, smiling sadly. 'If it were in my power to grant it then gladly, I would. But only the gods can do that for you now sweet boy!'

My spirits sank as a I realized what she was trying to tell me but still, I felt compelled to ask.

'Why Aurelia? Why can only the gods grant my wish?'

I began to feel a lump swelling in my throat as she led me over to a couch and sat me down next to her. She raised a soft hand to my face and gently stroked my cheek as she told me the worst possible news.

'Perhaps one month ago, Julia fell ill with a fever!' Tears began to glisten in her eyes as she quietly continued, not wishing to spoil the cheerful ambience of the room. 'There was nothing to be done and she succumbed two days before you returned with the captured brigands!'

I gazed into her eyes, wanting to read lies and seeing only the sad truth of it as a solitary tear slid down her sad face. She leaned slowly forwards and gently kissed my forehead.

'I am sorry my love. Take another girl tonight and remember Julia with fondness!'

With that she stroked my hair, stood swiftly, her composure once more regained, and mingled once more with her guests. Once more she wore the professional mask of the hostess and the tears for her lost Julia were gone.

I sat, for a little while, and thought of what the news meant to me. As far as I was concerned she, Julia, had given me the gift of completeness that night and I would never forget her for it. But, the fact also remained that she was a prostitute and whatever had been between us was part of a business arrangement. Nothing more. So why did I feel such a sense of loss? She was the first woman I had known intimately and perhaps I had wanted to explore her more and to learn more from her. That now would never happen and perhaps that was the loss I felt!

After a while I paired off with another of Aurelia's girls and satisfied the need within me. It was not like before. There was lust yes, but no passion. Just a need to perform a function, which the girl was happy to assist with, for a few coins. I never even knew her name, just took what I wanted and paid her for her time. Then I joined the others to return to the fort.

Having bidden Aurelia good night we set off. The weather had turned much colder now and snow had begun to fall, gradually covering the town with its white blanket. There was little wind as we trudged back through the thickening carpet and the usual banter kept us happy, distracting us from the icy touch of early winter. Windows were tightly shuttered now, protecting the inhabitants of the buildings from the frosty night. Still the odd hawker or beggar stubbornly held out in the hope of securing a few coins before bedtime, although even they were forced to shelter next to cressets or braziers to stay warm and, unlike before, they were not so keen to follow and pester the people they approached this night.

Soon enough the walls of the fortress rose in front of us, crenellations topped with soft snow, lit here and there by the glow of torches along the walls and in the gate tower. Although an imposing edifice, the fort looked strangely inviting that night, promising a warm bed, out of the way of the falling temperature. We passed by the guards on the gate, dropping in some food and wine as we passed. Something to cheer the two men as they kept their vigil that night. A *Contubernium* would man the gateway, sleeping in rotation throughout the night with men mounting watch in pairs for two hours at a time. Any trouble and there would be eight armed men available in a very short space of time.

Eventually, we entered our barrack block and made for the billet, shaking our cloaks off as we entered to rid them of the snow now caked on the shoulders and hoods. We moved quietly up the corridor after removing our boots, eliminating the noise of the studs on the floor which had been recently re-dressed with a layer of *Opus Signinum*. We opened the door as quietly as we could to avoid waking Secundus who had returned earlier and hung our cloaks in the ante room. Pudens eased the latch up on the dormitory door and pushed it slowly in with just the faintest of creaks.

'Gods!' He exclaimed in a shocked breath.

'What? What is it?' Said Pacatianus as we pushed into the room.

The light of the warming brazier made dancing shadows cavort around the walls as we stared in silence at the still form in the middle of the floor. Pudens approached and knelt down stroking Secundus' hair and shaking his head as we stood around in a semi circle and tried to understand just what had transpired that night.

He was curled up in a ball, on his knees. His head had fallen forward and rested on the cold, hard floor whilst his arms were tucked underneath him, still gripping the *gladius* steady that he had pushed into his stomach. A thick black pool had spread around him whilst the point of the *gladius* had just emerged from the small of his back, raising but not penetrating the wool of his tunic.

'Why did you have to do it, brother?' asked Pudens quietly as he gently stroked the dead man's hair.

'Everything he did from his first day here was done for the loved ones he lost!' Said Surus gently as he stared sadly at another of our fallen friends. 'He got his revenge. Now he can rest, at peace with his family!'

* * *

The loss of our friends had been bitter blows and we felt them deeply. The eight of us had toiled hard and overcome much hardship together. We had forged tight bonds of comradeship that took much to part. We had seen little action but already, only five of us remained. Two were dead, one by his own hand, and the other suffered a year's punishment for what he had done to one of Aurelia's girls. Small wonder why we questioned our bad fortune and the reasons why we suffered so.

We laid Secundus to rest, not far from Lupus, on the road leading north, towards his home. He went to his grave with our prayers for a happy reunion with the family he loved and lost. To echo those thoughts and to mark his resting place we dedicated a memorial stone to him which we set in the earth above his urn. Having poured libations on his grave we read the dedication out loud so that our friend would hear us once more before we left him to his rest.

'To the shades of the departed. In memory of Julius Appius Secundus. A soldier of the Fourteenth Gemina Legion. He died aged twenty two years, eternally devoted to his family. His comrades erected this for him.'

The pain of loss was real enough but it was not something we could allow ourselves the luxury of suffering for very long. We had to perform our duty so, with our goodbyes said, we turned once more to the business of soldiering. A new and glorious expedition was about to commence, by order of the Emperor. Our winter was to be spent preparing for what we were told was to be the most ambitious conquest of a foreign land ever undertaken.

Britannia was apparently a strange and enchanted island that lay on the other side of a wild and deadly sea off the north west coast of *Gaul.* I had heard tell of it but, in truth, I knew almost nothing about the place. Only that even the divine Julius Ceasar had attempted to conquer it on two occasions but had failed. Much talk had been put about, for well over a year now, that a new campaign was being planned involving the Northern Legions and that *Britannia* was going to be the focus of a huge invasion effort. Apparently, one of their Princes had fled the island and had sought the help of Rome to assist him in pursuing his interests back home. The Emperor had seized the opportunity for conquest and resurrected military plans already in existence from the time of the previous Emperor, Gaius. Now, we were to spend the winter preparing for this invasion, assembling all the necessary paraphernalia ready for an early march next year.

I felt the same as most others. A mighty General such as Caesar was not capable of claiming the island, which was not an encouraging sign and Gaius had not even landed. Preferring instead to assemble his troops on the shores of *Gaul* and humiliate them by making them collect sea shells. The memory of that little episode had stuck fast and, even now, left a nasty taste in the mouths of those who had been there. They would not take another such insult lightly. Claudius would need to handle the army very carefully if this was to succeed.

The majority of my time was spent working in the *fabricae* of the fortress, manufacturing and refurbishing weapons and armour for the coming invasion. Many old and damaged weapons had been sent in from outlying garrisons and now, if they could not be repaired, they were being melted down and reforged into brand new ones. Armour was being treated in the same manner and the task was being performed on such a scale that civilian contractors were being employed to assist in the drive to increase the numbers of available equipment.

The manufacturing drive didn't just apply to weapons. Weavers worked feverishly to produce vast reams of cloth of all descriptions while skinners and tanners turned out cured hides of varying qualities for myriad different uses. Tradesmen of all varieties laboured to create tools, pottery vessels, carts, wagons and crates. Thousands of arrows and *ballista* bolts were crafted and lead sling shot ammunition was cast, ready for use once we had landed. Some of the items were kept back at *Mogontiacum* whilst others were forwarded to the staging areas for the invasion. A vast war reserve of arms and equipment was being accumulated to equip new troops and replace lost and damaged kit as the invasion was to progress. Having only recently joined the Legion, we did not know that this process had started long before our arrival. This flurry of activity that we now participated in represented the last final push to arm and equip the vast force that would assemble early next spring.

Routine training continued throughout the winter to ensure that we were battle ready when the time came. Under normal circumstances we would not have trained so hard in foul weather but the early invasion date that the generals favoured ensured that we maintained our edge in some of the most gruelling conditions.

We endured freezing cold, driving snow and rain and dragged ourselves through cloying, strength sapping mud in order to remain at the peak of war readiness. Prolonged periods of leave were cancelled with periods of only around two days granted to allow us respite from the hectic pace we lived with. Once more we trained at the posts and drilled and drilled formations again until they were burned indelibly into our brains. Physical training continued with renewed intensity and we were fed on high quality rations to build strength and muscle over the long winter months.

I took the opportunity to visit Quintus and Curatia as many times as I could over the winter. When I had first joined the Legion I had been of a mind to think that I would probably always serve close to home. The reality of the situation was now far removed from my earlier ideas and reality had begun to bite. 'What if it is many years before I can return home?' I thought. 'What if I never return home? If I am killed in *Britannia*, then what?'

Suddenly, everything that I knew and was familiar to me had become so much dearer. I wanted to experience it as much as I could before we marched out and the fortunes of war decided my fate. Perhaps I drank a little more and gambled more freely. Aurelia's girls all became pretty much familiar to me as I pursued the pleasures of the senses as much as possible. If I was to die next year then I was determined to die as a man who had lived life, not one who sat quietly on a stool and watched it pass me by. All of us knew what could befall us in that so called cursed land across the northern sea and so it spurred us on to seek our pleasures like never before. There was little fighting amongst ourselves, or rivalry, my head just fills with the sound of laughter and women when I recall our times on leave. It was the only way to be!

The winter rushed by as we prepared for the great adventure to come. Departure time was almost upon us as final preparations were made to move the Legion out to the invasion staging point. We were to march to *Portus Itius* in north west *Gaul*, joining the other units that would cross the haunted sea to the weird and terrible land at the edge of the world. Auxiliary forces, already representing a huge force waited for us at the port. We had heard little of who the auxiliary units were likely to be and speculation was rife. What we did know was that we would form up with three other Legions to make a heavy infantry army of well over twenty thousand men strong. As well as ourselves we were told that Legio II Augusta was already in *Gaul* and ready to move west from their base in *Argentoratum*. Legio IX Hispana was already at *Portus Itius* having departed from their base in *Siscia* in the province of *Pannonia* the previous summer. Due to the great distance involved they had had to march early and winter in *Gaul* in order to be at the staging point in time for the sailings. Finally Legion XX Valeria would complete the force. They were based further north in *Germania* at *Novaesium* and would make *Portus Itius* at the same time as we.

Of all the rumour and gossip currently flourishing in the garrison, amongst the strongest related to what we would find when we made land, if at all, on the shores of *Britannia*. Much gossip had been touted about the inhabitants of the island and what happened there. Magic was a daily part of their lives and they were able to use sorcerer priests called Druids to bring blights and curses down on their enemies.

The native Britons were apparently huge people with wild eyes and ferocious in battle, preferring to fight naked from chariots than face an enemy on foot.

Caesar had had his fleet wrecked when he landed by a pack of these Druids summoning sea and wind demons to smash his fleet on their rocky shores. And what of the sea crossing itself? Everyone knew that the sea was teeming with sea monsters that could wreck a ship and devour its crew in an instant. A few fortunate men had returned from these shores with terrible tales of what had happened to them at sea, and what they had seen in *Britannia*. In fact the only reason they had been sent home was to warn people away from landing. The only people mad enough to sail there were greedy traders and the crews of their ships. Even then, everybody knew that sailors were the companions of death!

In an unprecedented move, the commanders of the invasion forces had released limited information to common soldiers concerning our port of departure and the numbers of soldiers involved in the invasion. Their hope was that, knowing that we were going to be part of a huge and seemingly invincible force, we would stop all this fearful talk of what awaited us over there. If we knew that we marched as part of the biggest army seen in recent times then, they reasoned, we would take courage and cease this scare mongering that infected the entire force. We would also be departing at the point where the sea is at one of its narrowest points, which would reduce the crossing time. The *Classis Britannica* would ferry us across in sturdy ships, many of which would be built especially for the job. They sailed the waters around the coast of northern *Gaul* and knew it well. We would be in safe hands, surely?

Winter had also brought about various personal changes for us all. Those of us who had completed training would now be posted to our respective units within the Legion. Initially we didn't know where we would be going and I became anxious that I and my friends might be separated to serve in different centuries or Cohorts but, happily, we had no need for concern.

Cohors III and IV had spent the campaigning season operating on the edge of the frontier, engaging war parties from hostile areas way east of the *Rhenus*. Fighting had been vicious and numerous lives had been lost on both sides in a battle for control of large tracts of disputed land. Rome was determined that lands immediately outside her borders did not pose a threat to her territory and citizens. Subsequently, various units were dispatched to push raiding tribes far beyond her borders to create a pacified zone, free from hostiles. The two *Cohorts* had performed their task well, but not without cost. We were to provide the units with replacements for the men lost in the fighting.

Upon their return, both *Cohorts* had reviewed their current strengths and reorganized accordingly. The five of us were sent to Cohort III and kept as a group, forming the bulk of a new *Contubernium* in the Century of Fatalis. Three old hands from the Century had been placed with us to make up the eight. Those five of us newly trained would make up the nucleus whilst the three experienced soldiers would mentor us and guide us in what seemed to be the approach of some testing times. Our new comrades fitted in with us almost immediately. We met them for the first time as we were allocated billet space together. Their jovial introductions at once instilling the relieving thought that there would be no 'them and us' atmosphere to overcome.

Both Marinus and Crispus had served for about seven years. They were experienced soldiers and had much to impart in the way of knowledge and experience. Of the two, Marinus was a larger than life character who enjoyed nothing more than to accompany us into town and celebrate just about anything we could think of. A lover of life in general, he also subscribed to the view that life was to be lived now, as you may not get another opportunity. Crispus took a more philosophical view of matters which he liked to debate, ad nauseam, when everyone had taken too much drink and were incapable of reasoned response. Always one for keeping a clear head, I was sure that he took his amusement from the drink induced confusion of his victims as he destroyed their feeble attempts at intelligent conversation. Many is the time that I and my comrades had engaged him in his craft and ended up slack jawed and silent as he sat there, a triumphal smile spreading over his face as we struggled with his logic.

Zenas was in charge of the *Contubernium.* A steady hand with over fifteen years experience in the Fourteenth, he had a wealth of knowledge to impart and all of us looked to him for our lead. We respected his decisions and obeyed his instructions when he felt it necessary to issue them. Although he would accompany us on our little expeditions into town he carried responsibility with him at all times. He seldom drank heavily and preferred instead to play dice and *tabula,* keeping an eye on us to ensure that we behaved ourselves. As time passed we became a close unit and I was happy with the knowledge that, if we had to embark on the road to war, then these were the right men to have at my side.

Inevitably enough, the day arrived when we were to depart for *Portus Itius.* On the eve of our departure we went into town and said our goodbyes to everyone we knew. We separated to make it quicker for us to bid farewell to the many acquaintances, friends and family that we had in the town. Soon, a new garrison would take up post in *Mogontiacum* and we would be posted far way from the place we knew as home.

'I can't believe that it is here!' Quintus shook his head slowly and sighed. 'Is it really time for the boy I once knew to march off to war? So quickly the time passes!'

I always knew that there was a chance that we would end up posted far away from home but somehow I never quite thought that it would happen. I had always thought that *Mogontiacum* would have been our permanent base and that I would see out my service there. To leave was going to be a great wrench, but duty demanded it and I would not shirk from it. Besides, what choice did I have?

Curatia's eyes had filled with tears and she lowered her face to the floor. She had not left the house this time, remaining instead to bid me farewell, she knew, for perhaps the last time. I reached forward and took both her hands in mine.

'Smile for me Curatia!' I asked as I gently squeezed her hands. 'You have been the mother I lost since I came here. Be strong for me now and give me the memory of a smile to take with me!'

She shook her head and tears ran down her cheeks as she stepped forward and hugged me.

'And you are the son that we never had. I couldn't bear to lose you now! Not after we have shared so much of your life!' She kissed me on the cheek and stepped away, the sorrow of her thoughts plain enough to see.

'Be strong for him now wife!' Urged Quintus. 'We cannot send the lad off with the memory of tears. Be happy and proud for him. It is his destiny!'

With that, Quintus clasped my forearm in the traditional Legionary manner and slapped his hard old hand on my shoulder.

'Make us proud, and honour the memory of your father!' He said, nodding gently. 'Remember what I taught you and where you came from. The future is uncertain but fortune will guide you on this campaign. I pray that it will bring you home safe and clothed in glory!' He swallowed hard as I fought back tears. 'Now go, and do your duty like the fine soldier you have become!'

For a moment there was silence as all three of us struggled to compose ourselves. I took both of them by the hand and squeezed once more. Then I turned for the door, feeling the greatest sadness of my life, as I lifted the latch and let the cold night air embrace me.

'Don't forget boy.' Quintus added, waving a finger at me. 'I know you can write. It was me who taught you. As soon as you have time send word, please!'

I paused, then ... 'Of course!'

It was all I could think to say as I stepped out into the freezing night and started to walk down the street. As I walked I could feel them watching me and, before I turned the corner I stopped and turned, taking one last look at the old house and workshop and the couple who stood, silhouetted in the warm glow of the open doorway. I raised my hand and waved slowly, receiving the same in return, then I turned my back and rounded the corner with a heavy heart, unsure if I would ever see them again.

As I trudged the muddy streets I could think of nothing but my own sadness, mixed with the apprehension of what I was about to do. I did not notice the hawkers, the street prostitutes or ordinary townsfolk going about their business all around me. As I walked, my mind was elsewhere. It drifted between the warm house that I remembered from my childhood and the cold, haunted shore that awaited me across a cursed sea. It never crossed my mind that, even now, fathers were kissing their children goodbye. Mothers were weeping for their departing sons. Never did I think that lovers lay in each others arms for one last time and a brother felt the pain of separation from his siblings. But, so it was. As the Fourteenth prepared to march out from its home, to invade somebody else's world.

Chapter 10

The March West

It was decided that, in order to reach our embarkation point on time, the Legion would have to set out from *Mogontiacum* no later than the middle of *Februarius*. And so the great column formed on a crisp, late winter morning which still glittered with the frost of the night before. Centuries of men made for marching positions within their Cohorts and slowly a huge line of men, six abreast, formed on the road leading west from the fortress. Most of the town had turned out to see the Legion move out. Nobody had seen such a display of force for many a year. It wasn't every day that an entire Legion took to the road just outside your home.

The crowd hummed with the sound of many things. Excitement, regret, salutations and sadness as the massive body of men were wrenched away from the community they had lived with for so long. Anywhere you cared to look in the assembled throng you would see someone waving frantically and cheering, their enthusiasm contrasted with a sad and lonely looking woman holding a small child, silently mouthing goodbye to a loved one in the column. Children ran back and forth, fighting mock duels with wooden swords while a man or woman offered prayers for the safe return of the Fourteenth.

As we stood, clad in our winter kit, I watched the steamy breaths of my comrades rising above the column. Now and again men would stamp their feet or walk on the spot to keep the circulation going. We wore thick, long sleeved woollen tunics and leather breeches with enclosed overboots above our *caligae*. Everyone wore a cloak of some description but still we were anxious now to get moving. The numbing cold of the morning was penetrating even the thick winter wear and the best way to combat it was to start marching.

We were some way along the road out of town, due to the order of march for the Cohorts. The first and second stretched out in front of us whilst the remaining seven Cohorts snaked out along the road behind us. Heading the column would be the Legion Commander, Titus Flavius Sabinianus, and his subordinates, all of whom were yet to arrive. Although leading the column, Sabinianus was protected by the cavalry and his own, hand picked, unit of bodyguards. These men were drawn from the finest soldiers the Legion had to offer and would fight to the last to protect him.

Leading the Cohorts themselves were the various standards of the unit. This included the powerful icons of the *Imago* and the *Aquila*, their approach being heralded by the *Cornicens* and *Tubicens* who always accompanied the sacred standards. Behind the Legionaries lay the transports for all the equipment accompanying the Legion. Mule trains and ox carts ferried everything from building and surveying equipment to specialist tools, tents and siege equipment. Following on from them were the camp followers. A few women had decided to continue their associations with the Legion, including prostitutes and mothers of bastard children who did not wish to remain behind. Tradesmen and sellers of all descriptions also made ready to march and in amongst those were the slave traders. Conquest of new land guaranteed a fine yield of marketable slaves as the army pushed deeper into the new territory. The slave traders would not be far behind, assisting the army by taking charge of non sensitive prisoners and returning them to the nearest slave markets for maximum profit. In all, the column stretched for almost a mile and a half in length.

Tiberius Claudius Fatalis stepped out from the head of our Cohort and craned his neck to try to ascertain whether there was going to be any movement. Our new Centurion was already in his late sixties but still held a formidable edge when it came to operational duties. The *phalerae* displayed on his armour giving ample testimony to the man's combat abilities along with the fact that he had been awarded the *Corona Vallaris* for being the first man over an enemy rampart during a siege. Fatalis favoured more functional looking equipment than some Centurions who, being paid around fifteen times more money than Legionaries, could afford to be a little flamboyant if they chose. He wore a plain shirt of *lorica hamata*, albeit constructed of very fine links and, on his legs, silvered *ocreae*. His helmet was tinned and he wore a black *crista transversa* atop it. The rest of his weapons were pretty much what the rest of us carried, although his were of earlier designs, reflecting his prolonged time in service. A tall, athletically built man of great fitness for his age, we learned rapidly that he was a fair leader who did not suffer fools gladly. The efficient, hard working soldier, however, had nothing to fear from him.

His *Optio*, Mestrius, had stepped out to the other side to see if he could get a view on anything but soon sent Fatalis a shake of the head in response to the querying gesture he had received. Mestrius was a little younger than Fatalis but shared many of the same attributes as the Centurion. He despised liars and laziness but would happily pass time with us sharing a drink and a laugh. Both men were a far cry from the likes of Fuscus, which came as a blessed relief to those of us who had just finished training.

'Look alive you lot!' commanded Fatalis after a short while. 'Something's on its way and I'm pretty sure it's not *Saturnalia!*'

As we waited in anticipation of receiving a command we could hear the roar of the troops behind us as they shouted their greeting to whoever it was travelling up the line. The shouted salutations became louder as Fatalis drew his *gladius* and shouted for us to take hold of our *pila*. Then came the order to turn right and, as we swung, Fatalis raised his sword and shouted the greeting:

'Ave Legatus!'

Each man thrust his *pilum* into the air and shouted the greeting again as the group rode past. The six tribunes of the Legion rode behind Sabinianus who sat astride a very tall and fine mount. Not one that you would ordinarily associate with the battlefield but a magnificent horse none the less. Taller and more elegant than the short, squat cavalry horses, the chestnut coloured horse was bedecked in red leather harness with silvered accoutrements and fittings. It wore a black leather chamfron over its face which was decorated with pierced bronze eye protectors and silver studs laid out in a scrolling pattern.

Sabinianus himself was an impressive looking man, typical of the features I had seen on the statuary of famous Roman nobles. A Senator of Rome, he exuded an air of arrogant superiority and hardly acknowledged us as he galloped by. He wore scarlet breeches and high red boots. His tunic was brilliant white with a broad purple strip bordering the hem and sleeves A bronze cuirass in the form of a muscular torso protected his body. It was adorned with silver figures and tied around the middle with a large purple bow of silk ribbon. On his head he wore an ornate helmet of Greek style finished with a plume of white ostrich feathers. A flowing bright red cloak was attached to the shoulders of his armour which billowed after him as he galloped to the head of the column.

Now that Sabinianus had taken his place at the head of the column it was a sure sign that we were ready to depart. Anticipation grew in the watching townsfolk, final shouts of 'farewell' and 'good luck' were shouted from the assembly and perhaps the crying of women and babies grew that little bit louder as we waited for the order to come. A faint shout from the head of the column soon turned into another as each Centurion echoed the order from the front.

'Prepare to march!'

Fatalis repeated the order and raised his right hand as he turned his attention to the rear of the column. As he did this we shouldered our loads and made ready for the next order. Fatalis would watch for the other Centurions to drop their hands in turn and cry 'ready' before repeating the action himself, for the benefit of the forward units. Presently, the response came from the rear formations and Fatalis dropped his hand and snapped his head round in the direction of Cohort IV.

'Ready!'

In a very short space of time I heard another order making its way down the column, Cohort II reacting to it as I heard the echoing shouts of their Centurions.

'Cohort II. Advance!'

Each Century of each Cohort had to be started off individually in order that the line did not become one giant stumbling mass as men tripped over each other trying to move off. The simple fact of the matter was that the Legion marching column was so big that it could never be moved with one order as it would never be heard by all. The great animal had to be started in stages. And stopped in the same way.

As Cohort II moved off, Fatalis allowed a modest gap to develop between us and them before we moved. Once he was satisfied that a sufficient gap existed between the two Cohorts he set us off on our long journey.

'Century. Advance!'

These were the first steps of an expedition that would lead us hundreds of miles across *Germania* and *Gaul*, finally crossing a sea to an unknown land populated by fierce savages. This was to be no ordinary invasion. What Roman army had ever invaded an enchanted island, defended by sea monsters and sorcerers? The emperor was asking a lot from mere mortals such as us!

For many weeks we marched across all kinds of terrain in difficult and strength sapping weather. We covered the regulation twenty miles a day and on some occasions exceeded that to reach more favourable ground for the Legion to set up camp on overnight. Every night a huge marching camp would spring up wherever we stopped. A defensive ditch and rampart would be constructed and the tents pitched inside the defences in the regulation order so that everyone would know exactly where they were in the camp. The camp followers and hangers on would have to make their own arrangements outside the defences. They had made their choice by coming. It was not the responsibility of the Legion to protect or shelter them and, for the duration of the march, fraternization was forbidden, by order of Sabinianus.

Every morning, the Centurions would visit the commanders' tents to receive their orders for the day whilst the vast encampment was dismantled and packed away. The defences would be filled in and any waste timbers burned. The camp followers would take the opportunity to lay any dead in the ditch of the camp, trying to provide a decent burial for those who had died in the night. Many is the time I saw mothers burying their children. Little ones who had perished from lack of food or had frozen to death in the harsh overnight temperatures. Even as we entered the first days of spring, the weather could still be bitter and unforgiving and I found myself wondering why they followed so devotedly as they lay their pathetic little bundles into the cold earth.

As we travelled, so we hit frequent supply points. The Legion was informed in advance of where these points would be and it would be imperative that we made these objectives, even in the worst weather, in order that rations and fodder for the pack animals could be replenished. Later on in the march we began to see more and more towns and cities that had grown from the time of Caesar's conquests. They made *Mogontiacum* look very much the poor relation with their great stone buildings and fortifications, theatres and aqueducts, supplying sophisticated water and drainage systems. I had never seen their like before and their beauty and technology were a great revelation to me.

'Could man really build all of this?'

It was true that great buildings existed in my own part of the world but not in such profusion. Huge Basilicas and Fora were surrounded by magnificent temples and bath complexes. Civic buildings gave way to small private homes and great houses and villas owned by the rich. All laid out in massive grid patterns. Everywhere were the trappings of civilization in such great quantity that I could never imagine *Mogontiacum* growing to become a city such as the ones I had lately seen.

If I was left impressed by the magnificent towns and cities and their sophisticated amenities then that was to be as nothing compared to the awe and amazement I felt when we made our approach to *Portus Itius*. The first we knew of our journey nearing its end were the countless columns of smoke rising into the grey sky from untold numbers of camp fires. As we drew closer even the more senior soldiers expressed surprise at the scene that extended in front of us. As we crested a low hill we could see nothing but men, everywhere! Great swarms of soldiers had settled on the land, waiting for the order to sail to *Britannia*. Huge camps had been set up to accommodate the three other Legions and a host of Auxiliary Cohorts, too numerous to take in properly.

As we marched towards the encampments ringing the port we came across massive corrals which housed the mounts of the Auxiliary cavalry *Alae*. Further stockades accommodated draught animals and tented accommodation lay close by for the wranglers and muleteers. Masses of temporary granaries and other storage sheds lined the roads. They had been used to stockpile massive amounts of grain and rations that had been harvested and collected from all over *Gaul* to support the invasion.

Fires burned everywhere. Either from buildings, campfires, or workshops and foundries. As we continued with the march towards the port the roads became hard to march on. Thick, slimy mud coated their surfaces to varying depths. Evidence of the constant movement of thousands of troops and animals crossing and re crossing the fields and roads. The horses and oxen adding to the mire with their own filth and contributing to the heavy stink of occupation that hung in the cold and damp air pushing in from the sea. Once inside the temporary camps we were marshalled along by our own cavalry contingent who had rode ahead to obtain the location of where we were required to camp.

Finally we arrived at a vast open field which still had a little grass growing on it and a fairly solid surface that had not, as yet, been churned up by thousands of feet. The field was surrounded by several other encampments, all of which seemed to be sharing a swollen brook for everything from drinking water to laundering clothes and the watering of animals. Immediately we set about establishing our camp and getting some shelter and warmth for ourselves. The day was beginning to darken and none of us wanted to be finishing off when night fell.

Eventually our work was done and we crawled into the dark interior of the leather tent. Soon a lamp glowed in a corner of the tent and then two more were lit from it. A small fire just outside the tent flaps was started and a hot stew was soon being prepared for supper. We could afford to take our time that night as we would not be required for guard duty until tomorrow evening. The night was ours. None of us wished to go off exploring, the march had been far too tiring, so we took the opportunity to lay out our bedding and rid ourselves of the filth caked tunics, boots and breeches that we had worn and swap them for fresh dry clothing. Eventually, with clean warm clothes on our backs and a belly full of hot stew, we settled down and slept like the dead.

Chapter 11

Mutiny

What I would have given for a trip to the baths while we waited at *Portus Itius* to start the invasion. Of all creature comforts, the restorative qualities of the hot baths and cold plunges were the ones I missed the most. We were able to afford ourselves limited washing facilities but it was nothing like a good visit to a half decent bath house. The port had its own baths complexes but, for the most part, they were off limits to the military. The local population were finding it increasingly more difficult to co exist with the presence of an army numbering nigh on fifty thousand men. Not to mention the thousands of camp followers that had settled outside the town. They had followed to be close to loved ones, to colonize and prosper in new lands or to make money from newly conquered territory. The port itself was not able to support such a huge increase in its population and soon found its infrastructure being overwhelmed by our presence. Demands on drainage and waste disposal were resulting in the streets being flooded with filth and rubbish was strewn everywhere, the whole place was beginning to stink. Because of the time of year the place also found itself awash, for the most part, in cloying, freezing cold mud as men and animals spread it through the streets and alleyways as they moved around the area.

Locals were beginning to complain to the civic authorities and, as a result, the military commanders imposed sweeping restrictions on what we could and couldn't do. The army was keen to foster goodwill amongst the locals but their efforts were coming to naught as resentments built on both sides. Naturally enough, the civilians had complained about the effect of such a large force in and around their town and we resented their complaints as they had made an already uncomfortable stay even worse with their troublesome complaining.

Our particular camp had by now turned into a great, sticky mire with the comings and goings of over five thousand men churning the ground up on a daily basis. For three weeks we had waited for the word to move out but to no avail. Nothing was going to happen until the weather became more settled and the prospect of a trouble-free sea crossing presented itself.

The decision to sail would be made by Aulus Plautius, who had until recently been Governor of *Illyricum*, a province on the River *Ister*. Now in command of the invasion force, he was an experienced and respected General, lately accustomed to commanding water borne operations whilst suppressing local resistance in his former province. The IX Hispana had been conducting operations in the area until recently and had been specially selected by Plautius for the job. Of all the four Legions, they were probably the most suited to the task that faced us.

'I'm sure that if the gods had meant me to spend my life up to my neck in water they would have given me fins!' complained Aebutius as he flung the tent flaps open and ducked inside.

'Well, you're almost there!' grinned Marinus. 'You stink like a damn fish. Now get in and close that flap will you? You're letting all the heat out!'

Aebutius threw off his damp cloak and sat on his bed, picked up a half loaf of bread and started pulling chunks off, shoving them eagerly into his mouth.

'Hoi!' shouted Pacatianus. 'If you're going to surround all of that bread with your skinny ribcage then you can damn well go out and bake some more. That's our last loaf!'

Aebutius stopped chewing and spread his arms wide, giving a hurt look just for good measure. For such a skinny frame, Aebutius had a tremendous appetite and thought nothing of taking any food lying around and claiming it as his own. On more than one occasion it had cost him a good beating from the likes of Marinus who had lost more than enough food to the permanently hungry scavenger.

Time was passing slowly and there was little to do in the camp while we awaited the order to move out. All the forces present had been drilled continuously on the use of the vessels we were to sail on. We were now well versed on how to embark and disembark quickly and efficiently. We learned how to stow and offload supplies and equipment and, where appropriate, the management of livestock and horses at sea. The training had been rigorous and not without cost. Even though the great barges and warships had stayed close to shore during these exercises, men and animals had been lost to the sea in the rough conditions that prevailed along the coast at this time of year. Many men had been injured on board vessels that had been tossed around like children's toys on the rolling ocean and slowly, discontent had begun to spread as men grew more and more aware of the enormity of the perilous mission they were about to undertake. The commanders had added to the bad feeling by shoving us out in some appalling weather on forced marches just to keep us occupied. They sought to prevent the simmering dissention from spreading. However hard they had tried to keep us occupied, the tension grew and manifested itself with spontaneous acts of disobedience and increasing instances of fighting between the various units who goaded and taunted each other as they stagnated in the now filthy tented camps.

'So when do you think we'll sail then, Zenas?' enquired Pudens as he sat on his bedding scraping at the dried mud that covered his shins and feet.

'How should I know?' snorted Zenas. 'I'm not privy to what the gods have planned for the weather and General Plautius certainly hasn't felt it prudent to confide in me!'

'Well, I'm heartily sick of this!' grumbled Pacatianus. 'The Generals are going to have to do something soon or there won't be an army to take to *Britannia*!'

I sat there listening as I tapped iron hobnails into the soles of my *caligae*, replacing the ones that had been lost on the recent marches. The conversation was moving in exactly the same direction as most of the others of late and reflected the depth of feeling around the entire camp. Morale was low and Plautius would soon be facing more than the noises of dissent. In a very short time, Plautius would face a mass rebellion and be unable to do anything about it. The Centurions could not possibly discipline every dissenter and nothing existed that could possibly pose a threat to such a huge army. The whole undertaking teetered on the abyss of revolt and there was seemingly nothing that could avert it.

Sooner than we thought the situation came to a head. Overnight the rain had stopped and the dawn rose on a crisp clear spring day. The Centurions attended their customary morning briefings and returned with fresh orders for the days activities.

'The General and his commanders have decided to exploit this break in the weather!' explained Fatalis after assembling the Century in the centre of the camp. 'We are to begin loading kit and supplies with a view to getting them aboard our allotted ships. If the weather holds long enough for us to complete this task then we will sail for *Britannia*. The invasion has begun. Now begin your given tasks!'

Momentarily we stood, looking about ourselves for a reaction to what we had just been told. Fatalis set us all with an icy stare and I saw his grip tighten on his *vitis*, an angry flush spreading across his face. Mestrius' hand went to the hilt of his *gladius* as he stepped up next to the Centurion.

'If I were an old woman accustomed to gossip then I would be inclined to hang around swapping tall tales!' growled Fatalis. 'Instead I command a unit of eighty fighting men who have never yet shirked their duties. Now fall out to your duties, as I will to mine and lets have an end to any thoughts of disobedience!'

The statement was calm and reasonable but the threat of looming violence was clear. If we failed to obey then Fatalis would act. There would be no negotiation. We were challenging his authority. If we failed to obey he would fight us to the death rather than suffer the ignominy of weakness in the face of disobedience. Mestrius would join him and there would be much bloodshed before the two were bested. None of us wished for such an outcome involving the death of two such well respected and liked officers. We reluctantly turned and made towards our allotted tasks.

By starting the process of making ready, the commanders had inadvertently made the situation far worse. Soldiers of the various units, moving between camps and docks, were now freely mixing with each other and fuelling the fire of revolt. As they passed by, they would ask each other where they were camped and what conditions were like. Inevitably, the reply came that they were living in filthy swamps or it wasn't fit for pigs to wallow in. Empathy was accompanied by more idle chatter and soon the men began to voice their fears about the sea crossing and what awaited them on the opposite shore. An atmosphere almost akin to hysteria spread through *Portus Itius* like a whirlwind as the army preoccupied itself with tales of wrecked ships, thousands of corpses choking the sea and fearsome naked warriors eating the flesh of slain Romans. The results were, predictably, calamitous for the invasion plans.

Rumours quickly spread of whole Cohorts and Centuries abandoning their duties and refusing to obey orders. Isolated fights broke out amongst various units and, as individual officers tried to re impose order they had been beaten down by their own men. As we loaded our own barges at the dockside, I saw one such incident take place.

Men from our own fifth Cohort were preparing to load artillery pieces onto a cargo vessel when a heated argument developed between them and the crew on the dockside. We watched from the quay above as shouting and pointing turned to shoving and punches. I couldn't hear what the argument was over but it soon became obvious that the situation was about to become very dangerous. As we watched, silently anticipating the inevitable, a Legionary landed a swift, crunching punch to the chest of one of the sailors who fell to the floor convulsing with pain. I shook my head slowly and placed the sack of corn I was carrying onto the dock. I looked over to Surus who returned a troubled expression and, almost despairingly, we continued to watch events unfold.

As men leaned over the dock shouting and cheering at the sudden fracas, one of the seaman's shipmates jumped from the deck of the vessel with a hefty wooden cudgel and split the belligerent soldiers skull open, dashing his brains over the slippery boards of the wharf with a series of vicious blows. The reaction of his comrades was spontaneous and brutal. As if engaging the enemy in battle they surged forward at the sailors, who stood trapped with their backs to the sea and the ship. Frantically they resisted the surge of the soldiers with what weapons they had to hand but, to no avail. In an instant two soldiers lay injured on the timbers while at least half a dozen sailors lay butchered, slaughtered by infuriated soldiers wielding wickedly sharp *Pugios*. A roar went up in the crowds of soldiers nearest to the incident and the word tore like lightning along the docks and into the town as men stopped what they were doing and refused to continue. Plautius now had an army caught up in the throes of mass mutiny.

The speed at which the atmosphere became so volatile was astonishing. Frustrations and resentments were vented amongst the men, manifesting themselves in the form of large brawls, individual beatings and isolated murders as rank and file soldiers claimed retribution for the unjust harshness of cruel officers who had pushed them too far or taken one too many liberty. The civilian population fled indoors as they suffered the kickback of sanctions imposed by their constant complaining at the army's presence. Had it not been for the reasoned and diplomatic control exercised by officers like Fatalis then anarchy would have reigned in *Portus Itius*. He and his like identified that the use of force was a lost cause and, instead, restored some semblance of order through a combination of skilful negotiation and plain speaking. The initial, violent flare up eventually died down to a surly and uneasy peace as the soldiers returned to their camps and flatly refused to participate any further in the great invasion.

For the best part of a month, the situation in *Portus Itius* remained a stalemate between the army command and the soldiers, now no longer under their control. On several occasions, large crowds of soldiers had assembled to listen to the remonstrations of the generals, but nothing had been achieved. The commanders urged the soldiers to take advantage of the better weather we were experiencing and put out to sea while it remained calm. Each time the men refused, citing the existence of terrible sea monsters and ferocious beasts in the cursed sea as their reason to stay. To say nothing of what awaited them in *Britannia*. The situation was becoming more and more ridiculous as hardened fighting men took on the semblance of a vast hoard of superstitious old women and snivelling children, scared of the unknown.

A relative stability now prevailed in the port however, as reparation was made to the sailors of the *Classis Britannica*. Much drinking and talking had taken place and all had accepted that the fighting that flared up had been an unfortunate by product of the aspirations of over ambitious Generals. Through such dialogues the IX Hispana had quickly formed a close bond with the men of the navy. They were accustomed to water borne operations and were able to share some common ground with the naval crews which they managed with enthusiasm over tavern tables when ever they could. Individual Legion Commanders had enjoyed varying degrees of success in rebuilding shattered relations with their troops. Of them all, perhaps the most successful was the commander of II Augusta, Titus Flavius Vespasianus. A seasoned and well respected General, Vespasian insisted on a close relationship with his soldiers and regularly shared in the hardships of life in the field. Rather than live in plush quarters and travel on horseback, he would regularly march at the head of his troops and sleep in their company. Such down to earth qualities were not shared by our own Commander, Sabinianus, a close relative of Vespasian.

The afternoon of Narcissus' arrival was much the same as any other of late. We sat outside the tent and prepared our main meal of the day. Crispus had acquired a leg of mutton which was an ideal, but very hard to come by, main ingredient for a hearty stew. The meat was stripped from the bone and cut into chunks while we waited for the water to boil, then thrown into the pot along with the bones. Pacatianus sat grinding flour with a small quern. When we had enough, I mixed it with water, herbs, eggs, a little milk and some seasoning to form a collection of nice plump dumplings to go with the stew. The fresh meat was becoming increasingly hard to come across as the army sat around eating itself stupid with the boredom of inactivity. When Crispus slipped into the tent with the cut of meat under his cloak we abandoned our plans to eat yet more dried bacon and *bucellata* and set about preparing our feast.

Mushrooms and vegetables were chopped and added to the pot, along with dried lentils and barley to thicken the mix further. Wild Garlic, sea salt and freshly ground pepper also went into the mix to add a little something and we all sat around the fire eagerly waiting for the stew to cook to perfection. Dough had been prepared earlier that afternoon, as was usual, and a short while before the stew was ready, we placed it under a *testum* next to the fire so that we could have fresh bread with our meal. Sitting on a smaller cooking stand was another pot which we had filled with red wine and spices to accompany the stew.

We chatted happily as the wonderful smells of the stew and the mulled wine wafted around the tent. The tendrils of aromatic steam mingling with the wood smoke of the cracking and popping fire. Soon the dish was ready and eager hands presented bowls to be filled with the thick brown stew and hot dumplings. Zenas dished the food out equally and beakers and cups were then filled up with the hot, spicy wine that had been simmering away over the fire. The *testum* was dragged from the ashes by the side of the fire and the glowing embers brushed from its top as the round soft loaf was retrieved from under it, adding its own tempting smell to the meal. The bread was distributed amongst us in equal portions and we sat around the fire ready to eat the best meal we had had in days.

Marinus said a prayer of thanks to the gods for our food and we each gave a small portion over as offerings, our thanks for their continued patronage, then we ate. We savoured the taste as we dipped our bread in the thick stew and shovelled the hot chunks of meat into our mouths, sipping on the pleasantly warming wine as we ate. There were no words. No conversation was needed as we savoured every last mouthful of the meal, the contented looks on our faces saying everything that needed saying as the food was eaten and the meal came to a pleasant end. I sat there, legs crossed. I appreciated the gentle warmth of the fire that touched my knees and face as I sipped the last of my wine and watched Aebutius rooting around in the bottom of the cook pot with a scrap of bread.

Had it not been for the excited voices coming from the other end of the camp I would have dozed off, wrapped in my cloak in the still afternoon. The voices grew louder and their excitement became very noticeable as I stood and peered over the rows of tents to see what was happening. Surus came running back towards the tent. He must have gone walking whilst I had been day dreaming by the fire. Pointing off in the direction of the docks with one hand, he frantically beckoned us to come to him with the other.

'You've got to come! You won't believe it!' He gasped excitedly. 'It's Narcissus. Narcissus is here, here in *Portus Itius*!'

What's he on about?' I said, puzzled. 'Who's this Narcissus then?'

'Great gods man!' exclaimed Marinus. 'It's only the Emperor's freedman. This man is an Imperial minister with almost as much clout as the Emperor himself. We've definitely ruffled some feathers if he's seen fit to pay us a visit!'

'Come on, let's get going!' urged Surus. 'The word is out that he wants to address the army down at the docks. He's travelled up from *Lugdunum* by river on the Emperor's bidding!'

'Right! Come on lads!' Zenas said as he stood and fastened his cloak. 'Let's see what a pampered former palace slave has to say to the likes of us!'

With that we were off. Running along the rows of tents, we were joined by our comrades as we streamed along the filthy roads towards the docks. An excited buzz hummed through the crowd as more and more soldiers joined the throng as it approached the harbour area and streamed along the wharfs and quays. Soldiers from all of the units were present as we crammed into the administrative area of the harbour and jostled to see what was going on. A suffocating press began to form as men thrust themselves forward, trying to get to the front to catch a glimpse of one of the most powerful and important men in Rome.

Slowly the vast crowd settled as men became satisfied with their positions and quietened down to listen to what was going on. Soon a hush fell over the assembled soldiers as they waited for Narcissus to show himself. Whispers and mutterings abounded as men questioned his presence at the port and became indignant at the thought of being addressed by a one time slave, albeit a very powerful one.

We did not have to wait long to see what we had all came for. A cacophony of chatter rose at the front of the crowd as the double doors of one of the warehouse buildings swung open and a large party of fully armed soldiers marched out towards a collection of wagons on the dock. The soldiers were very finely kitted out with gleaming armour and weapons, fine plumed helmets and black tunics and cloaks.

'*Praetorians!*' snapped Zenas.

'So that is what the Emperors personal army looked like!' I thought as I watched the body of men forge through the assembled masses of scruffy, dirty soldiers.

They drove the men before them as they shoved with their *scuta*, pushing towards their objective and lining a narrow passage as they progressed. Finally they halted at the wagons and waited, watching the crowd contemptuously, waiting for any sign of the onset of violence. Nobody was spoiling for a fight that day. If they had, the *Praetorians* would stand no chance. There were around two hundred of them and thousands of us. You couldn't help but admire the courage needed for them to face us down like this. Rarely were these soldiers seen outside the gates of Rome without the Emperor. Truly Narcissus was an important man if the Emperor had afforded him the protection of his own bodyguard.

Then began excited chatter as four *Praetorians* left the warehouse, swords drawn and shields levelled as they escorted a figure walking amidst them. Eventually, they reached the wagons and the figure was assisted onto the deck of a flat bedded cart. I was around fifty paces away as the figure rose up onto the cart and slowly surveyed the thousands of soldiers spread out before him. Men were muttering at the effrontery that this man had. A former slave about to address an army! Who did he think he was, a god?

Narcissus was a man of unremarkable stature. He had no distinguishing features and, had it not been for his fabulous clothing, you wouldn't have looked twice at the man. He wore a pure white tunic and toga which was trimmed in gold embroidered laurel leaves. Even at a distance you could see that the clothing cost more than some earned in years. He wore scarlet, high legged boots and a ring adorned his finger which no doubt carried his personal seal.

Two *Praetorians* mounted the cart with him and stood flanking him as he surveyed his audience. A gentle smile breaking on his face as he settled on the centre of the crowd and slowly spread his arms, as if to embrace us all.

'Soldiers of Rome!' Came the cheerful but resolute voice. 'Your Emperor sends you his warmest greetings!'

The smile grew wider and, with upturned hands, Narcissus gently bobbed his hands up and down and nodded affably towards us. This was too much! Who could he possibly think he was?

As if possessed of the same mind, the gathered crowd bellowed with one voice. 'Io Saturnalia!'

The shout seemed to freeze him in his tracks and his guards suddenly exhibited the first signs of nervousness as resentful noises spread through the gathered host. The self assured smile, however, did not leave his face as he composed himself to address us once more. He must have been aware that he and his men risked being torn to pieces if he provoked the crowd too much. The right choice of words would be crucial now if he and his men were to leave *Portus Itius* alive, let alone ending the mutiny as he had been tasked to do.

'Yes! Yes I do wear my master's clothes on this day!' he declared as he nodded his head and placed balled fists atop his hips. 'And what of you, soldiers? Whose clothes do you wear this day?'

A hushed pause fell over the crowd as Narcissus began to regain his composure and begin the battle for our compliance.

'There should be no need for me to ask this of you but I stand before you a confused man!' He cast another long glance over the assembled troops. 'Your

Emperor and my master has bid me to come and see what it is that goes on here. He knows that a mighty force stands poised to conquer a potential enemy of Rome but, whenever news arrives from this great army, all he hears of are the bleatings and worries of superstitious old women and weak willed souls frightened of dark places. Where is his army?'

The last, shouted question prompted loud replies from the men that they were there. Slowly Narcissus shook his head and silence descended once more.

'No, no! This cannot be it! Any army of Rome that I know is dutiful and ever ready to do its Emperor's bidding. This mass of scruffy, unwilling men in front of me have forsaken their sacred oath to the Emperor and to the standards. Where once stood a mighty army now only stands a hoard of renegades who terrify innocent civilians and disobey the proper authorities. This is no army!'

Instantly a rumble of lowered voices shot through the crowd with the odd voice rising to complain at the slight that Narcissus had just delivered. Narcissus was inflaming the crowd but he was gambling with the fact that honour counted for a lot with us. It was a dangerous tactic but he was going to play it. Slowly I started to admire him for his courage. Slave he may once have been but he had heart!

'What do I tell the Emperor when he asks me why the mightiest Roman army of recent times will not do his bidding? How can I return and tell him that his beloved soldiers languish in sodden, muddy fields and grow fat and lazy? Frightened to move because they have scared each other over the campfires with ghost stories!'

Slowly we started to look around at each other. Faintly ashamed now that the envoy's words had the ring of truth. Thousands of soldiers stood assembled for war. Many of them vastly experienced in the art of war and conquest, all of them now ragged and pathetic. Honourless and scorned by their masters for being afraid of mere rumours. As the reality of the situation dawned on us, Narcissus sensed the subtle change and pressed home his advantage. Stepping forward he thrust his finger towards the crowd and played on our shame further.

'In times to come, how will history see this army?'

He spread his arms wide and raised his face to the skies and rolling white clouds.

'The divine Julius made two thrusts into this unknown land. He did not succeed in conquering the land or bringing its people to heal but he showed them the might of Rome. He and his brave soldiers returned home with honour. The natives of *Britannia* remember this and they know that Rome will return and finish what Caesar began!'

Narcissus' head snapped down, the smile gone from his face as he stabbed his finger out once more to the assembly before him.

'Will you be remembered throughout time as the army that was beaten by nothing more than sinister bedtime stories?'

A thunderous 'no' echoed across the docks as the army bellowed its answer. Narcissus thrust his arms down at his sides, knowing that victory was his. Spreading his fingers wide and turning his palms up he shouted to the sky.

'Then are you telling the gods that you will embrace Caesar's legacy and be remembered as the army of Claudius, conquerors of *Britannia*?'

'Aye!' Shouted the soldiers as one, as if to shake the gods themselves and make them hear their pledge.

'Then go!' directed Narcissus. 'And prepare to take your place alongside history's heroes!'

The whole port erupted into thunderous cheering. Weapons were waved in the air and fists thrust high as pride was restored to the assembled force once more. Men whooped and yelled as they began to turn and hurry back to their camps, eager to prepare for the off. Narcissus remained standing on the wagon. The soft smile had returned to his face and he stood with his left hand extended and his right hand over his heart, slowly nodding as the crowd dispersed. Narcissus knew that he had placed his head in a lion's mouth and had lived to tell the tale.

In the space of two days we were ready for departure. Vessels were loaded with supplies and equipment and, as if blessing the invasion, the gods had given us fine sailing weather. Camps had been broken down and tents stowed on board ships. The next time they would be erected it would be on the soil of *Britannia*. Huge columns filed into the port area to embark upon the invasion ships. Shortly before we boarded, the traditional pledge of the Legionary echoed around the docks as we responded to a Tribune, yelling the question for all the gods to hear:

'Are you ready for a war?'

'Ready, aye!' ... 'Ready, aye!' ... 'Ready, aye!'

Chapter 12

The Shores of Britannia

Claudius should feel obliged to reward Narcissus very generously! Not only had he ended the potentially disastrous mutiny of a large army but the mood of optimism with which the men now turned to their task was a complete turnaround! Yes, there were still misgivings, but a new enthusiasm had now gripped us and the men were eager to embark in the pursuit of fame and glory. Narcissus had gained the grudging respect of the soldiers, standing before us as he did, the ex slave with the voice of the Emperor. What nerve! He had skilfully manipulated us with a combination of admonishments, shame and encouragement. The risk to his life was very real that day but his gamble had paid off. He had succeeded where Plautius and his staff had failed. The army would sail!

The Fourteenth would land as part of the second wave along with the XX Valeria and a large contingent of Auxiliary cavalry and infantry Cohorts. Our landings would be followed by the II Augusta, again accompanied by various auxiliary units including cavalry. General Vespasian was a renowned expert in the art of artillery warfare and it would be his job to land with the specialized weapons and then push down the coast to attack and secure *Portus Dubris*, giving the *Classis Britannica* a sizeable base to patrol the coast from. Many of the ports in this part of *Britannia* were well known due to the trading that had gone on with the Britons since before the time of Caesar and much intelligence had been derived from these activities.

The first wave had left port some hours before us. They would cross the *Fretum Gallicum* and land after dawn. Once on the beaches of *Cantium*, homeland of the *Cantiaci* tribe, they would quickly establish a beach head which they would hold until we arrived at around midday. Plautius had sent the IX Hispana across first as they were the Legion most suited to marine operations. Securing a safe landing area for the other forces would be crucial to the success of the operation. Landing with them were four Cohorts of Batavian Auxiliaries who were, amongst other things, specialists in fording large expanses of water in fighting order. A further four Cohorts of Batavians would be held in reserve. The Legion's cavalry force would scout for the presence of the enemy whilst the First Cohort of Hamians would provide withering streams of arrows if the advance party was attacked.

For long hours we had sat aboard the ships while they rose and fell on the swells inside the harbour of *Portus Itius*. I remember feeling my stomach starting to churn as I watched the endless numbers of ships rising and falling around me as we waited for sunset. We were close to large, broad beamed transport barges which carried scores of mules and the stink that emanated from them only made me feel worse. I yearned to sail just so that we could get some fresh air. The fetid atmosphere amongst the closely packed ships was almost too much to bear as more and more soldiers heaved the pits of their stomachs over the side. Their sour smelling vomit adding to the misery as I listened to the pitiful braying of the distressed animals below decks. How could anyone wish to be a sailor? This was torment. And we hadn't even put to sea yet!

At last! As the sun began to sink into the sea on the western horizon, the crews of the warships we were on began to busy themselves for the off. We were allocated at a rate of one Century per warship and were under strict instructions to act under the direction of the crews. The ships themselves were narrow of beam and carried sail as well as banks of oars. They were swift and manoeuvrable and a magnificent site to behold as scores of them put to sea in the first wave. Now it was our turn and I watched fascinated as the sailors swarmed over the rigging and decks, shipping mooring ropes and pushing the boats out of their berths while those aloft prepared to unfurl the sails to capitalize on the light evening winds.

As we cleared the harbour walls and entered the open sea I was suddenly aware of the vastness of the ocean around me and my mind flitted back to the talk of the dreadful monsters that waited in the deep. Terrible huge, scaly bodies and wicked, sharp white teeth waiting to shred the flesh of their prey. A shiver shot through my spine and raised the hairs on the back of my neck. Then the feeling was gone as I marvelled at the size of the enormous fleet of ships that had put to sea alongside us. What an awesome sight! What man, or creature, would dare to defy such an assembly? And this only represented a part of the force that would land on those strange shores. Surely the gods favoured us above anything else! As I stood, leaning on the rail, the sea spray whipped across the deck and stung my face, making me feel invigorated once more. Those of us on deck were oddly quiet and seemed deep in contemplation as I crossed to the hatch and went below. Best to sleep now, if I could, who knows what the next day would bring?

I woke just after dawn, rubbing my eyes and wincing at the cramps in my hips and shoulders after spending a restless night trying to sleep on the crowded lower deck of the creaking, pitching galley. I shivered with the discomfort of the draughts rushing through the ship and pulled my cloak tighter around me. I made my way towards the ladder that would take me up top and into the fresh air. It stank below decks of vomit and stale bodies. Of wet leather and wool. A foul mixture of odours if ever there was one! Aebutius was sat propped against the side of the ship scoffing great chunks of bread dipped in oil.

'Good morning!' He smiled benevolently as I passed, offering me a piece of the dripping bread. 'Here! Get that inside you!'

I retched and hurried past, waving the bread away as I went. I scrambled up the ladder, slippery with sea spray, and clambered out onto the deck into the grey drizzly morning. The warship pitched and rolled with the swelling waves but I immediately began to feel better as the fresh sea air entered my lungs. All around our vessel were the accompanying transports, spread out across the vast, heaving grey ocean. They were of varying shapes, sizes and functions and each carried formation pennants on their masts, identifying which unit they carried. This would be an important detail when landing the forces in the correct order, once we reached our destination.

The rolling grey clouds were full of rain but, for now, we were suffering a heavy drizzle and a reasonable temperature for the middle of Spring. If the conditions did not worsen then we would be well placed to make a successful landing without fear of loss to shipping or cargo. Most of our Century were milling around on the deck when Fatalis emerged from below decks with Mestrius. The *Optio* pointed to a small group of soldiers and instructed them:

'Everybody on deck now! If they're not here call 'em up here. Snap to it!'

The men scattered and disappeared down hatches. Soon shouts could be heard below us and men began to surface onto the rolling deck. Faces grimaced against the cold spray on their newly woken faces whilst others went straight for the rails and threw up over the side. Sailors continued with their tasks, grinning at the weak stomachs of some of their passengers as the men assembled and faced the stern where Fatalis stood talking to Mestrius.

'Right men, listen to me!' commanded the Centurion, shouting above the crash of the ocean and the wind slapping the sails as we all grew silent and waited for his instructions. 'In a couple of hours we should reach our landing sites and I want us to get ashore in an efficient and soldierly way!'

He looked out over our assembled heads as he braced his legs for balance on the moving ship.

'As a fighting unit you are only responsible for your own kit. You do not have to worry about anything else, just getting ashore safely! I do not expect to see any of you floundering around in the sea and losing items of equipment as you land!' he warned us sternly. 'If you are near the *Ballista* crew you will assist them ashore and if you drown, then may the gods help you. You know how I hate men leaving their posts without permission!'

We laughed weakly and Fatalis waved us silent once more to finish what he was saying.

'The Fourteenth is to engage any enemy that we encounter and will be part of a great push inland!' He informed us. 'When you are ashore, you will form the Century in extended line and move to join the rest of the Cohort. If we are attacked then remain calm, look for the standards and listen for the *Cornu*. You will not advance until you are formed up with at least three other Centuries. Clear?'

'Yes Centurio!' we shouted.

'Good! Now, make sure your kit is prepared and ready!' He told us. 'I want all of your equipment on deck in an hour! Meantime eat and drink as much as you can. I know some of you will want to part company with it very quickly but you must try. I don't know what we will find when we get there but I want you all to have the strength to deal with it. That is all!'

With that he turned, speaking briefly to Mestrius and went back below deck.

Reluctantly I joined the others in a simple breakfast below decks. I did not want to eat but I saw the sense of what Fatalis had told us. Who knew when we would get the opportunity to eat again? Once I had started to eat I began to feel a little better for having something solid in my stomach and refreshed myself with some well watered down *acetum*. After letting my breakfast settle I moved my equipment up on deck and waited there with the others for the first signs of land.

A little later we saw gulls skimming the surface of the waves and one of the sailors told us that it would not be long now. We sat on the deck, gathered in our *Contubernia*, fully armoured and equipped and waiting expectantly for the word to make ready. For a while we were quiet, just listening to the hiss of the spray covering the deck and the crash of the bow cutting the waves. Then, casually, we talked of the past. We remembered our friends, families and homes and all the things we had done since joining the Legion. Friends we had lost and actions we had fought, which in the case of most of us, was very little. I don't think any of us mentioned what we were about to do, our minds were elsewhere, wondering perhaps if we would ever see our homelands again.

High in the ships rigging a sailor shouted out above the slapping of the billowing sail.

'Land. Land on the western horizon!'

The master was directing the steersman when he heard the cry and responded immediately.

'Gather the canvas. Prepare to go to oars!'

Several sailors mounted the rigging and climbed for the top of the mast while another shouted down the deck hatch to those below.

'Oarsmen to posts! Stand by!'

As the ship seemed to suddenly swarm with activity I was aware of shouts echoing over the waves as the other ships' crews reacted to the sighting of land and made preparation for their approach. I looked out over the side and saw sails being taken in and signallers mounting the high sterns of their vessels, beginning to transmit signals with flags. Other vessels were putting out oars, ready to push for shore. I heard clunks and scrapes over the side of our ship and saw a bank of oars appear on the side nearest me. Poised horizontally for the order to row when they would plunge into the water and propel us to shore with powerful strokes.

All of us now peered out to where the sailor had indicated, trying to catch our first glimpse of *Britannia*. I felt a flutter in my chest, realizing that we were close now to this strange land from which so many odd tales had emanated. As the flapping sail raised, exposing a better view of the horizon, we glimpsed it. We shouted and pointed. 'There!' gesturing excitedly at the land and looking backwards and forwards at each other as the distant coast started to materialize in the drizzly haze hanging over the sea. No Roman army had seen this place for nearly a hundred years and now we were back! Determined that it be taken, for the glory of the Emperor and the people of Rome. It began to grow in the distance as I watched. The coast began to rise before us as the sail was taken in and the oars began to strike the surface of the sea with even, rhythmic splashes.

Our ship was part of a vast group of sleek, fast warships that struck out for shore first. As Fatalis had reminded us, we were going to be first ashore in this wave and the rest would follow. I looked behind me, seeing the distance between ourselves and the other transports increasing rapidly. A second fleet of vessels followed behind, along with a group of broad beamed barges which probably held cavalry to reinforce the horsemen already landed in the first wave. Signals were being passed between the ships all the time as the land drew nearer. Fatalis made his way to the front of the ship and shouted back.

'Bring the *Scorpion* to the front and as many bolts as you can!' he ordered. 'Make ready and prepare to give any covering shots as and when directed!'

The *Ballista* crew ran forward and placed the tripod stand on the deck, quickly setting the body in place and priming the weapon ready to shoot. As the galley surged forward the sound of our own *Ballista* being cranked was joined by the clatter of the ratchets from weapons on surrounding vessels also making ready. The loader placed an iron tipped bolt in the slide and busied himself searching for likely target areas on the far off shore whilst the trigger man waited for orders.

As the land grew closer I noticed that we were heading towards a wide inlet. Signal fires blazed on either side of the mouth, directing the approaching ships to the landing area. Many Roman ships were already moored in the channel, bobbing up and down awaiting our arrival. Fatalis jumped up by the *Ballista* and spread his arms wide:

'Form double lines either side of the ship and be ready to file towards the front and the gaps on the rail!' As he instructed us, the sailors lifted sections of the rail out on each side for us to be able to jump from the ship.

'The ship will beach in shallow water. As soon as we hit, move fast and make for the beach!' he shouted. 'Form the defensive line as soon as you have enough dry beach and then look for the Cohort *Signum*! Understood?'

'Yes Centurio!'

We roared the reply and I knew that I couldn't be the only soldier whose heart was pounding, my very body surging with the energy of impending combat. I gripped my sword hilt and gritted my teeth as we drew closer to the mouth of the channel. We entered the inlet sailing a short way up the centre until we approached another signal fire on a large outcrop of land on our left. Again I looked either side of me, awed at the speed at which we were closing with the land and watching the other galleys slicing through the water, their contingent of soldiers poised on the deck as we were. Soon enough the beach appeared before us, growing more distinct with each oar stroke until I heard the shout below:

'Raise oars!'

Swiftly, the oars completed their stroke and rose horizontally, pausing for the next order, Quickly the follow up was issued:

'Ship oars!'

At this, all oars were withdrawn and the ships glided towards the shore under their own momentum.

Fatalis placed one foot on the bow and leaned forward to see over the side as the waters grew more shallow on the approach to the beach. His hand raised above his head, waiting to motion us to move as the gap closed between ship and shore. It was then that I noticed that the area around the great signal fire was occupied by many men. Roman troops moved all over the outcrop of land, busying themselves in the preparation of defences over a wide area, securing the ground which had already been taken. There would be no great battle for the shoreline this day!

'Get ready! Brace yourselves!' warned Fatalis and his hand dropped to his side just as the ship ploughed into the soft, silty beach. We lurched forward as one and then we recovered our balance, ready to move.

'Off. Off!' ordered Fatalis as he swept both hands forward, motioning us to move off the sides and into the breaking waves.

We surged forward and jumped from the ship into the waist-deep water, forging through the waves and foam to make the beach and gain dry land. Finally my feet were planted on the shores of *Britannia*! In an instant we were formed up into an extended line as instructed and were looking for the *Cohort* standard. Three blasts from a *cornu* alerted us to its presence and Fatalis wasted no time in moving us into formation.

'Battle line!' He prepared us. 'Quick time, advance!'

The whole Century trotted up the beach in extended formation as Fatalis strode out in front of us. As we drew level with the *Signum* he turned us, halting us squarely behind the standard. In a very short space of time the whole *Cohort* was formed up behind the standard, awaiting orders and eager to engage an enemy who, apparently, was nowhere to be seen!

There was no time to waste! If the enemy had chosen not to engage us then we were to make good use of the time we had. We were immediately directed to join troops of the first wave in constructing vast defences which would secure our foothold on the coast. We soon found that, in the absence of any real opposition, Plautius would make capital from the lack of defenders and send Vespasian south with II Augusta and a force of Auxiliaries to secure *Portus Dubris*. Although this had been an original objective for the invasion it was not anticipated that such a push could take place so quickly but, opportunity had presented itself and the plan was altered. The land across the inlet, as with much of this part of the coast, was known to Roman traders and sailors. They knew the island as *Tanatus Insula*. The XX Valeria and accompanying units had landed over there as part of our wave and were, even now, spreading out from the landing point and pacifying the island so that it could be used as an offshore supply base. Once the island was secure then any attackers would have to cross the narrow channel to retake it. An ideal stronghold that was easy to defend, supply and reinforce.

For five days we remained in the area of the landings. Fortifications were raised and improved whilst cavalry and *Cohorts* made up of part infantry, part mounted soldiers patrolled the area and scouted for enemy forces. Several small scale engagements had taken place with the local forces. Auxiliary units had located the war bands and largely destroyed them without opposition. Within range of our fortifications lay several small settlements. They were simple farming communities, people of the *Cantiaci* tribe who worked the land to survive and cared little for the politics of warfare. They could tell us nothing of the defending forces, other than to warn us that fierce tribes would come from the west and destroy us if we remained. It was nothing personal! They had no particular argument with Rome but they had lived for years with the stories of the brutal struggles for power and land which raged further inland. They were simply telling us what they knew!

Once we had secured prisoners from some of the smaller engagements the *Quaestionarii* had set to work and we finally solved the puzzle of why there were so few defenders present.

In early spring a combined force of united tribes had indeed been present in the area waiting to repel any landing force which had appeared. Rapidly, word had filtered back across the *Fretum Gallicum* that, although a large Roman army was just across the sea, it was in the throes of revolt and was refusing to cross the sea to *Britannia*. Two warlord brothers, Caratacus and Togodumnus, commanded the defending army of some one hundred and fifty thousand men. Once they had heard of the mutiny in *Portus Itius* they had decided that the invasion would come to naught and dispersed their forces inland. Their mistake was that they had not waited for further intelligence informing them of the dispersal of the Roman army! Having made such a large tactical error it was now proving extremely difficult to re muster the forces previously at their disposal. Many of the warriors had made long journeys back to their tribal territories and reorganizing them was proving extremely difficult. Such an irony to think that we feared invading this land and by voicing that fear so loudly we had effectively given ourselves the best possible advantage!

However good the news was it certainly did not mean that we could afford complacency. The two brothers may have made a bad error of judgement but they would reform their forces and attack as soon as they were able. Their father, Cunobelin had set in chain many expansionist policies before his death and subjugated neighbouring tribes to build a huge kingdom ruled by the *Catuvellauni* and their neighbours the *Trinovantes*. Togodumnus and Caratacus would not let Rome threaten the territorial gains that they had made without a fight and there existed other reasons why the brothers would resist. King Verica of the Atribates had fled to Rome to ask Claudius for help against these brothers. Verica was not Claudius' only guest from *Britannia*. There resided with him also a Prince called Adminius who had also fled to Rome over two years previously to seek the help of the then Emperor Gaius. Adminius just happened to be the brother of Caratacus and Togodumnus. When the brothers had demanded the immediate return of the two defectors Claudius had flown into a rage and seized the excuse to invade *Britannia*. The impending war would have to be a total victory for either side as it now seemed very likely that any diplomatic compromises were out of the question. For the brothers it would be a battle, not only for their survival, but for their very way of life.

Whilst the landing areas had been reinforced, the *Classis Britannia* had been busy pushing up the coast, sailing the waterway that lay between the mainland and *Tanatus Insula,* taking strategic coastal features and settlements. The trading port of *Regulbium* had fallen to the navy and already a contingent of Auxiliaries were being shipped north to consolidate the gain. *Regulbium* would be crucial as a staging point for vessels to move in the more northerly waters helping to re supply units from the coast as we pushed further inland. Now that so much of the local coastline was in our control it became imperative for the push inland to begin. Scouting parties were already returning with news that hostile forces were moving across the countryside, driving livestock north west and destroying grain reserves and early crops to deny us re-supply opportunities during the coming thrust. In an attempt to stop this we used Adminius. He would never be allowed far away from the forward units as he was to be used to win over the local population and convince them that they would benefit from Rome's influence. He was a familiar figure in this part of the world and would prove very useful when quelling any dissention amongst the *Cantiaci* and the other, smaller tribes in the area.

Finally, we marched from the landing areas and drove westwards, a huge central force flanked by substantial cavalry cover from the auxiliary cavalry contingent. Legionary cavalry swept the ground before us looking for opposition forces and re supply opportunities. The defenders had not managed to completely wreck all food supplies and they were used as and when we located them, reducing the task of transporting supplies from the coast. As we marched we came across farming settlements, villages and isolated homes. These places were populated by simple people who had never seen such a force as marched through their land now. Those that had remained in their homes regarded us with a mixture of bewilderment and awe. Theirs was an unhappy position as they had been unwittingly caught up in the complexities of war. They were the innocents who would suffer most for the ambitions of powerful men! Having managed to preserve their supplies against their own army trying to deny the Roman forces, they were now having to surrender much of their produce to the invaders. This year would bring them to the point of ruin! These peaceful, hardworking people would pay a terrible price for the war and many would die from starvation to feed this new force!

As we passed the small settlements along the way, we saw the children standing at the side of the ancient trackways, watching us as we marched ever deeper into their land. Their work or play interrupted, they would stand at the side of the column and stare at the vast army as it advanced past their homes. The innocent eyes of the children stared from muck smeared faces, having not the first clue what was happening to their land. Long ago it seems, I saw the same eyes staring from the faces of *Mogontiacum's* children as they watched the Legionaries march out. The children of *Mogontiacum* however, were not watched over by parents who knew that a great upheaval was about to shake their world!

I never questioned for a moment why we were there, or what we had to do to achieve it! It was our duty as Romans to bring law and civilization to lands such as these! For centuries it had been so and for centuries it would continue. This land would benefit from our occupation and thrive in the coming generations, just as many had before it. We did not bring conquest to these people, we brought salvation, but first they must submit!

When I was first trained I was told that we were the weapon wielded by Rome and the Emperor. Nothing had changed since that day and, if the Emperor bade us to destroy the population, then so be it! Already in my short service I had witnessed the killing of innocents, destroyed those who opposed the will of Rome and driven nails into the living flesh of her enemies! My actions were not governed by thought or feelings, I was driven by orders and discipline, nothing more! If the people of an enemy land would not bend the knee then they would perish under our advance! I would never shirk from any unpleasant duty but I could not help but think, as we passed by these simple people and their wide eyed children, that the Gods were truly cruel!

Chapter 13

The Push Inland

We had never expected that we would come ashore with such little opposition. Each one of us was of the mind that the Britons would fight ferociously to defend their homeland and commit themselves to pushing us back into the sea that we had feared so much. Now we stood with our feet planted firmly in one of their kingdoms and none of the dreadful rumours about this place had come to pass. As a conquering force we could not have been more confident.The gods had seen fit to bless the invasion with much good fortune! *Britannia* was ours for the taking!

Although we had seen little in the way of resistance so far, it was now time for the next piece of the great invasion plan to be put into place. The *Cantiaci* had shown virtually no opposition to the landings in their territory and capital would now need to be made from their apparent acquiescence. Our objective would be to place Adminius in the heart of the kingdom where he could be used to good effect. That heart would be *Durovernum Cantiacorum*. An *oppidum* of considerable size, it lay a little less than a day's march inland. Located on reasonably flat ground close to areas of wooded swamps, the *Cantiaci* regarded it as their tribal capital.

The marching was easy enough. The countryside rolled gently and the vast majority of the forces could use the ancient trackways maintained by the native population. Even if the old routes were not always available the ground was reasonably firm and progress across the land was swift. The one thing we hated about the country involved the routine of having to dig out defences. It seemed that, everywhere we dug, there were flint deposits and worse! As soon as we cleared the topsoil we had to hack our way into hard packed chalky ground that tested the resolve of even the most seasoned excavators amongst us! Nothing was to be allowed to impede us however and the defences went up regardless of aching limbs and throbbing blisters!

By now we had had our first encounters with the enemy. Predictably, they would emerge from behind natural features at short distances and strike swiftly in an attempt to panic the forces and scatter the formations. They had never encountered anything like a Roman army before and their futile attempts to inject panic into the columns had cost them dear! They would generally attack the sides of the column in an attempt to break the line but always without success. Their infantry would not engage at this time, instead the Britons preferred to swoop down using war chariots and horsemen in swift moving strikes. The horsemen would hurtle fearlessly down on us on small and sturdy native mounts, much like our own horses. They wielded long slashing swords which they flourished enthusiastically above their heads or

108

carried long, thrusting spears which were twirled around in elaborate striking patterns as they came at us. Their lightening charges were accompanied by enraged, screaming war cries as they charged the lines which would react by closing up as a tight packed formation to meet the attack. Bareback they rode and many of them wore only leggings, preferring instead to clothe themselves in swirling designs painted onto their bodies with a thick blue paint or tattoos, etched deeply into their skin. To add to their wild and brutal image they often grew thick drooping moustaches and coated their hair in lime or chalk paste which they used to set their locks into spikes on top of their heads. Many of these warriors wore little or no armour in battle but I never saw any of them shy away from a fight. They seemed to revel in the glory of the fight and could only be stopped by the most mortal of injuries.

My very first impressions of these tribesmen were that they were an extremely formidable adversary. These were the men that I would have to fight in my first experiences of an all out war! They never wasted an opportunity to demonstrate their prowess to their opponents. Everything about the fighting Briton was intended to convey an air of menace and to intimidate their enemies. Perhaps the only piece of accurate information that we had been given about *Britannia*, when rumours flew thick and fast in *Portus Itius*, were about these warriors. They were indeed formidable in both appearance and ability and never to be taken lightly. These men would fight and die hard!

We had not seen a great many of their chariots yet but what we had seen more than demonstrated the skill and courage of these indomitable foemen. If the chariots were used against us they would always approach at breakneck speed in a head on course presenting a fast moving and small target. The chariots themselves were of an entirely wooden construction and of a very low profile, drawn by a pair of horses. Whilst one man drove another would prepare to attack his objective in various ways. He could engage the foe with spears from the back of the chariot or even by climbing up to the yoke and standing between the two horses. He could also discharge slings or strike with heavy wooden clubs and when he was ready to fight on foot he would dismount, kill and then remount the chariot, either making good his escape or circling for another sortie. The Britons would deploy their chariots either singly or in small groups, striking at vulnerable points in the enemy's forward lines. This may have been of great success against their own kind but, against us, it was futile! The Britons never knew how hard the Roman army trained, rehearsing endless drills to counter a variety of tactics and had never encountered such complex formations as they now faced. Whilst the Roman army operated as an entire body seeking to achieve one goal, the Britons preferred to engage almost as individuals. It was as though we faced thousands of warriors intent on single combat and not one army out to achieve a common goal. They could never hope to succeed!

When they threw their horses and chariots onto our columns the first two lines of troops nearest the threat would drop to their knees behind their shields while the line behind them would place their shields over the top of the front rank to create a sloping roof and then present their *pila* ready to throw. The front row already bristled with the points of their own *pila,* their slender iron shafts protruding from behind the shields like a row of defensive spikes. Even the hardy ponies of the Britons refused to charge directly into such a lethal barrier but ventured close enough for the rear rank to throw their javelins at them in one devastating wave which invariably broke the charge instantly. The same tactic was used against the fast moving chariots who also came under fire from *ballistae*. You could see the bewilderment on the faces of the Britons as their comrades were blasted from the back of their horses or chariots as the lethal iron-shod bolts took off with a mighty 'whack' and smashed into their unwitting targets. The carnage wrought by these weapons was something to behold. If the enemy were close enough and in tight formations the bolts would tear straight through them, often killing up to three men at a time before the tremendous force of their launch was dissipated. Shields were useless against such weapons as the bolts were easily capable of punching straight through them, piercing the man behind. Having no answer to these weapons and tactics, the Britons would disengage to regroup, only to have fast moving columns of cavalry falling on them from the flanks, butchering them with ease as they swirled around in chaos, reeling from the devastating shock of the withering defensive measures!

Finally, after many small engagements, we stood before *Durovernum Cantiacorum*, massed in battle formation and waiting to be deployed against the now visible enemy. The Britons stood directly between us and the *oppidum* in a single great formation which ranged across the rolling plain in front of us. Now that they had sight of the Roman army they stood, shouting and waving, goading us to attack as they roared defiance and whirled every kind of weapon above their heads. Behind them lay the town with its mass of round thatched roofs rising from behind the protection of the wooden palisade that protected the community within. Wispy grey tendrils of smoke rose from the houses and, apart from the presence of a large and hostile army outside its walls, it gave an impression of tranquillity, blending perfectly with its surroundings as though it had seemingly just grown there.

Gnaeus Hosidius Geta was second in command of the invasion force and was leading this phase of the advance whilst Plautius consolidated our hold on the landing areas and directed deployment of the third and final wave of troops that had come ashore. We were now spearheading the advance, along with several auxiliary and cavalry *Cohorts*. Vespasian and II Augusta would join us here and we would then push for the great rivers that stood between us and our later objectives. First however, we needed to sweep aside the seething mob that now stood before us, crying open defiance.

Geta had arrayed three *Cohorts* of Auxiliary infantry, I, II and III Gallorum, before us and had placed a *Cohort* of Hamian archers on our right flank. We stood in extended lines along with the First and Second Cohorts whilst the rest of the Fourteenth waited behind us in seven vast blocks of men. Two *Pannonian* cavalry *Alae* took up position, one on each flank and then the task of drawing the enemy out began.

Packed in a dense block formation, the troops of I Gallorum began the advance by moving forward, moving away from the extended lines of their comrades and coaxing the large force of Britons out towards them. As the ground between them closed, the Britons saw the opportunity to destroy the small force and began to move forwards in one great formation. Confident of being able to wipe out this small contingent, they streamed forwards howling and shouting as they came. Surely they did not think that we would fight with one unit at a time? Along with the forward units we began to cheer loudly and strike up a thunderous banging on our shields. Around ten thousand Britons now descended on I Gallorum as they advanced towards them. Suddenly the Roman formation moved sideways and began to run for the left flank, furthest away from the Britons. On the right flank there rose a great cloud of arrows as, seeing the field clear of friendly forces the Hamian *Cohort* began to rain arcs of streaking death down on the Britons. Screams rang out across the field as the shafts found their marks and the Britons began to fall, dead or wounded. Even as they started to think about retreat, the left flank cavalry had set off at a gallop and were moving behind the Britons, cutting off their return to the *oppidum*. The archers halted their deliveries of arrows into the tormented, howling mob as the cavalry swarmed their rear and began to drive the whole lot forward towards the waiting Auxiliaries. Panicking now, the Britons started to break away towards the right flank where they were met by the second cavalry *ala* who drove them back towards the central killing ground that they had so easily fallen into. As they surged backwards and forwards, desperately trying to break out of the tightening trap, the two reserve Auxiliary *Cohorts* charged.

As we stood overlooking the battle I was minded to think that the whole thing now looked like a wave breaking over the shore as the charging Auxiliary force swamped the leading edge of the doomed Britons. The tribal standards they carried slowly began to fall under the weight of the onslaught that engulfed them until, eventually, no more stood! The standards were captured and their bearers fell defending them! Now it was our turn! A call from the *cornu* started us off on a slow advance towards the mounting carnage in front of us and we began to close on the seething lines of Auxiliaries as they hacked their foe to pieces. I could hear the Auxiliaries own horns blaring out calls and knew that they would withdraw to allow us to smash what was left. Now my heart started to pound as I waited for the Gallorum to clear the field. The yelling and screaming of men caught up in ferocious combat grew deafeningly loud as we came ever closer to the massive press, intent on slaughtering each other! Quivers of tremendous energy shot up and down my spine as we drew closer to the vast line of bloody murder that stretched out across the field. I almost burst with the surging need to engage and fight!

A further series of rhythmic notes sounded over the chaos and the Auxiliaries broke off, running swiftly to the right flank and allowing us to charge into the now desperate mass of Britons that still stood in the middle of the killing ground. They did not give chase to the withdrawing forces, merely stood and braced themselves for the oncoming assault of the three Legionary *Cohorts* that now bore down on them. The dead lay before them, a sea of arms, legs, faces and the gods knew what else scattered about the ground! The wounded writhed around in their gory midst, screaming in pain, wailing or moaning as their life slipped from them! My body surged with incredible energy as I heard Fatalis give the order to draw swords. The hiss and scrape of the blades being pulled from their scabbards was accompanied by a thunderous shout as the *Cohorts* bellowed:

'Iuppiter, Optimo Maximo!'

The blades were slammed onto the sides of *scuta* at waist height and kept horizontal as they protruded from the line of shields. As we advanced we again began to beat the sides of the shields with our blades, the noise pounding rhythmically through the air, letting the gods know that the Fourteenth were about to fight! Then all at once the dam seemed to burst as one long note from the *cornu* signalled the charge and we fell upon the doomed Britons!

I can't seem to remember anything about the charge, or smashing into the packed mass of bodies before us. I just remember resistance. All the time, I could feel it! Every time I thrust out with the *gladius* it buried itself into a body! I twisted the hilt to free it and battered men in front of me with the boss of my *scutum*. My streaming sweat mixed with the spray of hot thick blood as it spattered through the air wetting my lips and stinging my eyes. My breath came in short rhythmic gasps as I pushed every last ounce of my strength into destroying the enemy before me! Men fell under the weight and force of the charge and were trampled into the ground by the stamping boots of their attackers. Hobnailed soles kicked out and ground down on upturned faces that struggled in vain to stand again in the packed mass of seething chaos! Furious shouts and animal grunts surrounded me as we continued the task of butchering the defenders of the *oppidum*. Then I heard another blast from the *cornu* and a shouted order to break off and fall back, loudly repeated by those who had heard it first. As the leading line, we were now being pulled out to rest whilst a fresh wave of Legionaries took over the killing! We moved swiftly to the back of the formation and again formed a line waiting to move forwards once more while the new front line fought with murderous, unrelenting efficiency, each time it was replaced. As I waited my chest rose and fell like a set of bellows. I wiped my face, only now realizing that my nose had been broken and was pouring blood onto my armour! I had no idea when it had happened and I didn't much care! I was fighting my first real battle!

Soon after we moved to the rear I heard multiple blasts from the horns and shouts to disengage and cease the killing! As the din of the battlefield died down, there was a brief moment of peace before the Roman forces erupted into triumphant cheering! Word quickly spread amongst the ranks that the Britons were beaten! What few who still stood had now surrendered and the way to the *oppidum* was open. I wiped the back of my wrist across my nose and mouth and looked briefly at the broad crimson smear on my filthy skin before I turned to look at Marinus who stood beside me. I smiled humourlessly and spat the congealing blood from my lips to the ground! He nodded his head slowly at me and then, smiling slightly, he turned his face to the front.

'Glory days brother!' He said quietly. 'These are glory days!'

Our whole force had soon been moved beyond the battlefield and we were arrayed in a wide formation on the approach to the *oppidum*. We waited in silence as Geta sent an envoy to the gates of the town with our terms for the surrender of the settlement. A party of cavalry had approached the gates and now sat astride their horses shouting up to a party of defenders who manned the palisade and gate tower. Their decision now would be crucial to their survival. If they chose to surrender then they would live and *Durovernum Cantiacorum* would be safe from destruction. Adminius would be installed as a client ruler and the people would prosper. If, however, they chose to resist then they would be besieged by the Roman forces until they acquiesced and then, they would be doomed. Any town or city, standing before a Roman army, that failed to accept terms was to be annihilated. The Roman Commander would allow his troops to enter the city and pillage at will for war booty. While this was happening every man, woman, child and animal within its walls would be slaughtered! It was the best way to let the world know that, if you defied Rome, you risked the ultimate penalty. Total and utter destruction! Much better for the army if they resisted. That way we got more loot out of it!

As we stood waiting for the outcome of negotiations the inevitable chit chat and small talk began to whisper through the ranks.

'Do you think they'll pack it in, or will we have to flatten them?' enquired Pacatianus.

'They're not stupid you know!' ventured Zenas. 'If I'm any judge they'll see that they are done and give it up! What's the point of standing against an army that has just wiped out your warriors and that you know can sweep up your little town of sticks in the blink of an eye?'

'Well that may seem sensible to us,' said Crispus. 'But they may have a totally different way of regarding the situation! What boils down to a simple question of survival for us may mean something totally different to this lot! I mean, we know next to nothing about them do we?'

Just then, Mestrius came stalking along the ranks and, striding up to the front of our *Contubernium*, a metallic clank rang out as stood before the front rank and swiftly rapped the head of his *Optio's* staff off Crispus' helmet.

'Crispus!' he said. A mildly amused tone present in his voice. 'Why, whenever I detect idle chatter in the ranks, do I almost always find that you are at its centre?

'I'm sorry *Optio*, but the newer lads were just wondering whether the Britons would give in or not!'

'Newer lads?' I thought! What a cheek! It was only Pacatianus that said anything and then the older ranks had carried it on.

'Oh! Well why didn't you say so?' Mestrius scoffed sarcastically. 'If I'd known you were sharing your vast knowledge on the subject I'd have invited the *Centurio* to come and learn from your observations as well!'

As he spoke, Mestrius leant forward, speaking directly into Crispus' face as he chastized the man, who shuffled his feet uncomfortably.

'Crispus?'

'Yes *Optio*!' came the wary reply.

'You seem to have far too much spare breath left after our recent engagement! It may be that I have to set you some special tasks later today to rid you of your extra wind. Meanwhile, if that jawbone of yours moves once more this afternoon, I will personally separate it from its hinges! Understood?'

'Yes *Optio*!' He shot the answer back as his back straightened and he looked directly to his front, looking for all the world as though he were back on the parade grounds of *Mogontiacum*.

'Now listen you lot!' Mestrius raised his voice slightly as he stepped back from the ranks. 'I haven't the first idea as to whether the Britons in that overgrown hovel over there will give up or not! That question is their problem and not yours! My problem is keeping order in a disciplined fighting formation, and I will have it! Now keep you traps shut and wait! You will know what is to be done soon enough!'

With that, he turned on his heel and walked off towards the right flank of the formation, surveying the ranks as he went, no doubt assessing the effect of the engagement on the Century and performing a mental head count.

After some time negotiating at the gate, finally Geta received an answer. There would be no slaughter here. The Britons would submit! The occupants of the fortified town swung open the great wooden gates and the envoy and his party entered within. After what seemed like many hours standing around watching parties of horsemen moving to and fro, in and out of the gatehouse, large formations of our troops finally began to move through the gates of the *oppidum*. A great sense of pride swelled within me as I realized I was watching history in the making as Imperial forces occupied their first major stronghold in *Britannia*! Our fear of this fabled land was unjustified. Like the rest of the world before them, the Britons were surely now destined to be ruled by Rome!

Before long we were dividing up into separate workforces to complete a number of tasks. The camp areas outside the settlement were already being established as men swung at the ground, breaking the chalky soil up with their *dolabrae* and carrying it off in baskets to be piled up into defensive banks. Whilst this carried on other men were laying out grids and erecting tents within the camp area. Fires already cooked the evening meals and the sound of axes striking tree trunks could be heard echoing round nearby copses as timber was felled for building and fires.

Lying not far away from all of this activity lay the now silent battlefield. The human cost of our first large engagement still lay where they had fallen. Roman dead randomly scattered in amongst masses of slaughtered Britons. The defenders of the *oppidum* vastly outnumbering the corpses of their attackers. In the sky, groups of crows and ravens circled, dropping down now and again and disappearing in amongst the sprawled bodies then hopping into view again as they perched on one of the fallen. Now and again they would flap and flutter around, cawing and squawking as another bird came too close. What need had they to squabble over such plentiful carrion as now littered the green field? There was more than enough to go round! Eventually they would settle. Pecking away with sharp black beaks, now and again pausing to look around suspiciously as they filled their bellies.

The wounded had been removed from the field as we had positioned ourselves around the *oppidum* and those enemy wounded that could not be healed and enslaved were despatched on the spot as we moved over the ground. I must have killed at least five of them as we made our way through. Mostly, it seemed to me that I was conferring a favour on these men. The only thing that was stronger than the pain in their eyes was the obvious desire for release. They fought with ferocity and bravery and commanded a soldier's respect. It was the least I could do to remove them from their pain and give them a warrior's death. Not a slow and agonizing passing without the comfort of anybody being there to see them on their way!

Each *Cohort* sent out a small party of men onto the field to retrieve the dead and strip them of their weapons and equipment. For the first time in battle I would be working in my role as a *Fabricensus*, examining the salvaged equipment and determining whether or not it was repairable or should be scrapped and recycled. We worked until nightfall. The bearers bringing in the dead and laying them in lines before a collection of carts we had acquired to transport the salvage. Men worked quickly and methodically to remove the kit from the corpses of men who had only recently woken to the dawn of that same morning and took their place next to us in the line of battle. I watched as they flopped lifelessly around, the stiffening limbs making it difficult sometimes to part them from their armour and equipment. I was glad that they had no inkling of how their once proud and vital bodies were now being irreverently pulled around and relieved of the accoutrements which they were once so very proud to carry.

Having been removed from its former owners, the equipment was placed in piles close to the wagons and there it fell to soldiers such as me to assess its worth. I lifted the bloodstained swords and dented helmets, examining them all for irreparable defects. Body armour such as *lorica hamata* and *segmentata* fell under my careful eye and, as much as I had a job to do, I could not escape the thought that every gouge, dent and blood stain told its own little story. Its very existence meant that perhaps a family or child somewhere would soon be receiving the worst possible news!

Still other parties scavenged through the corpses of the Britons, removing valuables and weapons alike. Anything that could be of use was taken from their bodies and carried to a cache close by where it would be sorted according to its value and usefulness. Jewellery and valuables went to the army coffers for conversion into hard currency and weapons and armour would either be melted down or retained to issue to locally recruited Auxiliaries once our foothold in the country was stronger. Particularly fine examples of weapons and finery would be held back for later. Soon they would make their way to Rome where they would be paraded through the streets with other booty. A victory procession to show the mob how mighty Rome really was!

Eventually, we finished with the fall of dusk and began to return to the camp. The Roman dead lay in neat lines, separated into the units which they came from and formed up with their comrades for the last time. A guard was posted over their bodies and they were covered with blankets. As I left, I looked over my shoulder to see two guards covering a small group of about twelve men with the blankets we had brought. These were the soldiers who would lie without a grave marker. So terribly disfigured in the brutal press that nobody knew their names any longer!

I was glad to be among the living once more! When we entered camp I made my way to the *Contubernium* tent and joined the others. The whole camp buzzed with excitement after the great victory we had just won ! Wine was being passed around and what rations we had were being supplemented with local kills of all kinds of animal from fox and badger to deer and boar. Rats and voles were also placed on skewers to roast over the camp fires as we prepared our victory feast. Whatever we could find was eaten but drink was strictly moderated! We were in an active area for the enemy and drunkenness could cost us our lives so overindulgence was strictly regulated by the prowling *Optios* and *Centurions*. We had all survived the day and the eight of us sat and talked. Ate and drank. Laughing and joking and commenting on the events of the day. After so much death and killing it would be hard to explain to an outsider why we were so jovial. Those who had never known a battle would never know how good it felt to come out the other side, still alive and with all of your friends with you!

'Curse it! It's going to take an age to get that out!' Aebutius complained loudly as he ran his finger over a deep notch in the blade of his sword. Muttering angrily he fished around in his pack, eventually pulling out a whetstone and beginning work on the damaged blade.

'I'm sure mine's bent you know!' mused Pudens as he cast his eye down the edge of his *gladius*. 'I'd just stuck it in some Briton's throat and was about to twist it out when "bang". This big seething idiot goes and clouts it broad side on with a club the size of a tree!'

'What? That little twig?' Zenas mocked him. 'Don't forget that I was standing next to you! A child could have stopped that one coming in. I saw the whole thing!' He laughed as he began to rub an oily cloth over his armour, the dried blood beginning to soften and loosen so that it could be removed with a light cloth, restoring a dull shine to its surface.

'Never!' snapped Pudens with mock indignation. 'Anyway! He didn't like the tap I gave him with my *scutum*! In fact I bet I could find his teeth marks if I look close enough!' He gave a low chuckle as he began to scrutinize the scratched and battered face of his shield.

'Are any more of those skewers cooked yet?' enquired Aebutius. 'Fighting gives me such an appetite!'

'Ha!' bellowed Marinus. 'How would you know? You hadn't even seen a decent enemy warrior 'til today!' he scoffed. 'Besides, you're just a pig! You'd eat until you burst if you could!'

Marinus sat and gave a huff of disdain, slowly shaking his head as he lifted the hem of his tunic and began to stitch a jagged rip in the garment.

'Lies!' Aebutius sprang up, pointing his finger at Marinus who continued to sew. 'I may not have been around as long as you but I've done my bit! I lost a brother in *Germania* while we hunted bandits!'

'So?' Scoffed Marinus, continuing his repairs and not even bothering to look up. 'Why don't you come back when you've got some more time in, and then tell me some more of your little laments, eh?'

Seeing that Aebutius was taking things too much to heart, I stood quickly and shoved him in the chest, pushing him back down onto his spread-out cloak. Aebutius had taken the loss of Lupus very much to heart. Since the day when the young boy had bested him in the boxing ring they had formed a close bond and his loss had been a heavy blow, for all of us, but especially for Aebutius. He made himself comfortable again and continued to grind at the notch on the blade of his *gladius*, scowling now and then at the seemingly oblivious Marinus.

'Give it a minute,' I advised him. 'There'll soon be some more food ready and you can have some of mine. I'm not that hungry!'

'What's up with you?' enquired Zenas, pausing and looking up from his polishing.

'Nothing. I ate some *bucellata* while I was assessing kit earlier. I'm fine!' I answered. 'Besides, we should count ourselves lucky that we have the choice! I saw some of our lads lying out on the field earlier who'll never feel the warmth of a camp fire again!'

'Luck doesn't come into it!' Zenas returned piously. 'It's the will of the gods whether you live or die! Simple as that!'

'Rubbish!' Marinus huffed, still busy at his repairs. 'I can't be bothered with all this divine will business! They made mistakes and they paid for it! Learn from that and give thanks that you can now have their share of the rations!'

An uneasy silence fell around the fire with just the sound of the wood cracking and spitting as fat dripped onto it from the browning meat placed above it. The noise from the other tents around us seemed to fade out as we all paused in silent thought, reflecting on the day's events. Eventually Pacatianus broke the silence as he stared into his wine cup, examining the reflection of the fire on its ruby surface.

'Say what you like but I'd be happier if they were all here, sharing a drink round the fire!'

Silently, we all nodded our agreement.

Eventually the warmth of the fire and the comfort of a full belly began to take its effect. The chatter died down to the odd muted conversation, which in turn gave way to our sitting round the fire, quietly gazing into the dancing flames. Slowly, we drifted off to our beds and the encampment fell silent.

Chapter 14

Aftermath

I slept soundly enough, until just before the dawn. My eyes seemed to snap open and instantly I was awake! Nothing had disturbed me and the others still slept soundly around me, save for Surus who had won the last of the watches for that night and was out, standing at his post. I pushed back my heavy woollen blanket and picked up the rolled up cloak that I had been using as a pillow. Quietly moving the tent flap to one side I stepped out into the chill of the pre dawn darkness and unrolled the *paenula*, pulling it round my shoulders and giving a slight cough as the cold air shocked my lungs. I walked silently through the camp towards where Surus had been posted. In the eastern sky a deep blue line was beginning to form on the horizon, heralding the arrival of the dawn. Even now the songbirds were beginning their morning chorus. Their cheerful sound accompanied the sound of snoring and the odd cough as I walked through the darkened lines.

Something else could be heard drifting on the air as I made my way through the camp. A distant wailing carried over the still air and caused me to cast my eye towards the settlement we now controlled. Here and there I could pick out the presence of small fires, their warm glow gently emanating from behind the palisade and amongst the thatched roundhouses. I realized that I was hearing the lamentations of the women in the *oppidum*. The *Cantiaci* had not taken up arms against the invasion in any great numbers but the warriors who had been present when the larger force of Britons had arrived to fight would have been obliged to join forces and defend their territory. Not being able to bear the shame of standing by whilst other tribes fought to defend their capital, or being slaughtered by their own neighbours, they had been obliged to join the battle!

Now there was nothing left for the women of *Durovernum Cantiacorum* but to mourn! Every able bodied man who had entered the field that day was gone! Those who had fought and died were still lying on the battlefield, cold and shattered, whilst the vanquished were now shackled and collared and waiting to be shipped to *Gaul*. Prime merchandise for the ever hungry slave markets, the only prospect they faced now was a life of hardship and servitude, many miles from the land of their birth and the arms of their loved ones. Many of the captives were fiercely proud and it would take much to bend them to their new master's will. I could see that many would not conform and that they would eventually receive the ultimate punishment for their rebelliousness! No doubt some of them would catch the eye of a *lanista* who would purchase them to fight in the arena. There, the weak and the disobedient would perish! Only the strong and intelligent would survive training and take part in the *Ludi*. If they were good enough, they would prosper and become famous. Wealth and adoration would be theirs, along with the attention of highborn women who would pay well to be pleasured by top fighters. Ultimately, they could win their freedom and perhaps return home. Such prospects would no doubt be a goal to aim for but the price of failure was high and could mean your blood seeping into the sands of the arena floor while slaves spiked your lifeless body with hooks and dragged you out of sight of the baying, pitiless crowd. Those men who now sat silently, once proud and free warriors now cruelly adorned by the iron chains that marked their enslavement, could have little idea of what was about to become of them.

After a short walk I found Surus. He stood, looking out over the defences, towards the battlefield which was layered with a fine ground mist, his breath appearing as small clouds of steam in the chill of the early morn. As I approached he turned, ready to issue a challenge but stopped when he saw me.

'Gods, Vepitta!' he hissed in a whisper. 'Are you trying to get yourself stabbed?'

'I know, I'm sorry!' I replied in a hushed voice. 'I just couldn't sleep!'

'Why didn't you tell me earlier?' He smiled. 'I'd have been glad to have taken your place in the tent so that you could have come out here to shiver as I have!'

'What?' I replied, gently mocking him. 'A big tough stone mason like you can't stand a bit of cool night air? Whatever next?'

'Cool my arse! It's freezing standing round watching that lot sleeping!'

He stamped his feet and hugged himself, laughing quietly then pointing to the dark shapes lying out on the field. I gave a muted laugh in response. It mattered little to me that hundreds of bodies languished close by! Man makes choices and has his destiny mapped out for him by the gods. If that destiny means that you lie dead on a battlefield in *Britannia* then so let it be! The Britons' own people would come and tend to them soon enough. We had our own men to bury later this day!

'How long do you think they'll keep us here?' Surus wondered.

'I don't know!' I answered him honestly. 'No doubt we'll have to wait for that turncoat bastard Adminius to turn up and for the rest of the assault force to join us before we go anywhere!'

'Hmm, I suppose you're right!' he replied. 'Have you seen this Adminius fellow yet? What a shit he is! Fancy fetching a bunch of foreign troops to do his dirty work! I bet his new subjects will love him for that!'

'The gods alone know how he'll get round that one!' I mused. 'He's not the only one, mind! There's another old king, if you can call him that, who's done the same thing!'

'Is there?'

'Oh yes!' I assured Surus, pleased with my knowledge of current affairs. 'Adminius came begging the mad Emperor Gaius for help. This old boy, Verica I think his name is, turns up in Rome not so long back also asking Claudius for his help. Apparently he kept getting pushed around by the two chiefs in charge of this lot we're now warring with and got fed up with it!'

'Vulcan's balls!'gasped Surus incredulously. ' What kind of people are these Britons? They would sell out to a foreign power just to get one over on the neighbours? How treacherous can you get? I know it's more gain for us but, if I were a Briton, I'd want to see this pair dead! It sounds like they'd sell their whole family and people into slavery if it suited them!'

'Ah!' I replied, ready to deliver the final piece of intrigue. ' This Adminius character stands to gain a fair bit from this, you know?'

'Does he? Why's that then?' Surus asked intrigued.

'Because these two chieftains who gather the tribes and try to unite them to resist us just happen to be his brothers!' I folded my arms and nodded smugly.

'Well I ...!' Surus was outraged. 'What a sordid little nest of vipers this lot are! It doesn't even seem that family, let alone their subjects, mean anything to them! Small wonder they need stamping out, I'm glad we're here now. This mess needs sorting out!'

We chuckled quietly and I slapped Surus cheerfully on the shoulder. We didn't have much to speak of but it was good to be able to gossip once in a while. It was a welcome diversion from the constant need to follow orders and routine. We were still human after all!

Later that morning I had reported to the temporary *fabrica* that had been set up to deal with the reclaimed weapons and armour that needed to be worked on. Our baggage train had arrived shortly after the battle, tools and equipment had been offloaded and tents hastily erected to shelter us as we worked. Piles of equipment had been laid out for us to work on and around twenty of us began the task that morning. My job was to strip down plate armour, removing damaged plates by chopping out rivets that held them to the internal leather strapping. Once this was done I would assess the plate as either scrap or worthy of repair. Repair invariably meant heating the plate, beating out the damage and then reshaping it ready to be re riveted back into the armour. I was glad that, of the tasks I could have won, mine was fairly light.

Aebutius had cursed his luck for being detailed to repair damaged ring mail, a job that required good light, skill and patience. He sat, hunched over a tree trunk and a small iron anvil, trying to make sense of the damage to the shirts. Separating the damaged rings from the holes torn through the shirts by the various weapons used on their owners, having a ready stock of wire he would coil new rings on an iron mandrel and cut them off one at a time, ready to apply them to the repair. Where possible he would heat the rings and beat the red hot ends together so that they fused into a solid ring which was then applied to the repair. Ordinarily the rings used to join the repair together would be closed by flattening the ends off and piercing them with a fine punch. Both ends could then be fastened to each other with a tiny bronze rivet. Battlefield repairs did not allow for such time to be spent on one repair so the jointing rings were just butt ended together. Although not as strong as the riveted product they could still easily stand the rigours of general wear.

My nose throbbed from the previous day and breathing was difficult through it. I now noticed just how much punishment I had taken the day before as all the aches and pains from the battle began to manifest themselves, making the wielding of hammers and chisels quite uncomfortable. As I worked I began to loosen off a little but my nose was becoming blocked from the smoke and hot gases from the small forge I worked at. My eyes began to water heavily as I beat at the buckled and dented plates I had cut from their strapping, but at least I did not have to rivet them back together again! The riveting was carried out by another soldier while still others replaced damaged strapping or beat helmets back into shape. Still others would be responsible for stripping the hilt and pommel assemblies from damaged swords whilst another would rework the blades with anvil and forge. Damaged shields would be stripped of useful components ready for refurbishment and scrap metals would be thrown into separate piles, ready to be melted down into small ingots once proper furnaces had been constructed.

The whole camp was a mass of activity as men moved around performing their allotted tasks! Building work was already starting on strengthening the whole area and teams of surveyors moved around with *gromers* and ranging poles, hammering in wooden pegs and wrapping string lines around them to mark the sites for timber buildings. Another team began laying out the course of a new road which would be pushed through from the landing site to where we now consolidated our position! I scarcely had time to pay attention to anything other than my duties but I did notice the burial parties march out onto the battlefield shortly after breakfast and begin the task of constructing funeral pyres for the Roman dead. The fallen would be cremated with the dead from their own units! Their positions on the pyres being carefully noted in order that their ashes could be gathered afterwards and a memorial stone erected to mark their final resting place. The unknown dead would be cremated together and a special ceremony conducted to honour them. Their ashes would then be gathered up and scattered over the land that they died conquering!

By mid day Plautius had allowed the Britons to set foot on the battlefield and begin the task of recovering their dead. Now and again I would look up to see women moving through the tangled spread of corpses that littered the ground. They would weep silently as they picked their way through the bodies of their men. Now and again they would pause and perhaps roll a body over or lift a head to check for the face of their missing man. If they found their loved one they would stand over the body and wail, tearing at their hair, beating their breasts and screaming curses at the Roman camp! It came as no great surprise. We had, after all, slaughtered their men folk. Those same men had taken up arms against us and paid for their defiance with their lives. Who cared what curses their women hurled at us? They were just words after all! The only things they had that could have hurt us were either dead or weighed down by slave chains!

The elders of the *oppidum* had requested that they be allowed to cremate their dead on the field of battle but Plautius and Geta had denied them their request. The bodies were to be taken a short way further south and buried. The army needed all available stocks of timber and such a large amount of bodies would require too much wood.

The next three days passed much the same as the first. Building and repair work carried on at an astonishingly fast rate. Vespasian had arrived on the second day with II Augusta and their Auxiliary contingent. Their contribution to the work effort had speeded things up immensely and *Durovernum Cantiacorum* was beginning to experience great changes as the war machine set about transforming their backward little world into a Roman stronghold! News had already reached us that a road was being pushed through from the original landing areas and that work had started on massive defences, docks and quays to turn it into a fortified port. It was to be called *Portus Rutupiae* and its immediate role would be as a key supply port landing goods, equipment and reinforcements from *Gaul* which would then be transported inland or shipped around the coast to be landed close to the army as it pushed further inland.

The port would also send cargo out as well as receive it and one of the outgoing cargoes would be the prisoners that still languished at the side of the battlefield. For two days they had been set to work removing the bodies of their fallen comrades from the field. A heavy and messy job, they had loaded the corpses onto ox carts and then followed under armed escort to the burial sites. It hadn't taken long for the battlefield to begin to reek of spilt blood and corrupted flesh as the days were now reasonably warm and pleasant. The Britons worked silently, handling the dead with great reverence and following instructions without complaint, but you could see in their eyes that all they wished for was to hold a weapon again! If the opportunity came their way then they would kill any unwary guard and gladly suffer the consequences as the reality of their situation became clearer to them. They would not, however, throw away their lives. It would be a warrior's death they would be after so weapons were kept well out of reach and the security of the chains checked regularly!

Nothing but the very bare essentials were offered to comfort these men! Water was plentiful and supplied by their guards but food was something that would have to be supplied by their own people. Their women would bake bread and bring it to the edge of the field every morning. It was as far as they would be allowed to go. No contact was to be allowed between them under any circumstances. The gods knew what might happen if the prisoners were fired up by the presence of their womenfolk! No shelter was provided while they awaited the arrival of the slave traders. After clearing the field they just sat at the edge of a track and waited in silence. The odd one died from his wounds or from exposure overnight and when that happened the body would be unshackled the next morning and cast into a nearby open pit under the supervision of the guards.

Eventually the slave traders had arrived in camp and the time came for the prisoners to be taken. A group of the traders had visited the men and examined them for their quality and saleability, closely checking every aspect of their bodies for strength, fitness and signs of disease. When they were finished they retired to the command tent and concluded business by drawing up a contract and agreeing a price for them. Eventually the traders returned, escorted by a unit of cavalry and began moving the men into a column which they prepared for the march to *Portus Rutupiae*. Once proud warriors now walked with their heads hung low, an emptiness of spirit plainly evident on their filth caked faces. They were still covered in the dried blood and gore of battle and had sat in their own filth for three days, stinking and humiliated! Hard to imagine that just a few days ago these were part of a fearsome and determined army! As the slave traders moved them off, taking the first steps of a very long journey that would lead them to who knows where, they shuffled along, hobbled by foot chains and joined together with great lengths of iron chain attached to broad metal collars. Now and again one of them would cast a glance over his shoulder, probably muttering a last farewell to a home and family that he was never likely to see again. As I watched the ragged column slowly disappear into the distance I found myself thanking the gods that I had not been on the losing side!

As the column of slaves had disappeared into the distance another wail rose from the *oppidum* as the women of the settlement had watched their surviving menfolk taken from them! They mounted the tops of the palisade and thrashed around making the most baleful noise I had heard so far. Eventually troops were sent up to pull them off the defences and drive them back to their homes. It came as no real surprise that they possessed an immense hatred for anything Roman after that! At a gathering of all of the leaders of the *Cantiaci*, Adminius was presented as client ruler and the tribe declared itself an ally of Rome, pledging non aggression whilst the forces that resisted were subdued. All this meant nothing to the women of *Durovernum Cantiacorum*. It was merely the political posturing of very powerful men. All the women understood was that they had lost everything the day Rome had invaded their world. It would take more than the language of politics and diplomacy to quell the burning hatred they harboured for us!

In just a few days we were ready to move once more. The commanders had decided on the next phase of the invasion and set their objectives. Their decisions were passed down to the men by the Centurions who attended the morning command briefing and received their orders. Fatalis had appeared before us on a cool and drizzly morning and outlined what was now expected of us.

'Tomorrow morning we begin the march to our next objective!' he began. 'You will make the necessary preparations today and be ready to move after breakfast tomorrow!'

He paused, collecting his thoughts to pass all of the recalled detail onto us.

'Further to the west lies the inland trading settlement of *Durobrivae*. We have known of it for many years as it is accessible from the sea via the great river that it sits on! Roman vessels have long traded there and we know that it will suit our purposes to capture it and once more establish a supply point to allow us to push for further objectives!'

He paused once more to look up and down the Century.

'So far, we have done well, with only three of our number injured and none of you killed. We did a good job of work by capturing this place but the next step is going to be much harder!'

He stood facing the middle of the formation and leant with both hands on his *vitis*.

'Our scouts report that the settlement of *Durobrivae* is now an armed camp and the largest force yet encountered is massing there to await our arrival! They are forming a large army on the opposite bank of the great river that we need to cross to further our objectives and already, they have dismantled the bridge that crosses to the settlement in an attempt to prevent us fording the river! We must now move swiftly to prevent that army from growing any bigger and to prevent them from doing anything else that will hamper our crossing of the river. Due to the importance of this objective we will be part of a large force comprising II Augusta, XX Valeria, four *Cohorts* of Batavian Auxiliaries and an accompanying cavalry force! General Plautius will personally lead the push accompanied by his second in command, Geta and our own Legion commanders! When there is more news concerning our role I will give you it when I have it. Now, fall out to your duties!'

With that, Fatalis spun round and walked briskly off to his tent as we broke formation and began to walk to our allotted tasks, eagerly debating the content of the briefing with our nearest companions.

'Yes!' hissed Zenas. 'That's what we need to be doing! Keeping these ignorant tribesmen on the back foot and not giving them chance to come back at us!'

'Surely they'll be expecting us?' queried Pacatianus, as we made our way through the lines, weaving around the tent ropes and fire pits of the *Contubernium* areas.

'Of course they will!' Marinus answered as though the point was obvious to us. 'They know we'll come but they won't expect to see us in such great numbers as before! They don't know how fast we can move and they don't know how fast we consolidate positions! They have never seen an army like this before!'

'That may be the case!' Crispus interjected as Marinus prepared to continue. 'But equally, we have never fought them! I don't think this is quite so cut and dried and I think the Britons are bound to have a few surprises for us yet!'

'You think too much!' snapped Marinus.

We moved out as planned the next day, marching westwards and slight north across the chalk downs to our new objective. Instead of marching in an extended column we had split into smaller battle groups and spread the advance into a broad band, sweeping across the country side, clearing the area as we went. Legionary cavalry galloped back and forth, maintaining communication with the units as we advanced and Auxiliary cavalry accompanied the separate columns, acting as both escorts and forward scouts. Most of the Fourteenth was on the march but *Cohorts* VIII, IX and X had remained behind to continue working on the building and civil engineering tasks that had been started. Their task would be to improve the efficiency of the chain of supply to the advancing force. Whilst we took a more direct course towards *Durobrivae*, the XX Valeria and a large force of Auxiliaries had followed a more northerly route and travelled parallel to us, being resupplied with the help of the *Classis Britannica*, navigating the northern coast of *Cantium* and sailing up the great estuary leading towards *Durobrivae*.

Although the weather had been fine and dry with the sun spending most of the day free of cloud, the wind had been very blustery and slowed the progress of the formation down somewhat. We carried heavy pack and large shields which caught the gusts and impeded progress. The other effect of constantly resisting the gusts was that you became tired quicker than normal and more rest stops were needed with the result that, at day's end, we had not achieved the required distance and were some three miles short of our planned camp area. Having been informed that the entire force was more or less in the same area, Plautius ordered that the formations should make their own arrangements for bedding down and prepare to assemble for an assault the next morning.

We quickly threw up the usual defences, becoming used now to the hard chalk and flint that made the digging of defensive ditches such an arduous task after a day's march. Soon we had our earth wall and ditch and had fortified it with *pila murali* lashed together in threes to form a tripod-like arrangement that presented spikes in multiple directions. These were then placed on the rampart wall to impede, or impale, attackers attempting to jump the ditch. Quickly we erected the tents and then dug fire pits to begin preparation of the evening meal. The wind had eased a little and allowed us the opportunity of establishing the cooking fires and building them up without having them blown all over the camp! Soon the air was filled with the aroma of stews and broths bubbling away in cook pots while men moved in and out of camp, collecting wild herbs and vegetables to add to their pots. Now and again the fortunate forager would return triumphantly with a hare or water fowl, ensuring that the evening meal would be just that little bit more interesting and tasty.

Despite the fact that the unit was now at rest for the evening the camp remained ever vigilant. Those that went foraging always ventured out in groups and always wore full armour. They knew always to remain within sight of the sentries who were posted as soon as the column put down its packs and started to dig. Even at night, boots would remain on and weapons were kept close at hand, the only concession to sleep was the removal of bulky body armour to facilitate much needed sleep, regenerating you for the next day's efforts.

As we sat down to our meal once more, we watched the sun dropping down behind the low hills, its dying rays lighting the sky up with a blend of wondrous colours, signalling the departure from the sky of *Apollo* and his fiery chariot for another day. Quickly, we finished our meal and retired for the evening. In the field of battle it was unwise to waste opportunities for sleep as conditions were often arduous and lack of sleep could cost a man dearly so we did not delay taking to our beds. There would be other opportunities for talk on other evenings but one last thing needed to be done before we slept.

As we sat on our bedding, Zenas took a small object covered in cloth from his pack and began to unwrap it. We sat waiting expectantly as the small clay figure was placed on its wrapping and then bowed lightly to it as it stood before us, a lightly moulded smile was visible on its shadowy face as it seemed to draw the warmth of the flickering lamplight to it. It was easy to imagine that the figure was glad to be free of its dark hiding place once more and savouring the light and the reverence of its human companions!

As our immediate leader, Zenas was keeper of the *Genius* of the *Contubernium* and officiated over this small ritual every night before we slept. Crispus placed a small earthenware bowl containing hot coals from our fire in front of the figure and withdrew while Zenas began the prayers.

'Sacred *Genius*, protector of we eight servants of the gods and great mother Rome!' he began solemnly. 'Share with us our meal this evening and grant us your protection for another day!'

Reverently Zenas broke a small piece of bread from one of our loaves and placed it on the glowing embers from the fire.

'Take this bread to sustain you and drink of this wine to refresh you!' Zenas then tipped a small amount of wine from out of his beaker onto the coals. A small cloud of pink steam erupted with an angry hiss as he finished the prayer. 'Watch over us while we sleep and grant that we live through tomorrow's battle in order that we can continue to be faithful to the Gods and the Senate and people of Rome!'

He placed his finger to his lips and then touched the small figure on the head. Quietly we copied his actions, then the lamps were doused and we settled down to sleep. Comforted that we had invoked the protection of our own special *Genius*.

* * *

'Alarm, alarm! Stand to, we're under attack!'

It seemed almost as though I had been asleep for a mere moment when the shouting snapped me back to consciousness! The first shout of 'alarm' had seemed to echo across the veils of sleep but the second shout registered loud and clear in my brain as I sat bolt upright and began to grab at my weapons! There was no panic as well rehearsed drills clicked into action and we rapidly prepared to leave the tent and man the defences. The tent flap was flung to one side and the faint light of the stars and dying cooking fires instantly created rapidly moving silhouettes moving towards the opening! In an instant we were out and throwing on our belts and weapons and grabbing up shields as other men emerged from their tents and swiftly began to equip.

Screams began to pierce the air from the direction of the southern defences as the raiders were engaged by armed sentries and the killing began. Nobody detoured from their pre arranged places as men ran to cover all points of the defences, regardless of where the main attack was taking place. It so happened that our assembly points were on the southern line so we snatched up our *scuta* and ran to defend that side of the camp!

Although none of us had donned body armour we had all equipped ourselves with helmet, shield, sword and at least one *pilum* each. As we fell behind the defences I saw one of our sentries lying dead, a spear transfixing his neck! His eyes were open and seemed to bulge with the shock of the mortal blow, his tongue poked grotesquely out of his wide open mouth. Shapes ran around shouting wildly in the blackness beyond the defences and, over the chaos I heard Fatalis' familiar voice bellow out:

'Double shield wall form! Archers! Light it up!'

At that moment I felt something rush past my cheek at a great speed, startling me as it passed and hitting something behind me with a thud. Again something else shot through the air and I heard a wet 'smack' and a scream of pain from our ranks!

'Shields up, they're using slings!'

As soon as the shout went up the shield wall raised higher and stones could be heard impacting with the faces of shields with fearsome thuds. All the time came the crazed screams of the as yet unseen attackers. Just than a wall of light erupted behind us as a flask of lamp oil was thrown onto a dormant fire and Legionary archers began to set light to arrows wrapped in cloth and pitch! As soon as the arrows began to blaze the bowmen sent them streaking out into the blackness. Shooting them along flat trajectories so that they ripped across the darkened field and hit the ground in front of the defences at varying distances. As the fiery trails zipped through the air like miniature comets the darkness began to diminish rapidly as the fire arrows lit up the night and set light to the surrounding undergrowth.

Now we could see them! About two hundred Britons were just short of the defences, armed with slings, spears and swords and carrying their lightweight shields, they now seemed shocked that the cover of night had been denied them and they had now become glaring targets in the newly illuminated field. Briefly, their momentum had failed with the shock of the initial response and we seized the opportunity to reply! The nearest Britons to us were around ten yards away and almost ready to recover their wits and charge the defences when Fatalis quickly bawled out another order:

'Ready *pila!*' He ordered and each man quickly hoisted his javelin into throwing position! Then immediately after:

'Loose!'

As a unit, we threw out a deadly rain of needle sharp iron points at the now charging Britons. The rushing advance faltered instantly as the shafts hammered into their targets! I don't remember seeing any one of those weapons missing their mark as the entire front row of attackers fell to the floor, screaming with the shock and pain as they were impaled by the deadly flying shafts! By now, around a dozen Legionary archers had placed themselves behind our ranks and Fatalis shouted the instruction for us to move to open order so that the archers could shoot between us. As we did, the bowmen began to loose their shafts at random into the Britons who were now running back and forth in fear and confusion. Very quickly the sound of bowstrings twanging was joined by the familiar sound of ratchets clattering and the meaty 'whack' of *Ballistae* loosing their deadly, heavy iron bolts at the hapless attackers! I watched as, one by one, the Britons fell to the deadly shower that beset them as they struggled to get away from the light of the fire arrows.

Dead and wounded lay scattered before the defences and here and there agonized screams and groans could be heard as the wounded cried out their anguish. Small fires lit up the night and grew in intensity as clumps of scrub caught fire, swirling clouds of rising smoke glowing light orange as they were illuminated by the flames. The grass smoke made me cough and my eyes water as the wind blew it into our ranks and then, I began to detect other smells! The spreading fires were also burning the bodies of the felled attackers and the stink of burning flesh, singed hair and smouldering wool filled my nostrils and slowly began to intensify until it became almost sickening to bear.

The Britons had fled in disarray and we stood behind our shields, peering out into the night, looking for the first signs of their return. We hadn't even drawn our swords, the enemy had never got close enough for that! Behind us, soldiers moved around and planted more *pila* into the ground behind us, preparing for another wave of attackers as the archers replenished their stock of arrows. About eight Britons had managed to clear the defences and enter the camp. They had entered via the track that crossed the ditch and killed another sentry before the alert had turned out the soldiers that would prevent them going any further and killing anyone else. Their heads had now been separated from their bodies and four had been stuck on the defence spikes whilst the remaining four were in the possession of soldiers who waved them around in the air and shouted crude insults in the direction of the fleeing Britons before eventually throwing them contemptuously into the defensive ditch along with their corpses.

We held our positions until the dawn rose, its weak light starting to display the results of the night's work in all of its brutal detail! Corpses lay scattered in front of the ditch, pale and bloodless. Many had more than one shaft stuck fast into their lifeless bodies while a few others seemed to have nothing wrong at all until you noticed the gaping hole left by a *ballista* bolt as it had sailed straight through their body, travelling on to claim another victim! Large, ragged black patches still smouldered from the grass fires which had started as the fire arrows had been deployed. Grey smoke drifted lazily around at ground level and climbed, here and there, into the pale dawn sky. It rose from the charred and blackened bodies which had been caught up in the fires. You could tell if they were alive or dead when they burned by how they looked! The ones who had died before being burned lay in slumped or flat shapes but the ones who had suffered the pain of the flames were arched and contorted, their gnarled hands and fingers and exposed, snarling teeth testifying to their agonizing demise!

I rubbed my eyes, which only now did I begin to notice were tired and sore from a sleepless and smoke filled night. I cast a glance up and down the front rank, taking in other weary faces, streaked with the grime from the smoke and made worse by tears caused by the stinging fumes that had rolled over us. Pudens stood next to me, loosening the laces on his cheek pieces and slowly rubbing his face with his finger tips.

'Well!' he sighed. 'So much for a good night's sleep eh?'

I nodded wearily and exhaled loudly, turning round to acknowledge the man on my other side. Marinus leaned on the top of his shield, watching me with a pair of grimy, bloodshot eyes. He stood straight and arched his back, groaning with the pleasure of the stretch and then sniffed the air lightly in my direction, looking me up and down. I regarded him curiously, unable to work out what he was thinking until at last, he shared his thoughts with me!

'You could do with a wash Vepitta!' He observed casually. 'You smell like an old camel!'

'What's a camel?' I asked, dismayed.

Chapter 15

The Battle on the River

As soon as dawn had spread its light over the camp and we could see into the distance we were stood down and allowed to take breakfast. Sentries still kept a watchful eye and their food was brought to them at their post so that they could maintain a watch. The night attack had been quite a surprise and demonstrated the unpredictable nature of the enemy, forcing us to remain ever vigilant. Mestrius had mustered us together and conducted a roll call to determine any losses the Century may have suffered. He would nod approvingly when he heard the shouted responses to the names he called out, but on three occasions however, he had been forced to amend the nominal roll inscribed onto the wax tablet he carried.

'Attalus!' He called as he came across the first of the missing. Initially, there was no response so he called again, peering into the ranks of the Century, hoping no doubt to catch the soldier daydreaming.

'Attalus. Claudius Attalus!' He tried again.

'Dead Optio!' A voice from the centre of the formation replied. 'He was on sentry when they attacked!'

My mind briefly revisited the action of the previous night and I remembered the face of Attalus as he lay dead, next to the defences with that spear rammed into his neck. No point dwelling on it now. It was done and Attalus was gone. Nothing would change that!

Mestrius looked up briefly then turned his attention to the tablet once more, briefly inscribing a note concerning Attalus' fate. He continued to call out more names until he reached the next of the missing men.

'Macrinus!'

'Dead Optio!' came the brief but adequate reply.

A few names further and he discovered the third and final victim of the night attack.

'Germanus!' He called out, only to be met with silence. 'Caius Velerius Germanus. Any information?'

He stood with his stylus poised over the tablet waiting for news of the missing soldier. I heard someone mutter at the back of the ranks then came the reply that Mestrius required.

'We think he's in the hospital tent Optio!'

'What do you mean, you think?' he snapped. 'Don't you know where your own comrades are?'

'He got his face smashed in by a sling shot Optio. It was a really bad injury so we don't know whether he's survived the night or not!'

'Right!' He barked angrily. 'This is not good enough! It is your collective responsibility to supply me with accurate information about your *Contubernia*. You should have found this out before roll call! If a man can't account for himself then you must do it for him. At the end of parade go off and find out. Then find me and kindly let me know what is going on with my own troops!'

'Yes Optio!' came the shout from the back.

Mestrius completed the roll call and closed the leaves of the tablet, tying it shut with a leather lace and sliding the stylus under the binding. Then he placed the tablet into a leather wallet suspended from a strap round his neck. Turning to face us, he concluded the parade with a brief critique of the night raid.

'Fatalis and I were pleased with how you acquitted yourselves last night!' he complimented us. 'You responded quickly and effectively to the threat, falling into your positions and repelling the enemy with the minimum of delay!

'As a criticism, I do not want bodies thrown into the defensive ditches of the camp. It minimizes the depth and stops the trench from twisting or breaking ankles as it is designed to do. In future, wait until it is safe to do so then dump the bodies away from camp. Clear?'

'Yes Optio!' We agreed. The ditch was cut in a sharp angle with a narrow trough at the bottom designed to twist a man's foot as he entered the trench. If this was covered by a body it would make life easier for any attackers. Lack of thought in the heat of battle had caused the error to occur. It would not happen again!

Mestrius paused for a moment before he spoke again.

'We lost two of our own last night.' he sighed, frowning. 'It may be that Germanus is not long for this world too! You should not dwell on these losses as they are very minimal and the first we have suffered in this campaign so far. From my own past experiences I know that war can be far more costly to the Century and am grateful that so many of us stand here this morning. All you can do now is offer a prayer for our fallen brothers and continue your good work.

 Now! To your duties, fall out!'

As we made our way back to the tent, we briefly discussed our lost comrades.

'Do you know Germanus?' Marinus made a general enquiry to us all, then without waiting for a reply he continued. 'We were in training together, I've known him for years. Let's hope he pulls through!'

'It would be good if he does!' agreed Pacatianus. 'He was always a good example to us newer lads!'

'What am I going to do about Attalus?' wondered Pudens. 'I'm in a bit of fix now!'

'Why?' questioned Zenas. 'What's he to you then?'

'He joined a couple of years before me but we grew up in the same place!' He explained. 'I told his parents I would look him up when I joined. I never expected this!'

' So what's your problem?' Zenas asked again.

'I don't know whether I should write and tell them of what has happened or not!' he replied, his usual cheer suppressed by the dilemma he now faced. 'They are old and frail. The news will be hard on them and I don't want to be responsible for causing so much grief!'

'Look lad!' sighed Zenas. 'I don't think Fatalis or Mestrius will find the time to write at this moment and anyway, would you have them ever wondering what happened to their son? You knew him, you know them and I think that they will take comfort from the fact that you were there when he died and you can tell them honestly that he passed with an honourable death, performing his duty!'

Pudens nodded gently, seeing the sense of the words.

'It will be good for you to write!' agreed Crispus 'Tell them exactly how it happened. That way, they will know that he did not suffer and that the end came quickly. It will sting at first but eventually they will accept it and be happy knowing that a family friend was able to tell them the story of their son. Yes?'

Pudens slowly began to smile, realizing that a little good could come from the otherwise sad situation.

'Yes, you're right!' he conceded. 'As soon as we can set up a more permanent camp I will write to them. That I can do for them at least!'

'Good man!' said Zenas approvingly and clapping his hand on Pudens' shoulder. 'Now let's go and get ready to move out!'

As it turned out, we were not the only camp to be attacked during the night. At least three other units had been raided by bands of lightly armed Britons operating under the cover of darkness. Most of the attacked camps had faired as well as ourselves and repelled their attackers with little difficulty. IX Hispana however, who had pitched camp around three miles from us, had suffered the loss of around forty men when a raiding party had briefly managed to penetrate their outer defences. Many of the dead had been killed whilst they slept. It came out later that their lines had been breeched due to a sentry that had fallen asleep at his post. He had sat down next to one of the tents and dozed off behind his shield, overlooked by the raiders as they slaughtered his comrades, he had eventually joined in the defence of the camp and survived the night.

As soon as they were able, his superiors had identified the breech in the defences and questioned him about his failure to alert the camp. The man could do nothing but admit that he had fallen asleep and automatically signed his own death warrant. In peace time, falling asleep at one's post attracted heavy punishment with hefty fines and on the spot beatings that could result in death. In time of war the punishment was clear. The offending soldier was instantly sentenced to *Fustuarium*, which was the case with the man from the IX.

Having caused the deaths of so many comrades and risked the lives of the others, he was executed the next morning, shortly after the facts had come to light. Stripped of his armour and weapons, his belt was taken from him so that he stood in just his tunic. His Centurion and brother soldiers then surrounded him and the sentence commenced with the Centurion delivering withering blows from his *vitis* until the guilty man fell to the floor. Then the rest of the unit stepped in and rained vicious blows on the man with wooden clubs and weapon pommels until he was dead. The body was then removed and dumped, the right to a decent and proper burial forfeited. There was, after all, no greater offence for a soldier, than to cost the lives of your comrades!

We commenced the march towards out next objective with somewhat less enthusiasm than normal. Prior to the start we had been told that our role would be to act as a distraction to the large force of Britons that would be arrayed on the opposite bank to us. Effectively, during the opening stages of the next engagement, we would not be taking an offensive role. Many of us were disappointed at this but, as disciplined soldiers, we would have to live with the Commander's decision and accept that the tactic was all part of a much larger plan to defeat the enemy in this latest engagement. We had marched the short distance to our objective in the early afternoon, locating and following the large river we were to camp on, a short distance downstream. As we progressed through the countryside we came across abandoned settlements and farms. Everything that the Britons could do to deny us had been done. The buildings burned and all tools and stores either taken with them or destroyed and spoiled. Livestock was driven off and whatever fields had been planted with crops had been either torched or ripped up to prevent us harvesting them later. It was as though we followed in the path of destruction left by a wrathful demon.

Eventually we reached our objective and camped on high ground, overlooking the river and the settlement of *Durobrivae*. On the opposite bank, the enemy watched our arrival. They had seen, and heard the deliberate display of force as we drew close to them and we had made as dramatic an entrance onto the field as possible. They must have heard our approach long before they saw us! We bellowed out our victory chants and sang songs of our past exploits to the accompaniment of our horns and the banging of our shields. The armour and equipment of the column added its own accompaniment of metallic clanking and jingling as we marched into view of the assembled Britons.

As soon as we had crested the low hill which had hidden us from view the thousands of assembled Britons greeted us with a terrific roar and began to hammer rhythmically on the backs of their shields. A war of bravado had already started as the *Cohorts* split into separate formations and we advanced towards the river in a broad line, shouting and bawling insults and threats and beating our own shields. 'Bang, bang, bang,' the sound of the shield backs being struck matched our foot fall as we marked time until each *Cohort* was separately halted and, one by one, fell silent. Nothing in the ranks stirred as the Britons on the opposite bank also quietened, puzzled no doubt at why we had suddenly ceased our display.

The early summer sun glittered on the flowing surface of the broad river as a gentle wind played along its edges, blowing along the banks and causing the *vexilla* and streamers and pendants on the standards to flutter lazily. Silently, the two armies faced each other as an incredible atmosphere of anticipation and rising excitement pervaded the ranks. Then, our own Commander, Sabinianus, rode slowly towards the front of the formation and halted on the bank. He turned to face us and, in doing so, deliberately turned his back on the enemy host. His six Tribunes joined him, three on either side and insulted the Britons in the same way. Slowly Sabinianus drew his magnificently crafted *gladius* from its sheath and held it low against his thigh. His exquisite armour glinted in the warm sunlight as he raised himself up in his saddle and shouted over our heads:

'Are you ready for a war?'

'Aye, ready aye!'

We bellowed the response three times as Sabinianus wheeled his mount around and thrust his sword out in the direction of his foe. Again, we hammered our shields and howled our curses at the Britons, who were shouting and screaming furiously now on the far bank until, eventually, the Centurions silenced us and we were turned about, moving off to where we would establish camp.

The usual defences were prepared, along with certain refinements to cater for the situation we now found ourselves in. The camp itself lay well back from the river and in clear ground, we placed it atop a low flat plateau so that any attackers would be overlooked but we made sure that the huge force of Britons across the river could be observed at all times. Closer to the river we erected special towers, upon which we placed our *ballistae*. That way we could rain bolts down on the Britons if they got too close on the opposite bank. To bolster this capability, we set up a dozen *onagers* which could easily hurl large boulders and other projectiles into their ranks as and when required. Not only had we used our own *onagers* but we also had other machines and their crews attached from IX Hispana, the main body of which were camped out of sight to the south east of us.

For the duration of the daylight hours, those soldiers not engaged on preparing defences were moved close to the river to maintain a show of force for the Britons who had now started to react to our presence. Their infantry still jeered us from the far bank and they had now drawn their cavalry and chariots closer to us. As they postured on the other side we watched them carefully as they performed their displays. They would flourish their weapons and perform elaborate movements, as though they were practiced gymnasts, to demonstrate their skill. Their cavalry thundered up and down the bank, both in groups and individually, showing us their prowess as horsemen and, once more we were treated to the site of their chariots as they reminded us of just how fast and versatile they could be. There was no doubting the skill and spirit of these men but, if they had set out to unnerve us with their displays, they may just as well have skimmed pebbles across the water at us!

'Have you seen these boys?' asked Marinus pointing across the river. 'They're brilliant! I'd love to see these in the arena back home! By the gods, those antics would go down a treat!'

'I'll tell you this!' added Surus. 'They're a bit stupid when it comes to tactics but they know how to fight!'

'Oh please! If they were that good at fighting they'd have shown up on the beaches and kicked our Roman arses back into the sea!' Marinus responded indignantly.

'Now don't forget that they thought that we weren't coming, you know?' Crispus pointed out. 'If they had, they probably would have turned up and given us just as many problems as they gave the Divine Julius!'

'Why, what did they do to him then?' enquired Pacatianus.

'Gods man! Don't you read?' criticized Zenas. 'He tried twice to take this land but couldn't, despite his best efforts to claim that he did!'

'Yeah, well? What of it?' replied Pacatianus.

'Well that's why we're here stupid!' interrupted Aebutius. 'If the old stutterer in Rome can pull this invasion off he'll have done what Julius Caesar couldn't and land the Empire with a very valuable new piece of territory!'

Fatalis was close by and, having heard the slight on the Emperor he stalked over and immediately lashed out at Aebutius, striking him hard across the thighs with his *vitis*. The hapless soldier howled in pain and fell to the floor clutching his bruised legs as the furious Centurion leant over him and snarled:

'Just as well I need all of my men for now Aebutius! Otherwise, I'd be beating the shit out of you for that remark! The Emperor is your supreme master, who you swore on oath to serve and honour. I don't call name calling honouring and if I hear you again I'll remove your tongue and stop it flapping forever. Understood?'

Aebutius nodded hurriedly, biting his bottom lip and trying to stifle groans of pain as the Centurion stalked off, leaving us all in a chided silence.

Eventually, things began to settle down and both armies made preparation to set in for the night. Cooking fires sent columns of smoke drifting lazily across the evening sunset and the aroma of cooking mingled with the sounds of equipment receiving last minute attention and men talking and joking. The Britons had settled out in the open and just a little way up from the bank. They had erected shelters and had fashioned wickerwork screens which they had placed along the bank to protect themselves from the attentions of arrows or slingshot. Scores of small fires glowed amidst their encampment and we could hear the sound of their laughing and singing floating over the river towards us.

As the reds and burnished gold of the setting sun succumbed to the dark blue and black of night I sat quietly and thought of those back home in *Mogontiacum*. I imagined Quintus shutting up shop for the night and retiring to the living quarters to take his evening meal with Curatia and I wondered if they would give me a thought this night. Did they know what was happening over here? Had they had any news of our success? Or did they worry that I was dead? If only *Mercurius* could speed me a message from the gods tonight to them to tell them that I was well and thinking of them.

What of Aurelia's house? I could not imagine that there would ever be a *Mogontiacum* without it! It was a place where I had spent so many good times and I had promised myself that I would return as soon as I was able. I wanted to share good times with my friends again and spend money on food, wine and those willing women once more! After all, was it not where I truly became a man? Ah yes, and then there was Julia! Wherever her shade now dwelt, I wonder, did she still remember me and hold me in such fondness as I would always hold her? She was a good soul and I prayed that the gods took care of her.

I knew none of the answers to the questions I asked but it was a comfort, as I sat quietly by the fire, to float back home and be there once more, even if it was only in spirit. As I pulled my cloak tighter around me to ward off the settling cool of the night I found myself looking skyward and wondering at the distant light of countless thousands of stars, twinkling round the crescent of the moon as it rose in the sky. It was the same sky that watched over my homeland but now, my view was different as I gazed at it from a very troubled but beautiful, deadly but fertile land. Other gods dwelt here and watched over their subjects. Were the very gods going to war with each other in the heavens tomorrow? A divine mirror of the battle played out by man, or did they gather together to watch the struggles of us mortals? Mocking us for our weakness and greed and treating the world as their own gladiatorial display. Preparing finally to punish us for our evils after we had entertained them with our puny power struggles. No! I go too far now! Too much thinking for one night, time to give in to sleep!

We were awake with the dawn. Throwing on our armour and moving formations towards the river bank, still wreathed by low lying mist coming off the water. The Britons were awake and assembled on the other side. Murky shapes at first, moving around in the gloomy grey light and veiled by the drifting mist, slowly taking substance and form as the mist began to evaporate with the quickening of the daylight. Eventually we stood, arrayed against each other, we in tight packed blocks of soldiers, they in a vast extended line, stretching along the line of the bank but around twenty paces back from the edge. Their cavalry and chariots were massed behind them and, once the formations had assembled, there was silence as we stood, coldly appraising each other.

From their rear formations came a single chariot, its driver moving the vehicle quickly but carefully through the masses in the forward ranks until it broke clear and halted, its warrior passenger standing behind the driver in defiant pose, scorn and contempt visible upon him, even at the distance that separated us. A man of unremarkable size and stature for his race, he was nevertheless of noble birth. Thick gold torques adorned both his neck and wrists and he wore a shirt of mail very similar to the Legionary pattern that we wore. A long sword hung from a decorated baldric crossing his chest and a red and brown checked cloak was broched on his shoulders. Unlike his men, he chose to wear his hair in a natural style with his dirty blond locks tumbling down his shoulders. As was the custom with his kind, he sported a thick droopy moustache.

'Romans!' he bellowed out across the water in coarsely accented Latin. 'You go no further into our land! Take your armies of murderers and thieves and leave! Withdraw your forces from our territories and we will spare your lives. Try to push any further into this land and the only soil you will win are the graves you are buried in!'

His words were brave but surely even he could see that, despite his superior numbers, we would overcome their defence and claim victory?

He stood, arms spread and turning to look up and down our formations, waiting for the reply that would not come until at last, he called an end to the suspense.

'So be it! Then by all the gods that protect this land know this, you have seen your last dawn and now, you will die!'

As he spat the words at us his assembled army erupted into gales of howling and cheering. He punched the air with his shield, yelling furiously at us as the Britons pelted us with sling shot which began to fly across the river dividing us. The front ranks threw their shields up as the stones struck home, banging off the faces of the *scuta* and ripping into the rolling waters, disturbing them with an eruption of small splashes as some of the shot landed around the bank area. Instantly we heard the familiar clatter of ratchets being wound back as the entire battery of *ballistae* and *catapultae* were made ready to loose their deadly messengers.

'Mark that man!' ordered one of the other Centurions as he shouted up to the crews on the towers, pointing at the Briton in the chariot. 'Bring that bastard down! A bounty to the man who fells him!'

Wooden support struts could be heard falling as the first of the crews tipped the *ballistae* off their supports and took aim at the fleeing chariot. Once more I heard the 'whack' of the bolts leaving the machines as their fearsome power was unleashed and the bolts could be seen streaking across the river to their targets.

I watched the chariot as it turned on a tight arc and sped away from the bank, the Briton on the back holding his long thin shield aloft to protect himself and the driver as the horses were lashed up to breakneck speed. For all the skill of the driver, they could not outrun the deadly bolts as they rained down in the area of the chariot. Men fell around it as the iron-shod heads bit into their flesh and hit the body of the chariot. Their target raised his shield just in time as a bolt hammered into it and blasted it from his grip, hurling the shield to one side but deflecting the bolt from its deadly course. The chariot gained speed and pulled away from the danger area as we shouted insults after him and cursed him for his luck. I did not know it at the time but this man, this Togodumnus, would soon see his luck run out during the course of this battle!

The initial exchanges had set the tone for the morning as the Britons massed around the bank area and assailed us with slings while we returned fire with *ballistae*. Their shock had been apparent when the first of the *onagers* had been deployed to hurl stone in both blocks and fragments at the foot soldiers assembled on the bank and behind wicker screens. The noise of the *ballistae* discharging was matched by the great bang as the throwing arm of the *onagers* shot forward and hit the leather damping pads, hurling their payload far into the air only for it to come down on the opposing forces with terrible consequences. Solid stone balls would smash the wicker shields to fragments, killing and injuring anyone behind them. The stone fragments would hit their marks with equally devastating effect as the sharp stones shattered bones and ripped flesh from limbs in great, bloody chunks. These terrible weapons caused absolute chaos amongst a huge army of men who had never experienced their like before.

The Britons soon learnt that it was no longer safe to approach the bank and dropped back, shouting and screaming insults and threats from a relatively safe distance. Now and again we would prove to them that they could still be easily hit at over three hundred paces by a well trained crew. There were very few shots taken however, as we needed to preserve ammunition for closer, more profitable shooting opportunities.

By mid morning we could see the Britons milling around excitedly and forming a mass of bodies around fifty paces from the bank as they swarmed around something that had caught their attention. Soon the crowd broke and we could vaguely see a group of men in their midst. As we watched we could see the men lurching around as they were pushed and kicked back and forth. There were about twenty or so and they were now being beaten and tormented with flaming torches. Soon it became apparent that the men were clothed in mail shirts and carried equipment very familiar to us. The Britons had captured a party of Roman cavalry scouts and were about to demonstrate their hospitality to us. Furious shouting rose amongst our ranks as we realized what was about to happen but we were forced to watch helplessly as the artillery crews were forbidden to shoot in case we hit our own men.

The Britons wasted little time in seizing an opportunity to demonstrate their hatred and contempt for us. They revelled in our furious shouts, taunting and goading us as they tortured their doomed captives. The screams of the men rang out across the gap between the forces as the Britons inflicted excruciating tortures on the cavalrymen. Fingers were broken or hacked off and ears sliced to the delight of the baying mob that surrounded the men. We roared blood curdling threats of vengeance as the men were stripped of their armour and clothing and beaten into the dirt. I never believed that I could feel such outrage and fury as I did when I watched the savage mob cut the men's genitals from their still living bodies and taunt them with their own parts, spitefully waving the dismembered flesh before their bloodied and pain wracked faces.

Eventually, the screams began to fade as, what tormented life the cavalrymen held onto, slowly ebbed away from them. We grew a little quieter as we saw warriors taking up position near to their unfortunate captives, the captors brandishing the men's own *spathas* as they prepared to end the cruel spectacle. The first blow delivered, the Briton surveyed the bloodstained blade, seemingly evaluating its quality as the severed head rolled onto the ground. Slowly he bent down and picked up the head and raised it in the air along with the captured weapon. Then he impaled the head on the blade tip, parading his new trophy to his comrades who whooped with delight. The remaining captives were quickly decapitated and the ritual of displaying the heads repeated for each until at last, it was done! The final act of the tragedy was played out by their cavalry who slung the headless corpses across their mounts and rode to the river bank. By the side of the river they shoved the shattered bodies off where they rolled down the bank and slipped into the silent water, there to drift lazily downstream with the current.

Orders were just being issued for a rider to gallop downstream with instructions for the recovery of the bodies when another commotion rose amongst the assembled Britons. As we watched we saw their cavalry race off in the direction of the bend in the river, about a mile and a half downstream from us. Their infantry began to fragment and a contingent began to move in the same direction along with a sizeable force of chariots. It must be the Batavians!

Unknown to the Britons, several *Cohorts* of Batavian Auxilia had moved into position beyond the large bend downstream in the river. They were expert in the art of fording deep waters in full armour and capable of emerging from the most arduous of swims ready to fight. Whilst the Britons had been distracted by our presence, the Batavians had obviously forded the river and their presence had now been discovered by the Britons who were racing to engage them before they were outflanked.

I could see livestock being hurriedly moved away from the land where the engagement was about to take place, their herdsmen were pushing cattle and sheep through the back fields in an attempt to deny them to Roman forces and move them further up river. Even now, every Roman on that bank knew that such an act was doomed to failure. We watched as their forces were drawn downstream and then cheered as a momentary panic gripped the remaining force. Now, they had discovered that another flanking force was approaching them from up river. II Augusta had skirted our positions in a broad arc the previous day and moved into position close to the crossing without the knowledge of the Britons. Having forded the river earlier in the morning they had waited just out of sight until word reached them that the Batavians had completed their crossing. A huge and deadly trap had just been sprung and the last thing the defending Britons should be worried about was the safety of their livestock!

For the next few hours, the Britons fought a desperate action on two fronts. Bravely, it must be said, pushing back at the tide of military might that threatened to engulf them. It was here that I saw Togodumnus fall.

He must have been part of the force that had first set out to defend against the Batavian crossing for I saw his chariot returning from that direction two hours later, along with a force very much depleted from the numbers I had originally seen leave. The chariots were making use of the flat land running alongside the river to speed their progress as they returned to engage Vespasian's force and that was to be his downfall. Almost as soon as they hove into view the artillery crews had spotted them and made their weapons ready. A detachment of Legionary *Sagittarii* ran down to the bank and also waited for their chance.

As the chariots and cavalry raced parallel to our ranks we jeered and called at them, hammering on our shields. Over the din of our calls I heard the wave of artillery being loosed and watched as the bolts ripped into the fast moving but tightly packed force. The archers let go their shafts and they soared into the sky, falling like black rain amongst the Britons with devastating effect. Togodumnus was almost level with my formation when the bolts struck. I saw the first of them rip into the neck of the nearest horse in his team. The animal fell instantly, pulling its mate with it and destabilizing the whole chariot, tipping it over so that it slammed into the earth in a shower of flying muck and splintered wood. The driver hit the ground head first and I saw his neck break instantly as his body rammed itself into the ground at an impossible angle. Togodumnus was thrown further away as he had been standing at the time the horse was hit. As he landed he was struck by another chariot. The impact must have broken his legs as he seemed to struggle frantically, pushing with his arms in an attempt to rise and stand, but to no avail. He spun as the first arrow hit him in the chest, its white fletchings clearly visible as it protruded from his mail shirt. The second arrow pinned his left hand to his leg and we heard him screaming in pain, even over our own triumphant cheering. It was as though a great hand had swatted him, knocking him backwards as the *ballista* bolt smashed into his face and travelled out of the back of his head, burying itself in the yoke of a ruined chariot and leaving him twisted and lifeless on the ground. Nobility he may have been but his death was just as miserable as the poorest of foot soldiers.

We stood in reserve for the remainder of the day as the battle raged before our eyes. We had nothing to do but watch the Britons race back and forth, desperately trying to repel the Roman forces on their flanks. every time their forces were pushed close to the bank we would rain artillery down on them, forcing them back and denying them any respite. The Britons put up a vicious defence of their side of the river and held our forces off until just before nightfall when the Roman forces were pulled back to regroup for the night and prepare for the final attack the next day.

What remained of the enemy force stayed in the field that night. There was no singing or merriment this time, just the now familiar sounds of men and horses giving voice to their pain and torment as they lay out on the far fields, wounded and dying. Their comrades who had survived without injury would be lying close to them, exhausted and knowing that tomorrow, it would all begin again.

As for us? For the rest of the night we remained on alert as we waited for the dawn to arrive so that we could finish the job. As time passed, the moans and screams grew less but the stench of death and battle began to rise and thicken, drifting over to us as we kept watch on the enemy positions. Little was said, we just ate and drank and waited patiently.

Fighting resumed just after the rise of the new dawn as II Augusta moved down towards *Durobrivae* in a concerted effort to smash the remaining force of Britons. Instead of moving to engage their attackers the Britons remained in position close to the settlement, choosing a standing fight rather than a running battle. In the early stages they had fought with speed and versatility, making great use of cavalry and chariots. The new day saw them with a battered and depleted mobile force and suffering heavy losses of foot soldiers. For all their spirit they could no longer stand the human cost of another mauling without risking total defeat.

The end had arrived with the rain at noon. By then XX Valeria had crossed the river and supported the push by II Augusta. Light, warm drops of rain fell gently onto the battlefield as Century strength wedge formations smashed into the assembled Britons, fragmenting them into groups that were engaged by running lines of Legionaries from the support force. Soon we could see native riders galloping frantically through the remaining packs of Britons, the order to withdraw had been given and they were beginning to disengage and run north.

Losing no time, we were formed up and marched to the crossing points upstream where we forded the river. So far the rain had not intensified and the river was not yet swollen so a rapid crossing was essential. Half of IX Hispana accompanied us whilst the other half took charge of our old positions and began immediate preparation to construct a bridge over the river. Our artillery was left in position in the unlikely event that the Britons would counter attack during the rout.

Within two hours of marching we had reached the settlement of *Durobrivae* and had formed up just short of the settlement waiting for orders. The dead lay all around us, sometimes in small heaps, sometimes in ones and twos. The gentle rain had began to wash the corpses of their grime and small crimson rivers meandered through the human debris, eventually settling and soaking into the soil. In an already rich agricultural land, *Durobrivae* would be fertile for years to come.

The familiar wailing of the women reached us from inside the compound and I knew that their fate was sealed. This had been no quick, decisive engagement such as *Durovernum Cantiacorum*, this had been a bloody, protracted battle that had cost the lives of many more Roman soldiers than the previous engagement. For the first time, we had witnessed our own soldiers being tortured to death before our very eyes. Now the Britons would have to learn why nobody should ever dare to stand against the will of Rome!

The gate to the settlement was opened and a middle aged man stepped forth, walking slowly up the track towards the waiting soldiers. He wore his hair tied back and was adorned with a simple natural coloured long woollen tunic. Some form of talisman was suspended around his neck and, even at a distance, it was apparent that his face, hand and arms were adorned with swirling blue tattoos. The ranks parted as Sabinianus rode towards the man and halted in front of him, leaning forward on his thigh with his elbow, waiting with mild curiosity for the man to speak.

'Great lord!' he began humbly in a voice which sounded as though he were more a native of Northern Gaul, 'I am Ademarus. Chief priest to the people within and spokesman for the community who have done nothing to harm you!'

He stood with dignity and courage as he pleaded his case before our commander. The very survival of his people depended on the words he would use now. As I watched him I realized that he was a brother of the Druid faith and I wondered if he would try to cast one of their foul spells on the General. Men began to mutter restlessly as they realized just what this man was and what he might try to bring down upon us.

'Your victory is complete this day, mighty Roman!' he continued. 'You have no need to harm the old men, women and children that remain and dwell in yonder homes. Take what you need and leave us in peace!'

Sabinianus drew his sword with a hiss and nudged his horse forward. Ademarus flinched when the blade appeared but defiantly stood his ground as the mount and rider casually sauntered towards him. The horse halted before the Druid, turning sideways as Ademarus stood, looking up at Sabinianus. He spread his hands wide, silently imploring him to grant his people mercy.

'As to taking what I need,' smiled Sabinianus, 'this will be done with, or without, your say so!'

Ademarus bowed gently in deference then raised his face once more to listen to Sabinianus.

'I will also confer peace upon you!' he continued. 'But I can only grant the peace of the dead!'

Sabinianus' smile changed to a mask of contempt as he plunged his blade into the Druid's throat and twisted. Shifting back in his saddle as the dying priest's blood spurted towards him in a sticky crimson arc and spattered his gleaming armour. Ademarus fell to his knees, a choking, gurgling sound bubbling from his mouth, then he fell forwards and lay face down in a spreading dark pool, his arms and legs twitching as death took a grip of him. Sabinianus turned in his saddle and shouted to us.

'See that this place never defies Rome again!'

A huge cheer roared out as the entire force ran like an undisciplined mob towards the stockade. I was cheering wildly as I ran and could hear my comrades whooping all around me as we descended on the settlement. Screams rose from inside as the undefended walls were swarmed and we spilled into the compound. Everything inside seemed to be screaming in stark terror as we began the killing. Human screams were accompanied by that of their livestock. The shrill piercing squeals of pigs being joined by the panicking bleats and wails of goats and sheep. Soon the roar of flames added to the chaotic din as we ran amok inside their homes, frenziedly killing and looting. It seemed as though the noises and the presence of stark fear and murderous death just maddened us further. Stealing and killing as we went, I felt nothing for the people that fell before me. They would slit my throat at the first opportunity. Better that I survive and they perish. Their women would only spawn more of our enemies and their children were mere bastards that would grow to fight us. They chose to oppose us and now they reaped their reward. It was that simple!

As the day turned to a rainy grey dusk, we finished with *Durobrivae*. Eventually, we made our way back to set up camp, pausing only to loot the bodies of the dead Britons for gold and other valuable items. Weary now, I looked over my shoulder and watched the great flames leaping into the air as they consumed the thatched roofs of the round houses. A small, hairy black pig flopped lifelessly under my arm. After a day such as this, that would taste good tonight!

Chapter 16

Towards the Tamesis

By mid morning the next day the process of clearing the aftermath of two days of vicious fighting was well underway. Whilst the XX Valeria and II Augusta had chased the enemy north with a large force of Auxilia, we had remained behind to establish another resupply base and construct a bridge which would allow road access to the area between here and the next great obstacle, a major river known to us as the *Tamesis*.

My head still felt fuzzy from the previous night's drinking and feasting when we gathered and celebrated our victory. Discipline had crumbled that night after Sabinianus had allowed us to sack and burn the helpless settlement before us. We had ran amok, killing, burning and looting. When it was done we had taken the best of the women that still lived and taken our pleasure with them. After so much killing we needed the release of self indulgent pleasure and the women that did not lay butchered owed us that price. Sabinianus was determined that the Britons would not fight to defend settlements once more and the best way to warn them off was to show them the price of that defence.

What women still survived the next morning lay curled up in corners or wandering the fields in a trance like state. The remains of their clothes were torn and ragged, flapping around over bruised, bloodied and filth stained limbs or clutched close to their breasts to protect what little dignity they had left as they drifted around the lines, sobbing quietly or muttering unintelligible gibberish as they went. Ignored now by the busy soldiers who had paid them so much brutal attention the previous evening.

As was customary in time of war, we had been allowed to take whatever we wished, our reward for the successes of the campaign so far and to act as brutal messengers for the army commanders. Now it was finished. Discipline had again taken hold and the duties of the day carried on as usual, punctuated only by the presence of these pathetic broken wraiths as they wandered a world that had changed forever. Eventually they were picked up by the slave traders who trailed the marching columns. They would grumble disapprovingly as they collected what little damaged merchandise they could. Shackling them in chains and stringing them out into spiritless lines of people who shuffled along, broken and violated, oblivious of what would become of them now.

Once more we set about reclaiming equipment from the field and I again found myself busy for days, sorting and repairing weapons and equipment ready for reissue. As I worked, all around me the efficiency of the war machine was in evidence. Bodies were removed and disposed of by various methods. The supplies and livestock that had been hoarded here by the Britons were now being inventoried and allocated space in a newly constructed storage area. The old settlement area was cleared of the charred remains of its buildings and new buildings were already being marked out and floors laid down as *Durobrivae* took on a new, Roman identity.

Across the river the IX Hispana worked steadily to extend the new timber bridge that would allow the carriage of men and supplies to our side. Men had swum the river with lines and we used them to haul thick ropes over to our side. These would guide the derrick they had constructed to drive piles deep into the river bed.

Once the floating platform had started its work the progress of the bridge was swift. Great wrought iron points had been forged in *Portus Rutupiae* and delivered to the site along with prefabricated sections of buildings. The iron points had been fitted to locally cut timbers and then fed out to the floating derrick as it placed them in the water. A huge timber block weighted with bags of earth was then hoisted above the tops of the massive timbers and dropped repeatedly onto the tops, hammering the piles down into the river bed. When sufficient numbers of piles were in place, carpenters followed and connected the piles with beams to complete the skeleton of the bridge before finally adding the deck.

For two weeks we concentrated on establishing the supply base and new headquarters that would be crucial in supporting a continued thrust north. From dawn until dusk, every day, all that could be heard was the clamour of the construction work. The sound of axes felling trees in nearby woodland drifted across to join the rasp of saws as timber was fashioned into the carcasses of buildings. Constant hammering rang out as nails and dowels were driven home or chisels were used to chop out joints in the fresh wood. Eventually, roofs began to appear over the level of the new defensive palisade and soon after that we received orders to move north and join the main force as they prepared to move from the crossing point of the *Tamesis* and push for *Camulodunum*, the greatest prize so far. Of any of the *oppida* known to us, *Camulodunum* was the most important of all. It was a major trading port lying a little way inland on another large river and, more importantly it was the wealthy tribal capital of the *Trinovantes* who, along with the *Catuvellauni*, were the two tribes who pursued violent expansionist policies and were actively resisting our advance. With Togodumnus dead, the fall of *Camulodunum* would be a great blow to the Britons and would hopefully reduce the will to fight of the surviving brother, Caratacus.

* * *

'Come on then! Let's get it on the shoulder or we'll be in the shit with Fatalis if were not fell in on time!'

Zenas had just overseen the packing and stowing of the tent onto the mule train and was now gathering the *Contubernium* to join the column. As instructed we pulled our equipment together. Shields were sheathed in their leather covers and slung on straps over our left shoulders, the *Pila* and *Impedimenta* were hefted onto our right shoulder and we made our way over to the column, the clanking and jingling of our kit mixing with the idle chatter as we took our place within the Century.

Fatalis stalked up and down one side of the formation, conducting a mental head count as Mestrius surveyed the other.

'Right, shut your chatter you animals!' snapped Fatalis as he continued to conduct his survey. 'We're about to start a route march. Not take a stroll down to the damn baths!'

We had only just picked up our equipment but, already I was starting to sweat with the weight of full marching order in the growing heat of the summer morning. I rolled my shoulders to position my load more comfortably as we waited to move. Pacatianus stood behind me and reached forward, untwisting my baldric strap and whispering forward as he straightened the leather.

'I'll dress you then, you scruffy bastard!'

Zenas looked back over his shoulder, grinning and mouthed the words, 'shut up!'

'Listen up you lot!' Instructed Fatalis as he addressed us one last time before we set off. 'We are an easy day's march from our next objective, which is the bridge over the River *Tamesis*!'

Having finished his head count he moved centrally to the column and stepped back so that he could see us all.

'The distance is easy but the day is going to be hot so I will allow us rest breaks every hour so that you can ease your loads and drink your fill! I don't want any spreading out at the stops as the land we are moving towards is apparently very marshy and the XX at least suffered losses to the terrain when they chased the Britons from *Durobrivae*, so stay close!

'There will be stops along the route where you can replenish your water supplies, so take the opportunity now to have a good drink and we will move out in five minutes!'

With that, Fatalis turned and walked over to a gathering of the other Centurions at the head of the column while we began to remove the stoppers from water skins and bottles and damp down, for me at least, an already growing thirst.

'Do you reckon we'll get any trouble on the march then?' asked Aebutius.

'No chance!' sneered Marinus. 'They've got to get through our lot on the *Tamesis* to reach us! They'd have to be stupid to try!'

'Yeah!' agreed Pacatianus. 'And we're not exactly a small force are we?'

'Maybe not,' contributed Zenas. 'But it doesn't mean that they won't try. They need to stop the advance force being bolstered up by us to save *Camulodunum*. With the local knowledge they've got they could find a way through the marshes and surprise us!'

'Oh right!' chided Marinus. 'So who suddenly turned you into a tactical expert eh?'

'Just shut your mouth Marinus!' snapped Zenas. 'And remember who runs the *Contubernium* will you?'

Marinus gave an indignant laugh and was poised to deliver his retort just as Fatalis returned and barked out his orders, effectively squashing any continuance of the squabble.

'Shoulder your loads. Prepare to move!'

Shortly after the march began the formation split into three smaller groups. The intention was to reduce the size of the column, thereby avoiding a large body of troops getting trapped in confined areas of the marshes if we were attacked. Smaller groups would have more room to operate and therefore mount a more effective defence, although in truth, the marshland we were entering was neither good for attack or defence so we felt ourselves reasonably safe.

As we pushed towards the *Tamesis* we came across small homesteads and settlements in the drier areas we were crossing. No longer did the occupants stand around and gawp at us as we passed through their land. Now they fled when we came into view, fearful now that the fate of *Durobrivae* would also be theirs and that the passing soldiers would slaughter them if they stayed. If we saw them making off we would hammer on our shields and shout and yell. Laughing as they fell over their own feet in their panic to escape. We knew that they would eventually return to their homes and had done so since our pursuing forces had passed this way previously, so nothing was done to the property they left behind. It would serve no purpose and besides, it was obvious that they already realized the price of resistance.

Fatalis had been true to his word and our march had been an easy one with no need to force the pace as in the previous marches from the landing areas. A party of cavalry had met with our own scouts and joined up with us to escort us through the marshland. Guiding us to the assembly points around the bridge that the Britons had carelessly left intact as they fled the pursuing army. As we made our way through the treacherous ground I could feel my feet springing in the soft ground and hoped that the track was a well tried and tested one. With all this equipment we carried, if anyone went under, they'd never come up again!

Many varieties of birds flew above us as we walked and we frequently disturbed flocks of water fowl as we progressed. At least there was a plentiful supply of food at hand with all these birds and, where there was water, there was usually fish. If we were to be camped here for a while, at least we would not starve! The thought of food made me suddenly hungry and I looked forward to the end of the march so that we could pitch camp and eat.

Once we had arrived at the bridge we were immediately moved across to the far bank and into the defensive area used by the XX Valeria. We were to relieve them on the hostile side so that they could withdraw back across the river and recover from the defence of the bridge. They and the other forces who had pushed up to the crossing in pursuit of the Britons had fought a defensive action for the best part of two weeks and they were exhausted. The Britons had kept up continuous raiding with small parties constantly harassing them and forcing the defenders of the bridge to remain in readiness until our arrival. It seemed, for now, that the Britons had learned to apply rapid attacks with small amounts of men, rather than engage the Roman forces in large costly battles.

Immediately that we had moved into position we were organized into defensive parties and allocated our own areas to defend. Rosters were drawn up for the manning of ramparts, day and night, and extra artillery was set up to deal with incoming raiders. Little of the artillery had made its way this far north as yet so the pieces that we had carried with us were of vital importance to the defence strategy.

Now that we had arrived to reinforce the area there would soon be a push to spread east along the north bank so that the area could be cleared of hostile forces.

Once this side of the river was secure along the stretch to the east we could sail the *Classis Britannica* down river to us and open up another line of supply. At present it was dangerous for shipping to sail so far down as they were vulnerable to attack from the bank and the risk of losing ships and supplies was unacceptable.

For around three weeks we concentrated our forces on the area around the bridge. Units were rotated regularly to avoid drops in morale, everyone sharing defence work, aggressive patrolling and general duties with equal measure. Eventually our control spread as intended and soon shipping was reaching us from the main supply ports bringing new equipment, provisions and limited reinforcements from Gaul. The Britons maintained their harrying attacks, but even they must have known that it was futile by now. A huge force had accumulated around the bridge and it was only a matter of time before we pushed for *Camulodunum*. The attacks now became more of an irritation to us as the Britons would charge in on their chariots and goad our forces. They quickly got the measure of the ranges of the catapults after their first forays had ended in disaster. Having lost too many men to the deadly machines they would stay out of range and attack patrols as they moved through the hostile areas.

Again we saw their preoccupation with the taking of heads. If they succeeded in their attacks they would parade triumphantly before us, careful not to venture within range of the artillery, and wave the severed heads of our fallen comrades at us, cheering savagely. On several occasions our cavalry chased them off but the Britons would never relinquish the heads, preferring to lash them to their saddles and then fight to retain them. It was only later that we learned that they believed that possession of an enemy's head meant possession of his soul and that the head was a magical and sacred talisman which they displayed at the entrances to their settlements. They believed that the head had the power to protect their property from evil and, in a curious sort of way, it was a mark of respect to their slain enemy.

With the appearance of the navy in the waters close to the bridge came the realization that we now controlled the *Tamesis* and the open waterways around its tidal estuary. Plautius' policy of aggressive patrolling had gradually allowed us to take control of the land to the east of us which would lead us to our prize at *Camulodunum*. Confirmation soon came that the river had also been forded further upstream and friendly forces were now in control of the ground over which we would march on the tribal capital. We moved out immediately, anxious to capitalize on our newly created advantage.

Our march was swift and unopposed as the great force bore down on its objective. Cavalry scouts had made various sightings of small forces of Britons but the encounters invariably came to naught as they merely monitored our progress, watching powerless as we closed inexorably with *Camulodunum*. Surely they must know now that it would be futile to resist us? They had never won against us and now, depleted and weary as they were, they had no chance of victory. Better to bend the knee now than be wiped from the face of the earth as though they had never existed.

The journey ended about ten miles short of *Camulodunum* on a broad, open plain. Awaiting our arrival on the top of a gently falling gradient was a considerable force of Auxiliary infantry and cavalry. Newly landed from *Gaul*, they had moved ahead of us to set up defence works of lines of sharpened stakes and artillery towers and there they waited, watching the lower end of the plain where the Britons waited to engage us in one final battle.

'I can't believe they still have the will to fight us!' said Surus incredulously as we settled in for the night.

'Perhaps they welcome death above the prospect of Roman rule!' observed Pacatianus. 'There is something to be said for their courage at least. They still face us, knowing that all is lost. How can they possibly win against a force this big?'

'I don't know.' said Aebutius. 'But I don't like this at all. Why would they want to fight when there is no point?'

'Use your head man!' snapped Zenas. 'You'll get used to seeing this if you live much longer. This is their homeland. They will fight to the last drop of blood to defend it! I hope Claudius gets everything he wishes for from this shit hole of a country because, as sure as you like, this place will cost us a lot of men before we're done!'

'Do you think we'll be army reserve tomorrow? Or will they perhaps let us have a go at those blue painted savages down there?' enquired Crispus.

'Who gives a damn anyway?' moaned Surus 'We've marched halfway across the world to chase these damn Britons about and play decoy for those glory grabbing bastards in the Twentieth and the Second. I'm bored with all this carry on now and, if I have to cross one more river in this damnable bloody country I'll go mad!'

'Why don't you shut that fat hole in your face boy?' snapped Marinus. 'I've got more teeth in my head than you've got months in this army and now you're bored? Go home if you can't take it, you snivelling little boy!'

'You call me boy once more and you'll have a few less teeth to be going on with. Why do you always think you're so clever, you spiteful old bastard!'

Marinus sprang up from the cloak he was sitting on and lunged forwards. As soon as I saw him move I jumped for Surus knocking him to the floor and pinning him down while Pacatianus and Crispus rushed Marinus, forcing him away from his quarry.

'Don't you test me boy!' He spat viciously as he stabbed his finger over Crispus' shoulder at Surus. 'I'll slip a piece of iron into your guts, then we'll see who's the clever one!'

Zenas shot up and stood between the two as they glared savagely at each other, eyeing one then the other.

'You!' He snapped pointing to Surus. 'You stay down or, by the gods, I'll sit you back down if you don't obey!' He whirled round to face the furious Marinus, still being restrained by Crispus and Pacatianus.

'And you!' He snapped accusingly, jabbing a finger at Marinus. 'Tomorrow any number of us could lay dead on that field out there! Do you think you have the right to take a comrade's life because you don't like what you hear?'

Zenas seemed frozen in time as he stood as still as a statue and stared at Marinus. Slowly Pacatianus and Crispus released their grip on him and the angry expression faded to a look of grudging compliance as he spread his hands and backed away.

'Any more trouble out of any of you and I'll be speaking with Fatalis and you can take the matter up with him. We fight for each other, not amongst each other. Now get some sleep, tomorrow is going to be a hard day!'

Chapter 17

The Test of a Man

Light drizzle and a gentle breeze drifted in from the distant coastline as we made final preparation for the coming battle. A light grey bar of sky lit the distant morning horizon while dark grey layers of thick rain clouds swirled ominously overhead. Last minute preparations were being made to the defences which would protect us from any advances the Britons were likely to make against our reserve areas and artillery positions. The morning was cool and peaceful but all knew that the peace was likely to be in stark contrast against what was to come this day.

Our very first task of the morning had been to seek the favour of the gods for the coming battle. We had formed up in *Cohort* formations and offered our prayers to the gods who could guide us safely through the coming endeavours. *Iuppiter* was father of the gods and it would be he who could strike the Britons with thunder and lightening and deluge them with rain, smiting them with the forces of the sky before they could even engage us. If it pleased him for us to engage them then *Mars* would give us the skill and strength to wage deadly warfare on the field whilst the goddess *Victoria* would ensure that the enemy were vanquished and Rome remained supreme over all. There was nothing to fear when the gods were with you!

Extra *ballistae* were being hoisted to the tops of the specially built towers as we began to form battle lines along the forward edges of the defences. The crews were already beginning to identify their arcs of fire and assess the ranges of reference points in the land. Soon they would send out ranging shots, allowing them to bring down instantly effective fire when required. The lethal efficiency of these machines had been proven time and time again through countless years of warfare with the enemies of Rome. The Britons had soon learned of their potency and would have to face them again if they wished to attack our reserve areas. They would also have to negotiate the anti cavalry stakes that bristled along the top of the slope, avoiding the deadly little traps that lay in wait before they even reached the more obvious dangers. Our formations had already been briefed on the clear routes through the fields of traps but the Britons would have no such knowledge and would inevitably fall foul of the waiting surprises if they ventured too far up. *Stimuli* lay in numerous concealed shallow pits in front of the wooden stakes. Painful and crippling surprises if the Britons were able to negotiate the ground forward of this which was liberally sewn with *caltrops,* able to cripple the unshod soldier or embed itself in the soft underside of a horses hoof.

Confident of our defences, we waited in the holding areas we watched as a party of cavalry set off down the slope accompanied by a delegation of officers.

The bright standards streamed behind them in the morning breeze as they made their way towards the centre of the ground between us and the Britons who, by now, were cheering and screaming wildly, banging thunderously on their shields. As the chaotic din echoed up the slope to us I found myself thinking that I was very glad that I was not part of the delegation that had just been dispatched to negotiate with the Britons.

The party halted at mid distance and held their ground nobly, given that they faced about thirty thousand warriors, all baying for their blood and craving possession of their severed heads. I had to admire them for their courage as they sat on their horses waiting to be joined by the envoys from the maddened horde arrayed before us. Eventually the sight of riders moving to the front of the massed warriors indicated that a delegation was on its way. A group of riders, far smaller than the waiting Roman party, slowly trotted up the slope towards their adversaries. As they drew closer, I noticed that they seemed to be grouped in threes. A central rider was flanked by two other warriors who bore shields and spears while the middle rider was bereft of armour or weapons save for a long dagger carried on his belt. The group halted and dismounted around thirty paces away from the Roman officers. Six of their number remained behind and held their mounts ready while the remaining number of around twelve made their way up the slope.

A similar party of Roman officers dismounted and met their counterparts midway between the two groups, who then began the talks that would either avert or plunge us into a large and bloody conflict that would ultimately decide who controlled the south east quarter of *Britannia*.

We waited silently for the outcome of the talks between the two delegations. Surveying the assembled host of Britons as we stood amidst the thickening drizzle, I began to tire of the sight of the waiting army and watching the droplets of water sliding down the backs of helmets as I looked around me. I wondered how many of these men would still stand if we did go into battle and what the outcome would be. How many of us would it cost to beat these damn Britons this time?

'Do you think they'll fight?' I said in a whisper. Addressing the question to nobody in particular.

'There's thousands of the bastards!' replied Pacatianus out of the corner of his mouth. 'They must outnumber us by at least ten thousand!'

'With odds like that, they'd have to be mad not to give it a go!' muttered Crispus, tucking his chin down to avoid being spotted by the officers.

'Who cares?' snorted Surus. 'Let's just get on with it and flatten them! They'll be raven food at the end of today. I know it!'

'Really? In the trust of the gods now are we?' sneered Marinus. 'How many of us will be raven food along with them then?' He asked, echoing my earlier thought.

'For the love of the gods!' exclaimed Zenas. 'Can't you lot shut it just for a bit? You're like gossiping old matrons, I swear it!'

'Eyes up !' hissed Pudens. 'They've finished. Here they come!'

The two parties had separated while we had been chattering idly and were now galloping back to their own lines. The Britons reached their own men first and I could see the riders shouting to their warriors and thrusting weapons in the air. Very quickly the whole host began to yell and scream and beat their lightweight shields with their weapons, thrusting swords and spears in our direction. The eerie sound of the *carnyx* cut through the air as they raised them in the front ranks and gave out great howling blasts on them. It reverberated around the field like a ghostly wailing amidst a cursed wind as we realized, without surprise, that they had chosen to fight.

The darkness of the cloud cover was not lifting and it seemed that there would be no prospect of better weather ahead as we watched the Centurions travelling to the rear command points to receive final briefings. Mestrius moved to the front of the Century and spied us out.

'Zenas! Is that your lot that I heard flapping their jaws around again?' he enquired, raising his head and looking down his nose at us.

'Sorry Optio!' replied Zenas. 'I did warn them!'

'Then you had better hope that they fight as well as they talk because I get the feeling that this little party is going to get very rough!'

'Yes Optio!' he replied. Embarrassment clear in his voice.

I regretted starting the small talk as Zenas had now been openly checked by the Optio, embarrassing him in front of the assembled Century. He was a good man and didn't deserve to be shamed by our lack of discipline so I resolved to apologize later for it. As I mulled over my apology I noticed three groups of three riders heading out from the enemy fronts and galloping towards us.

'What now?' I thought. 'Not more negotiations!'

As I watched, it became clear that these men were not coming to negotiate. They were actually charging us! Nine men sent to attack nearly twenty thousand troops? Madness! I could hear the drumming of the horses hooves as they closed on the front ranks of the formations forward of us and heard their war cries as they closed the gap with breakneck speed. Three of the riders hurled their light javelins at the formation and ripped their swords free, levelling them at our lines as they came on.

The officers at the front could be heard yelling out the order to form an anti cavalry wall and I could just see men falling into position as the horses came within range. Then, a wave of the javelins soared through the air, falling on the riders and mounts, felling the charge instantly in a jumble of flying clods of earth and screaming horses. While a couple of the horses thrashed round, trying to stand, the four riders who had survived the volley charged the lines on foot, screaming and whirling their swords above their heads as they came. I couldn't see what happened to them, just heard the thuds of their impact upon the shield wall and the ringing clang of metal on metal as they were engaged and cut to pieces by the front rank. A moment's silence gave way to a tumult of cheering from back down the slope as the Britons roared out after their dead warriors. Why in the name of *Dis* had they killed themselves like that? Surely, it served no purpose?

Whatever the purpose of their suicidal charge was, it galvanized our forces into action with the immediate return of the Centurions to their units and the pushing forward of Auxiliary infantry in preparation of the initial stages of battle. Cohorts I to IV Dalmatorum took front position and prepared to draw out the Britons while two Cohorts of their own Auxiliary cavalry waited on the flank to support them.

As we watched, two *Cohorts* of the Auxiliary infantry set off down the slope in tight blocks while the others took their forward positions, joined by two *Cohorts* of

Batavians acting as a reserve. It didn't take long for the Britons to charge out at the advancing force. Thousands of foot soldiers surged forward and charged up the hill to the first group of Auxiliaries who separated into Century sized formations and counter charged in wedges, slamming into the Britons and fragmenting their first wave. Fierce fighting waged at the foot of the slope as the wedges were almost engulfed in massive, loosely packed groups of Britons before the second *Cohort* charged in in running lines and engaged in brutal fighting with the enraged tribesmen.

Cavalry filtered across the head of the slope in front of us as one of the units made its way across to prepare for a charge from the left flank, leaving the other unit ready to move from the right. As the Auxiliary infantry began to draw back from the press, the Britons began to push after them in loose groups. Horns blew out from the cavalry troops and signals were exchanged between the two formations before they broke into a charge and swarmed down on the mayhem at the foot of the slope. Like a giant pincer, the cavalry smashed into the pursuing Britons on both sides simultaneously. The retreating Auxiliaries gained valuable time to regroup as the Britons now turned their attention on the cavalry. We cheered loudly in support of our forces, banging our shields and crying insults into the air, cursing the Britons for all we were worth. Suddenly, however, our cheers changed to shouts of dismay as we saw a massive force of enemy cavalry break ranks and charge towards the fight. Even at this distance, we could hear the thunder of the hooves and the jingling of harness above the shrill war cries as cavalry closed on cavalry and a chaotic battle erupted between foot and horse soldiers.

It didn't take long for the surviving Auxiliary cavalry to realize that they would be slaughtered if they remained in the fight and we watched with some relief as they pulled themselves out of the fierce fighting and galloped back towards us. As they returned the Britons had seized the initiative and were chasing them with their cavalry, rapidly closing the gap on the rear of the unit. As they drew closer the forward Auxiliary units deployed anti cavalry walls and artillery crews began to drop bolts onto their weapons, ready to fell the counter charge if they came too close.

Having got the scent of victory, the Britons closed for the kill on the Roman cavalry and came within range of the artillery which wasted no time in laying down a storm of bolts, firing over our heads and in front of the forward units. Once more we witnessed their deadly power and accuracy as the heavy bolts hurtled into the advancing Britons and destroyed the forward element as the wave of bolts hammered home. Horses pitched and screamed as riders flew through the air, thrown from their terrified mounts as the remaining force turned and fled.

The two fresh Dalmatorum Cohorts now formed tightly packed blocks as the Batavians did likewise and spread across the field in four distinct rectangular formations, allowing wide paths between each. The troops who had fought the opening engagements moved to the rear to regroup and prepare to be used in a later wave.

All across our front the order to pick up kit and prepare to move was shouted out by officers as the Auxiliary formation began to move slowly down the slope towards the seething, enraged force of waiting Britons. Fatalis appeared in front of the column, passing on his last verbal orders. From now on we would respond to signals and blasts of the *cornu* as a man could not easily make himself heard or understood in the chaos of battle.

'Listen up!' he shouted as he spread his arms as though to gather our attention. 'We follow the Auxiliaries down the hill in extended line and wait for them to engage. They will maintain the gaps you see between their formations in order to filter the enemy through in streams. As they emerge at the rear of the formations, we will engage and destroy them with rolling lines. Understood?'

'Yes Centurio!' we roared together.

'Two Pannonian cavalry *alae* are waiting in reserve and will deal with any flank attacks the Britons may try. Meantime, keep it tight and look for the order to fall back and refresh. Remember where the *cornu* and standards are and you will know where to look for signals, shout out any orders you hear so that the next man gets it! Now, Get ready to move!'

Now it was our turn. Excitement and trepidation started to build in me in equal parts as we waited for the order to move. A blast of the *cornu* and repeated shouts to shoulder *pila* came next and then we were on the move, tramping slowly down the wet slope behind the Auxiliaries while the waiting Britons jeered and chanted beyond the already countless bodies lying on the field, hammering their shields and threatening bloody murder at our approach.

Each of us concentrated heavily on our task now. We maintained an even, steady pace and looked to our sides, carefully maintaining the straightness of the line as we marched. Tight dressings were crucial if the formation was to be effective and avoid being shattered by a wild forward charge.

As we closed the gap I heard a huge roar rise from the Britons and saw their reaction to the coming threat. Caratacus had deliberately held his chariots back until we pushed him with a bigger attack. Now, with just such a threat presented to him, he unleashed the mighty force on the advancing Auxiliaries. As they sped forward they were joined by cavalry and foot soldiers in one massive, shattering charge.

Relentlessly we pushed forward as the first of the Auxiliaries were hit by the rushing mob and began to defend themselves. The hammering and screaming of battle rang out over our heads as we neared the forward units and watched the gaps between the *Cohorts* fill with charging Britons. Chariots burst forth beyond the rear of the formations and bore down on us with terrifying speed. *Cornus* sounded and the order was given to shoulder our *pila* and present shields to the front, preparing to meet the headlong charge. Swerving, the chariots swung their left sides to us and rushed along our fronts, the warrior on the back leaping from the vehicle and running screaming towards us. Many of their number seemed to surge with an elemental force. Either totally naked or, at the very most clad in breeches as they ran forwards. Their image was one of startlingly impressive savagery, with gleaming gold and bronze torcs round their wrists and necks and their bodies covered in swirling blue designs and representations of beasts. These men didn't need armour, they coursed with the force of the earth and trusted that to protect them.

The rumbling of chariot wheels, thundering hoof beats and the wild screaming of our foe grew deafening as they smashed into our ranks, slashing and hacking as they came on or stabbing wildly with spears, some of which carried razor sharp wavy edges, capable of gutting any man unfortunate enough to be impaled on one.

In an instant we had gone from a steady advance to the violent shock of impact and vicious fighting. The thrown wave of javelins had done little to assuage the fury of their assault as the Britons fell on us in droves. My shield slammed backwards as the first of the charging bodies hit it and I braced my feet, thrusting out with the shield to knock my assailant back then plunging the *gladius* into his naked torso. I gritted my teeth, grunting as I drove the weapon against the soft resistance of skin and muscle. The blade sunk deep into the twitching body and a pain wracked scream pierced my ears, already filled with the infernal din of war. A twist of the blade and another smack with the shield and he fell on the ground, muddy by now with the trampling of soldiers and the increasingly heavy rain fall.

Punch, thrust, counter punch, block and stab. The movements repeated themselves over and over again amidst the screaming, frenzied butchery of the savage battle while we forged forwards, fighting these blue painted demons, seemingly possessed of some supernatural force as they resisted every inch of our advance. Nothing could stop the slaughter, not even the anger of the gods as the sky grew ever darker with the thickening black clouds. Thunder shook the ground and lightening split the sky as men fell to the ground shattered and bleeding while their comrades fought on, slithering in the thickening, bloody mud as they strove to cut their opponents down.

The Briton rose before me like an enraged bear, his tightly muscled physique glistening with the falling rain and droplets of fresh blood, sprayed from the veins of his victims and brother warriors alike, mixing with the vivid colour of his body paintings and tattoos. His eyes glinted with a terrible spark as the long iron sword he was carrying flashed with the fire of the lightening, ripping down in an arc towards my head, water and blood flying from the blade as it sliced through the air. Instinctively, I raised my *scutum* and blocked the shattering chop, ducking under him and thrusting upwards in search of his stomach, the blade cramming itself instead between his ribs and lodging fast as I twisted and wrenched trying to free the weapon that would keep me alive.

I would have slammed the shield against him once more to free him from the blade, had it not been for another of their number hammering into my shield and flinging me backwards. The grip on my *gladius* now gone, I landed in the sucking mud, pinned between two corpses and with my shield covering my body as the enraged Briton sat atop it chopping at my face and screaming like some deranged *Lemur*. The sword he carried smashed down, cleaving a gash in the shield edge and hammering into the front of my helmet. Although the strike was numbingly painful, the brow guard of my helmet saved me from having my brains let out on the field and I struggled wildly, driven by choking fear as I pushed to free my arm from beneath the shield and grab at my *pugio*.

It seemed to feel unreal as I became aware that it was I who was now screaming, but in fear, and that my thighs were warming with the hot flow of urine that I could no longer hold in my bladder. I tried to bite him as me punched at my face and drew the blade of his sword back for another strike. My left hand became free and I lay there, staring upwards as if watching somebody else's hand as it soared upwards plunging the iron dagger into my attacker's chest. The scream hardly had time to form before the side of his face was cleaved off in one great slice and hit the mud next to me. A boot kicked the body off my shield and I heard a voice shouting at me;

'Rise boy! Get up, or you're dead!'

Fatalis grabbed the neck of my mail shirt and hoisted me up, covering me with his own shield as he lifted the edge of mine. I quickly snatched the shield up and yanked my *gladius* free from the body of my last kill, somehow being able to locate my father's sword amidst the carnage and weapons that covered the blood soaked ground. I had no chance to thank Fatalis as he disappeared as quickly as he had appeared. I resumed my place in the line and tried not to think about the sodden front of my tunic, now cooling in the air and lying heavy against my thighs.

Waves of soldiers fought against the Britons in this brutal, close up carnage for much of the day. We had been withdrawn earlier and Cohorts from the other Legions had taken their place in the line, experiencing a taste of the unrelenting savagery that raged at base of the slope. Withdrawing to our rear areas we delivered the badly wounded to the large tents that awaited them. Men sat outside being tended to by *Capsarii* who would wash the less serious wounds with *acetum* and dress them with clean bandages. A *Medicus* worked with teams of the orderlies, supervising their work and assessing the seriousness of their wounds as they arrived at the field hospital. The more seriously injured were taken inside the tents and treated under cover. Screams cut the air around the tent as men endured anything from having wounds cauterized to the amputation of limbs. It wasn't somewhere we liked to stay close to so we tended to leave as soon as we had delivered the wounded, trusting to the gods that we would see them again, fit and well once more.

By late afternoon the fighting was still raging and we were due to be sent in again. The Britons were being cleared off the field by Pannonian cavalry formations and their counterparts from the surviving Dalmatorum Auxilia. The vast stretch of field at the bottom of the slope was now littered with the dead and the ruins of chariots but the Britons were still a formidable and ever aggressive fighting force. Plautius wanted the last of the chariots to be taken care of and had dispatched the four available Cohorts of the Fourteenth to engage the Britons with three Cohorts of Batavians. *Ballistae* mounted on carts would be escorted by cavalry along the right flank and engage the chariots when they attacked the formation. Around twenty of these carts now waited below the rounded crest of the flank for the Britons to charge. Plautius knew that he would have to give the Britons Legionaries as well as Auxiliaries to attack otherwise they would probably not take the bait.

Once more, we marched down the slope towards the baying hordes, the Batavians marching on our flanks while we held the middle of the formation, a tempting prize for Caratacus' chariots and cavalry. We held the formation together as usual, keeping the extended lines tight and the pace steady as we neared the point at which we thought the Britons would charge. My heart began to pound as we drew closer and I gripped the shaft of my *pilum* tightly, determined that I would bury it in the first Briton who got close enough. They hammered their shields once more, shouting and taunting us as we drew closer until, at last, they charged.

The chariots thundered forward at the head of a mixed force of cavalry and infantry and we halted to form a defensive line, shields to the front and *pila* ready to throw, waiting for the *ballistae* to engage.

'Hold! Hold fast!' I could hear the orders being shouted up and down the line as a prickling sensation shot up and down my spine.

'Make ready. Hold fast!'

More orders as the chariots came within range and every muscle tensed in my body, waiting for the order to throw.

I heard the distant noise of *ballistae* discharging and soon saw their effect as the bolts ripped into the charging formation, cutting horses and passengers down alike as the chariots pitched over and horses ran around wildly, screaming in pain and fear. The order to make ready passed down the line in an instant and was followed immediately by the order to throw, the chariots now being around fifty paces to the front and closing fast. Waves of *pila* took to the iron grey skies and fell on the charging formation. I saw the result of my throw as it traced a high arc and plummeted down onto the driver of one of those damnable chariots. Knocking him off the back and causing the chariot to lose control, swerving into another as they hurtled towards us. I remember raising my shield as the horses ran in a blind panic towards us and then turned, avoiding the shield wall and slewing the chariot round, sending it crashing and rolling towards us. All I could do was watch as the tumbling mass of crashing timber somersaulted my way. In the tightly packed formation in which I stood, there was nowhere to go so I closed my eyes and waited.

I remember an impact, as though *Iuppiter* himself had struck me with his massive hand and then, nothing, just blackness.

I remember the awakening, slowly and painfully my consciousness began to return as my senses began to quicken, one by one. My head spun and pounded with a terrible pain that seemed to come from the very core of my head. My neck was stiff and sore and I had difficulty raising my head to see where I lay. Slowly my blurred and blackened vision began to adjust to the dim interior of the large tent and I blinked, trying to force my eyes to focus. The rushing in my ears began to subside and gradually my hearing adjusted to my surroundings, tuning in on the sounds of the other soldiers in the tent. Now I could hear them cursing their pain or groaning out their misery and discomfort at their injuries. Slowly I began to realize that I was in one of the field hospitals close to the battlefield.

I tried to raise myself on an elbow and screamed out in pain as a searing hot agony shot through my right forearm. Tormented, I rolled to my left and gingerly levered myself into a sitting position with my good arm. My head spun violently and I felt ready to spew as a wave of dizziness passed over me. Then it was gone and I began to take in my surroundings.

The floor of the spacious tent was covered with dry rushes and straw and, on top of that lay the soldiers, filling the floor space as they lay on thick army blankets some moving, some not. The scent of vomit and excrement filled my nostrils and, once again I felt myself starting to retch as the smell pervaded my nostrils. The centre of the tent was occupied by long narrow tables, some of which contained medical equipment and some of which were covered with bloodstained linen.

A soldier lay quietly on one with his hands folded across his stomach. As I studied his still form I realized that nothing more could be done for him. The bottom of the table was soaked with blood from his mangled leg, the worst of which had been removed below the knee. No doubt the pain and blood loss had been too much for him and he had succumbed, leaving this brutal world for a better, more peaceful place.

'Take this one out lads.' A quiet voice said as I watched the *Capsarius* enter my widening field of vision accompanied by two soldiers carrying a stretcher. He indicated to the still form on the table and watched solemnly as the two soldiers gently lifted the dead man and placed him on the stretcher, picking it up and moving to the flaps of the tent, carefully stepping between the legs of the wounded as they went.

He wiped the palms of his hands on his blood spattered brown woollen tunic and picked up a clean scrap of linen, wiping his forehead as he turned, finally noticing me as I remained sat up, watching him.

'Ah! You're awake then!' He smiled, stating the obvious. 'How do you feel?'

'You really want to know? I croaked, as I realized that my throat was bone dry. 'I'm thirstier than a horse!'

'Not yet my friend. I need to get a *Medicus* to check you over first!'

I groaned and tried to swallow as the *Capsarius* left the tent in search of the *Medicus*. Again I looked around me, searching the faces of my neighbours, wondering if anyone else I knew had ended up in here. I tried hard to focus in the dim light then slowly began to recognize the soldier lying on my immediate left. Zenas!

'Oh gods no. Zenas!' I gasped.

He looked a fright. His face was badly bruised and swollen on one side and his left eye was shut. A crust of dried blood wreathed his forehead where the rim of his helmet had dug into him and a thin line of black blood trickled slowly from the corner of his mouth. As I spoke his name his one good eye slowly opened and he looked towards me. A light smile curved his lips and his right hand stretched towards me. I grasped the hand, squeezing it as I looked on in despair at what had happened to him. He began to mouth something but I couldn't hear him properly. I leant closer and bent over his face, my own pain unimportant now. I was startled by a low cough which spotted my face with his blood. I tried hard to hear him as he strove to make himself understood but could only make out a low rattle as the blood frothed up in his mouth.

'Zenas, what ... Why are ... ?'

I couldn't find the words to express the shock I felt as I looked upon his broken body. I couldn't understand what had become of him, then, slowly I realized he had been very close to me in the formation as the chariot hit us. I looked to the eaves of the tent where our armour had been laid above our blankets. The *lorica segmentata* that Zenas wore was caved in all along its left side. Loose plates hung from torn leather straps and the armour was caked in mud where he had fallen onto the field. He must have been hit by the same chariot that I had. Even worse! I realized that it was my *pilum* that had felled the driver!

'Oh Zenas, I ... '

He squeezed my hand, seeming to know what I was thinking and slowly rolled his head from side to side, mouthing the word 'no'.

A wave of remorse engulfed me as I remembered how I had started the talking that got him a reprimand from Mestrius just before we had gone into battle. I remembered the look of embarrassment on his face and my heart weighed heavy with the knowledge that I was to blame and it would probably not now be possible to make amends for it.

'Zenas, I'm sorry. I didn't mean to get you in trouble!' I clasped his hand with both of mine and leant closer to him. 'Don't go. We need you with us to keep us in line. You must stay!'

Again he gave a thin smile as he struggled to lift his head. His mouth began to move again and I strained once more to listen. Softly the word passed his lips.

'...Victory...!'

His hand softened in my palms and I lifted my head to look at him, dreading what I knew I would see. Zenas was gone.

It seemed to last an eternity as I sat next to him, trying to remember all that we had done in his presence and what I had learned from him. I still held his cooling hand as I felt the presence of somebody behind me.

'The *Medicus* is here lad!'

I looked over my shoulder and saw the *Capsarius* standing there with Sextilli. Sextilli! I hadn't seen him for so long!

'I didn't think he'd last as long as this!' said Sextilli quietly as he nodded gently towards Zenas. 'His innards were damaged by a terrible impact and I expected that he would fade in the night. He held on though and made sure his hand was on yours throughout the night. Who was he?'

'Zenas. My *Contubernium* leader!' I said proudly.

Sextilli nodded his head and gestured to him once more.

'Then it looks like he stayed to keep an eye on you one more time. Just until he knew you were alright!'

I nodded sadly as I turned to look at him once more.

'Come on lad!' said Sextilli finally. 'He's done his bit. I need to do mine!'

I submitted myself to his examination, answering his questions and moving my limbs as requested. I could comply with the demands of the moment without thought but my mind was still out on the battlefield where we were all last together and I wondered what had become of the rest of my brothers. Were they alive or did they lie dead somewhere out on the field?

Eventually Sextilli allowed me to go. The injury to my arm was not serious enough to stop me marching with the baggage train but would keep me out of action for a while. The muscles had been badly bruised and a heavy gash had required cauterizing and stapling. All I could do now was clean the wound daily with *acetum* and dress it with clean bandages and a honey poultice. It would heal soon enough!

After promising to keep up with the treatment I was allowed to go. I collected my equipment and made for the shaft of daylight that pierced the gloom of the tent. Just something else needed to be taken care of before I went. I crossed over to where Zenas still lay and searched through his belongings until I had found what I needed.

Zenas always carried the little figure of the *Genius* in his armour when we fought. It would need a new guardian now. As I crouched by his side I fished around in my pouch, retrieving a silver *denarius* and turning it in my fingers. Normally a bronze coin was used for such things but I decided that Zenas' passage would be special. I gently prised open his mouth and placed the coin inside, before placing my hand over his heart.

'Safe journey brother, may the gods speed you on your way!'

Quietly, I gathered my things and left the tent.

Chapter 18

Hail Claudius!

I still felt a little shaky as I stepped out of the tent and into cleaner air. Although the day was grey and miserable the light still pained my eyes and a dull ache throbbed behind them. I wasn't too concerned as Sextilli had warned me of these symptoms and their persisting for a day or two so I set about carrying on with my business and ignoring them as much as I could. I stood for a moment, trying to take in the bustle going on around me. My first priority was to find my unit and rejoin them, but where? Things were so different here now!

The ground was now like a swamp, badly scarred by the ruts of cart wheels and pitted with the to and fro of men and horses. Muddy brown puddles filled the scrapes and men trudged through the sucking mud, cursing their luck for ending up in such a rainy, forsaken hole like Britannia. These soldiers however, were different. I rubbed the back of my neck and puzzled at the new shield insignias and, as well as these new men ... *Praetorians*! What in the name of *Iuppiter* were the *Praetorian Guard* doing here? I'd seen them once, in *Portus Itius*, but here? Why? I couldn't fathom things out. It was as though I had woken up in a new world. Everything was so different!

The bewilderment on my face must have been written large as I stood there trying to puzzle out what had happened. Before long, an Optio strode over to me and clapped his hand on my shoulder.

'What's the matter lad? You don't look as if you're rowing with all of your oars! Are you lost?'

'I need to find my unit Optio, but I can't see where they should be!'

I avoided his eyes and continued to cast around the campsite, trying to spot a familiar face. A dizzy spell swept over me and I began to sway before the Optio who clapped his hands either side of my shoulders to steady me.

'What unit are you lad?' he enquired, a slight look of concern on his face. 'I can see you're one of the Fourteenth boys!'

'Cohort III Optio. In the Century of Fatalis!'

'One of Fatalis' lads are you?' He rubbed his chin, looking me up and down. 'They got a bad mauling yesterday. A lot of them didn't see the dawn this morning. Were you in that lot then?'

The question echoed around in my head as my mind went back to the line and the charging Britons. The thunder and screams filled my ears once more as I saw the shattered frame of the chariot hurtling crazily towards the formation. I shook my head and snapped back to reality.

'Where are they now?' I asked.

'Gone!' said the Optio, in a matter of fact manner. 'Fatalis took what survived and moved out this morning for *Camulodunum* with the rest of Cohort III and Cohort IV as well. Half the battle group's gone there. They should be right on top of the place by now!'

'Fatalis lives?' I gasped, relieved.

'Of course he lives!' laughed the Optio. 'It'll take more than an army of dumb savages to snuff that old bastard's lamp out, although he lost many of his boys yesterday. Besides he's never been known to miss out on the glory and what more glory is there than to win the battle in front of the Emperor?'

'Praetorians! They've escorted the Emperor here. Gods!' Suddenly, realization dawned on me.

'The Emperor is here? Now?' I said in astonishment.

'Where have you been boy?' laughed the Optio. 'He arrived late yesterday, with two full *Cohorts* of *Praetorians* and an army of reinforcements. Look around you lad. These are nice, shiny new boys, they haven't so much as taken a piss in this shit hole yet, let alone fought a battle!'

'Apologies Optio. I was knocked insensible yesterday afternoon and have been unconscious until around an hour ago!'

'That's alright lad!' he grinned. 'We didn't mind you having a little nap while we did all the fighting. A baggage column moves out for *Camulodunum* soon. Trail along with it and see if you can find your lot at the other end!'

With that, the Optio turned and walked off through the sticky mud, cursing at the sucking mess as he went. I had to bite my tongue about the 'nap' quip but realized that he had meant nothing by it, although I would have given anything to have stayed in the line with my brothers. Now, I had not the slightest idea whether they advanced on *Camulodunum* or lay cold at the bottom of that slope. Curiously, I walked to the edge of the camp and looked out over the falling ground, down to where the dead lay. Thousands of them, Briton and Roman, united in death as field parties moved amongst them, salvaging equipment and beginning the task of removing the vast weight of slaughtered meat from the field.

The distant roll of thunder reminded me of yesterday, as did the dark and menacing clouds that boiled overhead, full of yet more drenching rain. This was summer! Did it always have to rain here? I stood for a while watching the rising smoke of countless fires and vast funeral pyres trailing upwards, tainting the turbulent sky with the stench of burning flesh. There was nothing to be done. If they were dead then, the gods have willed it. I could do nothing but carry on.

I returned back to the centre of the camp, towards the forming up point for the column that was about to leave. More unfamiliar things. I came across a new picket line of wooden stakes, an opening in it was manned by four *Praetorians*. As my eyes focussed beyond the defences I gasped in total shock at what I saw.

'Gods! What in the name of Mars are they?' I blurted aloud.

My mouth fell open as I tried to understand the nature of the beasts before me. Massive, with grey wrinkly skin and two huge white spears sticking out of their ugly faces. And that nose! Like some sort of massive writhing serpent, slithering around on the ground and waving in the air. As I watched, my mouth fell open with the unexpected shock of encountering these huge animals with their great flapping ears. As I examined them more closely, I spotted that they were chained to great timber stakes hammered into the ground. That was it! They were some strange animal, native to *Britannia* and we had captured them. I knew it! Truly this place is a cursed land! I resolved to go to the *Praetorians* and ask them about the beasts.

As I approached the gateway, the four guards turned to face me and one of their number stepped forward, holding the flat of his hand out.

'Where do you think you're going then?' He sneered.

'Nowhere! I just wanted to know where you captured those beasts from!'

Instantly the four of them broke into uproarious laughter and I felt myself reddening with embarrassment as they hooted and pointed mockingly at me.

'Those are the Emperor's pride and joy you stupid animal!' he snarled, condescendingly. 'They're war elephants from the other side of the world!'

My temper started to rise at the insult and I had to check myself from clapping my hand to the hilt of my *gladius*, injured arm or not.

'It was a simple enough question, friend!' I snapped 'I have never seen such beasts before and I just wanted to know what they were!'

The *Praetorian* thrust his fists into his hips while his three comrades fell silent, staring at me coldly.

'So now you have your simple answer, you can be on your way!' He said curtly. 'And don't call me friend. Now move on, or you'll need one or two more bandages you scruffy bastard!'

I seethed inside as I fought to control my rising urge to shove my *gladius* down his arrogant throat. I satisfied myself with the best spontaneous reply I could manage.

'I suppose it's a measure of the man who only threatens victims who are alone and injured!' I snapped, accusingly. 'Still! No more than I would expect from one who's worst battles have been won fighting off the attentions of over painted whores!'

With that, I smiled and turned away, leaving the guard stammering at my impudence, dignity restored once more. What did they expect? Respect for their revered status as palace fops? Maybe if they came out and got their hands dirty once in a while then they would deserve a little more respect than the negligible amount that they currently enjoyed.

I joined the column directly and marched along with another Legionary from the Fourteenth. Serenus was from Cohort III and under the command of the Centurion Pantarchus. He had lost two fingers from his right hand and had been kept over night in the hospital tents while he recovered from the shock of surgery to stem the bleeding and tidy up the injuries. As we marched under the leaden skies, we talked of many things. Where we came from, when we joined and who we knew. We talked of our own units and I voiced my worries to Serenus about my lost comrades and whether I would see them again.

'They are your brothers, I know!' confirmed Serenus. 'If they live then you will eventually find them, but the truth is that we are soldiers. It is our lot to suffer, and that doesn't always mean with the pain of our labours!'

He bit into a piece of flat bread as we marched and offered me a piece which I willingly took, my sense of nausea from the concussion now slowly subsiding. I watched the bread churning round his crumb ringed mouth as he chewed on the piece he had just bitten off, simultaneously dispensing his advice with flakes of spraying food.

'I have served ten years now and seen many good men lost to battle. Many of them I knew and felt close to. It is our lot to grow close to each other. When men face such things as we do, it is easy to become brothers and the pain of loss is very real, but we fight through. There is no shame in grieving for lost brothers, just as long as you make sure that you live their lost lives for them. Life is short. Honour them the best way you can, by being the warrior that they were!'

It made good sense. Once more, I realized that I could do nothing to change things and the gods would see that life carried on as ordained. I had to carry on with it. In that, there was no choice.

Before long, *Camulodunum* lay before us. Sprawled out over the vast plain, its sprawl of thatched roofs sheltering its beleaguered inhabitants against the churning rain clouds that threatened to break overhead. The *oppidum* was enormous. Deep ditches and high timber palisades enclosed it in their protective circle, stretching round to the great river that the tribal capital owed its wealth to. Wharfs and jetties stretched out into the rain-swollen current. Landing areas for the trading vessels that had conveyed the wealth of the Roman world to the land of the now immensely rich *Trinovantian* capital. Proudly, its dignity preserved it seemed, the great settlement lay before the conquering army at its gates.

Silently the massed Roman force stood arrayed before the great tribal centre. Battle smeared and indomitable, a huge spread of men and cavalry waited patiently for their Emperor to come and claim the rich prize as his own. A wide path extended through the assembled force to the very threshold of the town, the great timber gates thrown open now, a choice already made to survive rather than perish in the flames as *Durobrivae* had. The standards stood tall at the head of their units and scores of *vexilla* fluttered around in the breeze as we fell to the side of the ancient track way and waited for Claudius to claim his victory.

Soon we heard the distant sounds of horns and drums carrying on the wind to us and down to the assembled forces at the gates of *Camulodunum*. The great formations stirred as they turned to face up the track way in the direction of the approaching sound. A great roll of thunder crossed the hills to the north as even the gods heralded the arrival of Claudius, fourth Emperor of Rome.

First to crest the hill were the cavalry escorts, slowly riding down the track with their standards raised before them. Five hundred riders in their best finery with gleaming harness fittings and polished armour of silvered scale. Bright silk ribbons adorned their clothing and fluttered in the breeze as they rode past, the gleaming metal masks of their ornate helmets staring impassively ahead as they led the Emperor to accept the surrender of a beaten people. Then came the *Praetorians*, arrogant in their polished finery as they filed past. Not even glancing at the soldiers that lined the way, standing covered in the grime of a war fought to give Claudius his credibility as an Emperor.

At last came the elephants. Resplendent now in their decorated burden of miniature wooden castles mounted on their massive backs, draped with gold trimmed cloth and adorned with gold fittings. Archers held bows ready in the cradles while the riders pulled at the ears of the great beasts with iron hooks to steer them along the way as they strode powerfully along. I marvelled at the fact that man could even capture such powerful beasts, let alone control them. Then the watching column began to cheer wildly as Claudius rode into view. Even more magnificent than its companions, Claudius sat atop the biggest of the elephants, its finery even more breathtaking then the others. All around me the cheers erupted into the air, greeting the conquering Emperor as he rode along the route.

'Hail Claudius!'

'Ave Imperator. Domitor Britanniae!'

Over and over again, we chanted the greeting as he drew near. Standards were thrust into the air and waved before him as he went. A decorated wagon moved before his elephants and Nubian slaves as black as night threw gold coins from chests at the assembled soldiers. A gift of gratitude from the victorious Claudius.

I could see him clearly now as he came closer to where I stood. Double ranks of *Praetorians* flanked his elephant as they processed along, their eyes scanning the crowds suspiciously as they went. Along with everyone else, I was shouting and cheering wildly as the emperor drew level, his purple robes trimmed with embroidered gold laurel leaves. The white leather undershirt and gleaming golden breast plate tied with purple silk only enhancing the opulence of the great elephant he rode. My heart pounded like a hammer in my chest as I finally beheld my master, my ruler. The architect of all I had achieved. Gold coins showered down as I waved and cheered him on. I could see his face now as he waved gently at those he passed. His golden laurel had slipped on his head and he pushed it back into place. His ears seemed to be too big for his head and I noticed that he twitched and rolled his eyes. His mouth drooped on one side and was he slobbering? It mattered not, as I snatched at the falling coins and proclaimed him victor.

As quickly as he had arrived, he was gone. Moving ever closer to *Camulodunum* and the delegation of Chieftains that would formally offer their surrender, handing their land and people to the control of Rome forever. As I watched him fade into the distance I quietly opened my pouch and placed the small collection of golden coins inside then, gently, I removed the small bundle of cloth and carefully unwrapped it. The little figure of the *Genius* lay in my palm, smiling benignly up at me.

'At least you are still with me!'

I smiled contentedly as I turned and walked towards *Camulodunum*.

Glossary of Terms

Acetum - Bitter vinegar like wine. Drunk when diluted with water.

Ala - Roman cavalry regiment.

Amphora - Large earthenware jug, used as a container.

Apollo - Sun God, Greek in origin but worshipped in Rome. The sun crossing the sky was believed to represent the god riding his chariot from east to west.

Aquila - The eagle standard carried at the head of an entire Legion.

Aquilifer - Bearer of the Aquila.

Argentoratum - Modern Strasbourg, France.

Armatura - One-on-one weapons training conducted with blunt, heavy weapons. Particularly favoured by trainers developing speed and strength in gladiators. This method was common practice in the Roman army.

Atrebates - British tribe located around modern Wiltshire, Hampshire, Surrey, Sussex and Berkshire.

Augustus - formerly known as Octavian he was the first emperor of Rome, reigning from 31BC–14AD.

Auspices - Good or bad omens read from the entrails of sacrificial animals.

Ave Imperator. Domitor Britanniae - Greetings Emperor and victorious commander. Conqueror of the Britons.

Ballista - Catapult similar in design to a large crossbow. Used for hurling bolts or rocks.

Batavia - Roman province equivalent to modern-day Holland.

Bucellata - Staple ration. Oatmeal biscuits.

Caesar - First used by Augustus, this title was taken from the name of the Dictator, G. Julius Caesar and is the most familiar title associated with Rome's Emperors.

Caligae - Roman hobnailed military boots.

Caligula - See Gaius.

Caltrop - Small iron booby trap consisting of four spikes which were sown over approaches to defended areas and designed to hinder advances or charges.

Camulodunum - Modern Colchester, Essex.

Cantiaci - British tribe, natives of Cantium.

Cantium - The modern county of Kent.

Capsarius - Medical orderly.

Carnyx - War horn held vertically and with the outlet in the shape of an animal head such as a boar. The horn was common to the Celtic and Gallic peoples throughout western Europe.

Catapultae - A range of weapons developed for launching stones, bolts and other projectiles during sieges and when giving artillery support.

Catuvellauni - British tribe located approximately in the Southern Midlands, Oxfordshire and Buckinghamshire.

Centurion - Officer commanding a Century.

Century - Eighty man infantry unit.

Charon - The ferryman who transported the newly deceased to the realm of the dead.

Cingulum militare - Military belt consisting of waist belt and apron of straps at the front. Often highly ornate, it was one of the distinguishing signs of a soldier.

Classis Britannica - Roman Imperial Navy squadron.

Claudius - Fourth Emperor of the Julio-Claudian dynasty. He reigned from 41–54AD.

Clavi - Vertical stripes of varying widths and colour woven into a tunic.

Cohors - An infantry Cohort normally numbered 480 men (Six Centuries), unless it was the first Cohort of a Legion which had five double Centuries.

Contubernium - Eight man infantry section.

Cornicen - Player of Cornu horn.

Cornu - Large circular shaped horn.

Corona Vallaris - Rampart crown. High military honour made of gold.

Crista Transversa - Transverse crest worn on the helmets of Centurions.

Cupid - Roman boy god of love.

Denarius - Silver coin.

Dobunni - British tribe located around the Gloucestershire area.

Dolabrum - Tool used for construction work. Able to be used as a pick and also an axe.

Dis - Roman god of the underworld.

Durobrivae - Modern Rochester, Kent.

Durovernum Cantiacorum - Modern Canterbury, Kent.

Fabricae - Workshops.

Fabricensus - Armourer.

Fortuna - Roman goddess of fate, chance and luck.

Fretum Gallicum - Straits of Dover.

Fustuarium - Military punishment. Being beaten to death.

Gaius - Emperor known as Caligula reigned AD37–41.

Gaul - Roughly modern France.

Gladius - Roman short sword.

Genius - Guardian spirit that protects areas, places and groups of people as well as individuals.

Germania - Modern Germany, roughly speaking.

Gromer - Surveying device utilizing four plumb lines suspended from a cross piece on a staff.

Hamian - Auxiliary archer originating from Syria.

Haruspex - Priest who divines omens from sacrificial animals etc.

Illyricum - Province of; See Pannonia.

Imaginifer - Bearer of the Imago.

Imago - A standard carrying the image of the Emperor, cast in precious metal and carried at the head of the Legion with the Aquila.

Immunis - Soldiers with specialist skills which were exempt from general fatigues and duties.

Impedimentum - Soldier's individual marching kit.

Ister - The river Danube.

Iovi - See Jupiter.

Iuppiter - See Jupiter, (Iuppiter, Optimus Maximus. Jupiter, greatest and best.)

Jupiter - Chief god in the Roman panoply. Jupiter was also known as Iovi, Io and Iuppiter.

Juno - Chief goddess of the Roman panoply and wife to Jupiter.

Lanista - Trainer of gladiators.

Lares - Protective spirits guarding such places as households, buildings and specific locations such as crossroads.

Legate - Legion commander.

Lemur - Ghost. Evil or hostile spirit.

Libum - Cake made with cheese. This was either specifically baked as a sacrificial offering or as an ordinary dish.

Lorica - Armour.

Lorica Hamata - ring or chain mail.

Lorica Segmentata - Segmented iron armour articulated on internal leather straps. The name is a modern Latin title as the original Roman name is, as yet, unknown. This is probably the most familiar form of Roman armour.

Ludi - Games.

Lugdunum - Modern Lyon, France.

Luna - Roman goddess of the moon.

Mars Loucetius - The Roman god of war, Mars, combined with a provincial deity.

Medicus - Doctor or surgeon.

Mercurius - (Mercury) Messenger of the gods and herald of the new day.

Miles - Ordinary soldier (pronounced Mee lays).

Mogontiacum - Modern Mainz, Germany.

Novaessium - Modern Neuss, Germany.

Nymphs - Female spirits of woodland and water etc. Purported to be young and beautiful and having a fondness for music and dance.

Ocreae - Greaves. (Shin guards.)

Onager - Siege catapult powered by spring torsion and capable of hurling heavy stones. Translates as 'wild ass' because of its ferocious kick upon launch.

Oppidum - Native British town or large urban settlement. Usually fortified.

Optio - Second in command of the Century, the Optio was the Centurion's chosen successor, his *option*.

Opus Signinum - Smooth pink floor screed of crushed tile and aggregate, similar to concrete.

Paenula - Hooded, long woollen cloak.

Pannonia - Large Roman province covering the modern Balkan states and Austria. It's original northern and eastern borders were defined by the river Danube.

Papilio - Eight man tent made typically from goatskins.

Phalerae - Personal military decorations displayed over armour on a body harness.

Pilum - Heavy Roman javelin.

Pilum Muralis - Long wooden stakes tapering to a point at both ends. Used in the construction of defences and obstacles.

Portus Dubris - Modern Dover, Kent.

Portus Itius - Modern Boulogne, France.

Portus Rutupiae - Modern Richborough, Kent.

Praefectus Castrorum - Camp prefect. In simple terms, third in command of the unit and able to take charge when the Legate was absent.

Praetorian guard - The Emperor's personal bodyguards.

Principia - Headquarters building and administrative centre of a fort.

Priapus - Originating from Greece, this male fertility god was often depicted sporting a huge phallus. Although a revered deity, Romans tended to view him with amusement.

Probatio - Examination board for prospective recruits to the Legion.

Pugio - Heavy iron dagger.

Quadrans - Low denomination copper coin.

Quaestionarius - Torturer or interrogator.

Regulbium - Reculver, Kent.

Rhenus - The river Rhine.

Sacellum - Room and vault containing the unit pay chest and standards. Located in the Principia.

Sagittarius - Archer.

Sagum - Rectangular or square military cloak.

Samian - high quality reddish brown pottery from Gaul.

Saturnalia - Feast of the god Saturn. Held in December the festival is a rough ancient equivalent to Christmas where, amongst other things, slaves would be served by their masters and wear their fine clothes.

Satyr - Half man, half goat. These woodland spirits were associated with, amongst other things, lust.

Scopae - Straw or wicker archery targets.

Scorpion - See ballista.

Scutum - Rectangular and hemi cylindrical shield.

Signifer - bearer of the Signum.

Signum - Large standard for a Cohort.

Siscia - Modern Sisak, Croatia.

Spatha - Long sword used predominantly by Roman cavalry and auxiliary troops.

Speculatore - Messenger. Could also be scout or spy.

Stimuli - Iron or wooden spike set into shallow pits to injure advancing infantry or cavalry.

Suovetaurelia - Combined sacrifice of a bull, boar and ram to Mars.

Tanatus Insula - The Isle of Thanet, Kent. Now land-locked the island was once separated from the mainland of Kent by the Wantsum channel. A navigable waterway which ran from Richborough to Reculver.

Tamesis - River Thames.

Tesserarius - Keeper of the password, roughly equivalent to today's orderly sergeant.

Testum - Earthenware cooking pot. Similar in principal to a Dutch oven.

Tiro - Novice, beginner, recruit.

Tribune - High ranking staff officer normally drawn from the elite of Roman society. Each Legion contained six military tribunes.

Trinovantes - British tribe located around the Suffolk area, spreading towards North Essex.

Tuba - long straight horn, similar to a modern post horn.

Tubicen - Tuba player.

Turma - Thirty strong cavalry unit.

Varus - Publius Quinctilius Varus. Whilst leading an army of three Legions through the Teutoberger forest in 9AD, Varus was ambushed by the Germanic prince Arminius and his force was annihilated.

Venus - Roman goddess of love.

Veteranus - Veteran soldiers of the unit.

Vexillarius - Bearer of the Vexillum.

Vexillation - detachment.

Vexillum - Textile standard typically displaying information about a particular unit. Most commonly seen as a square of cloth carried atop an adapted spear shaft.

Via - Road (**Via Principalis** – the Principia road).

Viaticum - A payment traditionally representing travelling expenses for the new recruit. A modern equivalent would be the King's/Queen's shilling paid to soldiers on enlistment.

Victoria - Roman goddess of victory.

Vicus - Civilian settlement established outside a military base.

Vitis - A vine staff carried by the Centurion as one of his badges of office.